The Missing Mogul

A Tennyson Pierce Mystery

BARRY EATON

Primix Publishing
11620 Wilshire Blvd
Suite 900, West Wilshire Center, Los Angeles, CA, 90025
www.primixpublishing.com
Phone: 1-800-538-5788

Published by Primix Publishing: 08/11/2023

ISBN: 978-1-957676-59-3(sc)
ISBN: 978-1-957676-60-9(hc)
ISBN: 978-1-957676-61-6(e)

Library of Congress Control Number: 2023910715

Dedication

In memory of my parents:
Charles Homer Eaton (1915 – 1989)
Helen Miller Eaton (1918 – 2014)

Contents

Author's Note

This novel is entirely fictional, although the settings employed are based on historical information derived from the references cited in the appendix. For example, all of the streets mentioned in the story actually existed in 1886, as did many of the buildings visited by Pierce and Weston. Similarly, the food and drink selections are taken from restaurant menus and published recipes of the period. While the railroads employ the routes followed by the lines which ran through Texas in the late nineteenth century, the names were contrived to suit the narrative. Likewise, with but three exceptions, the characters are figments of the author's imagination; and any resemblance to actual individuals, whether living or deceased, is purely coincidental. The exceptions, who all appear in what might be termed "cameo" roles, are William Brown Miller, the builder of Millermore; Father Joseph Martiniere, the first pastor of Sacred Heart Church; and Professor E. B. Lawrence, the founder of the

Commonwealth Commercial College. Their names are used with the greatest respect for the contributions which these early residents of Dallas made to the city's cultural growth.

Preface

In her book *Texas Childhood* (Dallas: The Kaleidograph Press, 1941), my great-aunt Evelyn Miller Crowell wrote the following words about the home in which she was raised: "After making a careful survey of his land for a choice building site, grandpa chose a hill top overlooking the Trinity River valley and what there was to see of the struggling village of Dallas, five miles to the northwest. This is where the 'big house' was built in 1855, a large gracious white house with a wide center hall and rooms 20 x 20 feet." She was referring to Millermore, the stately residence constructed by my great-great-grandfather, William Brown Miller, which now stands in Old City Park near downtown Dallas. As a youngster in the 1950's, I spent many Sunday afternoons at Millermore, visiting my great-grandmother and viewing the intriguing collection of historical artifacts which were on display in the "Trophy Room." Recently, several boxes of materials from that special place came to my attention through the thoughtfulness of a distant relative. Among the many yellowed papers in the dilapidated cartons, I discovered several journals written by a certain Dr. Jarvis Weston. The oldest of the chronicles dated from 1886 and related a remarkable adventure that Dr. Weston had shared with a Dallas attorney named Tennyson Pierce. Believing that this story ought to be preserved for posterity, I set about organizing the material into chapters and filling in missing portions of the narrative with material from my family's archives. The result is presented here, and it is hoped that the reader will find the effort to be both entertaining and informative.

Barry Eaton
May, 2023

List of Principal Characters

Tennyson Pierce:
A Dallas attorney with a penchant for investigating mysterious crimes, he has an unfailing command of logic and an exceptional knowledge of topics pertaining to physical evidence.

Dr. Jarvis Weston:
A young physician who is trying to establish a successful medical practice following his arrival in Dallas, he finds a new field of interest after meeting Pierce.

Jack Lorentz:
A reporter for the *Dallas News* and confidant of Pierce, he has a wry wit and a nose for a good story.

Archer Pierce:
Tennyson's older brother, he is a useful source of information, thanks to his position with the United States Secret Service.

Henry Ward:
The Division Superintendent of the Texas & Louisiana Railway at Marshall, he has a problem which his own railroad police and the local sheriff seem unable to solve.

Jay Golden:
A New York financier intent on establishing a business empire without peer, he hopes to gain control of the Texas & Louisiana Railway.

Martin Donlevy:
A former Texan who now resides in Philadelphia, he has apparently made a good deal of money through land speculation.

Armand La Fourche:
The owner of numerous gambling interests in western Louisiana, he has a reputation for associating with known criminals.

Mrs. Hutchins:
The widow of a cotton broker, she owns the home at 211 Routh Street where Pierce leases the second floor.

Amy Hutchins:
A student at the Ursuline Academy with a talent for the natural sciences, she has developed what her mother considers to be an unfortunate interest in Pierce's methods.

George Riley:
A friend of Amy's who attends the Commonwealth Commercial College, he uncovers some revealing information at the Dallas County Courthouse.

Ambrose Dillon:
A leading member of the Dallas business community, he is an old friend of the Weston family and feels a paternal responsibility toward Jarvis.

Clair Whitman:
A prominent Dallas banker and close acquaintance of Pierce, he also owns one of the largest logging operations in East Texas.

Sheriff Lassiter:
A decent lawman but hardly an incisive thinker, he has the good sense to seek assistance from Pierce when confronted with challenging cases.

Choctaw Jones:
An army scout who sometimes works for Pierce, he knows the Piney Woods better than any man alive.

CHAPTER 1

A Fateful Meeting

It was in the spring of 1886 that I first met the man who would become my closest friend and with whom I was destined to share so many extraordinary adventures over the coming years. By now the name of Tennyson Pierce must be familiar to the reader; for despite a professed aversion to publicity, he has been lionized by the press due to his successes in solving a number of significant crimes that had baffled law enforcement officials throughout Texas. The occasion of our initial encounter was a reception hosted by the well-known William Brown Miller, a long-time Dallas resident with a large home a few miles south of the Trinity River. About two dozen people had been asked to the Miller estate on a Sunday afternoon to hear speeches by prospective candidates in the upcoming race for the office of City Attorney. I felt fortunate to be included on the guest list, having only recently moved to the area from Kansas City. My invitation was undoubtedly due to a favorable word from Ambrose

Dillon, a prominent local merchant who was an old friend of my parents.

While drifting through the group of guests gathered on the east lawn of the stately residence, I felt someone's hand against my back. Turning around, I found Mr. Dillon talking to a tall, lean man with auburn hair, an aquiline nose, and penetrating green eyes. The fellow appeared to be only a few years older than myself, and yet his bearing was that of an individual accustomed to commanding respect.

"Allow me to introduce Dr. Jarvis Weston," Mr. Dillon announced to his companion. "He has recently opened a medical office in the Curtis Building on Akard Street. Jarvis, this is Mr. Tennyson Pierce, one of our city's leading attorneys and an occasional consultant to the sheriff's office."

"It's a pleasure to meet you, sir," I replied. "A poor doctor feels somewhat out of place in such distinguished company. How are you, Mr. Dillon? My mother and father send their regards."

"I'm just fine, my boy. Tell your folks that I miss their company and wish them the best. Now, please excuse me for a moment while I track down our host. There's something that I want to ask him. Why don't you gentlemen use this opportunity to get better acquainted?"

With this comment, Mr. Dillon left us and walked toward the front of the house. In an effort to make polite conversation, I asked Mr. Pierce about his association with the sheriff's office.

"As you may be aware," he said, "there is an emerging recognition that physical evidence can play an important role in the apprehension of criminals. I have undertaken to familiarize myself with a number of rather uncommon subjects that may be useful in this regard. On several occasions, my knowledge has contributed to the resolution of cases where Sheriff Lassiter and his men had been making little progress."

Intrigued, I inquired about the nature of his studies. My interest seemed to please him, and he was more than willing to oblige it. However, our conversation was interrupted by the repeated ringing of a bell, followed by an announcement that everyone should proceed to the house for the presentation of the potential candidates. Since I had acquired some slight experience with forensics during my medical studies at St. Louis University, it was natural for me to wonder what methods were employed by Mr. Pierce. In order to satisfy my curiosity, I invited him to join me for supper that evening at the Quincy Hotel.

Over a leisurely meal a few hours later, I discovered that this unusual man had indeed accumulated a remarkable fund of knowledge, encompassing the geographic distribution of soils and plants, the actions and telltale signs of various poisonous substances, the types of ammunition employed in a wide range of pistols and rifles, the distinctive colors and odors of both domestic and imported tobaccos, methods for taking impressions of shoe and finger marks, and sundry other topics of a somewhat abstruse nature. I also learned that the two of us shared a variety of pastimes and personal habits. Our common inclinations included such diverse subjects as English history, the paintings of Edouard Manet, and experimental chemistry. In addition, it turned out that we both eschewed the use of tobacco, partook of alcohol only on social occasions, were in the habit of rising regularly at daybreak, and believed strongly in the adage of "a place for everything and everything in its place."

By the end of the evening, we were on a first-name basis; and Tennyson asked whether I planned to continue living at the hotel. It happened that I been looking for more permanent arrangements but had been unable to find anything suitable. When I told him this, his surprising response was that he leased the second floor of a good-sized house at 211 Routh Street and would not be averse to sharing these quarters. He then invited me to visit him on the following morning to see if his spare bedroom would suit me. Such an opportunity was clearly too good to pass up, and I readily agreed to stop by his home around 9:00 a.m. the next day.

On Monday morning, I arose to find a cloudless sky and a slight breeze out of the west. After breakfasting in the hotel dining room, I started off for Routh Street, following Tennyson's directions. The stroll in the fresh morning air was invigorating, and I arrived at Number 211 in a decidedly sanguine frame of mind. The house proved to be good-sized indeed, being a variation of the Louisiana Plantation style, with porches surrounding both floors and an outside staircase on the southeast side leading to the second level. Proceeding up the steps, I advanced to the front door and gave two quick raps of the brass knocker.

"One moment," came the sound of Tennyson's voice from within. As I waited for him to reach the door, I surveyed the surrounding neighborhood from my elevated vantage point, noting that the homes all bore an air of gentility and that the area abounded with large live-oak and elm trees. Shortly, the door opened; and I was confronted by the beaming face of my new friend.

"Good morning, Jarvis," he greeted me. "Welcome to my poor abode. Please come in."

As I crossed the threshold, I found myself in a wide hallway which ran the full depth of the house. Following Tennyson on a quick tour, I learned that his "poor abode" consisted of six good-sized rooms. At the front of the dwelling, the hallway was flanked by a spacious parlor on the right and a dining area on the left. Immediately behind the parlor was a cozy-looking library with a fireplace. Then came Tennyson's bedroom, which had two windows overlooking the back yard. Opposite the library, there was a vacant room measuring about tweve by fourteen feet, followed by the bathroom and an adjacent alcove that was filled with laboratory equipment.

"Well, what do you think? Will that empty room across the hall serve your purposes? Come, have a seat and let's discuss it," Tennyson remarked as he ushered me into the library.

At his invitation, I settled into a comfortable-looking

leather armchair at one side of a small octagonal table, while he took a cane-back chair opposite me.

"I suppose that I should tell you a bit more about the situation here before you make your decision," he continued. "This house is owned by a widow named Hutchins. She occupies the first floor together with her youngest daughter Amy, who is in her final year of studies at the Ursuline Academy. Mr. Hutchins was a cotton broker who died in an unfortunate accident at a compress. He left his wife clear title to the house and a modest income from his investments. However, with her other two children grown and moved away, she no longer needs so much space. I met Mrs. Hutchins through an acquaintance who handled some of the details of her husband's estate. When I ventured to suggest that I would pay her a generous rate for using the upper floor of her house, she graciously agreed. Since moving in about eight months ago, I have been very satisfied with the arrangements. It's also worth mentioning that the lady is an excellent cook and is happy to provide meals upon reasonable notice. These are usually delivered by means of the dumbwaiter which you may have observed in the alcove."

"You were certainly fortunate to have obtained such pleasant quarters," I commented, "and I must say that my weeks of searching have turned up nothing to compare. This would be an excellent location for me as well, since it's a fairly short walk to my office from here. However, I am frankly concerned that your asking price may be more than I can afford. My income is apt to be rather meager until my medical practice has developed."

"Don't give another thought to the cost, dear fellow. That vacant space is doing me no good, and you might as well make use of it. For the time being, let's say that the rent will be no more than what you are paying at the Quincy Hotel. Later, when your practice has grown as I'm sure that it will, you can assume a larger share of the monthly fee."

"How could anyone refuse such a generous offer? If you don't mind, though, I'd like to wait until next Saturday to move in, since I'll need to find some furniture."

"By all means, feel free to take up residence at your convenience. However, I believe that Mrs. Hutchins has some bedroom furnishings in storage, which she might well be willing to let you have for a modest sum. Let me find out."

"That would definitely make matters easier for me, but please don't go to any trouble. I am considerably in your debt as it is. And now, I had better take my leave so that you can get on with your work."

With that, we shook hands; and I departed. Proceeding along Routh to Ross Avenue and then turning southwest toward Akard Street, it took only about twenty-five minutes to reach my office. The walk gave me a chance to reflect that perhaps my luck was starting to change. Not only had I embarked on a new friendship and solved my problem of finding a place to live, but Tennyson's standing in the community might well prove helpful in building up my practice. Of course, I had absolutely no idea then that my association with this exceptional man would soon lead me into endeavors far removed from the field of medicine.

CHAPTER 2

A Journey to East Texas

My patient load continued to be unfortunately light over the next couple of days, and I was beginning to feel slightly dejected again. However, on that Wednesday morning, as I descended the hotel stairs, the desk clerk called my name and said that he had a message for me. This turned out to be a note from Tennyson saying that Mrs. Hutchins was willing to provide a bed, a dresser, and several other items of furniture for the very reasonable price of fifty dollars. Furthermore, she was agreeable to letting me pay this amount at the rate of a mere two dollars per week. I was sure that this last suggestion had come from Tennyson in consideration of my circumstances and was bouyed again by the thought of my good fortune in having made his acquaintance. After jotting a quick reply indicating my acceptance of these terms and adding an invitation to join me for supper that evening, I handed the note back to the clerk with instructions for delivery and proceeded to my office.

Around 11:00 a.m., having seen only one patient

all morning, I had just started to write a letter to my parents when I heard the tinkle of the bell over the outer door, followed by Tennyson's voice saying: "Are you occupied, Jarvis?"

Stepping into the outer room, I smiled at him and said: "This is a pleasant surprise. I hadn't expected to see you until this evening. What brings you to these humble surroundings?"

"As a matter of fact, I stopped by to offer my apologies," he replied. "Your kind invitation to supper arrived at an inopportune time, I'm afraid. A potential client has requested my presence in Marshall this afternoon, and I must leave on the next eastbound train. It occurred to me, though, that if your schedule permits, you might be interested in coming along. That part of the state is heavily forested, which makes for a nice change of scenery. I plan to return around mid-day on Friday. What do you say?"

"I'm not familiar with the town you mentioned. Where is it located?"

"Marshall is about a hundred and fifty miles east of here. It's an important railroad junction, serving as the meeting point of trunk lines from Dallas, Little Rock, and Shreveport. My business is with a Mr. Henry Ward, who is the Division Superintendent there for the Texas & Louisiana Railway."

"Well, as you can see, I am hardly beset by patients; and a diversion would be welcome just now. But are you quite certain that I won't be in the way of your business?"

"Not at all, my dear fellow. In fact, your thoughts on

the matter would be most appreciated. The situation is a rather strange one which may have some far-reaching implications."

"If you're certain that I won't be a hindrance, I would be more than happy to accompany you. What time does the train depart?"

"It's scheduled to leave the Houston Street depot at 1:36 p.m., which should give us enough time to stop by the Quincy Hotel for your bag and then have a quick lunch at the Market Street Cafe."

"Just give me a moment to prepare a notice for any patients who might come by, and I'll be right with you."

Returning to the desk in my consulting room, I took out a sheet of paper and wrote a note stating that I would be out of the office until Friday afternoon and that anyone needing medical attention during my absence should consult Dr. Everett on Harwood Street. After tacking this message to the inside of the outer door, I joined Tennyson in his buggy; and we set off for my hotel.

Following a brief stop, during which I quickly threw a few items of clothing and some sundries into my valise, we proceeded to the Market Street Cafe. There, we had a filling lunch of roast beef sandwiches and potato salad, washed down by tall glasses of lemonade. I offered to pay for the meal, but Tennyson wouldn't hear of it, saying that he had dragged me away from my practice and should therefore bear the expenses of the journey.

We arrived at the Houston Street depot about twenty minutes past the hour of one. After handing his buggy over to the care of a hostler, Tennyson approached the ticket window and requested two first-class seats to Marshall on the *Shreveporter*. Upon giving our names, however, he was informed by the passenger agent that instructions had been received from the Division Office for Mr. Pierce to be treated as a personal guest of Mr. Ward. When Tennyson commented that he was accompanied by an associate, the agent answered, "That's quite all right, sir. This directive specifies that we should accommodate any need which you may have."

The train, which was coming from Fort Worth, pulled into the depot at twenty-seven minutes past one by the station clock. It consisted of a baggage car and four coaches, pulled by a wood-burning Ten-Wheeler. After a brief delay while the tender was being replenished with wood and water, passengers were allowed to board. Tennyson and I were introduced to the conductor, a Mr. Johnson, who escorted us to seats which he had reserved for us at the rear of the last coach. Once we were situated, he drew a curtain across the aisle, providing us with a measure of privacy, although this was hardly needed in the sparsely occupied car.

After a couple of minutes, we heard two long blasts from the locomotive's whistle and felt a slight jerk as the train started to move. Our progress was initially slow as we traversed numerous turnouts and grade crossings on our way through the central area of town. Finally, the track veered to the southeast; and we proceeded at moderate speed through more sparsely settled neighborhoods, revealing aspects of the Dallas area which were unfamiliar to me. Another ten minutes or so of running at this pace brought us into open country. As the last reminders of the city were left behind, I began to feel a sense of relaxation mingled with anticipation for what lay ahead.

Turning to Tennyson, who had been sitting in deep thought since our departure, I ventured to ask whether he could share any further information regarding his business in Marshall. "It's always been my understanding that the major railroads retain their own attorneys on staff," I added.

"So they do, Jarvis," he responded. "However, my charge from Mr. Ward isn't concerned with the usual purview of the legal profession, at least not at this stage of the affair. The fact is that he wishes to consult me in connection with a rather intriguing crime involving railroad property. The line's own policemen and the local sheriff have been unable to shed any light upon the matter."

"What is it, if you don't mind my asking?" I inquired.

Lowering his voice almost to a whisper, he replied, "The situation could prove to be one with serious consequences. In fact, it's doubtful that even Mr. Ward appreciates the possible significance. As a result, I must ask for your discretion regarding what I am about to tell you."

"Of course. Anyone who undertakes to practice medicine must develop the habit of maintaining disclosures in confidence; and you may be assured that yours will be safe with me."

"I have no doubt of it, dear fellow, and apologize for broaching the subject. However, the early reports concerning this incident suggest that it was carefully planned by someone who recruited several accomplices. If those responsible are to be caught before achieving their ultimate aim, a cautious approach must be taken in pursuing the investigation."

"Well, you have certainly provoked my curiosity. The case sounds like one which may be rather challenging to solve."

"More than likely, although the local sheriff regards the crime as simply a prank. The basic circumstances are these: A locomotive disappeared from a siding between Marshall and Longview sometime during the late hours of last Saturday night or the early hours of Sunday morning, and a search of the line all the way from Shreveport to Dallas has failed to reveal any trace of it. Of course, the reduction in the pool of available motive power causes problems for the railroad because it affects the ability to maintain the published schedules. In addition, Mr. Ward is concerned that having an engine in an unknown location along the line could pose a danger to the division's crews, who might encounter it unexpectedly."

"That seems serious enough, not even considering the direct monetary loss," I commented. "Apparently, though, you're convinced the disappearance was a good deal more than a prank."

"If it was a prank, someone went to a great deal of trouble in exchange for a little amusement. No, the fact that the locomotive hasn't been found after three days of searching leads me to believe that there is a cunning mind behind this. I am very much afraid that the theft may prove to be only the first step in a larger plan."

"What sort of plan? Do you suppose that the thieves needed the engine to transport something?"

"That's a reasonable hypothesis, which remains to be tested. Our first task, if you would care to assist me, will be to see if we can determine how the engine was taken and in what direction it moved after leaving the siding."

Flattered at this unexpected invitation to participate in the investigation, I readily agreed to offer whatever help was needed. "However," I noted, "this sort of undertaking is well beyond my realm of expertise."

"You probably know more about such things than you realize," Tennyson responded. "The investigation of a crime is not unlike the diagnosis of a medical condition. In both fields, success depends upon careful observation of the 'symptoms,' coupled with rigorous reasoning from effects to causes. In any case, a second pair of eyes is always useful; and I would welcome your services in recording whatever facts we may discover. But there will be time enough to consider your role in the investigation when we reach Marshall. On Sunday evening, you expressed an interest in learning more about my chemical experiments."

With these words, Tennyson launched into a thorough description of his studies on the colligative properties of binary solutions. I listened intently, occasionally asking a question and marveling all the while at the range of knowledge which he possessed. It was clear that his understanding of chemistry exceeded my own, despite my medical training. We had been engrossed thus for some time when the voice of the conductor interrupted us with the announcement that the train was approaching its first station stop, in Grand Saline.

"How much farther is it to Marshall?" I inquired, poking my head through the curtain across the aisle.

"It's about another two hours," Johnson answered. "We're making good time and should arrive on schedule."

As I turned around again, Tennyson tapped me on the arm and said, "From this point onward, we need to keep a sharp lookout for any telltale signs near the right-of-way. The items of interest are tools, rails, ties, wagon ruts, freshly overturned earth, or anything that appears unusual. If you'd be good enough to take the south side of the train, I'll survey this side. Do you have something to write on?"

"I brought my journal, if that will suffice. What sort of notations should I make in it?"

"Simply record any observation which seems noteworthy, along with a brief description of its location relative to some recognizable landmark."

Extracting the journal from my valise, I moved across the aisle and took up a position at the window. The station stop in Grand Saline lasted but a minute, and we were soon rolling along through brushy terrain again. I had only the vaguest idea what should be considered "noteworthy," but made an earnest effort to watch the area beside the track carefully. Once in a while, I glanced over at Tennyson with a question on my lips; but he had such a look of intensity on his face that I hesitated to say anything.

The next station stop was in Mineola. As we came to a halt at the depot, I stood up to stretch and asked Tennyson if he had seen anything of interest thus far.

"Nothing worth mentioning," he said. "How did you fare?"

"The same, I'm sorry to say," I replied. "Of course, picking out small objects isn't easy at the speed we've been traveling."

"Admittedly, the task requires a sharp eye and good concentration. However, we mustn't relax our vigilance. There is still about an hour and a half to go before we reach Marshall, and the track ahead warrants particular attention. Please try to be especially alert in the vicinity of Longview."

As the train started moving again, I returned to my post and tried to focus on the task at hand. This became more difficult as the miles passed, with the steady clickety-clack of the train's wheels tending to lull me into a state of drowsiness. About an hour had passed when I was roused by Tennyson's voice advising that we were approaching the western outskirts of Longview. Shaking my head vigorously to ward off the feeling of lassitude, I began to carefully scan the area between the track and the adjacent woods. Shortly, I heard the conductor annnounce that passengers disembarking at Longview should gather their belongings.

As we drew nearer to the depot, the trackwork became busier, with numerous turnouts, sidings, and spurs, which made it difficult to take in all of the details. When we had come to a stop, I told Tennyson that I had still seen nothing remarkable, but couldn't swear that something hadn't escaped my notice in these labyrinthine surroundings.

He replied that we would certainly have to return for a closer inspection of the local vicinity at some point, since it was unlikely that the missing locomotive had been taken any further west than this before being diverted from the mainline.

The stop in Longview was another brief one, and we were soon underway once more. As I returned my attention to the view outside, Tennyson said, "It won't be long now. I know that close surveillance can be a tedious chore, but another half an hour or so should bring us to our destination."

Feeling that this remark must have been occasioned by my earlier difficulty in staying alert, I resolved to concentrate fully on watching the trackside area for the remainder of the journey. About ten minutes after our departure from the station, my efforts were rewarded when I observed a spot where the tall grass between the track and the adjacent woods had been trampled down. From the lay of the strands, it appeared that something had been dragged in the direction of the trees. After glancing at my pocket watch to note the time, I hurriedly made an entry in my journal, excited to have finally come across something which seemed worth recording. Not long afterward, we passed into a clearing where there were three fair-sized structures and quite a few stacks of logs. A spur ran into one of the buildings from the east, and the surrounding soil was criss-crossed with ruts which had obviously been made by wagon wheels. I concluded that the facility was probably a lumber mill, but decided that it still warranted a few lines of description.

The rest of the trip was pretty uneventful for me, as the remaining points of interest all seemed to be on the north side of the line. Two or three times, I heard Tennyson murmur some remark; but I restrained my curiosity and kept my gaze focused on the ground adjacent to the right-of-way. After awhile, I sensed the train slowing down and turned to see Mr. Johnson part the curtain across the aisle.

"We're approaching Marshall, gentlemen," he said. "If you'll kindly remain seated for a few minutes after the train stops, the stationmaster will come aboard and escort you to see Mr. Ward."

"Thank you," Tennyson responded. "I assume the Superintendent's office is not in the depot?"

"No, sir," Mr. Johnson replied, "it's in a building on the west end of the yard. A locomotive and caboose are standing by to take you there."

A few minutes later, the train came to a halt. I moved back across the aisle and watched through the window as ten or twelve passengers stepped onto the platform in front of the depot. Shortly, a uniformed man with a grizzled beard climbed aboard our coach and approached us.

"My name is Ted Wilson, gentlemen," he announced. "I'm the stationmaster here at Marshall. Mr. Ward asked me to greet you on his behalf and bring you down to the Division Office. Please come this way."

Following our guide out the forward end of the car, we were led into the depot, where a porter was waiting to take our bags. "We'll have these sent on to your hotel if that's all right," Wilson said.

Nodding our assent, we then proceeded into the rear part of the building and through a door marked "Trainmen Only," emerging beside a track where a small locomotive with a slope-backed tender sat coupled to a caboose.

"Watch your footing, now," Wilson said, as he indicated for us to board the caboose. Clambering onto the rear platform, I felt a twinge of excitement at this opportunity to see the working side of a railroad. The inside of the car was outfitted with a small table, four wooden benches, and a pair of bunkbeds. My first inclination was to climb straight into the cupola for a bird's-eye view; but yielding to professional decorum, I took a seat at the table beside Tennyson. After making sure that we were settled, the stationmaster stepped back onto the rear platform and gave the signal to get underway.

We seemed to be moving at hardly more than a walking pace as we threaded our way through the maze of track leading to the yard area. After traveling for what I judged to be little more than a mile, we came to a stop next to a two-story structure with clapboard siding.

"This is the Division Office, gentlemen," Wilson announced, motioning for us to follow him. Climbing down from the caboose proved to be more awkward than boarding it, and I suffered a slight twist of my right ankle in jumping the final foot or so to the ground.

Wilson directed us through a double door, along a corridor, and past an area where a number of clerks sat at desks piled high with papers. After climbing a stairway to the second floor, we emerged into a good-sized room whose walls were lined with track diagrams. On one side, a youngish-looking man wearing a visored cap sat at a bank of telegraph keys. Beyond him, at the far end end of the room, there was a small antechamber, which was assiduously guarded by a dark-haired woman of stern aspect. Approaching her desk, Wilson said, "Would you please let Mr. Ward know that we're here, Mrs. Freeman? He's expecting us."

Looking us over in a manner which made me feel distinctly uncomfortable, the woman rose slowly, then turned around and knocked lightly on a door labeled "H. J. Ward, Division Superintendent." She passed inside, closing the door behind her, only to return a few seconds later in the company of a well-dressed but rather stout gentleman who was chomping on an unlit cigar.

"These are our visitors from Dallas, Mr. Ward," Wilson announced.

My friend immediately stepped forward, extended his right hand, and stated, "I am Tennyson Pierce, sir; and this Dr. Jarvis Weston, who will be assisting me in the investigation of your problem."

CHAPTER 3

A Suspicious Message

After shaking our hands vigorously, Ward ushered us into his office, telling Mrs. Freeman as he did so that he was not to be disturbed for the rest of the afternoon. "Please be seated, gentlemen," he said, indicating a pair of leather armchairs which faced his desk. "Can I get you something to drink? I have some fine Kentucky sipping whisky."

"Just water, if you don't mind," Tennyson answered, looking in my direction.

"A glass of water would be most welcome," I agreed, glancing around the office. My attention was caught by a large line drawing of a locomotive on one wall. I started to ask about it, then checked myself as it occurred to me that the talking should probably be left to Tennyson.

Wilson, who had accompanied us into the office, walked to a credenza next to the door and poured out two glasses of water from a pitcher. After handing these to us, he took a chair at the far end of the desk.

"I don't mind telling you, Mr. Pierce, that this affair

has me thoroughly vexed," Ward continued. "That locomotive seems to have vanished from the earth."

"Perhaps you would tell us something more about the circumstances of its disappearance," Tennyson replied. "Please be as thorough as possible, for even details that seem trivial may prove to be helpful."

"That's why I asked Wilson here to join us," Ward said. "He was the one who turned in the first official report that the locomotive was missing. Ted, tell them how you learned about it."

"Well, I had just come on duty Sunday morning when Jim Burleson and Will Gosset stormed into the station cussin' up a blue streak. They had drawn the assignment from the Extra Board to pick up the Rusk Turn at Blanco siding and bring it into the yard. Blanco's about five miles west of the station, and the train was left there Saturday night because the yard lead was blocked by a derailment. But when Burleson and Gosset got to the siding just after sunrise on Sunday, there was no locomotive coupled to the train. They thought somebody was having a joke at their expense."

Wilson paused, apparently waiting for someone to comment on his account. "Please continue," Tennyson urged. "I'll save my questions until you have completed your story."

"Naturally, my first reaction was to consider the possibility of a runaway, which can happen if the brakes aren't set good and the fire isn't completely out. Enough steam pressure can build up to set an engine rolling. So I telegraphed the dispatcher right away and told him that he'd better alert the stations and operators east of here. Then I sent Gossett to roust out Steve Ellis and Frank Springer, who had brought the Rusk Turn in Saturday night. When those two got to the station, I grilled them pretty thoroughly about the steps they took to 'tie down' the train before leaving it. Their answers were right in line with the proper procedures, and there wasn't any reason to doubt what they told me. So it began to look like the locomotive might have been stolen, and I decided that I had better let Mr. Ward know."

With that, Wilson stopped and looked expectantly at Ward, who picked up the narrative. "I told Ted to meet me at my office and to bring Ellis and Springer with him. Upon arriving, I questioned the two men myself and was also satisfied that they were telling the truth. After directing the dispatcher to extend the alert across the entire division, I sent for Captain Stevens, the local head of our Railroad Police Bureau. He initiated a thorough search of the tracks from Shreveport to Dallas and seemed confident that the missing locomotive would be found quickly. When there had been no word of it by noon on Monday, I called in the Harrison County sheriff, Matt Peterson. He shared Stevens's view that the theft was nothing more than a prank and assured me that the engine was bound to be recovered soon. However, the search parties had still discovered no trace of it by Tuesday morning. It was then that I remembered hearing about you from Sheriff Lassiter of Dallas, Mr. Pierce; and I decided to telegraph for your assistance."

"Thank you, gentlemen," Tennyson said. "Your

reports have been most informative, although one or two of the points mentioned will need further elaboration. Before taking up those matters, however, I would ask that you favor us with a description of the missing locomotive, including its wheel arrangement and any distinguishing characteristics."

"Certainly, Mr. Pierce," Ward replied. "I apologize for not doing so earlier. It must be my agitation over this affair which caused me to overlook such a basic consideration. The stolen engine is Number 35, a Mogul of Class D-3, with six driving wheels and a two-wheel leading truck. She's one of ten identical locomotives that were erected for us by Brooks four years ago to haul heavy freights. You'll probably be able to see some other members of her class in the yard tomorrow. The engine which brought you down here from the depot is also a Mogul, but it's a lighter design used primarily for switching service."

"Is Number 35 a wood-burning locomotive?" Tennyson asked.

"Why, yes it is. Most of the engines on this division burn wood, due to the abundant supply of it from the Piney Woods."

"Very good," Tennyson commented. "Now, please tell me a bit more about this Rusk Turn that you mentioned. Is that a regularly scheduled run?"

"Yes, the Rusk Turn, which is also known as Train 17, departs Marshall at 6:10 a.m. every Tuesday, Thursday, and Saturday. It's a local freight that works a number of mills and logging outfits between here and

Rusk, as well as various other businesses along that branch, usually getting back here shortly after 8:00 p.m.," Ward answered.

"And what time did it return last Saturday?"

"Unfortunately, it was running about an hour late that day as a result of a lengthy wait for a flatcar to be loaded at the Hanley Brothers Mill. The train didn't pull into Blanco siding until a few minutes past nine."

"Are delays of that sort encountered with some regularity?"

"No, I wouldn't say so. Such things do happen from time to time, but our customers are pretty good about having their loads ready on time. They don't want to run the risk of missing a pickup."

"In that case, I will definitely need to speak with the crewmen later about what happened at the Hanley Brothers. Now, tell me about these derailed cars that blocked the yard lead. How did the incident occur?"

"As a matter of fact, the circumstances were rather curious. Normally, shunting activity in the yard on Saturdays is pretty well at a standstill by 8:00 p.m. But last Saturday, just as the yardmaster was about to shut things down for the night, he received a telegraphed message from the Missouri & Southwestern dispatcher in Shreveport, instructing him that a group of six cars needed to be set out for a special pickup early Sunday morning. The crew of Switcher 29 pulled the cars from Track 4 onto the yard lead and had just started to shove them into the interchange track when the first three cars derailed."

"What time was it when the derailment occurred?"

"From the reports of the incident, I would put it around half-past eight."

"And how long was it before the blocked track was cleared?"

"About three hours. We had a devil of a time because of the location. There wasn't any way to get our derrick car into position, so it was necessary to build a reaction frame and use a block-and-tackle to winch the cars back on the track."

"I imagine that this occupied most of your available personnel?"

"Yes, it did. Clearing the yard lead was our top priority. Until that track was opened, the yard was useless to us, which could have tied up the whole division."

"Has it been determined what caused the derailment?"

"It appeared that the point - that's the end of the moveable rail - on the north side of the switch into the interchange track had been bent away from the stock rail. Of course, the damage could have been caused by the derailment itself."

"What did Captain Stevens have to say about that?"

"I don't know that Captain Stevens was aware of the fact, Mr. Pierce. Do you think that he should have been informed about it?"

"I think, Mr. Ward, that someone obviously took a great deal of trouble to ensure that the Rusk Turn could not enter the yard on Saturday night."

"Ye-es, I see what you're driving at. So you think the derailment was part of an elaborate plan to steal the locomotive off that train?"

"That is a reasonable hypothesis, which we shall have to test by examining the physical evidence. First, however, I would like to know more about this message that the yardmaster received. Was it transmitted directly to him?"

"I'm afraid that I don't know, Mr. Pierce. My attention has been so occupied by the efforts to recover the missing engine that I really haven't given much thought to anything else. In retrospect, I probably should have, though."

"And why do you say so, Mr. Ward?"

"Because those cars that were moved on Saturday night weren't picked up until the Missouri and Southwestern's regular interchange run came through on Monday afternoon."

Tennyson's eyebrows arched noticeably as he remarked, "Then there was no special move on Sunday morning as allegedly indicated by the dispatcher in Shreveport?"

"No, there wasn't."

"That is certainly a telling fact. I'll need to speak with the yardmaster in the morning to learn more about that message and the movement of those cars."

"By all means, Mr. Pierce. Wilson here will be your escort tomorrow and will attend to whatever arrangements you require. Instructions have also been given for a locomotive and caboose to be placed at your disposal, so you can visit Blanco Siding and any other locations along the line which may be of interest. In view of the hour, however, I suggest that we adjourn for supper now. Will you and Dr. Weston do me the honor of joining me?"

"It would be our pleasure, sir," Tennyson responded; and I murmured my concurrence, as Ward escorted us out of the office.

CHAPTER 4

Confidential Disclosures

Over porterhouse steaks at the Delmont House, Ward briefed us on the operations of the North Texas Division of the Texas & Louisiana Railroad. As I listened to his descriptions of the weekly train movements, I gained a deep respect for the skill of the dispatchers who orchestrated all of this activity. I also came to realize how dependent railroads are on the telegraph lines. This thought had just struck me when I heard Tennyson saying, "Tell me, how are the train orders authenticated?"

"A unique call sign which identifies the dispatcher is included with each set of orders," Ward replied.

"How many people have access to these call signs?"

"Well, of course, there are the dispatchers themselves, the engineers and conductors, the stationmasters and yardmasters, the operators along the line who pass the orders up to the trains, and the road's officers."

"Is the same true for the Missouri & Southwestern?"

"Yes, the operating practice is a common one."

"Then, it would be a relatively simple matter for

someone to obtain one of these call signs and use it to send a counterfeit order, perhaps by tapping into the telegraph line at some remote location."

"I suppose that's possible, Mr. Pierce, although I am not aware of any instances of it. Do you have reason to believe such a thing was done?"

"Since there was no special move by the Missouri & Southwestern on Sunday morning, it is extremely probable that the telegram which was received by the yardmaster was not authentic. I am simply considering ways in which the message could have been transmitted. A better asssessment can be made after I have completed my interviews tomorrow. However, I should advise you that the signs point to this being anything but a simple case. As a result, the missing locomotive isn't likely to be found very quickly."

"You agree with me, then, that the theft wasn't just a prank?"

"I'm afraid that I do, Mr. Ward. In fact, I suspect that the disappearance of Engine Number 35 will be turn out to be only the first step in a scheme with very high stakes."

"Your comment worries me considerably, Mr. Pierce. What do you think the objective could be?"

"At this point, we can only speculate on the basis of common sense. For example, as Dr. Weston has observed, it's possible that the thieves needed a locomotive in order to transport something. Are you expecting any particularly valuable shipments in the near future?"

"Perhaps we had better continue this discussion at my office," Ward said, glancing around as though checking whether any of the other patrons were listening to our conversation. "Would you care for anything else before we go?"

"I couldn't eat another bite," Tennyson answered. "What about you, Jarvis?"

"No, thank you," I said, patting my overstuffed stomach. "That was quite a filling meal."

Ward, who was obviously well-known to the staff at the Delmont House, then waved at the waiter and rose to leave. I supposed that he kept a running tab with the owner for business purposes.

Back at his office, after he had offered us brandy (which we both accepted out of politeness), Ward said, "Gentlemen, no one else in the North Texas Division is aware of what I am about to tell you; and I must request that this information be held in the strictest confidence."

"You may rely upon both of us to do so," Tennyson responded.

"First of all, in answer to the question which you posed at the restaurant, Mr. Pierce, a consignment of gold bars from St. Louis is scheduled to cross our rails a week from this coming Friday. At Dallas, the train will be passed off to the Central Texas & Gulf Railroad for forwarding to Austin. The ultimate destination of the bullion is the state treasury. Naturally, every precaution will be taken to safeguard the shipment, which will be accompanied by federal agents."

"Nevertheless, such an enticing target might tempt

a particularly daring band of criminals. Moreover, in view of the rather considerable weight of the bars, a locomotive would prove quite useful in absconding with them. However, if I am not mistaken, you were intending to say something more."

"Ye-es, there *is* another matter which you probably ought to be told about. I have been debating with myself whether it can possibly have any bearing on the disappearance of the engine from Blanco siding."

"Please don't hold anything back. Complete frankness is essential if I am to have any chance of determining the reason for the theft."

"Of course, Mr. Pierce. My hesitation stems from the fact that this involves some extremely sensitive particulars concerning the railroad's future, and I am sworn to safeguard the details. Under the present circumstances, though, you should clearly be given at least an overview of the situation. It has to do with a possible merger and a struggle to prevent a rail monopoly in Texas. As you may know, with the completion of our line to El Paso two years ago and the negotiation of an interchange agreement there with the California Central, the Texas & Louisiana Railway was transformed into an important transportation link between its namesake states and the Pacific Coast. Even so, our access to the population centers of the Midwest remains limited. The board of directors considers it important for us to offer through service from El Paso all the way to St. Louis and eventually onward to Chicago. Toward that end, discussions were recently opened with officials of the Missouri & Southwestern about a possible merger of the two roads. An outside source of capital will be required to fund the transaction, and it is hoped that this will be provided by the investment banking firm of Woodward and Roche in Philadelphia. Mr. Woodward himself is planning to make an end-to-end inspection trip of the railroad in about two weeks. If news of the missing locomotive were to reach him, it would be a terrible embarassment, to say the least."

Tennyson had been sitting with his fingers tented and his head bowed throughout this intriguing tale. Momentarily, he said, "There are definitely some suggestive elements in that information, Mr. Ward, although I shall have to think about the possible implications. Can you elaborate on your comment regarding the attempt to prevent a rail monopoly in the state?"

"By all means. Perhaps you have read some of the accounts describing the devious transactions undertaken by the New York financier Jay Golden and his cronies. Their tactics have caused the ruination of several railroads in the East and have infuriated shippers in the affected areas. Now there is strong evidence that Golden intends to establish a rail monopoly in Texas. He has already gained control of the Central Texas & Gulf, and it is suspected that he has been secretly buying shares in the Texas & Louisiana through a number of businessmen who are acting on his behalf. This has lent a certain urgency to the completion of our proposed merger with the Missouri & Southwestern."

When Ward had finished speaking, Tennyson rose and said, "I believe that we have quite enough to contemplate for the time being. If you don't mind, Mr. Ward, Dr. Weston and I will retire to our hotel and see what we can make of all this."

"Surely, Mr. Pierce. It's time that I was getting home, anyway. I'll drop you off on my way."

Approximately ten minutes later, Ward's carriage drew to a stop in front of the Marshall Inn. When Tennyson and I had climbed down, our host said, "Ted Wilson will come by for you in the morning and remain at your disposal throughout the day. Please feel free to examine any part of the railroad which may be of interest. Let's plan on meeting again in my office around four o'clock to see how things stand. I hope that you have a restful night, gentlemen."

After bidding Ward good night, we proceeded to the desk in the lobby and inquired about our bags and our keys. A pair of rooms had been reserved for us on the second floor. As we approached the adjacent doorways, Tennyson remarked, "Well, have you reached any conclusions about this affair, Jarvis? Come in for a few minutes and share your thoughts with me."

Once inside Tennyson's room, I began to pace up and down while trying to organize my impressions of what we had heard from Wilson and Ward. Finally, I nervously ventured to say, "The message which the yardmaster received would appear to be the best starting point for your inquiries. It does strike me, though, that the thieves took quite a risk concerning the timing of the derailment."

"Splendid! Those are both perceptive observations, and I quite agree with the first. However, as *our* inquiries progress, I expect we will discover that there wasn't as much risk in the timing as it might appear."

"Why is that?" I asked, feeling a brief sense of gratification at Tennyson's compliment.

"There is good reason to believe that the movement of those cars onto the interchange track was carefully coordinated with the delay of the Rusk Turn at the Hanley Brothers Mill."

"So you believe that someone at the Hanley Brothers was in league with the thieves?"

"Very probably. After all, if the train had arrived back in Marshall at the usual time, it would almost certainly have been able to enter the yard before the lead track became blocked. The delay was an essential part of the plan."

"But couldn't the thieves have simply advanced the timetable for the events leading up to the derailment?"

"Not with any assurance of the desired result. If the spurious message had been given to the yardmaster earlier, he might still have waited until the scheduled shunting activities for the evening were completed before ordering those cars to be moved to the interchange track."

"I see what you mean. Then it looks like the theft was contrived by some sort of organized ring."

"As I stated earlier, this affair has the earmarks

of having been planned by a canny individual; and I suspect that he employed a number of accomplices to carry out the steps involved. Our inspections and interviews tomorrow should help to corroborate that hypothesis. Now, I suggest that we get some rest. An early morning is indicated."

Saying good night to Tennyson, I retired to my room and made ready for bed. Sleep came sporadically that night, however, as images of locomotives, train robbers, and boardroom meetings filled my dreams and periodically awakened me.

CHAPTER 5

Discoveries at Trackside

On the following morning, I awoke shortly after sunrise and dressed in moderate haste, anxious to get on with the day's activities. As I was about to leave my room, I noticed a slip of paper on the floor just inside the door. Picking it up, I found that it was a note from Tennyson saying that I should breakfast without him, but that he would meet Wilson and me in the lobby at about half past seven. Wondering where he could have gone at that hour, I proceeded to the hotel dining room and took a table which afforded a good view of the lobby. I was just finishing my ham and eggs when I saw Wilson come through the entrance door. After attracting his attention with a wave, I invited him to join me and told him of Tennyson's message. Over coffee, we chatted about the scheduled train movements through Marshall and the duties of a stationmaster. I then suggested that we move outside, since it was another splendid spring morning. We had just taken our seats on one of the benches in front of the hotel when

Tennyson approached, walking briskly and looking rather disheveled.

"Good morning, Jarvis, Mr. Wilson," he said. "I hope that you haven't been waiting too long. There were one or two points which I wanted to explore before we got underway."

"Not at all," I replied. "We have been having an interesting discussion about railroading procedures. But what have *you* been up to? Your appearance is frankly somewhat disarranged."

"Yes, I'm afraid that looking for evidence can be rather dirty work at times. If you can bear with me for another few minutes, I'll go and clean up a bit."

A short time later, Tennyson rejoined us in front of the hotel, looking a good deal more like the image of a respectable attorney. Wilson asked him what he wanted to do first, and he responded by suggesting that we start with a visit to Blanco siding. This surprised me a bit, since I thought that he wanted to speak to the yardmaster before heading out on the line; and I said as much.

"Yes, I had planned to do so," he answered. "However, I learned earlier this morning that both the yardmaster and the dispatcher who were on duty last Saturday night are still working the second shift."

"Yes, that's right," Wilson said, "but I can have them both come in this morning, if you want."

"No, let them get their sleep. We can interview them just before they go on duty this afternoon. In the meantime, let's make use of this fine morning to view the scene of the theft."

We then walked the quarter-mile or so to the station, where a switch engine and caboose were once again waiting. After telegraphing the dispatcher to obtain clearance for a westward move on the mainline, Wilson guided us aboard the caboose and signaled the engineer to proceed. Due to a speed restriction of six miles per hour within the city limits of Marshall, it took about twenty-five minutes for us to reach Blanco siding. As we approached its eastern end, the engineer braked to a crawl, whereupon Wilson swung down from the rear platform of the caboose and ran ahead to throw the turnout. Once the engine and caboose were in the siding, he re-aligned the switch for the mainline and walked back to where we had stopped. When Tennyson and I had joined him on the ground, he motioned for the engineer to pull forward a bit, then pointed at the track beside us and said, "This is about where Number 35 would have been sitting on Saturday night."

"Do you know how many trains have occupied this siding since then?" Tennyson asked.

"Four or five, I'd guess. The dispatcher can tell us the exact number."

"Am I correct in supposing that the only reason for any crewmembers of those trains to be on the ground here would be to throw the turnouts?"

"That's right, unless there was a problem like a hot box or a broken coupler."

"I see. Do occurrences of that sort show up on some kind of report?"

"Yes. The conductors are required to keep written logs of any incidents that delay their trains. A file of the records is maintained at the Division Office."

"Good. I'll want to see if there were submittals for any of the trains that stopped here since Saturday."

Tennyson then bent over and began walking slowly over the ground next to the track, moving back and forth in a serpentine pattern. Occasionally, he reached down, picked up something, and inserted it into an envelope which he took from the inside pocket of his coat. I had no idea what he was looking for, but concluded that my best course of action was to remain where I was until instructed otherwise. After about fifteen minutes of searching in this manner, Tennyson motioned for Wilson and me to join him at the edge of the woods.

"I can use your help now, Jarvis, and yours too, if you don't mind, Mr. Wilson," he said. "There is a good possibility that the thieves used the cover of this densely grown area to approach the siding. Our objective will be to see if we can discover signs of anyone coming through here recently. I would like for you to start about thirty yards west of this spot, Jarvis, and you about thirty yards east of here, Mr. Wilson. If each of us covers a swath about twenty yards wide, we can make reasonably quick work of the task. I suggest that you move back and forth in the manner that I employed just now and proceed as far into the woods as you can get within the next half-hour. In the event that you come across something of interest, please holler at me."

Some twenty minutes later, I heard Wilson yell, "Over here, Mr. Pierce!" Instinctively, I started to move in the direction from which his voice had come, then stopped as it occurred to me that I should continue scouring my assigned zone. The decision turned out to be a fortunate one, for shortly I stumbled upon a small clearing where the carpet of pine needles had been swept into a pattern of swirls. It appeared that someone had done this deliberately to obliterate the signs of their presence. On the northern edge of the open area, I came across what looked like a path that had been made by hacking away tree branches. This seemed like a significant discovery, so I cupped my hands to my mouth and called "Tennyson!" in a loud voice.

"Coming, Jarvis!" he shouted in reply; and after a short interval, I heard the crunching of twigs as he neared my position. Presently, he stepped into the clearing and said, "Well, well this is quite a find, my friend!"

"Yes, and come look over here!" I urged, trying to suppress my excitement as I showed him the opening into the woods. "Someone has evidently cut a trail through these trees."

"Indeed they have. This may well be the primary route which the thieves used to bring in the materials needed for their operation. Mr. Wilson has come across evidence that at least two men also entered the woods from the east. The clearing here probably served as a staging area where they waited for an opportune moment to approach the siding."

Tennyson then withdrew a small notebook from his coat pocket and began sketching in it. Upon finishing this task, he said, "Nicely done, Jarvis. You have made an excellent beginning, but we will leave it to Sheriff Peterson's deputies to follow that trail to its starting point. Let's be on our way."

I followed him back to the spot where Wilson was waiting, and the three of us proceeded out of the woods. As we emerged into the open, Tennyson glanced at his pocket watch and said, "I propose taking an early lunch in Longview, gentlemen. My treat, of course. If we start now, there should be ample time to carry out some inspections that I want to make along the way. Will your track clearance accommodate that, Mr. Wilson?"

After extracting a timetable from his back pocket and scanning it for a few seconds, Wilson looked at his own timepiece and said, "We'll have to remain here until the Number 104 freight passes on its way west. That should be about fifteen minutes from now. Otherwise, there are no trains opposing us for the next hour."

"All right. In the meantime, perhaps you can answer a few questions for me about track upkeep. If I am not mistaken, the ballast must be re-dressed at regular intervals; and it is occasionally necessary to replace ties which have deteriorated. Where is the nearest facility for storing the required supplies?"

"There's a fair-sized maintenance shed about six miles west of here."

"And what types of materials are stocked there?"

"The inventory usually includes enough crushed rock, ties, joiner plates, spikes, and the like to meet the needs of the track gang on this section of the line for approximately two months."

"What about segments of rail? I expect that replacements are occasionally needed for broken or damaged pieces."

"A few lengths are generally kept on hand for emergency repairs; but larger quantities would be brought out from Marshall on a work train."

"I assume that we'll have to pass the site of the maintenance shed on our way to Longview."

"Yes, but it's set back in the woods along a spur and can't be seen from the mainline."

"If your track clearance permits, I'd like to stop just long enough to take a look a quick look at the building and its surroundings."

"Sure, we should be able to accommodate that. Do you mind me asking, though, why you're interested in track materials?"

"For the moment, let's just say that I would like to test a conjecture. If anything comes of it, I'll tell you over lunch."

This exchange piqued my curiosity, and I was eager for a moment alone with Tennyson in order to ask what he had in mind. Before I could get him aside, however, he walked back to the siding and began examining the area beside the track once more. He was still engaged in this activity when I noticed puffs of smoke in the sky to the east. Upon seeing them, Wilson retrieved a lantern from the caboose and took up a position on the south side of the mainline. When I joined him and inquired about his objective, he explained that he was preparing to make a roll-by inspection of Train 104. Presently, the headlight of the distant locomotive came into view; and soon a faint chuffing sound could be heard. The noise grew louder by the second, rising to a thunderous bellow as the engine bore down on our position. When the last car had cleared the west turnout, Wilson crossed to where Tennyson was standing and said, "The rulebook requires a five-minute delay after a train passes before following it, but we should be able to run at a good speed once we're underway. Is there anything besides the maintenance shed that you want to see before we get to Longview?"

"Where does the Crockett Branch diverge from the mainline?" Tennyson asked.

"The wye is about three miles this side of the Longview yard limit."

"And how far along the branch is it to the Hanley Brothers Mill?"

"Around fifteen miles, I'd guess."

"We'd better leave that to another time then. Jarvis, where was that facility you noticed with a spur running into one of the buildings?"

"As I recall, it wasn't much more than ten minutes this side of the Longview station."

"Allowing for the time required to regain speed after

the train's stop, that would make the location perhaps nine or ten miles west of here," Tennyson said.

"Sounds like the Ferguson Mill," Wilson volunteered. "It's one of the oldest outfits in this area."

"If possible, I'd like to make a brief stop there as well," Tennyson returned. "We probably won't need to disembark, but the place warrants at least a passing survey."

"Whatever you say, Mr. Pierce."

After another few minutes, the three of us took our places in the caboose; and our train started moving very slowly along the siding. As we neared the west turnout, Wilson swung to the ground and ran ahead to align the switch. Once back aboard, he gave a highball signal to the engineer, who responded by rapidly increasing our speed to what felt like a pretty substantial rate. I soon became absorbed with watching the view out the window beside me and trying to count the seconds between successive telegraph poles. Thanks to this preoccupation, it seemed hardly any time at all before we slowed to a stop again.

"The maintenance shed is about sixty yards down that way, Mr. Pierce," Wilson said, pointing to a spur leading off from the north side of the track. "I'll come with you if Dr. Weston will agree to help me out with something."

"My services are entirely at your disposal," I responded, feeling a mild sense of importance. "How may I be of assistance?"

"The train has to be protected while it's stopped

on the mainline, which means flagmen have to be stationed both in front of us and behind us to warn any approaching traffic. I'll send the fireman up ahead, but I need for you to grab a lantern and a couple of torpedos and walk about fifty yards east. Place one of the cartridges on the top of the rail there, then continue another hundred yards or so and lay the other one. Next, take up a position roughly midway between them; and hold the lantern where the red aspect will be visible to any approaching train. When I give the signal to return, pick up the nearer torpedo on your way. Do you have any questions?"

"I don't believe so. The task seems simple enough."

Gathering the required equipment from a box at the rear of the caboose, I set off to take up my post. At the same time, Tennyson and Mr. Wilson started walking along the spur, quickly disappearing from view behind the brush that lined the track. Barely ten minutes later, while dutifully holding the lantern as instructed, I heard four long blasts of our locomotive's whistle. Turning around, I saw Wilson waving at me. When I reached the caboose, Tennyson announced, "Next stop, the Ferguson Mill."

We promptly climbed aboard, and Wilson motioned for the engineer to start. Soon the landscape was flitting past again; and the rythmic roaring of the locomotive, in concert with the sound of the wheels on the rails, made it difficult to converse. Tennyson sat looking out at the south side of the track, so I took my cue and kept watch on the north side. After a time, I heard him shout, "It should be coming up pretty quickly now." Wilson responded to this by stepping out onto the rear platform and giving an indication to slow down. Before long, we eased to a stop directly opposite from the site which I had observed on the previous day. "I'll handle the flagman duties this time," Wilson informed us. "Just let the engineer know when you're finished here."

Following Tennyson onto the rear platform, I was somewhat startled to see him ascend the ladder to the roof. "Come on up, Jarvis," he called. "The view is much better from this vantage point."

I cautiously scrambled up after him, then asked, "Are you looking for something in particular?"

"The missing locomotive, of course," he replied with a smile. "Actually, I would very much like to see the inside of that large structure and the area behind it; but for the moment, we'll have to be content with recording the general lay of the land here."

So saying, he took out his notebook and began sketching in it, occasionally pausing to gaze intently at some detail of the mill's configuration. When finished, he returned to the ladder and remarked, "This place definitely merits further investigation."

Once we had regained the inside of the caboose, Tennyson walked to the forward platform and managed to secure the engineer's attention. Four long notes from the whistle brought Wilson and the fireman running back to our train, and we quickly got underway for Longview. I decided to watch the south side of the track for this segment of our journey, since the features of interest seemed to lie in that direction. We all sat without speaking until I heard Wilson shout, "The junction with the Crockett Branch is just ahead." In another minute or two, we slowed as the maze of trackwork near the Longview depot came into view. Shortly, we braked to a stop beside a small two-story building.

Wilson hopped down, went inside, and emerged momentarily carrying a yellow sheet of paper, which he handed to the engineer. Climbing back aboard, he said, "We've been authorized to enter the yard and leave our train on Track 5, which is only a short walk from the Whistle Stop Canteen. I hope that'll be all right with you for lunch. They have pretty good food and generous portions."

"If you recommend it, Mr. Wilson, that's good enough for me," Tennyson replied. "Please invite the engineer and the fireman to join us as my guests."

"That's very kind of you, Mr. Pierce, but I'm sure that they would rather eat with the other crewmen at the company mess."

After threading our way through a number of turnouts, we came to a stop on a track which bordered a gravel-topped road. A short distance to the southeast, I could see a wider dirt road, along which there stood a row of what appeared to be commercial enterprises with false fronts. Pointing toward one of them, Wilson said, "That's where we're going."

Seven or eight minutes later, we were seated at a corner table in a sparsely furnished but clean restaurant which featured the hearty fare of the working man. Our guide ordered corned beef and cabbage, while Tennyson and I both chose the Irish stew. As we tucked into the abundant quantities of food on our plates, Wilson inquired whether anything of interest had turned up at the maintenance shed.

"You might say so," Tennyson answered. "I wanted to find out whether someone could have taken materials from the shed without being seen. My conclusion was that it would have been quite simple. The surrounding brush provides a very effective screen, and the lock on the door is of a type that can be easily opened with the point of a knife."

"But why are you interested in track maintenance materials?" I asked.

"Have you ever heard of a shoo-fly installation, Jarvis?"

"No, I can't say that I have. What is it?"

"Perhaps Mr. Wilson would be good enough to explain."

"Sure. A shoo-fly is a temporary set of rails built so that trains can bypass an area where construction or maintenance work is being done on the regular line."

"And these temporary rails can be laid very quickly, can they not?" Tennyson asked.

"That's the whole idea," Wilson responded. "Shoo-fly construction doesn't have to meet the usual track standards because the bypass is only used for a short time, with trains restricted to very slow speeds."

"I'm afraid that your point still eludes me, Tennyson," I said, feeling rather doltish.

"Put yourself in the place of the individual who planned the theft. You need a way to get the locomotive out of site quickly and keep it concealed for an extended period of time. What solution comes to mind?"

"I suppose he might think of storing it inside the large building at the Ferguson Mill."

"Possibly. However, a location such as that could serve as no more than a temporary hiding place. The person behind this crime would undoubtedly realize that every mile of track between Shreveport and Dallas was likely to be searched once the alarm had been given. Consequently, he would have sought some means to remove the locomotive a fair distance from the Texas & Louisiana right-of-way."

"It's my understanding, though, that the only connections of the North Texas Division to other railroads are at Marshall and Dallas. Isn't that right, Mr. Wilson?"

"Yes. We have a junction with the Missouri & Southwestern a few miles east of Marshall and one with the Central Texas & Gulf just west of Dallas."

"And what conclusion do you draw from that?" Tennyson asked.

"I'm really not sure," I replied, trying to fathom what he was implying. "It doesn't seem very likely that the thieves would risk taking the locomotive to either of those places."

"Precisely! An alternative had to be found. One which strikes me as entirely plausible is the construction of a shoo-fly track leading from the temporary hiding place to the nearby rails of another carrier."

"Why, such a thing would never have occurred to me! What other carrier is there in the vicinity of the Ferguson Mill, though?"

"Several private logging railroads operate in the Piney Woods, and I believe that at least two of them employ standard-gauge track. We shall have to see if the Harrison or Gregg County Land Offices have maps of their routes."

"Now I understand why you were asking about the lengths of rail, Mr. Pierce," Wilson commented. "However, there probably wouldn't have been enough on hand in the shed to build more than about a hundred yards of track."

"That might have sufficed for the purpose, depending on the alignments to be connected. Of course, there are also other potential sources for the rails if the quantity in the shed proved inadequate. For example, they could have been obtained from one of the logging railroads, pulled up from an unused line, or even stolen from the stock at the Marshall yard."

"I'm sure that Captain Stevens and Sheriff Peterson will be interested in hearing about this idea," Wilson said.

"Perhaps so, but I ask that the two of you keep it to yourselves for the time being. We must tread carefully in order to avoid alerting the thieves before discovering their intentions."

The rest of the meal was passed in casual conversation

about the local community. When we had finished eating, Tennyson said, "It had been my intention to undertake an inspection of the areas along the tracks on the outskirts of town, but I think now that we can make better use of our time by returning to Marshall. I'm anxious to interview Ellis and Springer about what happened at the Hanley Brothers Mill on Saturday."

We arrived back at Track 5 to find our engineer and fireman just climbing up into the locomotive. Wilson exchanged a few words with them, then told us that we would have to stop at the yard office again so that he could telegraph the dispatcher to obtain clearance for the run to Marshall. "While I'm doing that, the engineer will turn our train on the wye so we're heading east," he added.

It took about ten minutes for us to reach our objective, due to being held up at one track crossing while a long freight trundled past. Tennyson followed Wilson into the building, saying that he wanted to send a message to Mr. Ward, while I elected to stay on board so that I could ride around the wye. In fairly short order, we were ready to get underway for Marshall.

Once clear of the city limits, the engineer gave the locomotive its head; and we ran at a good pace for most of the return trip, slowing only for turnouts and posted speed restrictions. At precisely twelve minutes before two, we rolled to a stop next to the Division Office in Marshall. As we climbed down from the caboose, Wilson pointed to a locomotive on a nearby track and said, "The missing engine looks just like that one."

CHAPTER 6

Pieces of the Puzzle

After thanking the engineer and fireman for their services and giving each of them a generous tip, Tennyson proceeded directly to Mr. Ward's office and asked to be announced. The formidable Mrs. Freeman replied with disdain that the Superintendent could not be disturbed, but relented when my friend insisted and fixed a determined stare upon her. Wilson and I remained in the antechamber as Tennyson entered the office and closed the door behind him. A few minutes later, he returned and told us that Ellis and Springer were waiting in a room downstairs. "While Dr. Weston and I are speaking with them, Mr. Wilson, perhaps you would be good enough to arrange for the yardmaster and the dispatcher who were on duty last Saturday night to join us in about half an hour," he added.

"Certainly, Mr. Pierce. I'll attend to it," Wilson answered.

Back on the first floor, Wilson directed us to the room in question, then left to carry out his errand. When he was out of earshot, Tennyson said, "I thought that Ellis and Springer might be more candid if the stationmaster were not present."

Entering the indicated door, we found two men whose manner of dress immediately gave away their occupations. One was heavy-set, with graying hair and a weatherbeaten face. His attire consisted of denim overalls and a matching cap, accented by a red bandana tied around his neck. It wasn't difficult to surmise that he must have been the engineer of the Rusk Turn. The other man, who had a slender build with coal-black hair and a sallow complexion, was dressed in the same type of uniform that Mr. Wilson wore. I concluded that he was the conductor of the fated train. Tennyson looked from one to the other of them, then extended his hand and said, "Mr. Ellis, Mr. Springer, my name is Pierce; and this is Dr. Weston. We would like to ask you a few questions about what took place at the Hanley Brothers Mill during your run last Saturday."

The older man eyed us warily and remarked in a somewhat surly tone, "Not much to tell. Pretty routine run until we got the orders to take the hole at Blanco."

"Now Steve, you know that Mr. Ward told us we were to cooperate with Mr. Pierce," the other man interposed. "You'll have to excuse him, gentlemen. He's taking it kind of personally that his engine has gone missing."

"I quite understand," Tennyson responded. "Please be assured that our only interest is in discovering information which may aid in the recovery of Number 35. Whatever you tell us will be held in confidence. I am asking about what occurred at the Hanley Brothers on Saturday because Mr. Ward told us that you were delayed there for some time while waiting for cars to be loaded. Is that correct?"

"Yes, that's right, Mr. Pierce," the conductor responded. "We work the Hanley Brothers on the return leg of the trip because the turnout there faces south. Our Train Orders on Saturday called for us to pick up two cars of rough-sawn lumber from them. When I went to take care of the paperwork with the foreman, Tom Buckley, he told me that the loads weren't ready yet. Normally, in a case like that, we would have left the job for our next run; but Buckley insisted that we wait. Since the Hanley Brothers operation has been a good customer, I agreed."

"How long did it take for them to finish loading the cars?" Tennyson asked.

"A little over an hour. If I'd known that at the outset, I probably wouldn't have gone along with the request. Buckley initially told me that we'd only be held up about twenty minutes."

"Do you know what accounted for the additional time?"

"The story we heard was that they discovered there wasn't enough lumber on hand in the crib to make up the order, so the jacks had to go get some more logs and rip them."

"Had that ever happened before in your experience?"

"No, sir. The mills that we serve generally have their

loads waiting for us. When delays occur, more often than not they're due to problems with the paperwork."

"You must have been making pickups at the Hanley Brothers for quite a while now?"

"The railroad has been serving them ever since the Crockett Branch was finished six years ago. Frank and I have held down the Rusk Turn since the summer of '83."

"Has Buckley been the foreman there for all that time?"

"No, he was just hired for the post about three months ago. The previous strawboss, Ed Cooper, was getting up in years and was finally persuaded to retire."

"You have been very helpful, Mr. Springer. There is just one more thing that I would ask you to do for me," Tennyson said, guiding the conductor toward a blackboard which hung on the wall opposite the door. "Can you sketch the track arrangement at the Hanley Brothers and indicate the locations of their buildings?"

"I'm not a very good artist, Mr. Pierce, but I'll do my best," the conductor replied.

While Springer was drawing on the blackboard, Tennyson turned to the engineer and said, "Mr. Ellis, I'd like to ask you something about running Engine Number 35."

Ellis brightened noticeably as he said, "Go right ahead, Mr. Pierce. Nobody knows that Mogul better'n me."

"I've been told that every locomotive has its own individual characteristics. Is there anything in particular that someone would need to be familiar with in order to operate Number 35 properly?"

"Well, she's a really sweet engine, Mr. Pierce. Not a better one on the roster. Still, it takes a careful hand with the cutoff valve to keep her from belching black smoke when starting up. The fireman also needs to keep a real close eye on the water level when you've got a heavy train. That's about it."

"Thank you, Mr. Ellis, Mr. Springer. I appreciate your time. If you happen to think of anything else which might have some bearing on the events of last Saturday, please let Mr. Ward or Mr. Wilson know."

When they had left, I said, "That business with the lumber shortage certainly sounds suspicious. It appears that you were right about someone at the Hanley Brothers being in league with the thieves."

"The information which Springer provided is not conclusive, but it does appear that the delay at the Hanley Brothers was contrived. We shall have to learn more about their business and Mr. Buckley's background," Tennyson commented as he copied the drawing on the blackboard into his notebook.

Presently, a light knock on the open door sounded; and we turned to see Wilson in the company of a middle-aged man with the look of a veteran railroader and a bespectacled young man who was neatly dressed in the attire of an office worker.

"Mr. Pierce, Dr. Weston, this is Asa Bonnett, who was the second-shift yardmaster last Saturday,"

Wilson said, indicating the older man; "and this is Brian Simpson, who was the dispatcher on that shift."

"Please be seated, gentlemen," Tennyson greeted them. "I assume that Mr. Wilson has explained why I wanted to speak with you?"

"Yes, sir," Bonnett answered. "He said it's about the order that came in to set those cars out on the interchange track."

"That's right, Mr. Bonnett. Can you tell me how and when you received that message?"

"It was telegraphed to the yard office a little after 8:00 p.m. that night."

"Was there anything unusual about it?"

"Other than the time, no."

"There wasn't any reason for you to doubt its authenticity?"

"None at all. I'll admit to feeling a little peeved with the dispatcher in Little Rock for waiting until that time of night to tell me about the special move, but I figured he had probably just been too busy earlier in the evening."

"All right. Have you brought the message with you, as I asked?"

"Yes, sir. Here it is."

After perusing the piece of paper which Bonnett handed to him, Tennyson asked, "Did you copy this from the wire yourself?"

"No. It was taken down by one of the clerks."

"Can anyone corroborate that the message actually came in over the telegraph?"

"I'm not sure that I understand you, Mr. Pierce."

"Let me put it another way. Can you vouch for the integrity of the clerk?"

"Well, I don't know anything about his personal life; but he's been pretty reliable on the job. What are you driving at?"

"It's conceivable that there wasn't actually any telegraph transmission. In other words, the clerk might have written down a counterfeit message while pretending to copy it from the wire. Would the circumstances have allowed him to carry out such a deceit?"

"I'd have to admit it's possible, but the idea seems awfully far-fetched."

"Perhaps it is. I am not accusing the young man, mind you. However, the possibility that someone in the yard office was involved in the scheme to steal the locomotive cannot be overlooked."

Turning his attention to the dispatcher, Tennyson continued, "Tell me, Mr. Simpson, what do you know about the alleged telegram?"

"Very little, sir," Simpson replied. "I didn't even know that it existed until Mr. Ward informed me what happened."

"Orders such as this are normally sent to the Marshall dispatcher and then relayed to the yard office, aren't they?"

"That's correct. However, if a move is carried out strictly within the yard limits, the dispatcher doesn't have to be informed."

"What actions would you have taken if this message had been received at the dispatching station?"

"After recording the transmission as it came in, I would have confirmed the contents with the Missouri & Southwestern dispatcher in Little Rock. Then I'd have written out two copies and sent one to the yard office with a messenger while posting the other for the third-trick man."

"A sensible procedure, but one which I assume is not reciprocated by the clerks in the yard office."

"Pardon, sir? I'm afraid that I don't understand what you mean."

"Simply that the dispatcher is not provided with copies of the messages which are received in the yard office."

"Oh, I see. Not unless an order affects the movement of a train or engine outside of the yard limits."

"Very well. Now, I understand that you asked the dispatcher in Little Rock whether he had sent any message about moving those cars to the interchange track and that he denied having done so."

"That's right. Mr. Ward called me in about an hour ago and told me to find out if the directions for the unscheduled interchange had really come from the Missouri & Southwestern. I telegraphed Wayne Tarpley, who was on duty in Little Rock last Saturday evening. His answer was that he hadn't transmitted the order or received any request to confirm it."

"And yet, this is his call sign at the bottom of the

sheet?" Tennyson asked, holding up the copy of the message so that Simpson could see it.

"It appears to be, sir."

"Could one of Tarpley's co-workers possibly have sent the message without his knowledge?"

"I don't really know, but he did say that none of the other dispatchers in Little Rock knew anything about a special move being planned for Sunday morning."

"All right. Thank you for your time, gentlemen. Please don't discuss this matter with anyone other than Mr. Ward or Mr. Wilson."

Tennyson then rose, shook hands with the two men, and added, "I want to caution you, Mr. Bonnett, not to say anything to your clerk that might lead him to think that he is under suspicion."

When Bonnett and Simpson had left the room, Tennyson said, "I told Mr. Ward that we would meet with him at four o'clock to report on our findings today. In the meantime, I want to take a look at the track diagrams upstairs. While I'm doing that, Jarvis, perhaps Mr. Wilson would be good enough to direct you to the Harrison County Land Office. See if you can find any records which show the locations of the logging railroads that operate in the Piney Woods."

"I'll do my best if Mr. Wilson will point the way," I replied.

"Certainly. In fact, I'll be glad to accompany you," Wilson said. "The Land Office is only a block from the County Courthouse, and I know the clerk there.

We'll hitch a ride back to the station, and then it's just a short walk from there."

As Tennyson headed for the stairway, I followed Wilson to the main entrance. We walked around to the back of the building, where he told me to wait while he crossed to an adjacent track and spoke to the engineer of a light switch engine. Momentarily, he shouted for me to join him, adding a warning to watch my step. When I reached the locomotive, he said, "Climb aboard. Ed has agreed to run us down to the station. I'm afraid there's no caboose on hand, so we'll have to ride in the cab."

Never having seen the controls of a steam engine at close quarters, I was delighted at this prospect, but tried not to show it. The first step of the ladder was a long way from the ground, and I felt a definite strain in my right calf while climbing up. Once we were aboard, Wilson introduced me to the two crewmen, who both nodded without saying anything. I watched with unabashed interest as the engineer gave two tugs on the whistle cord, then manipulated various valves and levers to start the machine moving.

Not quite ten minutes later, our conveyance drew to a stop behind the station. After thanking the enginemen for the ride, we climbed down and set off toward the town square. Upon reaching the County Courthouse, Wilson pointed to a street behind it and said, "The Land Office is over there. We can cut through this way."

Our destination proved to be a narrow building whose two front windows each bore a sign proclaiming "Harrison County Land Office" in large black lettering.

As we entered, a man behind the counter looked up and exclaimed, "Why, Ted Wilson, you old rascal! I haven't seen you in a coon's age. Don't tell me you're in the market for some property."

"Hello, Howard. It's been awhile, all right," Wilson replied. "I wouldn't mind having a few acres if the price was right, but our business today concerns the railroad. You've probably heard about the locomotive that went missing last weekend. Well, an associate of this gentleman has been retained by Mr. Ward to help us find out what happened to it; and we need some information from you."

Stepping up to the counter, I extended my hand and said, "My name is Dr. Jarvis Weston. I'm not quite sure how to go about this, but I need to locate the routes of the private logging railroads in this county."

With a rather flaccid handshake, the clerk responded, "Howard Newton, Dr. Weston. I'll be glad to show you what we have. It would help, though, if you could tell me what part of the county you're interested in."

Pausing a moment to consider, I replied, "The area south of the Texas & Lousiana mainline between Marshall and Longview is probably the best starting point."

"Okay. Let me see what I can find," Newton said, disappearing through a doorway behind him.

Before long, he returned carrying three large folders, which he set down side-by-side on the counter. Opening one, he began running a finger across the page, commenting that our search would go faster if we each took a set of plats. Wilson and I then turned back the covers of the remaining files and began to scan the sheets for any indications of railroad rights-of-way.

We had been looking through the drawings in silence for five or six minutes when I heard Newton exclaim, "Here! I think I've got something."

Moving closer to see where he was pointing, I noted the usual symbol for a rail line in the northeast sector of the page which he had been perusing. Excited at this discovery, I quickly examined the remainder of the survey to orient myself, then called Wilson over and asked, "Isn't that about where the Ferguson Mill is located?"

After studying the map for a moment, he answered, "I believe it's on the section of land just northeast of this one."

Without saying a word, Newton turned over a couple of pages in the folder and directed our attention to the top portion of another plat. Wilson peered at it and said, "Yep. That's the site of the Ferguson Mill. You sure do know your records, Howard."

Since our finding seemed noteworthy, I requested a piece of paper from the clerk and carefully sketched the location of the rail line, taking care to note the reference numbers of the two surveys. When I had folded the sheet and placed it securely in my wallet, I looked at my pocket watch and said, "We'd better be starting back if we want to be on time for the meeting at four o'clock. Thank you very much for your assistance, Mr. Newton. You have been extremely helpful."

Taking our leave, Wilson and I strode rapidly down the street and cut across the lawn of the County Courthouse, arriving back at the station just twelve minutes before four. Proceeding to the rear of the depot, we were surprised to find the same locomotive and caboose that had carried us to Longview earlier. The engineer stuck his head out of the window and said, "Mr. Ward sent us to get you. Better hurry."

We quickly scrambled aboard the caboose, and Wilson immediately signaled the engineer to proceed. With two long toots of the whistle, we started backing slowly along the siding. The trip to the Division Office seemed to take forever. As we finally braked to a standstill, I glanced again at my pocket watch, which indicated two minutes before the hour. Jumping to the ground, I fairly ran to the front of the building, with Wilson trailing behind me.

Taking the steps of the stairway two at a time, I reached Mrs. Freeman's desk short of breath and had difficulty in getting out the words to ask if Mr. Pierce had already arrived. The redoubtable secretary eyed me with an air of derision before declaring in a disapproving tone that Mr. Ward and Mr. Pierce were waiting for us. Moving gingerly around her desk, I knocked on the office door and then opened it part way.

"Come in, Jarvis, come in," Tennyson enjoined, sounding quite jovial. "Mr. Ward and I have been discussing English history. It seems that he is descended from the sixth Earl of Chelmsford, for whom one of my ancestors once performed a service of some significance.

Perhaps history is destined to repeat itself. But tell me, did you discover anything of use at the Land Office?"

"I believe that we may have," I replied, taking a seat next to Tennyson, while Wilson drew up a chair at the end of the desk. "With the aid of the clerk there, we found a plat showing a rail line that runs through the quarter-section of land just southwest of the Ferguson Mill."

Withdrawing the paper from my wallet, I handed it across, then commented that there wasn't time to look through the surveys covering the areas farther to the south. "Another visit to the Land Office may be in order," I added.

"Excellent! This is more than I had hoped for," Tennyson commented, as he glanced at the sheet. "You have been a tremendous help today, Jarvis. As have you, Mr. Wilson."

While I smiled spontaneously in response to the compliment, Ward asked, "Has Dr. Weston found further evidence to support the hypothesis which you were telling me about?"

"Perhaps," Tennyson answered. "It is more accurate to say that the facts we have uncovered so far, when fitted together as pieces of the puzzle, seem to yield a believable portrait of what occurred. There is much more to be done before we can determine the motive for the theft, but I believe that we have made a good start today."

"If you don't mind, I would like to hear more about the piecing together of these facts," Mr. Ward said.

"By all means," Tennyson responded. "Let's consider the day's results in chronological order. Early this morning, I walked through the yard area, where I made a close inspection of the turnout leading to the Interchange Track. The bent rail had already been replaced, of course; but, fortunately the damaged piece was still on hand. Examining it under a magnifying lens, I found scrapes near one end such as those which would be made by the prying side of a crowbar or similar tool. In the corresponding location on the mating rail of the turnout, I found another set of marks where the heal of a crowbar might have rested. Our first finding is thus that it appears likely the point of the turnout was deliberately bent in order to cause the derailment.

"While in the yard area, I happened to notice a six-coupled locomotive which was being oiled by a fellow whom I took for an engineer. I struck up a conversation with him and confirmed my surmise that the engine was a Class D-3 Mogul. The crewman was good enough to allow me into the cab and to answer my questions about the functions of the various valves and levers. He also explained quite clearly how to go about getting a cold engine under steam. From this information, I concluded that the men who took Number 35 from Blanco siding must have had more than a passing familiarity with the operation of steam engines and probably had experience with this particular class of locomotives or very similar ones from the same builder. This, then, is our second finding.

"I next took the opportunity to watch a brakeman

coupling and uncoupling cars as shunting operations were carried out. With a bit of persistent persuasion, he demonstrated the operation of a coupler for me on a stationary car. This was simply to satisfy my curiosity about the amount of time required to engage or disengage a car from a train.

"On my way back to the hotel, I stopped to have a conversation with Sheriff Peterson. For the time being, the details of our discussion are better not disclosed. Suffice it to say that he agreed to undertake certain inquiries for me. If anything of consequence arises from them, I will naturally inform you.

"At the hotel, I found Mr. Wilson and Dr. Weston waiting patiently for me; and the three of us set out for Blanco siding. There, we uncovered telltale signs of the thieves' presence. Near the track at the east end of the siding, about where Number 35 was left on Saturday night, I came across a number of faint but discernible footprints, as well as the remnants of some cigarettes and cigars. The tobacco from these will be subjected to chemical tests when we return to Dallas and may possibly yield some information about their sources. However, the most significant findings at that site are due to Dr. Weston and Mr. Wilson, who discovered the paths by which the thieves apparently entered the nearby woods and the clearing that was probably used as a staging area where they waited for an opportune moment to strike. This collection of physical evidence constitutes our third finding.

"From Blanco siding, we proceeded to the storage

shed which is located about six miles west of there. I made a close inspection of the lock on its door and concluded that even an unskilled burglar could easily gain entrance. Moreover, the surrounding brush provides a very effective screen for anyone approaching the shed. Hence, our fourth finding is that the thieves had ready access to track maintenance materials.

"Our final stop before lunch was at the Ferguson Mill, where I made a sketch of the general layout, including the track arrangement and the adjacent topographical features. My purpose was to evaluate the possibility that the thieves had used the facility as a temporary hiding place for the locomotive. I concluded that it was quite feasible that they had done so, and this amounts to our fifth finding.

"Following a tasty meal in Longview at a restaurant recommended by Mr. Wilson, we returned here in order to question the gentlemen whom I had asked you to make available. From Mr. Ellis and Mr. Springer, I learned enough to conclude that the delay of the Rusk Turn at the Hanley Brothers Mill on Saturday was contrived. This constitutes our sixth finding. I also found out from Mr. Bonnett and Mr. Simpson that the message about moving the cars to the interchange track probably did not come from anyone at the Missouri & Southwestern and may not even have been transmitted by telegraph. This is our seventh finding.

"Lastly, with Mr. Wilson's kind assistance, I dispatched Dr. Weston to the County Land Office to look for the locations of the private logging railroads in this vicinity. You have already heard his report of a rail line near the Ferguson Mill, which represents our eighth finding."

When Tennyson paused after this lengthy summation of the day's activities, Ward said, "I am impressed with the amount of information which you have collected, but must confess that I don't really understand how all of these discoveries fit together."

"As I mentioned earlier, at this stage of the investigation, they are simply pieces of the puzzle," Tennyson replied. "My arrangement of those pieces must be regarded as hypothetical for the moment and remains to be tested through further inquiries. However, the chain of reasoning is simple enough. First, the evidence suggests that the theft of the locomotive was a highly coordinated effort, involving the activities of participants at four different locations: the yard here in Marshall, the Hanley Brothers Mill, Blanco siding, and the Ferguson Mill. Second, the fact that the missing Mogul has not been found after a thorough search of the Texas & Louisiana line indicates that it was somehow taken off the property. Third, it is unlikely that the thieves would risk coming back through Marshall or running all the way to Dallas, for fear of being seen. Therefore, the engine was probably transferred to one of the private logging railroads in the Piney Woods. Fourth, the existence of such a line in close proximity to the Ferguson Mill suggests a convenient means of removal through the construction of a connecting track using materials stolen from the nearby maintenance shed."

"Your inferences certainly seem plausible, Mr. Pierce," Ward remarked. "If what you say is true, though, the thieves obviously took exceptional pains to achieve their end. That would seem to suggest they expect a substantial payoff."

"Yes, it would, Mr. Ward. The men behind this affair undoubtedly have an objective of some consequence. In view of that, additional precautions should be taken against the possible theft of the bullion shipment. I plan to visit Colonel Yarbrough at Fort Worth tomorrow afternoon and ask for his assistance in providing protection for the train. Even so, I admit to being concerned that the actual objective in this affair may be something far less obvious."

"What can we at the railroad do to help?"

"Please let me know immediately if anything out of the ordinary occurs in your operations or if you learn of any activity involving the railroad in which there is a significant financial consequence."

"Very well, Mr. Pierce. I am grateful for your assistance, although the possibilities which you have described are certainly troubling ones. In fact, I am beginning to wonder if the road's president shouldn't be briefed about all of this."

"I would ask that you refrain from doing so for at least a few days yet, Mr. Ward. In fact, I would urge both you and Mr. Wilson not to speak of these conjectures outside of this office. The chances of thwarting the thieves' plans could be greatly diminished if the details of our investigation become too widely known. I will keep you informed of further developments after my return to Dallas and will send prompt notice of any action which appears advisable on your part."

"In that case, I will leave the matter in your hands, Mr. Pierce. After all, you seem to have made a good deal more progress in a single day than Captain Stevens and Sheriff Peterson have in several. I trust that you and Dr. Weston will be able to join me for a home-cooked meal this evening. Mrs. Ward is anxious to meet both of you and has promised an appetizing menu. If it's convenient, I'll send my carriage to your hotel around half past six."

"That will be fine. Please thank your wife for the gracious invitation and tell her that we are looking forward to making her acquaintance."

"Good! Ted, will you see to it that Mr. Pierce and Dr. Weston have a ride to wherever they need to go?"

"Please don't bother. It's a nice afternoon for a walk, and we can use the exercise," Tennyson said, as we rose and took our leave.

CHAPTER 7

A Possible Lead

At the Ward's home that evening, we enjoyed an excellent meal of roasted chicken, sweet corn, and yellow rice, topped off with blueberry pie. Mrs. Ward proved to be quite a good cook, as well as a skilled conversationalist. Our discussions about art and the cultural activities in Marshall were a welcome diversion from the problem of the missing locomotive. After supper, Tennyson conferred in private with our host for a few minutes. When they had finished, a servant drove us back to the Marshall Inn.

The next morning, I was awakened before dawn by a series of loud knocks, followed in short order by the sound of Tennyson's voice calling my name. Stumbling across to the door and opening it a crack, I found the cheerful countenance of my friend peering at me. "Rise and shine," he urged energetically. "An early breakfast is called for if we want to make the most of our day. There are some matters that I need to discuss with Sheriff Peterson, and a quick stop at the Land Office may be worthwhile."

"Just give me a moment," I answered groggily. "I'll meet you downstairs."

Ten or twelve minutes later, having hastily dressed and shaved, I joined Tennyson at a table near the front window of the hotel dining room. He apologized for waking me and asked if I had slept well. "Moderately so," I replied. "The implications of what we learned yesterday kept running through my head."

"Yes, I'm afraid that's one of the hazards of investigative work. It's always difficult to set a puzzle aside until the solution has been found. Well, perhaps you can get a bit of rest on the train. Tomorrow should also provide a change of pace, since we will be pretty-well occupied with getting you settled into the house."

"The move! With all that's happened, it completely slipped my mind. I'll have to find someone to help transport the furniture."

"You needn't bother. Two able-bodied young men who are acquaintances of Miss Amy have agreed to provide their services for a very modest fee."

"Making those arrangements was a very thoughtful gesture, Tennyson. I really can't thank you enough for allowing me to share your residence."

"Nonsense, Jarvis. You have already thanked me through your assistance with this investigation. Your findings yesterday were invaluable to me."

"Hardly that. Still, I'm pleased to have contributed something worthwhile. In return, if it isn't being too presumptuous, would you mind telling me what you discussed with the sheriff?"

"Not at all. I didn't want to mention the specifics in front of Mr. Ward and Wilson, because they might have inadvertently altered their behavior toward the personnel involved. However, even before our interview with Asa Bonnett, I suspected that someone in the yard office was involved in the transmittal of the counterfeit message. When I visited Sheriff Peterson, I explained the basis of my suspicion and asked that he check into the backgrounds and associates of the employees who had access to that building. Before we leave this morning, I want to tell him what Bonnett related to us and request that some men be dispatched to find the other end of the trail which you came across at Blanco siding."

"You also mentioned the possibility of stopping by the Land Office. Am I correct in supposing that you want to review the plats for the southern part of the county?"

"A few of them, at any rate. While your discovery of a rail line near the Ferguson Mill is an important clue, I'm also interested in looking at the surveys which cover the vicinity of the Hanley Brothers Mill and the region southwest of there."

Upon finishing our breakfasts, we immediately set out for the sheriff's office, which was located about midway down the east side of the town square. Tennyson introduced me to Sheriff Peterson, then withdrew his notebook and repeated what Asa Bonnett had told us on the previous afternoon. He also related the details of the clearing and trail which I had found in the woods next to Blanco siding, supplementing these with copies of the sketches which he had made there. After agreeing on a schedule of communication, we left and headed toward the Land Office.

As we walked along the street, I ventured to wonder why Tennyson hadn't asked the sheriff to look into Tom Buckley's background. He replied that there was a more discreet way of gathering the needed information, but didn't elaborate on his plans.

At the Land Office, it was my turn to handle the introductions. Newton said that he was surprised to see me again so soon, but willingly trotted out the same three folders which Wilson and I had been shown on the previous afternoon. When Tennyson explained what area he was interested in, the clerk immediately opened one file and called us over to take a look. "This is where the Hanley Brothers Mill is located," he said, pointing to the lower left-hand portion of the plat. "You can find the adjoining surveys by looking at the designations on the tops of the pages."

After thanking him and taking a moment to orient ourselves, we turned to the preceding map, which depicted the quarter-section of land just west of the one which Newton had shown us. Scrutinizing it carefully, I saw no indication of a rail line and was prepared to move on to the consideration of another page. However, Tennyson took out his notebook and directed my attention to the name listed under "owner" at the bottom of the plat: The Easton & Monroe Logging Company. "Did you happen to notice the name of the owner on the survey where you found the rail line, Jarvis?" he asked.

Feeling slightly chagrined, I admitted my failure to do so, but quickly moved to the applicable folder and found the map in question. Scanning down to the bottom of the drawing, I read "The Easton & Monroe Logging Company."

"Splendid!" Tennyson responded. "Let's just examine a few more of these, and we can be on our way."

When we had checked the plats representing the quarter-sections directly north, south, and east of the one containing the site of the Hanley Brothers Mill, we thanked Newton for his help and departed.

On the way back to the hotel, I inquired with evident eagerness whether Tennyson thought that the missing locomotive might be hidden somewhere on the Easton & Monroe property.

"Quite possibly," he replied, in a purely matter-of-fact tone.

"Hadn't we better stop and alert the sheriff?" I urged, convinced that haste was called for.

"That would be unwise at this point, Jarvis. You must bear in mind that our goal is not simply to recover Number 35, but to prevent the person who planned the theft from achieving his objective, whatever that may be."

"But how are we going to discover whether the locomotive is actually on that property unless the sheriff searches it?"

"It happens that I am acquainted with an old army scout by the name of Choctaw Jones who knows the Piney Woods like the back of his hand. When we return to Dallas, I intend to give him a commission to explore the area in question. If the missing engine is anywhere in that vicinity, you may be assured that he will find it. Moreover, he will do so without alerting the thieves to his presence."

This answer brought home to me the fact that I was a novice at the art of investigation, and I resolved to refrain from making any further suggestions about the conduct of the case.

Upon reaching the hotel, I was surprised to find Mr. Ward waiting in the lobby. As we approached him, he rose from his chair and said, "I wanted to wish you a comfortable journey back to Dallas and thought you might need a ride to the station."

"That is most considerate of you," Tennyson replied. "Were you able to address the matter that we discussed last night?"

"Yes. I took care of it first thing this morning."

"Good. Please let me know without delay if anything comes of it. Just give us a few minutes to collect our bags, and we'll be with you."

Hurrying up the stairs to our rooms, I couldn't help wondering what it was that Tennyson had requested of Ward. However, I refrained from asking about it since he apparently didn't care to share the information with me.

When we rejoined Ward in the lobby, he told us that our bills had been paid. Without further ado, we followed him out to his carriage; and a ride of only a few minutes brought us to the familiar environs of the depot.

Wilson was on duty in the station and had our

tickets already made out. The train for our return trip to Dallas was the *Pecos Limited*, which provided through service from Shreveport to El Paso. It arrived at 8:12 a.m. by the station clock, pulled by an elegant-looking Ten-Wheeler with a red cab roof and polished brass trim. Ward introduced us to the conductor, a Mr. Sutton, and instructed him to make sure that our needs were met. Then we said our farewells and took our seats at the forward end of the first coach.

Tennyson and I spoke only a few words to one another during the journey. For the most part, I sat gazing out at the passing countryside, enjoying the scenery and trying not to think about the missing locomotive. Occasionally, I dozed off, soothed by the rhythm of the train's wheels passing over the joints in the rails, only to be roused again by the sound of the whistle as we approached grade crossings or stations. For his part, Tennyson sat with bowed head in the pose which he customarily assumed when thinking earnestly. We exchanged pleasantries during the station stops in Mineola and Grand Saline; but otherwise, I left him to his contemplations.

The train pulled into the Houston Street depot in Dallas at 11:57, just four minutes behind schedule. Sutton opened the door at the forward end of our car to provide a private exit for us, so that we were able to beat the rush of passengers heading onto the platform. Tennyson hailed a porter and sent him to retrieve his buggy from the livery stable, then asked if I was hungry. When I replied in the affirmative, he suggested that we have lunch at the Market Street Cafe again. I readily agreed, subject to the stipulation that he allow me to pay for the meals this time.

It took almost ten minutes for the porter to return with the buggy and another short while for us to reach the restaurant. Due to the time of day, the place was quite crowded. However, as soon as the proprietor saw Tennyson, he greeted him enthusiastically and escorted us into a private room at the rear of the building.

As we enjoyed a filling repast of baked ham, candied yams, and apple cider, I summoned the nerve to apologize for having taken issue with Tennyson over the disclosure of our findings at the Harrison County Land Office. It still seemed to me that Sheriff Peterson should have been informed of them, but I was prepared to accept my friend's judgment in the matter.

"No offense was taken, dear fellow," he replied affably. "I certainly don't claim to be infallible, and your thoughts about the case are always welcome. If I responded somewhat brusquely over that particular suggestion, it was only due to my preoccupation with the implications of the information."

"I'm afraid that I was caught up in the excitement of what seemed to be an important discovery," I said.

"Your reaction was entirely natural. The discovery *was* an important one, but I needed to think about how it fit into the emerging picture of the crime. However, there will be time enough to discuss that after we have gotten you settled in your new quarters. For this afternoon, the order of business for both of us should be to see how our practices fared while we were away."

After I had paid the bill (despite Tennyson's attempt to take it from me), we set off for Akard Street. Our progress along Commerce was slowed by the multitude of buggies and pedestrians that clogged the central business district. As a result, it was almost half-past one when we drew up in front of the Curtis Building. I thanked Tennyson for the ride and agreed to be at the Hutchins home around nine the next morning to oversee the movement of the furniture.

CHAPTER 8

New Prospects and New Friends

Upon opening the outer door of my office, I found an envelope lying on the floor inside. This turned out to contain a note from Dr. Everett asking me to call upon him at my convenience. Having no reason to delay, I deposited my valise on a chair in the back and was about to depart for Harwood Street when a young woman carrying an infant entered the waiting room.

"Dr. Weston?" she inquired. "I do hope that you can help me. My name is Mrs. Wright. My sister works for Mr. Dillon, and he told her that you had just opened a practice here. My baby has had a fever for two days now, and he won't eat. I'm worried that he has contracted something."

"Here, let me have a look," I said. Feeling the child's forehead and noting that it was definitely warm, I escorted the woman into the consulting room. After taking the boy's temperature and finding it to be 100.2°F, I listened to his chest, examined his ears and throat (which were both slightly red), and probed his stomach. "Well, Mrs. Wright, it appears that he has a mild case of febrile influenza," I concluded. "It's nothing to worry unduly about, but you should make sure that he gets a lot of fluids. A little oil of peppermint will help to settle his stomach. Use just a drop or two diluted in about four ounces of water. If you don't have any, it's available at Oldenburger's Pharmacy, which is just down the street on the corner of Akard and Young. I would give it to him about every three hours. It will also help his breathing to add a little camphor to an open pan of warm water and place it near his crib. If the symptoms haven't improved by Monday morning, let me know."

"Oh, thank you, Dr. Weston. I was afraid that it might be something serious. But what about his refusal to eat? Is there anything that I can do about that?"

"The oil of peppermint should help, but he probably won't have much of an appetite until the fever breaks. You might try giving him a little chicken broth later today and see how he responds to it."

"All right. I am most grateful for your help. How much do I owe you?"

"Oh, you needn't pay me now. Let's wait and see whether I need to examine him again. However, I would appreciate it if you would mention my location to your friends. There aren't very many people who know of my practice yet."

"Certainly. I'm sure that a number of women in the Cumberland Hill area will be glad to learn that there is such a nice doctor nearby."

After Mrs. Wright had departed, I tacked a note to the outer door and started off for Dr. Everett's office.

When I arrived, his nurse told me that he was with a patient; so I took a seat in the waiting area. There were a number of people sitting there, and it struck me that Dr. Everett seemed to be doing a booming business. Six or seven minutes later, a middle-aged woman emerged from the door behind the nurse, who then called to me and said, "He will see you now."

As I entered the consulting room, Dr. Everett came forward, shook my hand energetically, and said, "Thank you for coming, Dr. Weston. I was anxious to have a word with you."

"I trust that it wasn't too much of an inconvenience having my patients referred to you while I was out of town," I replied. "The trip arose on short notice, and there wasn't time to inform you before my departure."

"No, no, that was quite all right. There were only a few people who said that they came here because of the note on your door. In fact, it was one of them who put me in mind of talking with you. He happened to mention that he worked for Ambrose Dillon, who assured him that it would be easy to see you because of your light case load. That started me thinking that we might be able to help one another. You see, my practice has grown to the point that there is sometimes a delay of a day or two before a patient can get treated. Matters become particularly acute during an outbreak of disease, as with the influenza that is going around just now. Most of those people in the waiting room are probably here for that."

"Their appearances suggest as much. As a matter

of fact, I examined an infant with a mild case of it just before coming here."

"Well, what I wanted to propose is this: I could have my nurse start sending patients to you when my schedule gets backed up. Of course, you'd be able to specify what types of cases you are willing to handle. This wouldn't be a matter of just offering you the crumbs from my table."

"At this point, any cases which you care to refer to me would be acceptable, Dr. Everett. I will be candid in telling you that I am still struggling to become known in the community and find that I have a good deal of time on my hands at present."

"Then the arrangement should be beneficial for both of us. If it's all right, I'll have Nurse Mackenzie start directing patients to you tomorrow."

"Unless an emergency arises, I would prefer that you wait until Monday. I'm going to be moving tomorrow from my quarters at the Quincy Hotel to a residence on Routh Street."

"Very well, then. Monday is certainly soon enough. I must say that it will be a relief to have some help."

We shook hands again to seal the arrangement, and I took my leave. During the walk back to my office, I reflected on Dr. Everett's proposal with mixed emotions. Naturally, I was pleased at the prospect of growing my practice; but I was also concerned that an increased case load might prevent me from further participation in the affair of the missing locomotive. I had found my brief involvement in investigative work to be stimulating and was hoping that Tennyson would allow me to continue assisting him.

The next morning, I awoke to a clap of thunder and looked out the window of my hotel room to see dark clouds moving in from the northwest. Deciding that I had better hurry if we were to get the furniture moved before the storm arrived, I quickly donned an old pair of denim pants and a chambray shirt and hastened downstairs. On my way to the dining room, I stopped at the front desk and asked the clerk to have a buggy brought around for me. By the time I had finished my bacon and eggs, the conveyance was in front of the hotel; and I headed for Routh Street with the horse at a gallop.

Although it was not quite twenty minutes past eight when I arrived at the Hutchins home, I found a couple of stalwart-looking young men struggling to carry a good-sized dresser up the outside staircase. Approaching the one on the lower end, I offered to help; but he waved me aside. At the top of the stairs, I saw Tennyson guiding them around the corner. "Good morning," I greeted him. "I'm glad that you didn't wait for me. It looks like the rain is about to start coming down."

"Yes, in fact there have already been a few sprinkles here," he answered. "I thought it advisable to go ahead and get started. Let me introduce you to our helpers."

Leading me into the hallway, he said, "Jarvis, may I present George Riley and Joshua Thomas. Boys, this is Dr. Weston. George and Joshua are students at the Commonwealth Commmercial College. They agreed to help us today for the princely sum of a dollar apiece plus refreshments, although I suspect that they actually came for the opportunity to spend some time with Miss Amy."

The young men grinned at this last comment; and Tennyson continued, "Leave the dresser there for now. We had better collect the remainder of the furniture as quickly as possible."

The four of us then hurried downstairs and around to the storage shed behind the house. George and Joshua hoisted a sturdy bedframe and started back for the stairway, while Tennyson and I followed with a feather mattress, which almost got away from us when it was caught by a gust of wind. A second trip to collect a bedding chest and a nightstand was completed just as large drops of water began to fall. In another minute, the heavens opened up; and we were treated to a prime example of a Texas thunderstorm.

Since I hadn't known just what items of furniture were included in the lot that I was purchasing from Mrs. Hutchins, I wasn't prepared to tell the boys where to place the pieces in my bedroom. It took me about three-quarters of an hour to finally settle on an arrangement that I liked. By then, the downpour had transitioned to a gentle shower; and Tennyson suggested that he take me downstairs to meet Mrs. Hutchins and her daughter.

As we rounded the corner of the porch on the lower level, I observed a woman standing near the front door, gazing out toward the street. She appeared to be in her middle forties, with an attractive face framed by dark brown hair that was just beginning to show touches of gray. Tennyson bade her good morning and introduced me.

"I am so glad to meet you at last, Dr. Weston," she said. "Mr. Pierce told me

last Monday that you would be joining his household. I hope that everything is to your liking."

"Decidedly so, Mrs. Hutchins. I am most grateful for your willingness to let me have the bedroom furniture at such a good price. Please be assured that you shall receive the full amount within a few weeks."

"Oh, there really isn't any rush about it. Mr. Pierce has vouched for your integrity. Besides, I may have need of your professional services sometime. It will be a great comfort to have a doctor on the premises."

At that moment, the front door opened; and a striking young lady in a blue gingham dress emerged. "The cookies are almost done, Mother," she declared. Then, seeing Tennyson, she added, "Oh, hello, Mr. Pierce. Did Josh and George show up on time?"

"Yes, both of them were here bright and early; and they completed their chores in good time. Amy, this is Dr. Weston."

"How do you do, sir?" she replied, extending her hand in a very ladylike gesture and making a slight curtsy.

"I am very pleased to meet you, Amy," I said. "Mr. Pierce tells me that you are in your final year of studies at the Ursuline Academy. Have you enjoyed the curriculum there?"

"For the most part. We've gotten a good grounding

in all of the classical subjects, but my favorite courses are the ones in mathematics and the natural sciences. I'm afraid that my mother considers those to be a man's domain, though."

"You could probably use some refreshments after your morning's labors," Mrs. Hutchins interjected. "We've made shortbread cookies and lemonade. If one of you wouldn't mind going after the boys, Amy and I will finish setting things out."

I soon collected George and Joshua; and we joined the others in the dining room, where a platter of warm cookies and a pitcher of lemonade stood at one end of the table. Amy handed out plates and tumblers as we trooped past, while Mrs. Hutchins poured the lemonade and invited us to help ourselves to the cookies. We spent a pleasant half-hour in small talk; and then Tennyson and I excused ourselves, after thanking our hostesses for their hospitality and paying the boys for their services.

Back upstairs, Tennyson told me that he had to leave shortly for Fort Worth to see Colonel Yarbrough and would return around seven that evening. Since I still had to collect my belongings from the hotel, I offered to give him a ride to the train station in my hired buggy. Then I asked if there was anything that I could do for him while he was gone.

"As a matter of fact, there is, Jarvis," he replied. "You might stop by the Dallas News Building and ask for Jack Lorentz. Tell him that you are there about the matter which I discussed with him yesterday afternoon. He should have gathered a number of back issues of the old *Dallas Herald* containing articles about Jay Golden's activities in the state. I would appreciate it if you would bring them back to the house. In fact, if you can spare the time, you might begin reading through them and jot down any points which strike you as salient."

"Certainly," I responded, feeling gratified at this indication that I was to be allowed to continue my involvement in the investigation.

When Tennyson had changed clothes, we made a dash for the buggy. Although the rain had decreased to little more than a drizzle, the earlier downpour had turned the streets into something resembling black gumbo; and our journey to the Houston Street station was slow and uncomfortable. The canvas top of the buggy afforded some shelter from the rain, but did nothing to keep us from being splattered by the mud that was thrown up by the wheels and the horse's hooves. Tennyson had donned an oilskin ulster, which served to keep his suit from being soiled; but I had no protection from the continual pelting. By the time we reached the station, I was thoroughly begrimed.

After letting Tennyson off at the platform, I went on to my hotel, where I washed up, changed clothes, and put on a light topcoat and a felt hat. I then walked to the Dallas News Building, which was only about three blocks away. Fortunately, the streets that I had to traverse were paved with bois d'arc blocks, which spared me from further exposure to the mud. Upon arrival at my destination, I approached a counter that stood just inside the entrance and asked a young man where

I might find Jack Lorentz. He pointed to a hallway behind him and said, "His office is the last one on the right."

I proceeded to the end of the hall and was about to knock on the indicated door when it opened suddenly. Before I could move out of the way, a man rushed out and barreled straight into me. As we recovered from our mutual surprise, I noted that he appeared to be in his mid-thirties, with a jovial face and a mass of unruly black hair. "I beg your pardon," I said. "Are you Jack Lorentz?"

"The one and only," he answered. "What can I do for you?"

"My name is Dr. Jarvis Weston. Tennyson Pierce asked me to stop by and see if you had managed to find the back issues of the *Dallas Herald* that he requested."

"Oh, yeah. Come on in, and I'll show you what I've got."

Every nook and cranny of Lorentz's office was piled high with paperwork, and I wondered how he ever managed to find anything. However, he went straight to a stack on a bookcase behind his desk and handed me a bundle of newspapers.

"I searched the *Herald's* morgue back through the beginning of '82 and found six issues with stories about Jay Golden," he said. "I also looked through the old copies of the *News*, but apparently nothing has been written on Golden since we started publication last October."

"Do you mind if I take these with me?" I asked.

"Tennyson went to Fort Worth for the afternoon, but he's anxious to have this information. We'll take good care of them."

"That's fine, as long as I get them back eventually."

"All right. Thank you very much for your help. Perhaps the three of us can have lunch together one day next week."

"I'll look forward to it. Just remind Tennyson that I get the scoop when he solves this case."

After shaking hands with Lorentz, I tucked the newspapers inside my topcoat to keep them dry and started back to the Quincy.

When I reached the hotel, I realized that it was past lunchtime, so I stopped off in the dining room. While waiting for my order of braised beef with mushrooms and rice, I started to look through the stack of newspapers which Lorentz had given to me. The earliest one was dated February 16, 1884. It carried a two-column article telling of Golden's involvement in a scheme to raise freight rates in Illinois and Missouri. The writer went on to point out that Golden had managed to obtain financial control of more than fifty percent of the railroad mileage south of St. Louis and west of Little Rock and that he was known to covet control of the lines in Texas. It was speculated that he intended to extend his rate-fixing trust throughout this region.

The waiter arrived with my order just as I finished reading the article, and I put the newspaper aside to give full attention to enjoying the meal. As usual at the

Quincy, the food was cooked just right. After scraping every last bite from the plate, I paid the bill and went up to my room to collect my belongings. It took three trips to load everything into the buggy. When I had finished, I settled my account at the front desk and started off for my new residence.

The rain had finally stopped, and the streets had dried a bit; but I was still thankful to have the protection of my topcoat. Without the resistance of the heavy muck that we had encountered earlier, the horse's burden was lighter; and our progress was correspondingly quicker. It was not quite half-past two when I drew up in front of the Hutchins home. George and Joshua were still there, sitting on the porch with Amy. When they saw me start to unload my effects from the buggy, the boys got up and came over to help. We made quick work of transferring the goods to my bedroom, and I set about putting things away.

When my belongings were arranged to my satisfaction, I took the back issues of the *Dallas Herald* to the dining room and laid them out in chronological order on the table there. For the next couple of hours, I read and re-read the articles about Jay Golden, making notes about points which I thought would be of interest to Tennyson and trying to think of connections with what Henry Ward had told us.

A little after 5:00 p.m., I was roused from my deliberations by the sound of the brass knocker. Opening the front door, I found Amy standing there, with George and Joshua hovering behind her. "I'm sorry to disturb you, Dr. Weston," she said, "but Mother wanted me to see if you and Mr. Pierce would like to have supper with us."

"That's very kind of her," I replied. "However, Mr. Pierce has gone to Fort Worth; and his train won't get back to Dallas until about seven."

"Oh, that's all right. We don't mind waiting for him. Please do say that you will join us. We're going to have fried chicken, and Mother is baking a blackberry pie for dessert."

"How could I refuse such tempting fare? Please tell your mother that Mr. Pierce and I gratefully accept her invitation. Is there anything that I can do to help with the preparations?"

"Thank you for offering, but Mother wouldn't hear of making a guest work for his supper. Besides, Josh and George can be pressed into service if the need arises."

"Actually, I could use a hand myself, if one of you wouldn't mind, boys. I have to return my hired buggy to Hofstetter's Livery and then meet Mr. Pierce at the Houston Street station. It would be worth a half-dollar to me if one of you would follow me to the livery in Mr. Pierce's buggy. I'll need to leave here about a quarter past six."

"Why don't you go, George?" Amy said. "Josh can stay here in case Mother and I need something done."

George consented politely enough, although his disappointment at Amy's apparent favoritism toward Joshua showed clearly in his face. After arranging to meet him on the porch downstairs at 6:15, I retired to the library and looked over Tennyson's diversified collection of books. Selecting a treatise on Sir Walter Raleigh, I passed a pleasant hour refreshing my knowledge about the Age of Discovery.

At the agreed-upon time, George and I set off for Hofstetter's Livery, which was situated just a block from the Quincy Hotel. When I had turned in the hired rig and paid the attendant, I joined George in Tennyson's buggy; and we proceeded to the Houston Street station. The train from Fort Worth pulled in at three minutes before seven, and I quickly located Tennyson as he disembarked. Within another couple of minutes, we were on our way back to Routh Street. While we drove up Elm, I informed Tennyson of Mrs. Hutchins's invitation for supper and also mentioned that I had obtained six back issues of the *Dallas Herald* from Jack Lorentz. However, showing what I thought was admirable self-restraint, I suppressed my eagerness to tell him what I had read about Jay Golden, assuming that he wouldn't want to discuss the matter in George's presence.

Darkness had fallen by the time we arrived at our residence, and an inviting glow shone from the windows on the lower floor of the house. While George put the buggy away, Tennyson and I went upstairs to wash our hands and faces, then descended the staircase to find Amy waiting for us. "Supper is served, gentlemen," she said; and we followed her into the dining room. I soon concluded that Tennyson's comment about Mrs. Hutchins's cooking had been an understatement. The meal was delicious, and I couldn't have asked for more congenial company. As I finished the last bite of my blackberry pie, I felt grateful that I had found a home with these good people.

CHAPTER 9

Influential Contacts

After thanking Mrs. Hutchins and Amy for a delightful evening and bidding good night to George and Joshua, Tennyson and I retired to our quarters. As soon as we had bolted the door for the night, I showed him the articles about Jay Golden that were laid out in the dining room and handed him the notes which I had compiled about them.

"Your time was obviously well-spent today, Jarvis," he said. "Did you have any difficulty with Jack?"

"Not at all. He was quite willing to let me bring the papers back to the house. I promised that we would take good care of them and suggested that the three of us might have lunch together one day next week. He *did* ask me to remind you about your promise of an exclusive story when you solve this case, though."

"Ever the newshound, eh? Well, he's a valuable ally, despite his insistence on publicizing my occasional successes. I appreciate your taking the time to go see him. Let me just glance through your remarks for a moment."

When Tennyson had finished reading my synopses of the news items, he asked whether I had drawn any conclusions concerning Golden's activities in Texas.

"These accounts seem to lend credence what Mr. Ward told us concerning an attempt to establish a rail monopoly in the state," I said. "The first report, from February of 1884, certainly indicates that Golden has ample experience with such schemes."

"Indeed it does. If he *is* trying to gain control of the Texas & Louisiana, we'll need to learn the identities of the other participants in his endeavor."

"Do you think that objective could be connected somehow with the theft of the locomotive?"

"We don't know enough yet to make an informed judgment, but the possibility definitely warrants further exploration."

"How do you plan to go about determining who else may be involved?"

"A good start on the task can be made by securing a list of all the individuals and companies that have purchased sizeable amounts of Texas & Louisiana stock in recent months."

"Isn't information of that sort difficult to come by?"

"Not for someone with the right credentials. I haven't told you about my brother, have I, Jarvis?"

"No, you haven't. In fact, I wasn't aware that you had a brother."

"Archer and I don't see much of each other these days. For the past five years, he has resided in St. Louis, where he heads the local office of the Secret Service.

As you may know, that's a division of the United States Treasury Department, which affords my brother access to a wide range of financial records. I sent a telegram from the train station before leaving for Fort Worth, asking him to obtain the names of all Texas & Louisiana stockholders who have purchased a hundred or more shares within the last year. It will probably take a few days to gather the information, but the results should provide some additional avenues for us to pursue."

"I had no idea that you had connections in such high places, Tennyson. It will be interesting to see what your brother turns up. But tell me about your visit with Colonel Yarbrough. Did you achieve your objective?"

"Let's just say that the trip was worthwhile, and some necessary groundwork was laid. I acquainted Colonel Yarbrough with the situation regarding the bullion shipment and obtained his agreement to provide additional protection for the consist. Guards will be stationed near a number of key turnouts to ensure that the car containing the gold isn't diverted from the mainline, while another train carrying a contingent of troops will follow at a discreet distance."

"Then you really believe that an attempt will be made to carry off the bullion using the stolen engine?"

"No, I still suspect that the individual behind the theft of the locomotive has a less conspicuous objective than the gold. Even so, prudence dictates taking suitable measures to safeguard such a valuable commodity."

"From your remark about laying groundwork, I gather that you had some additional purpose for meeting with Colonel Yarbrough. Is it something that you can share with me?"

"You are quite perceptive, Jarvis. However, the other matter which I discussed with the colonel concerns something which is no more than a vague notion at this point. I need time to ponder the ramifications before deciding whether to proceed with the idea."

Tennyson then turned his attention to the back issues of the *Dallas Herald*, while I retreated to the library and took up the volume on Sir Walter Raleigh once more. By a quarter of ten, I was ready to retire for the night. Looking in at the door of the dining room, I saw Tennyson sitting with his fingers tented and his head bowed. Although I was reluctant to disturb him, I thought it only polite to say good night and did so in a soft voice. Looking up, he returned my greeting and added, "I hope that this first night in your new home will be a restful one."

The labors of the day had fatigued me more than I realized, and I fell asleep fairly quickly and slept reasonably well for the first time in several days. On the following morning, I was awakened by a clattering noise, which turned out to be the dumbwaiter arriving in the alcove with a steaming teapot and two cups. Donning my dressing gown, I splashed water on my face to chase away the remnants of sleep, then joined Tennyson in the library.

"Good morning," he greeted me cheerfully. "Mrs. Hutchins has been good enough to send up a little orange pekoe. Would you care for some?"

"By all means," I replied. "That sounds just the thing to start the day."

"I'm planning to attend the 9:00 a.m. service at Sacred Heart Church, if you would care to accompany me."

"Certainly. It happens that I recently registered to become a member there."

After lingering a while over our tea and dressing in our "Sunday best," we started off for the church, which was located just a few blocks northeast of my office. The mud had dried considerably overnight, but the journey was still rather unpleasant due to the ruts which were left in the streets. In spite of that, we arrived early enough to find spaces in a pew near the pulpit. The altar was resplendent with tulips and crocuses, and the choir was in fine form. Father Martiniere's sermon was a bit lengthy, but it was delivered in a lively style that held one's attention. Following the recessional hymn, Tennyson and I paused in the vestibule to pay our respects to the pastor. We then drove to the nearby Bluebonnet Cafe and had a late breakfast of thick hotcakes with maple syrup. When we had finished stuffing ourselves, Tennyson said, "I think that we are both due for a little recreation. What would you think of taking in the matinee at the Dallas Opera House? I believe the Rial Biggers troupe is putting on *Fortune's Fool.*"

"That sounds like a welcome diversion," I replied. "What time does the performance start?"

"The Sunday matinee usually begins at one o'clock.

We can stop at the box office to check and then while away the time with a stroll down by the river, if that's all right with you."

"I'd like nothing better. In fact, we might consider walking across the bridge at the foot of Main Street. A patient told me that the wildflowers on the west bank are worth seeing."

Having agreed on the day's entertainment, we set off for the Opera House, which was located at the corner of Commerce and Austin Streets. Once we had verified the starting time of the play and purchased our tickets, we left the buggy at a nearby stable and walked back to Main Street, where we turned southeast. Another three blocks or so brought us to the iron span which was the sole means of crossing the Trinity on foot. As we reached the middle of the bridge, I paused to gaze at the river, which had been transformed from its usual sluggishness by the rains of the previous day. Looking at the water rushing beneath me and reflecting on its inevitable course to the Gulf of Mexico, I was reminded of the predestined path of a train following the rails to a distant city. That brought my thoughts back to the problem of the missing locomotive.

Tennyson had gone on ahead, and I hurried to catch up with him. When the opportunity arose, I casually asked if he had spoken to Choctaw Jones yet about searching the Piney Woods.

"No, I haven't," he responded. "Choctaw can make himself scarce when he wants, but I left word with the garrison at Fort Worth to have him get in touch with me. He'll probably show up within a few days."

"Oh," I said, somewhat disappointed at Tennyson's apparent lack of urgency about pursuing the possible connection with the Easton & Monroe Logging Company.

Evidently my tone betrayed my reaction; for he added, "Remember that recovering Number 35 is not our primary objective. It's far more important to discover the purpose behind the theft. Naturally, I'm curious to find out whether there is any evidence to support my speculation concerning the shoo-fly track. However, now that the preparations for protecting the bullion are in place, patience will be of greater avail than haste."

"But if the stolen engine were retrieved, wouldn't that prevent the thieves from carrying out their plan, whatever it might be?"

"Your reasoning assumes that the criminals are lacking in resolve, but we have already concluded that their leader is playing for high stakes. If his men were deprived of the locomotive, it's likely that he would simply shift to an alternate plan to achieve his aim. No, the course of justice and the interests of the railroad will best be served by letting the fellow proceed for awhile without interference."

"I can't help feeling uneasy about the risk involved in doing that. Shouldn't the authorities at least be informed of your intentions?"

"Unfortunately, the minions of the law are generally more inclined to action than to cogitation. The last thing that I want at this stage of the investigation is for some headstrong deputy to start poking around. However, perhaps it will help ease your mind to know that I spoke with Sheriff Lassiter on Friday afternoon about certain aspects of the case; and he agreed to go along with my recommendations."

"All of this is really none of my business, of course; and I apologize for presuming to question your judgment. It's just that I can't stop worrying about the implications of what we discovered at the Harrison County Land Office."

"My dear fellow, your comments and your concerns are well-founded. An intelligent critique of one's ideas is always useful, but let's try to set aside our thoughts of the case for at least a few hours and enjoy this fine day. I see a few wildflowers over yonder, and there may be more beyond that rise."

As we walked in the direction that Tennyson had indicated, we passed close to a small patch of Indian paintbrush, interspersed with a few black-eyed Susans. Continuing up the mound beyond them, we came upon a hillside that was completely covered with bluebonnets. Although the blooms were not quite at their peak yet, they were still an impressive sight.

The terrain on the west side of the river was far hillier than that on the east, and we soon found ourselves on a high bluff which afforded a panoramic view of the central area of the city. For a few minutes, we stood there in silence, looking out at the scene before us. If I had any lingering doubts about my decision to settle in Dallas, they were removed then and there. The sight of this growing center of commerce rising out of the black soil of the prairie inspired me with a sense of confidence in my future undertakings. It occurred to me, too, that those endeavors were going to be far more varied than I had expected, thanks to my new friend. I was roused from this reverie by the sound of Tennyson's voice saying, "We had better start back if we want to be on time for the beginning of the performance."

Our wanderings had taken us farther than I realized; and even walking at a good pace, it required about forty minutes to reach the Opera House. By the time we passed through the entrance on Commerce Street, the announcer was already on stage, preparing the audience for the opening curtain. However, the matinee wasn't heavily attended, so that we had little difficulty in getting to our seats. The play was entertaining in the characteristic fashion of a melodrama, and Will Marion gave a splendid portrayal in his role as the leading man. When the cast members had taken their final bows, Tennyson and I waited for the audience to disperse, then exited through the side door and retrieved his buggy from the stable.

As we drove along Austin Street toward Main, Tennyson asked if I would mind making a stop before returning home. Naturally, I consented, although I was mildly curious about his destination. Continuing on to Elm Street, he followed it all the way to Harwood before veering northwest and proceeding to the intersection with San Jacinto. There he turned to the right and soon drew up in front of a substantial-looking two-story residence constructed in the Georgian Transitional style.

Stepping down from the buggy, Tennyson said, "I thought that we would just take a moment to pay our respects to my friend Clair Whitman."

"That name sounds vaguely familiar," I commented, joining him on the flagstone walkway leading to the front steps of the house.

"It should, judging by the amount of publicity he has received. Mr. Whitman is a prosperous banker who is well-known for his civic contributions. He also happens to own one of the largest stands of timber in East Texas."

"Oh yes, I recall reading something about his involvement in the efforts to make the Trinity into a navigable waterway," I said, with the dawning realization that this was not merely a social call.

I followed Tennyson to the front entrance, where he gave two polite raps of the elegant brass knocker. Shortly, the door was opened by a smartly dressed Negro, who took Tennyson's card with a bow and asked us to step inside and wait for a moment. The servant disappeared to the rear of the house, returning presently to tell us that Mr. Whitman would be with us in a few minutes. He then guided us into a richly furnished sitting room which contained several marble busts of historical figures and a number of oil paintings depicting pastoral subjects. I was admiring one of these, an evening scene by Daubigny, when I heard a deep voice saying, "Mr.

Pierce! It's good to see you. To what do I owe the honor of this visit?"

Turning, I saw a distinguished-looking gentleman of medium height and build, with light gray hair and a small moustache. Tennyson shook hands with him and replied, "How are you, Mr. Whitman? I hope that you don't mind this intrusion. We have just come from the matinee at the Opera House; and I thought that I would take the opportunity to introduce Dr. Jarvis Weston, who has recently moved here from Kansas City."

"I am pleased to meet you, Dr. Weston," Whitman responded. "How do you like our community so far?"

"Quite well, thank you, sir," I answered, stepping forward to offer my hand. "Dallas seems to be a city of great opportunity, and I have been fortunate to meet some very gracious people."

We chatted briefly about the similarities and differences between Kansas City and Dallas before Tennyson interjected, "Dr. Weston's parents are old friends of Ambrose Dillon, whom I believe you know."

"Yes, Ambrose and I go back a long way," Whitman returned. "We came here about the same time, almost thirty years ago. In fact, he was the one who convinced me to go into the timber business."

"How is your logging company doing these days?" Tennyson asked.

"Not badly at all, particularly since you took care of that matter for me last year. But please be seated, gentlemen. May I offer you something to drink? A glass of Chablis or some Madeira, perhaps?"

Tennyson and I both chose the Chablis; and Whitman pulled a bell cord, which caused his man to quickly appear at the entrance to the room. Within a few minutes, the servant returned with three glasses of wine on a silver tray. As we sipped the excellent vintage, Tennyson continued, "If Jay Golden succeeds in his effort to establish a rail monopoly in the state, I suppose that it could have a pretty significant effect on timber prices."

Whitman's face showed mild surprise as he said, "So you know about that? Yes, Golden's reputation for using onerous freight rates to drive competitors out of business has a lot of the local merchants worried."

"I've read of the rate-fixing schemes which he has implemented in other states, but thought that he was simply using his control of the railroads to reap large profits on the movement of freight."

"He is doing that, of course; but he has also been buying interests in various businesses and then giving favorable freight rates to those companies while raising the rates for their competitors. The fellow is as ruthless as they come."

"To your knowledge, has he acquired interests in any of the logging outfits or mills operating in East Texas?"

"I don't have any real proof, but there have been some financial transactions over the past year that lead me to think so."

"Might I presume to ask a favor of you, Mr. Whitman? It happens that I am currently engaged in a case which turns upon some occurrences in the Piney

Woods, and an insider's perspective would be beneficial. Does Colin Drake still manage your timber enterprise?"

"Yes he does, and I regard myself as fortunate to have him. How can he help you?"

"There is a good chance that he knows or can obtain some information that I'm seeking. If it isn't too much of an imposition, I would greatly appreciate having a letter of introduction from you, asking that he cooperate in my inquiries."

"Gladly, Mr. Pierce. I consider myself in your debt after the service which you performed for me, and I welcome the opportunity to be of assistance. Can you tell me what this matter concerns?"

"All I can say for the present is that it is an extremely sensitive matter which could have far-reaching effects on the growth of commerce in the state. As soon as circumstances permit disclosing the details, you shall be one of the first to hear them."

"Fair enough. If you'll excuse me for just a moment, I'll withdraw to my study and draft the letter right now."

When Whitman had left the room, I turned to Tennyson with a grin and said, "So this is your 'more discreet way' of finding out about Tom Buckley's background. How many other tricks do you have up your sleeve?"

"At least one or two," he answered, the corners of his mouth curling ever so slightly. "It doesn't hurt to have a wide circle of acquaintances, especially when those individuals have a certain amount of influence."

Before long, Whitman returned and handed an

envelope to Tennyson. "I believe that this will meet your needs," he said. "Even without it, Drake would probably be willing to cooperate with you. He's a good man and knows most of what goes on in the Piney Woods."

"I am grateful for your time, Mr. Whitman," Tennyson replied. "Now we had better be on our way and leave you to enjoy the remainder of your Sunday afternoon. Thank you for the hospitality."

"Please accept my thanks as well," I added. "It was a pleasure to meet you, sir."

"The pleasure was mutual, Dr. Weston. I hope that you will continue to find Dallas to your liking. Please stop by again."

After we had climbed into the buggy once more, Tennyson remarked, "No one is likely to know more about the personnel at the Hanley Brothers Mill or the Easton & Monroe Logging Company than Colin Drake. I'll have to make another journey to the Marshall area in a day or two."

"I'm afraid that I may be too busy to accompany you this time," I commented. "There appears to be an outbreak of influenza in the city; and Dr. Everett has asked me to take on some of his patients, starting tomorrow."

"That's quite all right, Jarvis. Your professional responsibilities certainly take precedence over the investigation. If you can manage to spare the time while I'm gone, though, I would appreciate your help in looking through the information that Archer is sending. The list may be rather extensive."

"Certainly. I should still have my evenings free and will be glad to do anything that I can. As a matter of fact, after what Mr. Whitman told us concerning the rate-fixing scheme, I am quite anxious to learn more about Golden's holdings."

"Yes, it's becoming apparent that Golden is intent on establishing a financial empire of tremendous scope. If the Texas & Louisiana falls into his hands, I'm afraid that the consequences could be disastrous for the state's economic development."

"I understand now why you said on the train that this case might have some serious implications. However, I must admit that I'm still unable to conceive what use the thieves intend to make of the locomotive."

"When we have figured that out, unraveling the remainder of the mystery will be easy. There are a couple of possibilities that come to mind; but until some supporting evidence is found, they aren't worth discussing. Perhaps by the end of the week, we'll be in possession of enough facts to form a plausible conjecture."

As we headed back to Routh Street, I couldn't help feeling disappointed at Tennyson's guarded attitude. If he suspected that a connection existed between the events at Blanco siding and Golden's plan to establish a rail monopoly in Texas, I certainly wanted to hear his ideas. Even though such things were unquestionably beyond my realm of experience, I believed that collaboration was the best way to solve any problem. However, it had become clear that my new friend couldn't be persuaded to reveal his deductions before he was good and ready. My curiosity about the motive for the theft would have to go unsatisfied for a while longer.

CHAPTER 10

A Visitor from the Panhandle

The following day, I discovered that Dr. Everett's nurse had apparently taken her instructions to heart, as I was beset by a continual stream of patients. Most of them were suffering from respiratory influenza in various stages of progression. Fortunately, none of them exhibited particularly severe symptoms, which made for fairly rapid diagnosis and repetitive prescription of treatment. Still, the frequency of their arrival in my waiting room meant that I was unable to take time out for lunch. My only consolation, beyond the gratification of helping the ill, was that the majority of the referrals paid for my services in cash. Consequently, I ended the day with more money in my pocket than I had enjoyed for some time. As the last of the patients departed shortly before 6:00 p.m., I realized that I was exhausted and hungry. After sitting down to rest for a few minutes, I decided to treat myself to supper at Stockton's Restaurant on Main Street. The walk there took only some five minutes but still helped me to shed some of the day's tensions.

Despite arriving during the height of the evening trade, I was seated straight away, although my table was a small one near the kitchen. As soon as the waiter came around, I ordered a thick-cut sirloin steak with a baked potato and spring peas. A plate heaped with the restaurant's renowned cornbread had just been delivered when I heard someone call my name. Looking around the crowded room, I finally picked out Jack Lorentz waving to me from a table about ten feet away. He was seated with another man, and the two of them seemed to be in good spirits. I walked over to them and said, "Good evening, Mr. Lorentz. Tennyson was most appreciative of those back issues which you gave me. They proved to be quite helpful."

"I'm glad to hear it, Dr. Weston," he replied. "I saw you sitting over there by yourself and thought that you might want to join us. This is Clyde Starrett, the editor of the *Abilene Journal*."

"Jarvis Weston, Mr. Starrett," I responded as the stranger rose to shake my hand. "But I don't want to intrude if the two of you are talking business."

"Don't give it a thought," Lorentz said. "Please have a seat."

I wasn't about to abandon my plate of cornbread, so I excused myself for a moment to retrieve it and inform the waiter that I was moving. Then I joined the two newsmen and asked, "What brings you all the way from West Texas, Mr. Starrett?"

"I'm here on behalf of the Panhandle Cattlemen's Association. Its members have come to depend pretty heavily on the rail line through Abilene, and they are concerned about the rumors that freight rates may be going up. I agreed to look into the situation for them. Of course, it doesn't hurt that there may be a good news story in it."

"I've read some of the speculation about what might happen to the charges for shipments if a rail monopoly is established in the state, but I wasn't aware that there were imminent prospects of increases," I commented.

"The reports aren't widespread yet," Lorentz interposed. "However, the Central Texas & Gulf has served notice to its customers that a new schedule of tariffs will be distributed next month. The action came right on the heels of the stock deals that brought the line under the financial control of Jay Golden. Naturally, it's assumed that the new fees will follow the pattern of escalation which he has put into effect elsewhere."

My interest piqued, I remarked that I was under the impression that the ranchers in West Texas drove their herds to railheads in Kansas.

"That used to be the case," Starrett explained, "but so much of the open range has been fenced with barbed wire in the last few years that long trail drives aren't practical any longer. Once the Texas & Louisiana built through West Texas, a lot of the ranchers started shipping their cattle to the stockyards near Fort Worth. From there, the beeves go up to Denison on the Central Texas & Gulf and then to Kansas City via the Hannibal & Fort Gibson."

"Since the segment of the haul on the Central

Texas & Gulf isn't very long, wouldn't the costs for the shipments be dominated by the other two lines?"

"You're right, of course. However, the Association's members are afraid that once the new tariffs are published, the Texas & Louisiana might raise its charges to the same levels."

"The volume of business involved must be pretty considerable. I would think that the railroads might be willing to negotiate long-term agreements with the cattlemen at favorable rates," I observed.

"You'd make a good businessman, Dr. Weston," Starrett returned. "That's exactly what I hope to accomplish this week. In fact, I have an appointment with the General Freight Agent of the Texas & Louisiana on Wednesday morning."

I considered mentioning that I knew Mr. Ward and suggesting that Starrett deal directly with him, but decided that I had better tell Tennyson about this conversation first. As I was musing over what might happen to a freight contract if Golden gained control of the Texas & Louisiana, Lorentz suddenly slapped the table and said, "I don't know why it didn't occur to me before, Clyde. My friend Tennyson Pierce is an attorney, and he happens to be pretty familiar with railroad operations. It could be a big help to have him on your side in the negotiations. What do you think, Dr. Weston?"

"That's certainly a reasonable suggestion, although he is quite busy just now and may not want to take on the task. If you'd like, though, I can broach the subject with him tonight."

"Then you're going to be seeing him later?" Starrett inquired.

"Yes. We share living quarters in a residence on Routh Street."

"Would you mind if we accompanied you there after supper?"

"I don't know what Tennyson's plans are for this evening. However, if you want to take a chance that he can give you some time, it's fine with me."

"This is admittedly a brash imposition, Dr. Weston; but a newsman learns to seize an opportunity when it presents itself."

"That's quite all right. There may come a day when I'll need a favor of some sort in return."

This discussion was interrupted by the arrival of our food; and for once, I was grateful that the servings at Stockton's were plentiful. For the next twenty minutes, the three of us gave our attention to the savory fare on our plates, while exchanging only a few words of small talk. When we had finished eating, I reminded Lorentz that I had promised him a meal and offered to pay the bill. Starrett wouldn't permit it, however, saying that the cost of a dinner was a small price for intruding on my evening. I didn't protest too strongly, since I assumed that he would be reimbursed by the Cattlemen's Association.

It was a pleasant evening, and I elected to take a somewhat roundabout route to Routh Street. Proceeding along Main to Harwood, then across to Ross, we walked at a leisurely pace, chatting about the weather, the condition of the streets, the newspaper business, and the growth of Dallas. By the time we reached the front steps of my new home, it was nearly half-past seven. Mrs. Hutchins and Amy were sitting on the porch, evidently also enjoying the mild temperature and the gentle breeze. They greeted me cheerfully, and Amy commented that I looked tired. Her mother frowned at this, but I quickly affirmed her conclusion and mentioned the considerable number of patients that I had treated over the course of the day. I then introduced my two companions, only to find out (as I should have realized) that Lorentz was a regular visitor. After a few more words of polite conversation with the ladies, I led the newsmen up the stairway to the second level and asked them to wait while I advised Tennyson that he had callers.

Opening the front door slightly, I peered in to make sure that no other guests were present. When I had verified that the parlor and the dining room were both unoccupied, I made my way to the library, where Tennyson was sitting with a large tome in his lap and papers scattered about him on the floor. "Good evening," I said. "May I disturb you for a moment?"

"Good evening, Jarvis. You appear anxious about something. Could it be the visitors who are waiting outside?"

"How did you guess?"

"There is no great mystery about it. I observed you

approaching the house in the company of Jack Lorentz and another man, but heard only one set of footsteps in the hallway. The obvious conclusion is that you left the two of them on the doorstep, which suggests they are not here for a social call."

"No, I'm afraid that they aren't. That's why I asked them to remain outside until I determined whether you were occupied. The other fellow's name is Clyde Starrett. He's the editor of the *Abilene Journal*, but has come to Dallas as a representative of the Panhandle Cattlemen's Association."

I then related what Starrett and Lorentz had told me at the restaurant about the Central Texas & Gulf instituting new freight tariffs and the cattlemen wanting to negotiate a rate agreement with the Texas & Louisiana. When I had finished, Tennyson sat quietly for a moment before saying, "You had better show your guests into the parlor. I'll be along presently."

Stepping back out onto the porch, I told the newsmen that Tennyson had agreed to speak with them, but cautioned that they shouldn't take up too much of his time. After ushering Lorentz and Starrett into the parlor and inviting them to be seated, I returned to the library. To my considerable surprise, Tennyson was standing with his face up against the front wall. I started to ask him what he was doing, but he hushed me with a finger to his lips. Drawing closer, I was astonished to find that he had been peering through a sight glass which was mounted in the lathwork. He motioned for me to come have a look, and I reluctantly stepped forward and pressed an eye close to the lens. Evidently the device contained specialized optics, for it afforded a panoramic view of the adjacent room. I felt guilty for spying on our visitors in this manner, however, and quickly turned away. Tennyson smiled at my discomfiture and murmured, "I'm sorry if this offends you, Jarvis; but it can be a very useful tool." Then he added, "Let's go see if I can be of some service to Mr. Starrett or perhaps vice-versa."

We proceeded to the parlor; and I allowed Lorentz to introduce his friend, who apologized for calling without notice. Tennyson assured him that it was no trouble and commented that he was impressed with the rapid growth of Abilene since the coming of the railroad. This provided just the opening that Starrett needed to recount his mission on behalf of the cattlemen. At the conclusion of his tale, he hesitantly added, "I wonder if you might be available to provide legal counsel during the negotiations, Mr. Pierce?"

"It's possible that I may be able to assist you, Mr. Starrett," Tennyson answered. "At the very least, I can accompany you to the meeting on Wednesday, and we can see what transpires. How long will you be in town?"

"My plans are to remain through the end of the week."

"Good. There are one or two issues that must be resolved before I can agree to accept your assignment. If circumstances permit me to act on behalf of the Cattlemen's Association, it may be advisable for us to visit the railroad's Division Office in Marshall on Thursday. Would that pose any difficulty for you?"

"No, I suppose not. What's behind the recommendation?"

"The General Freight Agent of the Texas & Louisiana here in Dallas probably doesn't have the authority to accept the sort of agreement you're proposing without obtaining approvals from his superiors. Consequently, we may find that it saves time to deal directly with Mr. Henry Ward, the Superintendent of the North Texas Division."

"I understand. Should I request an appointment to see him?"

"That won't be necessary. Mr. Ward communicates with me regularly, so I'll make the necessary arrangements."

"It looks like Jack was right about you being a good man to have on my side, Mr. Pierce. Is there anything that I ought to do in preparation for the trip?"

"Just be certain that the statistics in support of your proposition are accurate and succinct. Now what time is your meeting with the General Freight Agent on Wednesday?"

"It's scheduled for 10:00 a.m. Will that be convenient for you?"

"Yes, that's fine. I suggest that we rendezvous at the Dallas News Building about half-past nine. You won't mind sharing your office for a bit, will you, Jack?"

"Not if you promise to give me the low-down on what happens."

"I'll leave that for you gentlemen of the press to work out, provided it's agreed that nothing will be published about the negotiations without my review."

After Starrett had provided some further information on the proposed rate agreement, the two visitors thanked us for our time and took their leave. When they had departed, I accompanied Tennyson back to the library and said, "I hope that I did the right thing in bringing them here. When they told me about the tariff changes, I thought that their information might have some bearing on your investigation into Golden's activities. I'm sorry there wasn't time to send word ahead that they were coming."

"Don't apologize, Jarvis. Your reaction was quite appropriate. This business with the cattle shipments may well help us discover another piece of our puzzle."

"At the very least, it would seem to strengthen Golden's motive for wanting to gain control of the Texas & Louisiana."

"That's quite true, all the more so if we consider the situation in relation to what Mr. Whitman told us."

"I'm afraid that you have lost me again."

"This is pure speculation, mind you; but it does fit with what we know of Golden's ambitions. You're probably aware that Texas ranchers supply a considerable fraction of the beef which is purchased by the large packing houses in Kansas City and Chicago. Suppose that you owned substantial cattle operations in another state, such as Iowa, and wanted to reduce the competition as a means of driving up the delivered prices. One way of accomplishing your goal would be to raise the shipping costs for Texas herds to such an extent that they become effectively excluded from the Midwestern markets."

"What you are suggesting sounds ambitious even for Golden. Do you really think that he would attempt something like that?"

"I wouldn't put it past him. Of course, I have no evidence that he actually has financial stakes in any cattle ranches. Still, it would be consistent with his efforts to control other fields of commerce."

"Perhaps you're right. It's just a little difficult to believe that one man could achieve such widespread dominance."

"The fact is that he couldn't do so by himself. Despite an obvious talent for financial dealings and a cunning mind, Golden would be unable to succeed in his grand designs without the aid of a large number of accomplices. That's why I'm anxious to see the list that Archer is putting together for me. It's likely that at least a few of our state's businessmen are in league with Golden and have been induced to purchase stock in the Texas & Louisiana Railway on his behalf."

"I don't suppose that you have heard anything more from Mr. Ward?"

"Nothing of consequence. However, I did receive some interesting news from Sheriff Peterson this afternoon. His men found the other end of the trail that you discovered in the woods. It came out into a field owned by a farmer named McClure. Although there were some wagon and horse tracks present, the rains on

Saturday made them difficult to follow. Unfortunately, McClure hadn't seen any strangers around his property; but there are a couple of hired hands on the farm that haven't been questioned yet. You may recall that I also asked the sheriff to look into the backgrounds of the men who work in the yard office at Marshall. He reported that one of the clerks, a young man by the name of Dennis King, has a real fondness for poker. Further inquiries revealed that the youth isn't very good at the game and often ends up owing money to the other players. That would make him an easy mark for someone seeking an unwitting participant in the plan to steal the locomotive."

"I take it that this Dennis King is the person who passed on the alleged telegraph message about moving the freight cars to the interchange track."

"He is, indeed; and I'll wager that he did so without knowledge of the consequences. When I travel to Marshall on Thursday, one of my objectives will be to discover who suborned him. Incidentally, I must leave for Austin first thing in the morning and won't get back until fairly late tomorrow evening."

"Does the trip have some connection with the case?"

"Indirectly. It concerns the steps required to ensure that the bullion arrives safely at the state treasury."

"Is there anything that needs to be done while you're gone?"

"Thank you for offering, Jarvis, but there's nothing that won't keep until I return. Besides, I expect that you'll be kept busy enough with another influx of

Dr. Everett's patients. Judging from your worn-out appearance, you must have treated quite a number of people today."

"Yes, I admit that the pace was a bit more than I had bargained for; and having to miss lunch didn't help. Of course, it's nice to finally have some business; but I hadn't planned to have quite so much of it."

"Well, perhaps your caseload will taper off to a comfortable level after the influenza outbreak runs its course. Until then, you had better try to turn in early and get enough rest to deal with your demanding agenda."

I readily accepted Tennyson's suggestion and retired for the night. However, I had trouble falling asleep, despite my fatigue, as speculations about Jay Golden's plots kept running through my head. It must have been well after eleven before I finally slipped into a light slumber. This would prove to be a typical pattern for most of the following week.

CHAPTER 11

Spadework and Subterfuge

On Tuesday morning, I arose just as Tennyson was about to leave. He told me that Mrs. Hutchins had sent up a breakfast of poached eggs, biscuits, and tea, which awaited me in the dining room. I thanked him and wished him a safe journey, then washed my face and sat down to eat. The back issues of the *Dallas Herald* were still on the table, although placed in a neat stack now. Extracting the paper dated August 21, 1885, I leafed through it until I found the article about Jay Golden's attempt to obtain control of the Hannibal & Fort Gibson Railway. I wanted to gain a better understanding of the methods used to take over a company against the wishes of its directors. In this case, according to the reporter, Golden had planned to distribute a large quantity of counterfeit stock certificates, with the aim of forcing the trading price for the railroad's shares to an artificially low level. Evidently, he hoped that many of the stockholders would panic and sell their holdings at bargain rates. After Golden had acquired a majority of the legitimate shares, he would arrange for the fraudulent certificates to be revealed as invalid, leaving him in a position to call for the election of a new board of directors. Fortunately, this scheme failed when a certificate from the first batch of fake ones was detected by an alert broker at the Chicago Stock Exchange. A warning was issued to the public, and trading in the railroad's shares was suspended until suitable precautions could be put in place. Naturally, Golden had isolated himself from the details of the stock transactions; and the authorities were unable to link him to the deception.

While pondering the avarice of the man, my attention was caught by a heading on the adjacent page of the newspaper which read "Lumber Outfit Expands." The accompanying article stated that the Easton & Monroe Logging Company had purchased the Ferguson Mill along with 640 acres of neighboring land in southwestern Harrison County. This information was clearly relevant to the case, and I excitedly made a note of it.

When I had emptied my teacup, it dawned on me that time had gotten away from me. Hurriedly shaving and dressing, I set out for the Curtis Building at a lively pace. Upon reaching the outer door of my office, I found three people already waiting there. It looked like I would have another busy day, and so it proved. However, after a fairly steady flow of patients throughout the morning, the rate of arrival tapered off a bit. As a result, I was able to get away long enough to have a hasty lunch at the Bluebonnet Cafe.

I was just finishing my roast beef sandwich when Ambrose Dillon entered the restaurant. Walking over to him, I said, "It's nice to see you, Mr. Dillon. I'd like to thank you for introducing me to Tennyson Pierce. The two of us found that we have a number of interests in common, and he offered to share his living quarters on Routh Street with me. I moved in last Saturday and consider myself fortunate to have found such a congenial arrangement."

"Well, I'm glad to hear it, my boy," he replied. "Mr. Pierce is a man of unusual talents and has helped me a time or two with business matters. From what my wife tells me of Mrs. Hutchins, I would also say that you're in good hands with her as a landlady. How is your practice coming along?"

"As a matter of fact, it has taken a sudden turn for the better, thanks to Dr. Everett. He has begun referring patients to me, with the result that I had more business yesterday than I could comfortably handle. This morning was also quite busy for me."

"Your parents will be happy to hear that. I know they were concerned about your decision to leave Missouri."

"Yes, I'm afraid they still think of Texas as the wild frontier. This city is really beginning to feel like home to me, though. In fact, there is something about the atmosphere here that I find invigorating."

"I quite agree with you, Jarvis. That's why I settled in Dallas some thirty years ago, and I have never had cause to regret it."

"Speaking of those early years, Tennyson and I had

the pleasure of visiting Clair Whitman last Sunday. I understand that you and he are old friends."

"We certainly are! Clair drifted to town a month or so after I did back in the fall of 1856, and we soon fell in together. Talk about a pair of greenhorns! Why, there wasn't anything that seemed too big for us to take on. I guess the young are always blind to the obstacles that lie ahead."

"Well, it's apparent that you and Mr. Whitman managed to overcome the obstacles pretty well."

"If so, it was because we had a lot of help along the way."

"I didn't mean to keep you from your lunch. Please come sit down. If you don't mind, there is something that I would like to ask you about before I go."

Once we were seated at the table, I continued, "My question concerns the companies that supply the merchandise for your store. It may seem that I'm simply being nosy; and if you prefer not to answer, I'll certainly understand. However, I assure you that my interest derives from a matter of some consequence. You are undoubtedly aware of the increases in freight rates for rail shipments that were put into effect about two years ago in Illinois and Missouri. The question that I have is this: Was any attempt made to displace your established sources for goods in the aftermath of those increases?"

"I might expect a question like that from Mr. Pierce, but I can't imagine why you are concerned with such things, Jarvis. In any event, the answer is in the affirmative. A number of the farm implements and tools that I sell are manufactured by firms in Illinois, and my costs for them rose about twenty percent after the freight rates went up. Then, just before Christmas that year, I had a visit from a man named Lawson, who told me that he represented a company called the Belleville Ironworks. He said that they would guarantee to undercut what I was paying for hardware items by fifteen percent if I would sign an exclusive contract with them."

"May I ask if you accepted his offer?"

"I most certainly did not. Loyalty is something that I have always prized highly in both my personal life and my business dealings, and I wasn't about to throw aside my long-time suppliers for some opportunist."

"It doesn't surprise me that you reacted in that fashion, Mr. Dillon. Would you happen to know how to get in touch with this Lawson?"

"He gave me a business card, but I threw it away some time ago. All I can recall from it is that he resides in Waco."

"Thank you very much for the information. With any luck, I'll soon be able to tell you why it was necessary to impose upon your good graces in this way. Now, I had better be getting back to my patients. I hope that you have a pleasant afternoon."

After paying for my meal, I hurried back to the Curtis Building, where there were once again several people waiting to see me. Fortunately, however, the afternoon wasn't as busy as the morning had been; and

I was able to end my day's labors shortly before six. I felt tired, but less so than on the previous evening. Since I hadn't yet finished the letter to my parents which I had started writing on the preceding Wednesday, I decided to take the time to do so. A lot had happened to me since my last note to them, and I ended up spending a good forty minutes telling about my experience in meeting Tennyson, my new living quarters, my arrangement with Dr. Everett, and even my journey to East Texas (although I thought it better not to mention the reason for it). When finished, I reverted to habit, walking to the Quincy Hotel and dining there on venison with rice and asparagus.

It was nearly half-past seven when I reached 211 Routh Street, and Mrs. Hutchins was again sitting on the porch. As I approached the front steps, she stood up and said, "A messenger delivered a telegram for Mr. Pierce this afternoon. Would you mind seeing that he gets it, Dr. Weston?"

"Gladly, Mrs. Hutchins," I replied, taking the envelope which she held out. "Incidentally, I've been meaning to tell you how much I appreciate your willingness to accept me into your home. I know that it must be something of a bother putting up with another tenant."

"Not at all, Dr. Weston. I am pleased to have you. As a matter of fact, I think that your living here might turn out to be a good influence on Amy. She's an exceptionally bright girl, and it would be a shame to see her talents wasted. With the money that Mr. Hutchins left, I can afford to see that she gets a good education. Perhaps you could help to direct her interests toward a career in medicine."

"I would consider it a privilege to discuss the various opportunities in the medical profession with Amy. Furthermore, if there is ever anything that needs to be done around the house or grounds, please don't hesitate to call upon me."

"That's very considerate of you. Please sit down and relax for a little while. I have a pitcher of lemonade inside, if you would care for some."

I accepted her offer; and we talked for half an hour or so about the spring flowers, the play that Tennyson and I had seen on Sunday, our mutual acquaintance with the Dillons, and my family back in Kansas City. Then, with the last glow of twilight rapidly fading, I excused myself and went upstairs.

Settling into the leather chair in the library, I picked up the volume that Tennyson had been perusing when I interrupted him on the previous evening. It turned out to be a history of railroad construction and consolidation in North America, illustrated with a number of lithographs by Currier and Ives. I remembered reading that Golden controlled more than half of the rail mileage south of St. Louis and west of Little Rock, and I was curious just which lines were involved. Most of the maps in the book were taken from surveyor's drawings, which made them somewhat difficult to read; but I managed to piece together a pretty good conception of the rail network in the southwestern part of the country. My attention was so firmly focused on speculations about the extent of Golden's empire that I didn't hear the front door open. As a result, I received quite a start when Tennyson suddenly called my name. Scrambling to my feet, I advanced into the hallway to greet him.

"How was your trip?" I inquired. "Did you accomplish your purpose?"

"The journey was pleasant enough," he replied, "but it will be a few days before the results can be assessed."

I hoped to learn something more about his meeting at the state treasury, but he changed the subject by inquiring how my day had gone.

"It was another busy one, but less hectic than yesterday. I was able to get away for lunch at the Bluebonnet Cafe, where I encountered Mr. Dillon. We had an interesting conversation, and he told me something that I think might be of use in the investigation. But before I forget, Mrs. Hutchins gave me a telegram that came for you this afternoon."

Retrieving the envelope from the table in the library, I handed it across to Tennyson. He slit it open with his pocket knife, extracted the folded paper, and nodded with satisfaction as he read the message.

"Good news?" I queried.

"In a sense," he replied. "This is a response from Mr. Ward to a request which I made of him yesterday. It indicates that certain preparations for my journey to Marshall on Thursday have been set in motion."

"Do you still intend to take Mr. Starrett along?"

"That decision must await the outcome of our

meeting with the General Freight Agent of the Texas & Louisiana in the morning. However, I believe that Starrett might be of some use to me, provided I can persuade Jack to cooperate in a slight bit of subterfuge."

"Lorentz seems like an amiable enough fellow. What is it that you need him to do, if I may ask?"

"Give me a moment to freshen up, and I'll tell you what I have in mind."

Returning to the library, I took a seat next to the octagonal table. After a few minutes, Tennyson came in, absent his coat and tie. He graciously insisted that I move to the leather chair, while he occupied an adjacent cane-back one. When we were situated, he said, "At this stage of our investigation, we are like hunters whose quarries have gone to cover. A way must be found to flush them into the open without their suspecting that someone is lying in wait. For the time being, let's take it as a working hypothesis that the ultimate goal of those involved in the theft of the locomotive is to gain control of the Texas & Louisiana Railway. If it were to become known that the railroad's customers are trying to negotiate long-term, unbreakable freight contracts, it might provoke the conspirators to accelerate their plans. That's where I need Jack's assistance. I want him to publish an article which gives the impression that I am representing a sizeable number of shippers in rate discussions with the Texas & Louisiana. My journey to Marshall with Starrett can be cited to lend credibility to the story."

"I am certainly thankful that you're on the side of

the law, Tennyson. You would probably make a first-rate confidence man."

"I'll take that as a compliment, Jarvis. After all, the best way to catch a criminal is to think like one."

"Perhaps so, but it's just as well that there aren't many people who are inclined to the practice. Tell me, how can you be sure that Jack's story will be seen by the intended audience?"

"I can't be be absolutely certain, of course; but the odds will be favorable if the report about the negotiations is widely distributed. That will require convincing the editors of major newspapers throughout the state to carry the article."

"Aren't you asking a lot? Even if Lorentz agrees to your request, is there any reason to think that the editors of the other papers are likely to go along with it?"

"Jack is well-respected among his fellow newsmen, and he can be quite persuasive when properly motivated. Besides, there ought to be widespread interest in the story due to the effect of freight rates on prices for goods in local stores."

"The concern about that *does* seem to be growing, all right. While we're on that subject, let me tell you what I learned from Mr. Dillon. You probably know that he sells a wide variety of merchandise, including a lot of farm implements and tools. He told me that most of those items are made by companies in Illinois. As a result, his costs for them went up about twenty percent when Golden put his rate-fixing scheme into effect over there. Well, shortly after that happened, a man by the name of Lawson visited Mr. Dillon and tried to convince him that he should start buying his hardware items from a company called the Belleville Ironworks. The sales pitch included a promise to undercut the existing suppliers by fifteen percent in exchange for signing an exclusive contract."

"Indeed! When did this occur?"

"In December of 1884."

"It appears then that Golden's associates may have been active in Texas for some time. Did you happen to learn where this Lawson resides?"

"Mr. Dillon didn't keep the fellow's card, but remembered that he was from Waco."

"We shall have to see if the McLennan County sheriff can provide an address for him. If Lawson *is* associated with Golden, even in a remote way, he could lead us to some of those involved in the conspiracy. You have done well once again, Jarvis."

"There is something else, too, although you may already be aware of it. I came across an article in the *Dallas Herald* for August 21, 1885 which indicated that the Easton & Monroe Logging Company had purchased the Ferguson Mill and 640 acres of adjoining land."

"Yes, that item caught my attention when I looked through the back issues. You are to be commended for taking note of it, though. We may yet launch a second career for you as a detective."

"All jesting aside, I wish that the demands on my time weren't so heavy just now. This affair seems to grow more involved by the day, and I don't see how you can possibly unravel it without a good deal of assistance."

"You are quite right, Jarvis. Solving a case of this complexity requires a lot of spadework, and I certainly can't undertake all of it myself. Remember, however, that Sheriff Peterson, Sheriff Lassiter, Colonel Yarbrough, and my brother Archer are all engaged in carrying out various tasks for me. Within another few days, Choctaw Jones should be added to that list. So please don't feel any sense of duty in connection with the investigation. Your increased participation in my inquiries would certainly be welcome, but the local citizens are undoubtedly in greater need of your medical care."

"So they are, as long as this epidemic continues. Nevertheless, I find my thoughts continually returning to the question of how the missing engine could be involved with the plans of Golden's confederates."

"A vexing issue, to be sure. However, I'm afraid that your worry over it will have to be endured for at least a few more days. By then, I hope to have received some information from my brother which may help in discovering the answer."

"Are you referring to the list of Texas & Louisiana stockholders?"

"No, this concerns another subject. Unfortunately, I am not at liberty to tell you about it just yet without violating a professional confidence."

"Now you have really whetted my curiosity. Well, perhaps it's a good thing after all that I find myself deluged with patients this week. Otherwise, I would probably be driven to distraction trying to figure out what it is that you're withholding from me."

"My dear fellow, I am truly sorry that you must be kept in the dark for the present. Please believe that a serious obligation compels it and that all of your questions about the matter will be answered as soon as circumstances permit. Now, if you don't mind, I think that I'll retire for the night. There are a few things that must be accomplished before my appointment with Starrett in the morning, which will require rising at an early hour."

After Tennyson left, I remained in the library for a time, mulling over what he had told me. Unable to reach any conclusions that made sense, I finally decided to turn in, although I doubted that I would be able to sleep. My apprehension proved correct, and I spent the night tossing and turning, powerless to stop thinking about the enigma of the missing locomotive and its possible connection to Jay Golden. Sometime well before dawn, I heard Tennyson moving about; and by the time I arose just after sunrise, he was gone. Due to my restless night, I was still in a bit of a stupor when I left the house and made my way to the Quincy Hotel for breakfast. A cup of tea soon helped to ward off my grogginess, and a steaming bowl of oatmeal provided the energy that I needed to take on the day's labors.

When I reached my office, I was relieved to find that only one patient was waiting for me, although another appeared shortly afterward. As the day wore on, the rate of arrival turned out to be steady but manageable, giving me time to perform my examinations without rushing and to briefly engage each patient in polite conversation. It was gratifying to provide the care that people needed without wearing myself out, and I finished the day feeling contented with my practice for the first time.

Despite the fact that it was only a few minutes after five when I locked up and departed, I decided to go straight home. I was anxious to find out what Tennyson had learned in the meeting that morning and hoped that he would consent to join me for supper. It was therefore a disappointment to discover that he was nowhere to be seen when I entered our quarters. As I glanced at my pocket watch and deliberated over whether I should wait for him, I heard the clap of the brass knocker. Swinging open the front door, I was agreeably surprised to behold the charming countenance of Amy Hutchins.

She smiled and said, "Good evening, Dr. Weston. I was watching for your return to pass on a message, but you dashed up here too quickly for me. Mr. Pierce left word that he had some business at the sheriff's office and would like you to join him for supper at the Grand Windsor Hotel around seven, if that's agreeable."

"Thank you, Amy," I replied. "I'm sorry for making you climb the stairs."

"Oh, it was no bother. As my mother keeps pointing out, I'm young and healthy."

"That would seem to be true enough. How is your schoolwork coming?"

"Just fine. I hope you realize that I was only joshing about Mother's attitude toward my interest in the natural sciences. Although some of her ideas are a bit old-fashioned, she has been very supportive.”

“I’m sure that your mother wants you to receive a good education. With your aptitude for technical subjects, a career in the medical field might be worth considering. Have you ever thought about studying to become a doctor?”

“One of the teachers at the academy has discussed the possibility with me a few times. I’ve been told that it can be pretty difficult for a woman to be accepted as a practitioner, though.”

“It’s true that there aren’t many women in the field presently. However, the ones with whom I am acquainted are every bit as well thought of as their male counterparts. I would be glad to answer your questions about the profession sometime. In fact, if you and your mother would consent to have lunch with me next Saturday, we could spend an hour or two discussing what it’s like to practice medicine and what preparations are needed to obtain admission to a medical curriculum.”

“That’s very kind of you, Dr. Weston. I’ll ask Mother and let you know.”

When Amy had gone, I washed my face, combed my hair, and straightened my tie, then set out once again for the central area of the city. A detour over to Live Oak Street afforded a chance to see the many clusters of azaleas that adorned the yards of the elegant homes along that thoroughfare.

The Grand Windsor, which billed itself as “the most

elegant hotel in the South," was located on Commerce Street, across from the Opera House. I arrived there about half-past six, purchased a newspaper from the vendor in front of the building, and took a seat in the lobby. A few minutes before seven, I glanced up from my reading just in time to see Tennyson come through the entrance. After a few words of greeting, we made our way to the station where the maitre d'hotel kept a watchful eye on the dining room. Evidently Tennyson was known to this rather officious individual, since we were promptly conducted to a table, with a marked show of deference.

As soon as we were seated, I inquired about the outcome of the meeting with the General Freight Agent of the Texas & Louisiana.

"It went as I expected," Tennyson replied. "The agent listened courteously to Starrett's proposal, stated that the Panhandle Cattlemen's Association is one of the railroad's most important customers, and then indicated that he would have to consult with his superiors before accepting the proposed terms."

"Then Starrett will be accompanying you to Marshall tomorrow?"

"He will. The agent's deferral of a decision on the rate agreement provided just the pretext that I needed to justify the trip from Starrett's standpoint."

"Did you have an opportunity to ask Jack Lorentz about writing the article that you mentioned?"

"As a matter of fact, I just came from discussing it

with him. A good deal of 'arm-twisting' was required, but he finally agreed to do what I wanted."

"I hope that it will have the desired effect. Amy said that you had gone to the sheriff's office. Was that also in connection with the investigation?"

"Yes, it was. Sheriff Lassiter sent word that he needed to see me about the arrangements for safeguarding the bullion shipment. It turned out that the request was actually occasioned by a message from Choctaw Jones. He wanted me to meet him in a secluded spot on the other side of the river, since he doesn't feel comfortable in cities."

"I take it that you saw him, then. Did he agree to search the Piney Woods for the locomotive?"

"He accepted the assignment which I offered him, but finding the location of the missing engine is only a part of the task."

"May I ask what else you expect of him? Does it have something to do with the Ferguson Mill?"

"That facility will certainly come in for a fair amount of attention, but my primary interest centers on the vicinity of the Hansen Brothers Mill and the area south of there."

This discussion was interrupted by the arrival of the waiter, who recommended the table d'hote, featuring ragout of mutton with potatoes francaise, marrowfat peas, and peach fritters. Since the menu was in French and my command of that language was minimal at best, I accepted his suggestion. Tennyson, on the other hand, ordered something unfathomable which I later learned was sea turtle with truffles, ravioli, and kale greens. When the waiter had departed to hand in our orders, I returned to the topic of what Tennyson hoped to discover in the Piney Woods.

"Do you think that the thieves could be using the area south of the Hanley Brothers Mill to prepare for the next step of their plan?" I ventured.

"You may solve this case yet, Jarvis," Tennyson responded with a twinkle in his eyes. "There are several good reasons for supposing what you suggest, but this is not the place to discuss them. Tell me, are you still struggling with a heavy load of patients? You look a bit careworn again this evening."

"My appearance is due to the fact that I didn't get much sleep last night for thinking about this confounded puzzle. However, I had a rather satisfying day at the office. The pace was fairly busy but less rushed than earlier in the week."

"I'm glad to hear that your practice seems to be settling into an agreeable level of activity. Even so, if discussions such as we had last evening are going to cause you to sleep poorly, perhaps we had better adopt a policy of not speaking about the investigation after supper."

"That might be wise. You apparently have the ability to set questions aside until enough information has been gathered to answer them. Unfortunately, I find myself quite unable to do so."

"The trait is one which can be acquired with practice

my dear fellow. It depends upon learning to control emotional reactions in favor of logic."

"I have always been regarded as a logical individual, but must admit that emotions often influence my behavior."

"Human nature being what it is, you can't expect to completely exclude the effects of feelings on your reactions and decisions; but their hold on you can be substantially reduced through the consistent application of a few basic principles. I have written a short treatise on the subject which you might want to read sometime."

For the next several minutes, the conversation shifted to more ordinary subjects, including the new fairgrounds being constructed in the community of East Dallas, the proposed ban on curbside trading of cotton, and the feasibility of making the Trinity River into a navigable waterway. We were still discussing the latter topic when the waiter arrived with our food.

Thankful for the interruption, I eagerly turned my attention to the well-presented cuisine. The Grand Windsor was renowned for its epicurean delights, which were said to rival those of the finest restaurants in New Orleans; and my meal did nothing to diminish its reputation. From the tender mutton in the ragout to the peach fritters with their slightly crisp exteriors and moist interiors, each item on my plate was delicious. Judging by the expression on his face, Tennyson must have found his fare equally appealing (although I confess that sea turtle and kale greens didn't sound very appetizing to me). Only a few words were exchanged between us as we concentrated on savoring each bite of food. When the last morsels had been consumed, Tennyson suggested ordering the cold custard *a la chantilly* for dessert. I was afraid that this might be a bit rich, but agreed to try it and was pleasantly surprised at the wonderful flavor. Following this course, we were served a plate of Camembert cheese and water crackers in the continental tradition. However, we both partook sparingly of these and called for our bill as soon as the waiter came around again. Flush with funds from my marked increase in business over the previous three days, I offered to pay for both meals. Although this gesture was naturally resisted by Tennyson, I managed to prevail by stubbornly insisting that it was my turn.

As we proceeded through the crowded lobby toward the front entrance, Tennyson asked me to wait for a moment while he walked over to a counter where the hotel maintained a telegraph service. I saw him write out a message and hand it to the operator along with some coins, then utter something in apparent response to a question. After he had rejoined me, we threaded our way to the door and headed south along Austin Street. Ambling along for a couple of blocks, we came to the livery stable where Tennyson had left his buggy and were soon rolling along Commerce Street toward the familiar environs of Akard. From there, we followed the usual route to Routh Street. However, the darkness, which was broken only by the occasional feeble rays of the gas-fired street lamps, caused the landmarks along the way to take on unaccustomed appearances.

Because of the inability to see obstacles very far ahead, Tennyson held the horse to a slow pace; and it was about forty minutes past eight by the time that we reached Number 211. When the buggy had been put away in its spot next to the storage building behind the house and the horse had been taken to the small barn that Mrs. Hutchins shared with three of her neighbors, we climbed the stairs to our quarters.

Once inside, Tennyson reminded me that he was departing for Marshall on the following morning, although I was well aware of the fact. It came as a bit of a surprise, though, to learn that he probably wouldn't be returning until midday on Tuesday. In view of this extended absence, I again inquired whether there was anything that needed to be done while he was away; but he politely declined the offer. My lack of sleep on the previous night was catching up with me, so I decided that I had better retire early. However, I wanted to find some way to keep my mind off of the mystery of the missing locomotive. To this end, after saying good night to Tennyson, I selected a volume of Matthew Arnold's works from the library and took it to my bedroom. After donning my nightshirt, I propped myself up in a position to catch the light from the one lamp in the room and began reading *Discourse in America*. This had the desired effect of absorbing my attention; and in half an hour or so, I found myself starting to nod off. At that point, I set the book aside and doused the lamp. Within a short time, I was sleeping rather soundly for the first time that week.

CHAPTER 12
A Troubling Report

On Thursday morning, I arose just after sunrise, feeling rather refreshed for a change. Tennyson had gotten up a few minutes earlier and had beaten me to the washstand. As I waited in the alcove for him to finish, I heard the clatter of the dumbwaiter. Sliding open the chamber door, I found a tray with a pot of tea and two plates of bacon, eggs, and hominy grits. Evidently Tennyson had requested Mrs. Hutchins to prepare breakfast so that he wouldn't have to stop somewhere before catching the train. Feeling grateful for this convenience, I carried the tray to the dining room and arranged its contents on the table. After I had washed, shaved, and dressed, I joined Tennyson there.

"Good morning, Jarvis," he said. "I hope that you slept better last night."

"Good morning," I replied. "Yes, I slept pretty soundly for a change, thank you. I started reading one of Matthew Arnold's treatises, and his style of prose turned out to be well-suited for inducing sleep."

"Arnold is an insightful writer, but hardly one noted

for being economical in his use of words. At least you have found a practical use for his discourses. In any case, I'm glad that you were able to get some rest."

"It was definitely a relief to spend a night without being bombarded by thoughts about the investigation."

"On that subject, if it isn't too much of an inconvenience, I thought you might be willing to drop me off at the Houston Street depot before proceeding to your office. That would save me from having to pay the livery stable for several days' boarding and would allow you to have the use of my buggy while I'm gone."

"Of course, I'll be glad to. Are you quite sure there isn't anything that needs to be taken care of here during your absence?"

"It occurred to me after you went to bed last night that there *is* one matter which you could check on. I asked young George Riley to look up some property tax records at the County Courthouse. Provided your schedule allows, you might stop by the Commonwealth Commercial College sometime in the next day or two and see how he is coming with the task."

"Certainly. Would it help for me to review his findings?"

"Possibly. I'm interested in learning what property in Dallas County was originally deeded to the Central Texas & Gulf Railroad and whether any of those holdings have changed hands since Golden acquired financial control of the company. If George has managed to compile the information from the tax records, you might read over the material, keeping an eye out for anything that appears out of the ordinary."

"Can you give me an example?"

"The most obvious one is a recent deviation from the historical pattern of land sales, such as the transfer of multiple tracts to a single individual or company. There may be nothing to find, but I'm hoping that Golden has used the railroad's land grants as a means of rewarding his associates. If that proves to be the case, the ownership records could lead us to some of those involved in his schemes."

"I must say that such a possibility would never have occurred to me."

"Unfortunately, fraudulent transfers of real property are encountered all too frequently in the legal profession. However, we had better stop talking and start eating, or I will surely miss the train."

After hurriedly consuming our breakfasts, we hitched up the buggy and set off for Houston Street at a lively speed. Once I had let Tennyson off in front of the depot and wished him a safe trip, I headed up Wood Street and handed the buggy over to the care of the hostler at Hofstetter's Livery. From there, I continued on foot to my office via the route that I had traversed so many times while living at the Quincy Hotel.

Once again, I was called upon to treat a considerable number of patients during the course of the day. For the most part, however, they arrived at reasonable intervals, other than during a short span right after lunch. I even had time for a nice chat with Mrs. Wright, who stopped by to tell me that her baby was back to eating normally and didn't seem to be suffering any lingering effects from his case of influenza. Fortunately, the pace of arrivals slowed as the afternoon wore on, so that I was able to close the office promptly at five-thirty, feeling well-satisfied with my day's labors.

Since it was too early for supper, I decided to take a chance on finding George Riley at the Commonwealth Commercial College, which was only a few blocks away. I knew that the school advertised that it offered evening classes for the benefit of those who worked during the day. Sure enough, when I reached the two-story structure at 317 Main Street, the entrance proved to be unlocked. As a matter of propriety, I knocked, not really expecting an answer. When there was none, I opened the door and stepped inside, finding myself in a wide foyer whose walls were lined with benches. Not a soul was in sight, but I could hear faint voices coming from somewhere in the rear part of the building. Calling 'hello,' I began to advance down a hallway which apparently led to a number of classrooms. Presently, a dapper-looking gentleman came out of an opening on the left and approached me. He introduced himself as Professor E. B. Lawrence, the headmaster, and asked how he could help me.

"I'm Dr. Jarvis Weston," I responded. "Would you happen to know if George Riley is here this evening? I need to have a word with him."

"Ah, yes, Mr. Riley is one of our most diligent students. I believe that he is in the last room on the right, working on his accounting exercises. There's nothing wrong with his health, I trust?"

"No, this isn't a professional call. Mr. Riley was engaged to perform some legal research for a friend of mine, a local attorney by the name of Pierce. Since my office is nearby, I volunteered to see how the work is coming."

"I am well-acquainted with Mr. Pierce. He has used the services of our faculty and students with some regularity during the last few years, and we have usually benefited from the experiences. If there is any way in which I can be of assistance with the present undertaking, please let me know."

"That's very considerate of you, sir. I'm sorry for the intrusion and promise not to keep Mr. Riley from his studies for more than a few minutes."

"There is no need to apologize, Dr. Weston. Visitors are always welcome at the Commonwealth Commercial College, and I hope that you will come to see us again. Please give my regards to Mr. Pierce."

Upon entering the room indicated by Professor Lawrence, I found George in the company of two other students. All three of them were holding pencils and peering intently at sheets of paper on their desks. Not wishing to disturb their concentration, I stood quietly for a few minutes, watching as they periodically made entries on the pages. When George paused to stretch, I tapped him lightly on the shoulder and said, "Excuse me. Could I speak to you for a moment?"

Evidently I surprised him, for he swiveled his head

rather abruptly and then replied, "Oh, good afternoon, Dr. Weston. I didn't see you standing there. It's easy to become completely absorbed in the calculations when working on some of these ledgers. You happened along at an opportune time, though, since this is a convenient point for me to take a break."

"I'm sorry to bother you at school, George," I continued; "but Mr. Pierce wanted me to find out whether you had made any progress in looking through the tax records at the County Courthouse. Is there someplace where we can discuss the matter?"

"Let's go up to the front of the building, if that's all right. We can talk there without disturbing anyone."

Walking to the foyer, which was still deserted, we took seats on one of the benches near the entrance. George then faced me and began apologetically, "I haven't had a chance to finish going through all of the files. You know, it's been more than fourteen years since the Central Texas & Gulf first built through Dallas County, so there are a lot of records involved."

"Mr. Pierce didn't expect you to have completed the assignment, George," I commented in order to relieve his anxiety. "He would just like to know how the search is proceeding. Your studies obviously must take precedence."

"Well, I thought it best to start with the most recent files and work back to the earliest ones. I've gotten through 1881 so far, but it will probably take me another week or so to get all the way back through 1872."

"I think that you have approached the task correctly.

The information for recent years is probably of greatest interest to Mr. Pierce. Could I see your notes on what you have found?"

"I'm afraid that I don't the summaries with me today. If you'd like, I could drop them off at your residence this evening."

"There's no point in making a special trip, George. Why don't you just bring the results to the school tomorrow, and I'll stop by around noon to pick them up."

"All right. They'll be ready for you."

"By the way, I invited Amy and Mrs. Hutchins to have lunch with me on Saturday. Would you possibly be interested in joining us?"

George perked up noticeably as he said, "I'd like that very much, thank you, Dr. Weston."

"I thought we would dine at the Quincy Hotel. You could meet us in the lobby there around 1:00 p.m., assuming that suits your schedule."

"It suits my schedule just fine."

"Good. Then I'll see you tomorrow. Have a good evening."

"You also, Dr. Weston. And thank you again for the invitation."

Once outside, I turned my steps toward the Dallas News Building in the hope that I might find Jack Lorentz in his office. Luck was with me, as I arrived to find his door open and mumblings coming through it. Sticking my head in, I saw that he was scribbling rapidly on several pieces of paper, which were all but lost among the clutter on his desk. I waited to see if he would notice me, then cleared my throat to attract his attention. When he looked up, I said, "You know, I still owe you a meal, Mr. Lorentz. If you can get away, I could use some company for supper."

"Well, well, if it isn't the good doctor," he answered. "As a matter of fact, I'm so hungry, I could eat an armadillo. But you've got to stop calling me Mr. Lorentz. To my friends, I'm Jack; and I've got a feeling that we're going to become boon companions. Give me a couple of minutes to finish this, and I'll be with you."

"Take your time. I wouldn't want you to miss a deadline."

Shortly, Jack put down his pencil and said, "All done. So where are you taking me for this sumptuous feast?"

"I happen to have Tennyson's buggy this evening, so our choices are pretty well open. Do you have any suggestions?"

"There's a place called Rousseau's that I've been meaning to try. It's on Cedar Springs Road out in the Oak Lawn area."

"I'm not familiar with that part of Dallas; but if you can show me the way, I'm game. We'll have to collect the buggy from Hofstetter's first, though."

"Let's go, then. I wasn't joking about being hungry."

We covered the few blocks to the livery stable at a brisk pace and were soon rolling up Wood Street toward Akard. Turning northwest at that corner and proceeding past my office, we continued for another three-quarters of a mile or so to an oblique intersection with a well-travelled route. Jack informed me that this was Cedar Springs Road, and I duly swung to the north on it. Letting the horse find its own gait, it took about fifteen minutes more to reach the restaurant.

When we had been seated at a reasonably secluded table, I opened the conversation by inquiring, "So what big news items are you working on this week?"

"You mean besides our friend Tennyson's chicanery?"

"I wasn't going to mention that. In fact, his proposal struck me as somewhat unethical, despite the good intention behind it."

"At least he really is representing the Panhandle Cattlemen's Association, so there is some truth to the report that he wants me to publish. I was willing to go along with him because it looks like there may be a lot at stake. If his suspicions turn out to be correct, I could end up with a major story. But for the moment, I guess the big news has to be the gold shipment that's coming from St. Louis."

"I had almost forgotten that it's due through here tomorrow. Did Tennyson tell you about the precautions he arranged with Colonel Yarbrough to prevent the train from being robbed?"

"Some of them, anyway. Naturally, I had to promise not to write anything about the details until the bullion has been safely handed over to the state treasury."

"It concerns me that the whereabouts of the missing locomotive are still unknown. I hope that our friend knows what he's doing."

"You may have a point, but I wouldn't worry too much about the plans for safeguarding the gold. In the four years that I've known Tennyson, he hasn't yet put a foot wrong when it comes to outfoxing criminals."

At that point, the waiter arrived to take our orders. Quickly scanning the menu, I selected the filet of whitefish in madeira sauce accompanied by sweet potatoes and Elgin sugar corn, while Jack settled on the roast beef with mashed potatoes and English peas au gratin. When the waiter had left, I decided that it might be wise to change the subject, so I asked Jack whether he was acquainted with Clair Whitman.

"Sure, I know him," he responded. "Whitman has a lot of influence in both local government and the state legislature."

"I understand that he also owns one of the largest stands of timber in East Texas," I remarked.

"So I'm told. The word is that he bought the land a long time ago. Then, as settlers began pouring into Texas from other states, he was in a position to provide the lumber that they needed to build their homes. Of course, he has quite a few competitors now. Why are you interested in Whitman?"

"Tennyson introduced me to him last Sunday, and I got the impression that he is one of the area's leading businessmen. I was just thinking that a drastic increase in freight rates would probably affect him almost as much as it would the cattlemen in the western part of the state."

"Could be, although his lumber shipments don't have as far to travel as the cattle."

"Do you know anything about the Easton & Monroe Logging Company?"

"Only that they're a pretty big outfit. Why?"

"I was wondering how their operation compares to Whitman's."

"You've got me there, but I can probably find out. Does this have something to do with Tennyson's investigation?"

"It very well could. Whitman told us that Golden has been buying interests in companies and then giving preferential freight rates to those firms so they can undersell their competitors. I think he might be planning to do that with the lumber business in the Piney Woods."

"That's an interesting speculation. Does Tennyson agree with you?"

"I believe so, although he hasn't been particularly forthcoming with his thoughts on the matter. Hopefully, his trip to Marshall will afford the opportunity to learn more about it. He plans to interview Whitman's foreman, Colin Drake."

"I can see that I'm going to have to start spending more time with you, Jarvis. You're a regular fountain of information."

"Perhaps I've said too much, but I assumed that Tennyson had taken you into his confidence."

"Don't worry. What you've told me will stay between

us until you say otherwise. I'll do a little digging and see what I can turn up about the Easton & Monroe outfit."

Presently, the waiter appeared with our plates; and we suspended our conversation. For the next fifteen minutes, we spoke only intermittently while giving our attention to enjoying the chef's handiwork. The quality of the food compared favorably with that at the Quincy Hotel, I thought. When we had finished eating, Jack suggested ordering brandy to top off the meal. I would have declined, but didn't want to offend him. Fortunately, the restaurant lived up to its French name by offering a fine cognac. After we had drained the last drops from our goblets and I had paid the bill, we boarded the buggy and started back toward the central area of the city.

The sky was darkening rapidly as sunset approached, and Cedar Springs Road proved to be devoid of lighting once it passed into the open fields beyond Hood Street. Consequently, I proceeded very cautiously along the unfamiliar route until we came to the intersection with Akard. From that point on, I picked up the pace a bit. It occurred to me that I didn't know where Jack lived and that he might want me to take him to his home rather than to his office. Upon inquiring, I learned that he resided in a boarding house on Patterson Street, less than a quarter of a mile from my office. After dropping him there, I headed back up Akard to Ross and soon arrived at 211 Routh Street. I drove to the rear of the house and was in the process of unhitching the buggy when Amy came out of the back door.

"How are you this evening, Dr. Weston?" she inquired. "My mother asked me to give you this telegram that was delivered about an hour ago. She also said to tell you that she would be happy to join us for lunch on Saturday, but wondered if you wouldn't rather have her fix something here."

"I'm quite well, thank you, Amy," I replied. "Please tell your mother that I am most reluctant to pass up another opportunity to sample her cooking. However, it wouldn't do for me to extend an invitation and then expect her to provide the food. I planned for us to dine at the Quincy Hotel, if the two of you don't mind. The staff members there know me and will ensure that we are seated at a table which affords us some privacy."

"That sounds fine to me. Mother will probably enjoy being waited on for a change, anyway."

When I had taken the horse to the barn, I went upstairs, lit the lamp in the library, and opened the envelope containing the telegram. The message was from Tennyson and read as follows: "Starrett's goal achieved. Do not be alarmed at news tomorrow."

I took the first sentence to mean that Mr. Ward had agreed to the rate terms which were proposed by the Panhandle Cattlemen's Association. That was a relief and made me feel that I had done the right thing in allowing Starrett to come to the house on Monday evening. However, I couldn't begin to guess what Tennyson was trying to tell me in the second statement. Resolving not to let my curiosity keep me from getting a good night's rest, I prepared for bed and resumed reading the essays of Matthew Arnold. Once again, his words produced the desired effect; and before long, I nodded off.

Friday morning turned out to be another busy one for me, with patients arriving at pretty much the same rate as on the previous two days. One difference was that there were fewer cases of influenza, indicating that perhaps the peak of the outbreak had passed. As noon approached, the intervals between patients began to increase; and around a quarter to twelve, I found that the waiting room was temporarily empty. Quickly putting up an 'out to lunch' sign, I grabbed the opportunity to dash over to the Commonwealth Commercial College.

This time, when I stepped into the foyer, there were a number of people milling about. I approached one studious-looking young man and asked if he knew where I might find George Riley. He responded that George was in the second classroom on the left side of the hallway, talking to one of the professors. Not wanting to interrupt a conversation about schoolwork, I took up a position opposite the entrance of the indicated room and waited. Several minutes later, the door opened; and George appeared in the company of Professor Lawrence. The two of them must have noticed me at the same instant, for they called my name almost in unison.

"Good day," I greeted them. "Please excuse this imposition. I just need another minute or two of George's time."

"It's a pleasure to see you again," Lawrence

responded. "I'll leave you to your business. Feel free to use this classroom if you need to talk in private."

Accepting the suggestion, I followed George into the room and closed the door. He then withdrew a portfolio from his satchel, set it on a table, and untied the ribbon that bound it.

"These are my notes on the tax records back through 1881," he said, handing me a dozen or so sheets of paper. "I didn't copy everything in the files at the courthouse, but I think all the information that Mr. Pierce wanted is there."

Leafing through the material he had given me, I could see at a glance that the task had been approached very methodically. Each sheet was divided into columns labeled as 'property description,' 'location,' 'date of acquisition,' 'date of sale,' and 'current owner.' When I had finished glancing at the entries, I replaced the papers in the portfolio and thanked George for his efforts.

"Don't forget about lunch tomorrow," I told him as we exited the room. Then, with a knowing wink, I added, "Perhaps after we have eaten, I can keep Mrs. Hutchins occupied for awhile so you can talk to Amy."

"I guess it's pretty obvious that I'm sweet on her," George replied with a look of embarrassment. "She seems to like Josh better than me, though."

"Maybe she just doesn't know you well enough. I think you're probably a lot like I was at your age, George, a serious student who is a bit unsure of himself around young ladies. We'll have to see about arranging some opportunities for Amy to appreciate your better qualities. With any luck, our outing tomorrow should provide a good start on that objective."

"Thanks, Dr. Weston. I admit to being a little self-conscious around girls, especially with Amy. It's awfully nice of you to help me out."

"I'm glad to do it, George. Remember, one o'clock at the Quincy Hotel."

We shook hands, and then I walked back to the foyer and departed from the building. Once outside, I headed for the Bluebonnet Cafe to have a quick lunch before returning to my office.

As the waitress conducted me to a table, I noticed Mr. Dillon waving at me from the far side of the room. I walked over to say 'hello,' and he invited me to join him. When I was seated and we had both placed our orders, he asked, "Have you heard about the robbery?"

"No, I was kept rather busy all morning and haven't spoken to anyone but young George Riley since leaving my office," I answered. "Who was robbed?"

"The bullion shipment that was on its way to the state treasury was stolen over near Longview," he replied, to my considerable astonishment.

CHAPTER 13

Unanswered Questions

For a moment, I couldn't fully comprehend what I had heard. With all the precautions that Tennyson had taken, it didn't seem possible that anyone could have made off with the gold. Fully a minute must have passed before I recovered sufficiently to inquire how the theft had occurred.

"I don't have many details yet," Mr. Dillon said. "Sheriff Lassiter told me about it on my way over here. He had just received a telegram from Sheriff Peterson of Harrison County. Apparently, a locomotive that had recently gone missing from the Texas & Louisiana was involved in the theft somehow. I understand that the *Dallas News* is putting out an extra edition about the incident this afternoon."

So Tennyson misjudged the situation after all, I thought. It really *was* the bullion shipment that the locomotive thieves were after. I knew that we should have informed the authorities of our suspicion about the shoo-fly track at the Ferguson Mill. If a search of the Easton & Monroe property had been carried out earlier in the week, the Mogul would probably have been recovered; and the loss of the gold could have been averted. Now, because of my friend's mistaken belief about the motive for taking the engine, the criminals had succeeded in stealing a fortune.

Continuing my thinking out loud, I said, "It's hard to believe that anyone could have gotten past all those troopers. I would really like to know how the robbers evaded them."

Mr. Dillon looked at me sharply and remarked, "You appear to know something more about all this than I do, Jarvis. Where were these troopers supposed to be? The published information indicated that the train was guarded by agents of the United States Treasury Department who were riding on board."

Fortunately, I recovered my presence of mind in time to stop myself from revealing Tennyson's involvement in the plans to protect the shipment. Responding truthfully but incompletely, I simply remarked, "It was my understanding that a company of cavalry from Fort Worth had been deployed along the right-of-way between Marshall and Dallas as a precaution."

"I hadn't heard that," he rejoined, "but it seems like a reasonable measure to take. If the army *was* guarding the route, I would have to agree with you that it's difficult to see how the thieves managed to escape. Perhaps Sheriff Lassiter can shed some light on the matter."

"I suppose that the point will be addressed in the newspaper story when it comes out this afternoon. Might I ask you to do a favor for me?"

"Certainly, if I can."

"My patient load has been fairly heavy all week, and I'm afraid that I may not have an opportunity to get away from my office during the afternoon. If I'm not mistaken, the route back to your store from here will take you near the Quincy Hotel. Would you mind stopping in and asking the desk clerk there to have someone bring a newspaper to me as soon as the extra edition is on the street?"

"I'll be glad to. However, if I may say so, you seem to be unduly troubled by this incident, Jarvis. The theft is certainly a significant event, but I fail to see why you should take the matter so personally. Is there some reason for your singular interest in it?"

"I suppose that my reaction does seem a bit peculiar. Unfortunately, I am not at liberty to divulge the reason for my concern just now. If you'll bear with me for the time being, I promise to provide you with an explanation of my behavior before long."

"First your questions about my suppliers, and now an undue misgiving over a distant crime. One would think you were a lawman, rather than a doctor, Jarvis. You're not working for the Pinkerton Agency on the side, are you?"

"You've found me out," I replied with a laugh, thinking that his jest was closer to the truth than he realized.

Just then, the waitress arrived with our orders. Realizing that the hour was approaching one o'clock, I quickly downed my ham sandwich and lemonade.

When I had finished, I thanked Mr. Dillon for his consideration, paid my bill, and left.

During my walk back to the Curtis Building, I continued to ponder what could have gone wrong with Tennyson's plans to prevent the gold from being stolen. His strategy of having sentries stationed at key points along the route had seemed like an excellent safeguard. I tried to envision where the thieves could have intercepted the bullion train and what avenues of escape were available to them. Perhaps another shoo-fly track had been constructed at the Ferguson Mill. If so, it must have been torn up again before the train carrying the troopers had arrived there. That didn't seem very likely, since the timing for such a plan would certainly have been critical. Then, as I struggled with further speculations about what might have happened, the words of Tennyson's telegram came back to me: "Do not be alarmed at news tomorrow." Was he possibly referring to the robbery, I wondered? Surely not, because that would mean he had known about it in advance. Still, he *had* commented on the previous Sunday that the man who planned the disappearance of Engine Number 35 should be allowed to proceed for awhile without interference. Suddenly, a disquieting idea occurred to me. Suppose that Tennyson had deliberately allowed the bullion to be stolen as a way of tracking the thieves to their ringleader. Would he have taken such a risk? Even if he had been foolhardy enough to try it, would the authorities have gone along with him? After all, such a scheme could hardly have been managed without some degee of cooperation from Colonel Yarbrough and Sheriff Peterson, not to mention the Secret Service. On the other hand, Tennyson had told me repeatedly that he was convinced that the men who took the locomotive were after something other than the gold. If he really believed that, he would have had no reason to anticipate the robbery. But what other interpretation could there be for his cryptic message?

I arrived at my office in a state of agitation and for once was glad to find that there were several patients waiting at the door. At least the effort involved in diagnosing and treating their ailments served to divert my attention from the disconcerting news of the theft. As the afternoon wore on, I was confronted with a workload that was not much different from that of the previous two days. In order to keep from thinking about what Tennyson's words could have meant, I extended my time with the patients by asking about their personal and family histories, then recording relevant information for my files. Shortly after half-past three, a runner from the Quincy Hotel showed up with a copy of the extra edition issued by the *Dallas News*. After thanking the boy and giving him a generous tip, I set the paper aside until an opportunity arose to read it all the way through.

Around forty-five minutes later, I found myself with a little time available when a lull developed between patient arrivals. Settling into the chair behind my desk, I started to peruse the newspaper account of the morning's occurrence. The story indicated that the train carrying the bullion departed from Marshall at 10:13

a.m., with a boxcar and two passenger coaches behind a fresh 4-6-0 locomotive. The gold was in the boxcar, sandwiched between the two coaches, which carried the Secret Service personnel. As the train slowed for a speed restriction about eight miles east of Longview, a number of armed men on horseback rode out of the dense woods adjacent to the track, creating a great commotion by repeatedly firing their weapons into the air. While the guards were distracted by this disturbance, a member of the raiding party managed to approach the track on foot and pull the coupler pin on the aft end of the first coach. Two more of the outlaws boarded the locomotive and forced the engineer to proceed down the track for about a mile, where the engine and its abbreviated consist were diverted into a spur at a lumber mill (probably the Ferguson Mill, I thought). The fire was then dumped into the ashpan, disabling the Ten-Wheeler. In the meantime, the rest of the train had rolled to a stop on the mainline. Badly outnumbered, the remaining guards were compelled to surrender, after which the bandits disconnected the trailing coach from the car containing the bullion. Shortly, another locomotive came down the tracks from the east. This engine, which bore the number '35' on its headlight and tender, coupled onto the boxcar and steamed away with it in the direction of Longview. By the time the Secret Service agents were able to reach the nearest lineside telegraph station and raise the alarm, the robbers had disappeared without a trace.

There were several collateral stories dealing with the

purpose of the shipment, the loading of the bullion in St. Louis, the involvement of the Treasury Department, and the progress of the train before it reached Marshall. I skipped over these as not being particularly relevant, but drew up short at a heading which read, "Missing Locomotive Used in Raid." This article reported the disappearance of Engine Number 35 from Blanco siding almost two weeks earlier and told of the unsuccessful search for it by the railroad and the Harrison County sheriff. The account was brief and to the point, with few particulars given. Even so, I was somewhat surprised that it had been published, in view of Mr. Ward's desire to keep the incident from being disclosed to the public. Apparently the enormity of the bullion theft had made it impossible to suppress the facts about the missing locomotive any longer. However, I wondered what effect this news might have on the funding that was being sought for the railroad's proposed merger.

I sat for a few minutes more, mulling over what I had read. It struck me as odd that there was no mention of the soldiers who were supposed to be stationed at key points along the right-of-way. Considering what Tennyson suspected about the involvement of the Ferguson Mill in the theft of the Mogul, he would almost certainly have arranged for the siding there to be watched. Perhaps the guards at that spot had been overpowered by the robbers. If so, why wasn't that reported in the story? There was also the question of what had happened to the troopers who were following behind the shipment aboard another train. How long had it taken for them to reach the scene of the holdup? Did something prevent them from pursuing the fleeing engine and boxcar? Surely, these were questions that any competent reporter would have asked.

Further theorizing on these topics was interrupted by the entry of two patients into the waiting room. These were followed a few minutes later by three more, keeping me quite busy for another hour or so. Nevertheless, I was able to close the office by forty minutes past five. In my consternation over the theft of the gold, I had forgotten all about the tax records which George Riley had delivered. Luckily, I was in the habit of putting the consulting room in order before departing for the day; and I found the portfolio sitting on top of my supply cabinet. Taking it and the newspaper with me, I set off to find Jack Lorentz.

I had expected the Dallas News Building to be buzzing with activity related to the extra edition, but all was quiet when I arrived there. In fact, the only indication that the place was open for business was the young man behind the counter in the foyer. He recognized me from my previous visits and said, "If you're looking for Mr. Lorentz, he's left for the day. However, you might try the Mustang Saloon on Main Street. That seems to be his favorite spot for relaxing in the evenings."

"Thank you," I replied. "Isn't it unusual for him to leave this early?"

"He's normally here until at least six, when the evening shift comes on duty. I guess he was probably pretty tired today, though, with the added work of putting together all the stories for the extra edition."

"That must have been quite a chore, all right. Well, I'll see if I can catch up with him. Thanks again."

Saloons were generally distasteful to me, and the patrons of those on Main Street were infamous for their wild behavior. However, I was anxious to talk to Jack about the morning's events, so I suppressed my aversion and headed for the Mustang. Pausing at the door to steel myself, I gingerly stepped inside and looked quickly around the crowded room. Jack was standing with two other men at one end of the bar. Although I realized that they might not appreciate the intrusion, I approached them and uttered a hearty greeting.

"Well, look who's here," Jack returned. "I didn't know you were a drinking man, Jarvis."

"Only on occasion, Jack," I said. "However, I would gladly buy a round for you and your friends if I could have a moment of your time."

"That's the best offer I've had today. If you're going to stand drinks for these guys, I guess I should introduce them. The ugly one is Frank Willis, and the mean-looking one is Matt Hogan. Fellows, this is one of our community's leading physicians, Dr. Jarvis Weston."

I shook hands with Jack's companions and motioned to the bartender. Willis and Hogan both asked for bourbon, Jack followed suit, and I ordered a brandy just to be sociable. After paying for the drinks, I maneuvered Jack aside and broached the subject of the train robbery by saying, "I guess that the gold shipment turned out to be a bigger story than you expected."

For some reason, Jack took pains to avoid looking at me as he responded, "That's sure the truth!"

"Has there been any further news about it?"

"You mean other than what we printed in the extra?"

"Yes. I thought something more might have turned up since the newspaper went to press."

"Not that I know of. According to the last report, the lawmen haven't picked up the trail yet."

"Tennyson certainly missed the mark this time, didn't he?"

"Now wait a minute, Jarvis. You know that our friend took every reasonable precaution to see that the shipment was protected."

"Oh, yes, you *did* tell me that you knew something about his arrangements with Colonel Yarbrough."

"That's right. There was the nothing wrong with the plan that they devised."

"Then why wasn't it even mentioned in the newspaper accounts?"

Jack was clearly taken aback by this question and hesitated noticeably before answering, "The authorities wouldn't let us print anything about the involvement of the troopers from Fort Worth."

This statement didn't ring true, and it was obvious from his expression that Jack knew it. He tried to change the subject by bringing up Tennyson's success in helping Clyde Starrett to negotiate a favorable freight rate for the Panhandle Cattlemen's Association. I acknowledged this accomplishment as a useful counter move against Jay Golden, but added that it paled in comparison with the loss of the bullion. It was apparent that Jack felt very uncomfortable with our discussion, and I decided to let him off the hook by saying that I had to be on my way. Following a brief exchange of small talk with Willis and Hogan, I left the saloon and walked to the Quincy Hotel, still harboring a good many unanswered questions about the robbery.

CHAPTER 14

A Fresh Line of Attack

Over a supper of baked veal pie with mashed potatoes and black-eyed peas, I began to read the material that George Riley had assembled from the property tax records. I knew that the Central Texas & Gulf Railroad had been deeded every other section of land along its right of way through Dallas County, with the plats alternating on the east and west side of the tracks. George had done a good job of distilling the information on all of these holdings into a form that was easy to understand. As I looked over the entries that he had made under the heading "current owner," I noticed a name that appeared multiple times: the Donlevy Company. A little further along, I found another repetitive listing: Molloy & Wilber. In both cases, the firms had acquired the indicated pieces of property within the preceding four months. These transactions might have been perfectly legitimate. On the other hand, they could have been just what Tennyson was hoping to find: payoffs from Jay Golden to his associates. This thought led me to realize that the threat to the Texas &

Louisiana remained, even if Tennyson had been wrong about the intended use of the stolen locomotive.

When I had finished my meal, I carefully placed George's notes back into the portfolio, then started for home at a leisurely pace. Walking always helped to clear my head; and as I strolled along Ross Avenue, my dismay over the theft of the bullion began to subside. In its place, there arose a growing sense of curiosity about what had really occurred that morning. The omissions in the newspaper accounts and Jack Lorentz's reluctance to talk about them, coupled with the obscure message in Tennyson's telegram, made me suspect that all was not as it seemed. However, it was clearly fruitless to speculate about the matter without additional information. Since there was little prospect of learning anything more until Tennyson returned on Tuesday afternoon, I resolved to devote my attention in the meantime to discovering more about the Donlevy Company and Molloy & Wilber. As I pondered how to proceed, it occurred to me that Mr. Dillon might well be familiar with the firms because of his position in the Dallas Merchants' Exchange. By the time I reached 211 Routh Street, my earlier agitation had largely given way to a strong sense of purpose. The thought struck me that perhaps this was what Tennyson had meant about controlling emotional reactions in favor of logic.

Once I was settled in the library, I continued my perusal of the listings that George had extracted from the county tax files. I found four more entries for the Donlevy Company and another three for Molloy &

Wilber. A quick calculation showed that these two firms together owned over 10,000 acres from the original land grants of the Central Texas & Gulf. There were several other names that appeared more than once in the summary; but in each case, the total holdings amounted to less than 2000 acres. This disparity certainly seemed to warrant investigation, and I decided that a visit to the Dillon Mercantile on the following afternoon was called for, to see if Ambrose Dillon could tell me anything about the businesses in question. I also concluded that it would be useful to have George Riley look up the addresses to which the property tax statements for the two companies were sent.

Despite my determination to stop worrying about the day's news, I was too wrought-up to sleep very well that night. Consequently, I awoke on Saturday morning feeling rather lifeless. Even splashing cold water on my face failed to chase away the sense of lethargy. However, Mrs. Hutchins soon came to my rescue, as the dumbwaiter arrived with hot tea, poached eggs, bacon, and biscuits. This unexpected repast provided just the lift that was needed to revive me, and I was touched by the lady's thoughtfulness in sending it without being asked. After consuming the tasty meal, I took a moment to write a note of thanks, adding a reminder that I would call for her and Amy around a quarter of one. I then placed the note on the serving tray, returned it to the first floor on the dumbwaiter, and departed for my office.

Upon arrival at the Curtis Building, my first action

was to post a sign stating that the consulting room would close at noon and that anyone needing care after that should see Dr. Everett on Harwood Street. I didn't know how many patients to expect on a Saturday under our referral agreement and wanted to be sure that I would be able to get away in plenty of time for my luncheon engagement. It turned out that this was not a problem, as only nine people showed up during the morning, although the last one came in just a few minutes before twelve. He was a laborer at the Harry Brick Manufacturing Yard and was suffering from a persistent rash, which I diagnosed as a reaction to the silica that he encountered on the job. Quickly applying a salve to the affected areas, I wrote out a prescription for him before locking up and hurrying back to Routh Street.

As soon as I reached Number 211, I went straight to the backyard and hitched up Tennyson's buggy. After driving it around to the front of the house and setting the brake, I dashed upstairs to wash my face, comb my hair, and check my apparel. The opportunity to treat my landlady and her daughter to lunch, while also assuming the role of mentor, had me tingling with a sense of anticipation. Wanting to be precisely on time, I extracted my pocket watch and nervously waited until the hands indicated fifteen minutes before the hour. Then I descended the staircase, walked around to the front entrance, and knocked once. Amy opened the door almost immediately, looking delightful in a pale yellow skirt and a white ruffled blouse. Momentarily,

Mrs. Hutchins appeared, wearing an attractive dress of beige linen with a pleated bodice. I bowed and said, "Your carriage awaits, ladies."

As we made our way to the buggy, Mrs. Hutchins asked, "Are you sure that you don't want me to fix something here, Dr. Weston? It really wouldn't be any trouble."

"Your offer is most kind," I responded. "However, I can hardly pass up the opportunity to be seen dining at the Quincy in the company of two such lovely companions. Admittedly, the fare there is no match for yours; but I think that you will find it acceptable."

"What a glib tongue you have, Dr. Weston. Very well. If you are determined to spend your money on us, we certainly can't refuse."

Some ten minutes later, we drew up in front of the Quincy Hotel. After helping the ladies down, I handed the buggy over to the attendant and led the way into the lobby. George was sitting on a sofa near the dining room, neatly attired in sharply-creased tan trousers and a starched white shirt. He rose as we entered and came forward to greet us. When Amy saw him, she exclaimed, "Hello, George! You're all dressed up today. Are you waiting for someone?"

Before he could answer, I quickly explained, "I hope you don't mind that I invited George to join us. He has been doing some research for Mr. Pierce, and I thought that he deserved a lunch as a token of appreciation. It also crossed my mind that he might be able to contribute something to our discussion of career choices."

Amy didn't say anything, and I couldn't tell how she had reacted to my announcement. Fortunately, Mrs. Hutchins broke the silence by remarking, "It's nice to see you, George. I'm certainly interested in hearing what you plan to do after completing your studies."

Maneuvering the three of them into the dining room, I found a table in one corner, which afforded a measure of seclusion. George was a model of politeness, pulling out a chair for Amy and guiding her into it, while I did the same for Mrs. Hutchins. The special of the day was young capon with hollandaise sauce, accompanied by brown rice, sugar-snap peas, and queen olives. From my months in residence at the hotel, I knew that this was one of the better meals offered there, so I heartily recommended it. The others accepted my suggestion and agreed, as well, that iced tea would be a suitable beverage.

While we were waiting for our food, I opened the conversation about careers by briefly relating the development of the medical profession in modern times. Knowing of Amy's interest in mathematics and the natural sciences, I emphasized the significant advances that had been made over the previous half-century as trial-and-error treatments and folklore had given way to the application of the scientific method. In order to illustrate this point, I cited the discoveries that had been made by Thomas Addison, Gerhart Hansen, Thomas Hodgkin, Gregor Mendel, James Paget, and Louis Pasteur. I also described my own experiences as a medical student at St. Louis University.

When I paused, Mrs. Hutchins commented, "That was a fascinating account, Dr. Weston. Don't you think so, Amy?"

"Oh, yes, it certainly was," Amy answered quickly. "I hadn't realized how much the practice of medicine has advanced in recent years."

"Well, after hearing a little about the field, do you think that you might be interested in studying to be a doctor?" I asked.

"I'm really not sure. The opportunity to use what I've learned about the natural sciences is appealing, but I don't know whether I could cope with some of the things that a physician must do."

"Your reaction is understandable. Unfortunately, the treatment of injuries and illnesses can involve some rather unpleasant experiences; and a lot of people are put off by that. However, such an aversion doesn't have to keep you from pursuing a career in medicine. The need for medical researchers is growing rapidly. Rather than dealing directly with patients, these doctors devote their time to determining the causes of diseases and developing methods for preventing them or reducing their effects. This sort of work might be better-suited to your temperament."

"That *does* sound like something worth considering. How can I learn more about what's involved?"

"I'd be happy to lend you some of my reference books. After you have had a chance to look through them, we could discuss the subject further."

"What schools offer the type of training necessary to pursue such a career?" Mrs. Hutchins inquired.

"My alma mater, St. Louis University, would be an excellent choice; but there are also a few institutions closer to Dallas that offer suitable courses of study. For example, the college of medicine which the University of Texas recently opened in Galveston would be worth considering. Perhaps we could take a trip down there sometime to let Amy see the facilities and talk with a few of the students."

"I think that's an excellent idea," Mrs. Hutchins said. "What do *you* think of the suggestion, Amy?"

"If it's all right, Mother, I'd like a chance to review the material in Dr. Weston's books before visiting any schools. A decision like this shouldn't be rushed."

"Of course. I'm just anxious about your future. The graduation ceremony at Ursuline is less than two months away now. Besides, it was very gracious of Dr. Weston to extend the offer, and we can't expect him to accommodate his schedule to our convenience."

"Please don't be concerned about that," I interjected. "With a little planning, we should be able to find a mutually agreeable time for the journey."

At that juncture, the waiter arrived and set our plates on the table. He then excused himself and went back to the kitchen, returning momentarily with a plate of hot rolls and a pitcher of iced tea. When he had departed again, Mrs. Hutchins asked me to say grace. After reciting a standard blessing, I asked the others to tell me how they liked the capon. To my relief, all of them commented favorably on it. Soon the conversation lagged as the four of us became absorbed in the business of eating. In order to fill the void, as well as to focus a bit of attention on George, I commented that I had enjoyed meeting Professor Lawrence at the Commonwealth Commercial College on Thursday. Using this as an opening, I added, "He told me that you are one of his best students, George. Have you decided what sort of occupation to pursue after your graduation?"

"I plan to become an attorney," George responded. "My father insisted that I get a good grounding in business principles first, but I've wanted to be a lawyer since I was twelve years old. Mr. Pierce has offered to recommend me for admission to the law school in Austin and to help me find a position after I pass the bar."

With a look of some surprise, Amy said, "I didn't know you were interested in a legal career."

"There are probably a lot of things about me that you don't know," George returned, lowering his eyes.

"Mr. Pierce must have a lot of confidence in you if he is willing to go to that much trouble," I observed.

"Oh, I think he just knows that I'll work hard to live up to his expectations."

"Well, I'm impressed with your determination, George," Mrs. Hutchins declared. "There aren't many young men today who have such clear-cut goals."

Suppressing a grin with some effort, I reflected that my attempt to elevate George's standing seemed to be having a beneficial effect, if not on Amy, then at least on her mother.

"While we're on the subject of jurisprudence," I ventured to say, "that's another field where a strong background in reasoning can be put to good use. If you decide not to follow a career in medicine, Amy, it might be advisable to have a talk with Mr. Pierce about the various opportunities associated with the administration of our nation's laws."

"As a matter of fact," Amy answered, "Mr. Pierce has already told me quite a bit about his studies on the use of physical evidence to catch criminals. I'm looking forward to reading some of the monographs that he has written."

"That isn't quite what I meant," I quickly explained, seeing Mrs. Hutchins looking at her daughter in a manner which suggested a combination of aggravation and anxiety.

Amy replied to the unspoken admonishment by saying, "Of course, my mother thinks that women shouldn't concern themselves with solving crimes. Her views might be different, though, if she'd take the time to learn more about the techniques employed by Mr. Pierce. He's really doing nothing more than applying the scientific method to the cause of justice."

The thought struck me that his approach wasn't always successful, however, as Mrs. Hutchins countered, "The good Lord has blessed you with a fine mind, Amy; and tracking down people who break the law is certainly not the best use of it. Please promise me that you will think seriously about what Dr. Weston has told us and spend some time examining the books that he mentioned."

"I have every intention of doing that, Mother; and I'm sorry for upsetting you. Dr. Weston's discussion of medicine has given me a new perspective on the subject, and I definitely want to find out more about the type of work performed by medical researchers."

A change of topic appeared to be advisable, so I suggested that we order dessert, noting that the peach tapioca pudding was an especially good choice. Mrs. Hutchins and Amy went along with my recommendation, while George decided to have a piece of blueberry pie. When we had finished eating, I persuaded my guests to join me in a stroll to the Star Art Gallery, where a number of landscape paintings by local artists were reported to be on display.

As we walked along Akard toward Elm Street, I deliberately allowed the two young people to draw ahead a bit so that they could talk more freely. This also gave me a chance to tell Mrs. Hutchins that I regretted having contributed to the discord between her and Amy.

"Oh, that was nothing," Mrs. Hutchins assured me. "In any case, please don't blame yourself for our little contretemps. I know that Mr. Pierce has become something of a public figure because of his work with Sheriff Lassiter, but it caught me by surprise to hear Amy express such an interest in his activities. Although I would never admit this to her, I think she would probably be very good at that sort of thing. However, I am old-fashioned enough to regard such endeavors as a man's domain. On the other hand, the practice of medicine would seem to be a natural outlet for my daughter's talents."

"It isn't my place to say so," I remarked, "but I'm in complete agreement with you. Although I've only known Mr. Pierce a short time, I have already learned a fair amount about his investigative techniques. Amy is correct in saying that he utilizes the scientific method, but there is a lot of field work involved in doing so. From my own experience in assisting him with a case, I can tell you that searching for clues can be a strenuous undertaking, with some degree of risk on occasion."

"I feel very fortunate that you are willing to spend time acquainting Amy with the medical profession. For her own good, I intend to insist that we accept your kind offer to show us the school in Galveston. Will you let me know when the trip can be fit into your busy schedule?"

"By all means. As soon as my patient referrals from Dr. Everett have tapered off a bit, I should be able to get away for a few days. We could take the train down on a Friday morning, spend Saturday looking around the campus and speaking with some of the students, and devote Sunday afternoon to viewing the sights on the island. An early departure on Monday would have us back in Dallas by suppertime. How does that agenda sound to you?"

"Quite acceptable, as long as it's understood that I will bear all the expenses of the journey."

"A gentleman doesn't impose on a lady's purse, but

rather than contest the point now, let's leave it until the occasion arises."

Presently, we rounded the corner to Elm Street and came upon a short queue of people at the doorway of the Star Art Gallery. Taking our places in line, we had only a brief wait before being admitted to the room where the paintings were on display. The subjects ranged from the sandy beaches on Padre Island to rugged scenes from the Chisos Mountains, and we spent a pleasant half an hour viewing the skillful renderings. After we had made a complete circuit of the room, I offered to retrieve the buggy while the others waited there. However, the ladies indicated that they preferred to walk back to the hotel.

When we reached the Quincy, I signaled the attendant to have our carriage brought around, then asked George if I might have a word with him. Making our excuses to Amy and Mrs. Hutchins, we stepped aside; and I explained what I wanted to find out about the tax statements for the Donlevy Company and Molloy & Wilber. George appeared to be expecting my request and readily agreed to undertake the task. He also thanked me earnestly for inviting him to have lunch with us.

In another couple of minutes, a hostler returned with the buggy. I helped Mrs. Hutchins climb aboard while the two young people said their farewells. Once George had assisted Amy into the seat, I released the brake and let the horse proceed at his own pace. Heading along Wood Street, I decided to continue on to Harwood before turning. Soon, we were rolling along Live Oak

Street at a moderate speed, chatting about the impressive homes that we passed and the colorful flowers that adorned their yards.

As we approached 211 Routh Street, I noticed that a wagon was sitting in front of the house. After pulling up behind it and aiding Mrs. Hutchins and Amy to the ground, I looked around for the driver. Momentarily, a young man in a Railway Express uniform came around the corner from the southeast side of the porch. He was carrying a parcel and frowning. Upon seeing me, he hurried forward and asked if I was Mr. Tennyson Pierce.

"No, my name is Dr. Jarvis Weston," I replied. "However, if that package is for Mr. Pierce, I can accept it on his behalf. We share these quarters."

"I guess that would be all right," he said with a tone of uncertainty. "I've been waiting quite a spell for someone to show up. The station agent told me not to come back without delivering this. You'll have to sign for it, though."

Taking the receipt book that the boy held out, I used the porch railing as a support and signed "Jarvis Weston, M.D. for Tennyson Pierce, Esq." The messenger peered at the signature for a prolonged interval before handing over the parcel, as if he wasn't sure whether I could be trusted. However, it seemed to placate him when I proffered a half-dollar to make up for his long wait. When he had departed, I looked more carefully at the label on the box, which indicated that the shipment had been entered at St. Louis, Missouri by one A. F. Pierce. With a sudden feeling of anticipation, I realized that I was undoubtedly holding the information which Archer had gathered concerning the stockholders of the Texas & Louisiana Railway. As I stood there pondering whether it was appropriate for me to verify the contents before informing Tennyson of the delivery, I became aware that Mrs. Hutchins was speaking to me.

"Is that something which Mr. Pierce was expecting?" she inquired.

"Yes, I believe so," I answered. "Judging from the point of origin, it appears to be some records that he mentioned needing in connection with one of his cases. I was just deliberating whether to send a telegram notifying him that they have arrived."

"We'd best leave you to your business, then. Thank you so much for the delightful lunch and the informative discussion about careers in medicine."

"Yes, I want to offer my thanks as well," Amy added. "The meal was delicious, and it was awfully nice of you to take the trouble of explaining the opportunities in the medical profession."

"It was my pleasure, ladies," I said, bowing slightly. When they had gone inside, I carried the package upstairs and left it in the library. Then I returned to the buggy and set out for the central business area again.

My objective was the Dillon Mercantile facility on Young Street, where I hoped to get some answers from Ambrose Dillon about the Donlevy Company and Molloy & Wilber. Having discovered this fresh line of attack thanks to George, I wanted to see how far it could be pursued before Tennyson returned from Marshall.

CHAPTER 15

Signs of Collusion

Some fifteen minutes later, I parked the buggy near the subtantial-looking three-story building that housed the city's leading supplier of hardware, tools, and farm implements. The street directly in front of the establishment was crowded with wagons being loaded with merchandise. Maneuvering through this bustle of activity, I made my way to the staircase at the rear of the structure and climbed to the third floor. There, I walked straight to the familiar door marked "Private" and knocked twice. A resonant voice from within sounded a hearty "Come in!"

"Good afternoon, Mr. Dillon," I intoned upon entering. "Are you busy?"

"Never too busy for you, my boy," he replied. "How can I be of assistance today?"

"Please excuse me for disturbing you during business hours, but I find myself in need of some information once again. It's your misfortune, I'm afraid, that I don't know anyone else who is likely to have the answers to my questions."

"Does this have something to do with our recent discussion about that Lawson fellow?"

"Indirectly. You're probably wondering why I have been so inquisitive lately, and circumstances now warrant revealing the reason. Tennyson Pierce has enlisted my assistance with an investigation that involves the attempt by Jay Golden to establish a rail monopoly in Texas. Due to the sensitive nature of the case, it has been necessary for us to pursue our inquiries discreetly. If I have asked about things that don't seem to concern me, it's because we are trying to learn the identities of people who may be associated with Golden's scheme."

"That's extraordinary, Jarvis! I wasn't far wrong in accusing you of acting like a Pinkerton agent, was I? But take a seat and tell me more about all of this."

"It's very considerate of you to put up with this imposition. I don't mind admitting that there aren't many leads in the case yet."

Drawing a straight-backed chair up close to the desk, I sat down and continued, "The problem which concerns me at the moment is discovering who the principals are in the Donlevy Company and Molloy & Wilber. Within the last four months, those two firms have acquired a good deal of land along the route of the Central Texas & Gulf Railroad in Dallas County. I thought that you might know something about them because of your involvement with the Merchants' Exchange."

"I'm not familiar with the Donlevy Company. However, Molloy & Wilber is a big building supply outfit in Waco. It was originally owned by Arnold

Molloy and Hiram Wilber, but they sold out last year to a syndicate from Philadelphia. A man named Lyle Benedict is in charge of the operation now."

"What sort of building supplies do they sell?"

"Primarily lumber, brick, and pipe. They're the major source of construction materials for the central part of the state."

"Then Molloy & Wilber might be an outlet for the products of the Ferguson Mill or the Hanley Brothers Mill?"

"It's certainly possible."

"What do you think they could want with around 4000 acres of property in southern Dallas County?"

"I really couldn't say. That's more land than would be needed for a branch in this area. In any case, there haven't been any rumors about them expanding."

"And you don't know anything at all about the Donlevy Company?"

"Nothing whatsoever, I'm afraid. How much real estate have they acquired?"

"Approximately 6000 acres in the northern part of the county."

"That *is* a rather considerable amount, isn't it? You might try asking Clair Whitman about them. If they've had any large financial dealings in the community, he'll probably know the details. I also vaguely remember him mentioning a man named Donlevy many years ago."

"You've been very helpful, Mr. Dillon; and I'm grateful for your patience. Perhaps I could treat you and Mrs. Dillon to supper sometime as a small token of appreciation."

"My wife and I would certainly enjoy dining with you some evening, Jarvis; but please don't feel any obligation toward me. It's always a pleasure to see you, even under these unusual circumstances. Just promise to exercise caution in the further pursuit of your inquiries. The men whom you are trying to identify may very well be dangerous."

"I realize that all too well and definitely don't plan on taking any undue risks. Naturally, I would like our discussion today to be kept between the two of us. Thus far, there are only five or six people who know about the investigation. The number will inevitably increase as the case progresses, but limiting it as much as possible is obviously desirable. That's probably the best way to minimize the likelihood of retaliation by Golden's associates."

"Rest assured that your secret is safe with me, Jarvis."

After thanking Mr. Dillon again for his time, I took my leave, walked back down the stairs, and picked my way through the still-crowded store to the street. Once aboard the buggy, I headed for the Western Union office on Main Street, where I sent a telegram to Tennyson in care of the Marshall Inn. Assuming that he would know what I meant, the message read simply, "Information from St. Louis has arrived." With that duty accomplished, I started back toward Akard Street. When I reached the Curtis Building, I stopped long enough to pick up the books that I had told Amy about, then set out once again for home.

As I rambled along Ross Avenue, I reflected on what I had learned from Mr. Dillon. The fact that Molloy & Wilber had been purchased by a syndicate from Philadelphia suggested a possible link to Jay Golden. In addition, their location in Waco seemed noteworthy, since that town was also the home of the man Lawson who represented the Belleville Ironworks. Moreover, there could be a relationship between the building supply firm and one or both of the lumber mills that Tennyson was investigating. Perhaps the pieces of the puzzle were beginning to fit together. I still couldn't figure out how the locomotive and the bullion came into the picture, however.

Upon arriving at Number 211, I put the buggy away, tended to the horse, and retired to the library, where I continued my deliberations. It was tempting to open the package from Tennyson's brother, because I was quite anxious to see the names on the list of stockholders. However, my authority to view official documents from the Treasury Department was questionable. While mulling over this dilemma, an idea gradually dawned on me. Once formed, it was so obvious that I couldn't understand why the thought hadn't occurred to me before. The stolen bullion would provide the conspirators with the funds required to purchase a majority interest in the railroad! This explanation tied everything together, while also imparting a new urgency to the investigation. Now that these men had the gold, they would undoubtedly move quickly to execute the takeover. There was no time to waste if they were to be tracked down and arrested before accomplishing their goal. I considered sending a telegram to inform Tennyson of my conclusions, but decided that I dared not do so, for fear that the message might be intercepted by someone in the employment of Golden's confederates.

With a feeling of considerable frustration, I tried to think of the best course to follow under the circumstances. Even though my standing in the case was entirely unofficial, I clearly had a civic responsibility to do something about the impending threat to the state's economy. The only choice seemed to be approaching Sheriff Lassiter after church on the following day, in order to find out how much he knew about the suspicions concerning Golden's scheme. If it appeared that he was fully aware of the situation, I planned to inform him of my findings. Otherwise, I would have no alternative but to wait for Tennyson's return.

Admitting that there was nothing more to be done that evening, I took down a volume of John Stuart Mill's works from the shelves and began reading his treatise *On Liberty*. An hour or so of this was as much as I could take at one sitting, however; and around six, I decided to go out for a light supper. No sooner had I stepped from the stairway onto the lower porch than Amy came around the corner.

"Oh, I'm glad that I caught you, Dr. Weston," she said. "Mother and I were wondering if you would like to eat with us. We're having shrimp salad and brown bread with cream cheese."

"That sounds delicious, Amy," I replied, grateful for the opportunity to enjoy a home-cooked meal and some pleasant company.

Proceeding into the dining room, I greeted Mrs. Hutchins and thanked her for the invitation. Then I remembered the reference books that I had brought home for Amy and excused myself to retrieve them. When I returned, the ladies were about to sit down at the table, so I set the volumes aside and helped them into their chairs. Mrs. Hutchins once again asked me to say grace, and I responded with a simple prayer of thanks that I had learned from a Jesuit teacher.

The shrimp salad was quite good, with an unusual flavor that I couldn't place. It was just the thing for a warm spring evening, and I commended Mrs. Hutchins on her culinary skills. She demurred and adroitly changed the subject by commenting on our lunch at the Quincy Hotel. Taking advantage of this opening, I said, "Allow me to apologize again for inviting George to join us without consulting you. He had done such a fine job with the research for Mr. Pierce that I wanted to reward him. I hope that you didn't mind his presence too much."

"Not at all," Mrs. Hutchins returned. "George seems like a very nice young man, and it was interesting to hear about his plans to become an attorney. Didn't you think so, Amy?"

"The news came as rather a surprise, actually," Amy

answered, looking a little embarassed. "I was under the impression that George was going to work for his father when he finished his studies at Commonwealth."

"What sort of business does his father have?" I inquired.

"He owns a cotton oil mill down on south Lamar Street."

"That must be a fairly profitable enterprise."

"It probably is, but I'm glad that George has decided to follow a different path. He would be wasting his abilities working there."

"You may be right, Amy," I remarked, thinking that she appeared to have more interest in the young man than he realized. "From my dealings with him, I would say that George has a first-rate mind and should be quite successful in the legal field."

"Perhaps you could tell us a little more about what led you to become a doctor," Mrs. Hutchins interjected.

"Well, I suppose you could say that I came by my interest in medicine naturally. My maternal grandfather was a physician. He was born in England, but received his medical training in Edinburgh, Scotland. In 1834, he emigrated to the United States and established a practice in Lancaster, Pennsylvania. Then in 1846, he moved to St. Louis. That's where my family lived until 1870, so I saw my grandfather frequently when I was young. Once in a while, he allowed me to accompany him to his office and look at his instruments. I became intrigued with the methods employed to diagnose and treat illnesses. When the time came to choose a career, I decided to follow his example."

"You were fortunate to have someone like that to influence your decision. I'm not sure that Amy knows it, but one of her great-grandfathers was an army surgeon who served in the War of 1812."

"No, I don't recall being told about him. What was his name?"

"Jonathan Parmiter. He was my mother's paternal grandfather," Mrs. Hutchins responded. Then, with a meaningful glance at Amy, she added, "Unfortunately, no one in the family since his time has taken up the medical profession."

"I promise to give it serious consideration, Mother," Amy said. "However, there *are* other respectable occupations, you know."

"Of course there are, dear; and the decision is yours to make. It *would* be nice to have a doctor in the family, though."

Sensing a need to take up a less sensitive topic, I mentioned that there was a performance of a play called *Dad's Girl* at the Dallas Opera House on Sunday afternoon. "Would the two of you consider accompanying me to see it?" I asked.

"With pleasure," Mrs. Hutchins answered. "According to the newspaper, the title role is being played by Lizzie May Ulmer, who is one of my favorite actresses. Would you like to join us, Amy?"

"I'm sorry, but I've already agreed to go on a picnic

with George tomorrow afternoon. Thank you for inviting me, though, Dr. Weston."

"Well, it should be a fine day for an outing. Your mother and I will just have to enjoy the play without you."

When we had finished eating, I offered to help with the dishes; but Mrs. Hutchins wouldn't permit it, saying that I was a guest and ushering me into the sitting room. Along the way, I paused to pick up the reference books that I had brought for Amy. Once we were all comfortably seated, I opened one of the texts and started to leaf through it.

"This is a treatise on the scenarios for a number of commonplace diseases, including influenza, measles, scarlet fever, smallpox, tuberculosis, malaria, and diptheria," I explained. "It lists the most up-to-date findings on the probable origins of these maladies and describes the tests upon which the conclusions are based. For example, there is a nice summary of the work by Robert Koch that led to the discovery of the bacillus that causes tuberculosis. The articles should give you a pretty good idea of the types of activities performed by medical researchers."

"It sounds like a very interesting volume," Amy observed. "I'm looking forward to reading about the techniques used in the experiments. What's the other book?"

"That one is a compendium of information on the formulas and actions of various commonly prescribed medications. You might find the contents helpful in understanding the role that chemistry plays in the development of treatments for various symptoms."

"I can see that it's going to take a while to go through these. When do you need them back?"

"There's no rush; but please take care not to lose them, since replacement copies are somewhat difficult to obtain."

"You have my word that they won't leave the house. It's awfully nice of you to loan them to me."

"I'm more than happy to do it, Amy. Don't hesitate to consult me if you have any questions or comments about the material. Now, with your permission, ladies, I had better take my leave. There are still a few things that I need to accomplish tonight. Thank you for a delightful supper."

As I rose to leave, I added, "If it's all right, I'll call for you around a quarter past noon tomorrow, Mrs. Hutchins. That should give us ample time to reach the Opera House before the opening curtain. Considering the popularity of *Dad's Girl*, there may be a good-sized crowd for the matinee."

"A twevee-fifteen departure will be fine, Dr. Weston. Would you like for me to send up breakfast in the morning?"

"If it isn't too much trouble. As a matter of fact, I've been meaning to ask if you might consider doing so on a daily basis. It would be a tremendous convenience for me, and I would be willing to pay a premium price for your wonderful cooking."

"I'll be more than happy to prepare something for

you every morning, and there's no need to pay me. The rent that I receive from Mr. Pierce is more than adequate to cover the cost of a few added meals. Besides, it's a welcome change to have someone in the house who has a good appetite."

On that gratifying note, I bade the ladies good evening and returned to the library upstairs. The sight of the parcel from Archer Pierce returned my thoughts once more to the risk which the Texas & Louisiana Railway faced from Jay Golden. For a few minutes, I paced up and down, debating whether I could justify opening the package. After all, I reasoned, Tennyson *had* requested my help in looking over the list of stockholders. Surely, he wouldn't want me to wait for his return before getting started. In addition, the theft of the gold had added a new urgency to the situation. A delay of two or three days might well allow Golden's collaborators to succeed in their objective. In the end, I convinced myself that the circumstances warranted examining the contents of the box. Extracting my pocket knife, I cut the twine with which it was bound and pulled up the flaps. Underneath a stack of old newspapers inside, I found an envelope addressed to Tennyson and a portfolio that was stamped with the seal of the United States Treasury Department. Setting the envelope aside, I hesitantly opened the folder and started to read its contents.

At the top of the first page, an introductory paragraph indicated that the material which followed was a list of all individuals and companies that had purchased 100 or more shares of stock in the Texas

& Louisiana Railway since December of 1883. It was stated that the information had been extracted from the files of the Treasury Department on corporate securities and had been cross-checked against the records of the New York and Chicago Stock Exchanges. Below this explanation was a roster of names that ran to some thirty pages. For each entry, the report included an address, the total number of shares owned, and the dates on which the shares had been acquired. I decided to take these sheets into the dining room, where I could arrange them on the table as I looked through them.

For the next hour and a half, I carefully studied the tabulation of names, first extracting and writing down all of them with addresses in Texas and then sorting those by the number of shares held. When I had finished my compilation, I found that it contained thirty-one entries, comprised of twenty-six individuals and five companies. Their holdings ranged from a respectable 106 shares to a very substantial 9245 shares. Significantly, this last figure belonged to a familiar firm, the Easton & Monroe Logging Company, which had purchased all of this stock within the past six months. Another name that caught my attention was that of Ralph Lawson, who was listed as residing in Waco and owning 2362 shares of stock, most of it acquired since the first of the year. These discoveries seemed to support my earlier conclusion about the link between Golden's confederates and the events that had taken place in East Texas. Excited by what might prove to be a significant development in the case, I realized that another restless night lay in store for me unless something were done to counter my restive mood. Even though it was well past sundown, a short walk seemed the best prescription, short of a sedative.

Heading southeast along Routh, I strolled over to San Jacinto, then followed it down to Leonard Street. While ambling along, inhaling the pleasant night air, I made an earnest attempt to erase all thoughts concerning Jay Golden's schemes. Even so, a certain anxiety remained, arising from the strong conviction that Tennyson should somehow be informed of my findings as soon as possible. In a moment of weakness, I even permitted myself to gloat a bit, imagining his reaction when he learned how much progress had been made without him. Fortunately, by the time my meanderings took me back to Routh Street, this feeling had subsided somewhat. As a result, I arrived home feeling at least a little more at ease.

Although the walk had helped me to relax, sleep didn't come easily that night. Several times, I was awakened by vivid dreams of fierce-looking train robbers presided over by the sneering visage of Jay Golden. It was a relief when dawn arrived, giving me an excuse to escape from my bed. After washing, shaving, and donning a freshly pressed suit of clothes, I opened the dumbwaiter to see what culinary delights it held. Mrs. Hutchins surely didn't disappoint me, as the tray was laden with a pot of tea and a plate bearing a generous serving of French toast and sausage. Carrying these into the dining room, I dawdled over the meal while thinking about the day's prospects. Then, wanting to purchase a newspaper before Mass, I harnessed Tennyson's buggy and set out for the Quincy Hotel.

It was a pleasant morning, with a moderate breeze from the south and a few white clouds off to the west in an otherwise clear sky. Finding myself with plenty of time, I took an indirect route to the central business area. Upon drawing up in front of the Quincy, the *Dallas News* vendor there recognized me and immediately came out to the curb. "Paper, Dr. Weston?" he inquired, holding up a copy of the Sunday edition.

"Yes, thanks, Johnny," I said, handing him two nickels. "Is there anything new in here about the train robbery?"

"We've got a piece that starts on the front page; but to tell you the truth, it's mostly a rehash of what was printed two days ago."

"That's surprising. Something more about the search for the criminals should be known by now. Well, have a good day."

Proceeding along Akard to the Curtis Building, I parked the buggy at the curb and took the newspaper into my consulting room. There was still nearly an hour before the start of Mass at Sacred Heart Church, which left ample time to peruse the day's news stories. Naturally, I started with the article on the theft of the bullion. Just as Johnny had indicated, it appeared to be nothing more than a condensed version of the information that had been printed earlier. A few editorial comments had been added, but there was still no mention of the role played by the troopers from Fort Worth in guarding the train. Neither was anything reported concerning the actions being taken to track down the thieves. This struck me as extraordinarily curious, and I resolved to have another talk with Jack Lorentz at the earliest opportunity.

The remaining stories on the front page dealt with local issues, including the upcoming political races, the growing congestion caused by the curbside trading of cotton, the need to expand the fire department, and the attempt to organize a carpenters' union in the city. As important as these topics might have been, they held little interest for me in my state of mind on that day. What I was looking for was something that might be related to the activities of the men who were plotting to take over the Texas & Louisiana. Turning to page two, my attention was arrested by a bold heading in what appeared to be 18-point type, which proclaimed, "Shippers Negotiate Rates." The accompanying text stated that a number of local businessmen had engaged the well-known attorney Tennyson Pierce to represent them in trying to establish long-term agreements on shipping rates with the Texas & Louisiana Railway. It was explained that this action was being taken to guard against future increases in tariffs that might adversely affect the competitive positions of local products. Mr. Pierce was said to have travelled to the divisional headquarters of the railroad in Marshall on the preceding Thursday to begin the negotiations. This was obviously the article that Tennyson had persuaded Jack Lorentz to print in order to draw out the conspirators.

I continued to go through the paper, scanning the headings for anything of possible significance. Finally, on page six, I came across an item that struck me as worth reading. Under the title, "Cotton Cartel Expands," there was an account which related the lease of a large tract in southern Dallas County by a group of cotton producers from the Houston area. The story indicated that the cartel controlled more than 25,000 acres in southeast Texas, as well as owning two cotton mills and a weaving firm. It was speculated that their intrusion into the Dallas market would not bode well for local growers. My interest was piqued by the mention of the land that was leased. Although an exact location wasn't given, I couldn't help wondering if it might be part of the property that had been acquired from the Central Texas & Gulf Railroad by Molloy & Wilber. At least the prospect seemed to warrant investigation. This could well be another sign of collusion among Golden's cronies.

CHAPTER 16

Tentative Deductions

When I had finished my survey of the newspaper, I locked the office and started off for Sacred Heart Church, arriving in time to hear the fine choir practicing the hymns for the service. A Benedictine priest from Chicago concelebrated the Mass with Father Martiniere and preached an instructive sermon of reasonable length. Following the recessional, I stopped briefly to meet the visitor before hurrying on my way to see Sheriff Lassiter.

The sheriff's office was located on the first floor of the County Jail, an impressive-looking three-story structure, which might easily have been taken for a hall of learning rather than a place of incarceration. A short distance inside the entrance, a gated wooden railing barred further progress. It was guarded by a grim-faced deputy, who bluntly asked me to identify myself and state my business. Handing across a calling card, I explained that I was an associate of a local attorney and needed to speak with Sheriff Lassiter on a vital matter. This apparently made no impression, since the man insisted on conducting a search for weapons before allowing me to pass. Proceeding across a fairly large open area, I approached a glass-paneled door bearing the inscription "Dallas County Sheriff" in gold leaf. A knock on the pane was quickly answered by another deputy, whose manner seemed decidedly more friendly. He informed me that the sheriff had stepped out for a few minutes, but would probably return shortly. When I declined his offer of assistance, explaining that my business was confidential, he directed me to a bench just outside the office. Taking a seat there, I whiled away the time by thinking over the best method of questioning Lassiter without disclosing any sensitive information. Not knowing how much Tennyson had told him, it was clearly necessary to broach the subject of the conspiracy in an oblique fashion.

Some quarter of an hour later, the sheriff came through the front entrance. After pausing to exchange a few words with the deputy on duty there, he started toward my position, reading from a sheet of paper while walking. When only a few paces separated us, I stood up and said, "Sheriff Lassiter, I'm Dr. Jarvis Weston. You may recall that we met at the Dillon Mercantile a couple of months ago."

"Why, sure, Dr. Weston, I remember the occasion." he replied. "As a matter of fact, Mr. Pierce mentioned your name to me recently in connection with one of his cases. What brings you to the County Jail on a Sunday morning?"

"Could we speak privately for a few minutes?"

"Certainly. Come on inside."

Opening the door, Lassiter motioned for me to precede him into a cramped room where the friendly deputy was working at a desk located between two rows of file cabinets. From this area, we continued through another opening into a more spacious chamber that was outfitted with new-looking furniture. After ushering me into a padded armchair and situating himself behind the desk, the sheriff asked, "How can I be of service today, Dr. Weston?"

"Evidently you've already been informed about my role in the matter which Mr. Pierce is currently investigating."

"Yes, that's right. He told me you were helping out with this business of the locomotive which disappeared from the siding over near Marshall."

"Then perhaps it's also no secret that I was apprised of the measures being taken to safeguard the bullion shipment."

"The subject *did* come up in passing last Wednesday when we were trying to coordinate the preparations."

"This may seem like an odd request, but I'm rather worried about a telegram which Mr. Pierce sent to me on Thursday afternoon. The message read, 'Do not be alarmed at news tomorrow,' without any further explanation. I was wondering whether you might know what he could have meant."

"Not offhand. Why ask *me* about it?"

"As a representative of the law, you're the most likely candidate for him to trust with a confidential disclosure. What troubles me is that the only news of any significance on Friday had to do with the train robbery."

"So you think his message concerned the holdup?"

"Possibly. I was frankly hoping this interview would enlighten me on that point, as well as several others. For example, how were the bandits able to get past the troopers who were stationed along the tracks?"

Lassiter squirmed a bit in his chair as he answered, "I guess they must have picked just the right place to strike."

"For some reason, there wasn't anything in this morning's *Dallas News* about the ongoing efforts to track down the culprits. With all the lawmen that are surely participating in the hunt, some trace of the trail should have been picked up by now. Can you tell me what progress has been made?"

Looking slightly uncomfortable, the sheriff said, "I'm afraid that no leads on the gold's whereabouts have been found yet. Considering the cover afforded by the woods over in East Texas, the search is apt to take a good while."

"Don't you suppose the robbers will probably try to convert their bounty into currency pretty quickly? After all, the bars are far too bulky for ready use as legal tender."

"That makes sense, I guess. What's your point, though?"

"Figuring out the potential destinations where the bullion might be taken for exchange could allow a trap to be set."

"You're obviously a pretty sharp fellow, Dr. Weston; but poking into this situation really isn't a good idea. The whole affair is being handled by agents from the U. S. Secret Service, and they don't want any outside help."

"Very well, then. Let's move on to a different subject. Mr. Pierce told me that he was planning to consult you concerning the activities of a man named Lawson from Waco. Has he had an opportunity to do so?"

"Now that you mention it, he *did* ask for assistance in obtaining an address for a Lawson from the McLennan County sheriff. I haven't followed through on the request yet, though, because it didn't sound like there was any real urgency about the matter."

"New circumstances may have made the information more important than originally thought. Incidentally, I happened to learn yesterday that the man's first name is Ralph."

"Okay. I'll get in touch with Sheriff Hicks this afternoon. Do you know why Mr. Pierce wants to find this character?"

"Apparently he has some connection with a problem concerning one of the lumber mills in East Texas," I responded evasively, watching the sheriff closely for any reaction. When none was evident, I decided to try another tack and inquired, "Are you familiar with the Easton & Monroe Logging Company?"

"To some extent. They're reportedly a pretty big outfit, with timber holdings in the Piney Woods almost as large as Mr. Whitman's. Why do you ask?"

"In looking through the records at the Harrison

County Land Office for locations where the stolen engine could have been hidden, it appeared that the Easton & Monroe property was strategically situated. I thought the fact might have come up in your discussions with Mr. Pierce."

"No, he didn't mention any ideas along those lines. Of course, that's not my jurisdiction over there. Maybe you should be talking to Sheriff Peterson. In fact, the Easton & Monroe property may even extend beyond the boundary of Harrison County."

Lassiter's response seemed genuine, and I concluded that he was entirely unaware of Tennyson's suspicions concerning the conspiracy. Unfortunately, that made it imprudent to disclose my findings. Disappointed, but resigned to holding the information for another two days, I stood up and said, "Please excuse me for taking so much of your time this morning. The report that the missing locomotive had been used in making off with the gold shipment was pretty disturbing, and I wanted to find out how the search for the robbers was coming along. Perhaps you wouldn't mind letting me know when some news is passed on by the Secret Service agents."

"I'll be glad to, Dr. Weston. Naturally, you'll do likewise in the event there's any word from Mr. Pierce that might have a bearing on the case?"

"Of course. I only hope his next message is less cryptic than the last one."

We shook hands, and the sheriff escorted me back up to the vicinity of the building entrance. His presence undoubtedly saved me from being searched again by the stern deputy, who eyed me warily as I left.

Climbing aboard the buggy once more, I headed for the intersection of Commerce and Austin Streets. There, I stopped in front of the Opera House long enough to purchase two tickets for the matinee performance of *Dad's Girl*. With decent seats for the show assured, I returned home feeling that I had at least accomplished something.

It was not quite half-past eleven when I drew up beside the house. Having time to kill before calling for Mrs. Hutchins, I went upstairs to the dining room, where the stockholder records sent by Archer were still spread out on the table. The newspaper article concerning the cotton cartel from Houston had provoked my interest, and I wondered whether that organization or any of its principals might own shares in the Texas & Louisiana. Looking over the summary which I had compiled on the previous evening, I found listings for twelve individuals with addresses in the city of Houston. However, the corresponding holdings weren't large enough to generate any suspicions. Continuing to scan the tabulation, I stopped at an entry that struck a faint chord of remembrance: Armand La Fourche, on the Crosby-Lynchburg Road in Harris County, with a sizeable 3518 shares of stock. The surname seemed vaguely familiar, but I couldn't immediately recall where I had heard it. A few minutes of intense concentration restored my memory of the incident, however. The occasion was the lunch which Tennyson and I had shared with

Ted Wilson at the Whistle Stop Canteen in Longview. Someone sitting at a nearby table had said, "Tell La Fourche that we need money for expenses." The words hadn't meant anything to me at the time, but they now suggested a possible connection with the theft of the locomotive. Here was another lead that would need to be investigated, and I made a note to ask Jack Lorentz what he knew about this man.

As I reflected on the continuing progress of my inquiries, I began to feel as though the widening circle of suspects made the situation rather hopeless. By the time my conjectures were confirmed, it would probably be too late for appropriate countermeasures. Once the conspirators had converted the stolen bullion into legal currency, there would be nothing to stop them from buying a controlling interest in the Texas & Louisiana. It seemed to me that the only chance for thwarting the takeover was to recover the gold before the thieves could dispose of it. I sorely wished that I knew what Tennyson had been doing since the robbery.

Deciding that it was better to stay occupied than to worry over something which I couldn't control, I began inspecting the pages on the table again, looking this time for addresses in Philadelphia or New York City. Golden might have acquired a considerable amount of stock in the railroad through his confederates in Texas, but I reasoned that he had probably purchased shares through his Eastern associates as well. Not surprisingly, the list of stockholders included the names of a good many individuals from the nation's two major centers of finance. I had copied nineteen of them when it occurred to me that I had better check the time. A glance at my pocket watch showed that the hour of my engagement with Mrs. Hutchins was almost upon me. After taking a few minutes to wash up, brush the dust from my shoes, and straighten my attire, I descended the stairway, pulled the buggy around to the front of the house, and knocked lightly on the lower entrance.

Mrs. Hutchins promptly opened the door, looking quite elegant in a dress of pale green cambrie accented with white velvet rosettes. A silver necklace supporting a small cameo provided an appropriate finishing touch. Before I could find the words to comment on her appearance, she said, "How dapper you look today, Dr. Weston."

"Thank you," I replied. "That is indeed a compliment, coming from someone of such obvious good taste. Your costume is lovely, and I consider myself extremely fortunate to have the company of such a charming lady."

"What bald-faced flattery! I admit to enjoying the attention, all the same. It isn't often that I hear such words from a gentleman."

"Then the fault is obviously with the beholders. Forgive my impertinence, but you really are a very attractive woman. The unmarried men of the city ought to be lined up at your door."

"You certainly have a way with words, Dr. Weston, although I don't believe them for a moment. But hadn't we better be going?"

"There's no need to rush. I bought the tickets this morning to make sure that we would have good seats. Still, an early arrival may save us from having to make our way through a throng of people."

"Well then, let's not dally. It's never pleasant to be jostled by a crowd."

When I had helped Mrs. Hutchins aboard the buggy, I set off for the Opera House at an unhurried clip. Proceeding down Ross Avenue to Akard, then across to Commerce, it took about twenty minutes to reach the theater. Despite a moderately long line at the ticket office, I had no difficulty in pulling up directly in front of the main entrance. Two hostlers were on duty at curbside to take customers' carriages to the livery stable on Austin Street. Handing the reins to one of them, I climbed down and aided Mrs. Hutchins to the ground. Once inside the building, we found our way to the fifth row of the parterre and squeezed past several patrons to our seats. Approximately ten minutes later, a man dressed in formal wear came out onto the stage and proclaimed that the play would begin shortly. Following this announcement, he read a list of the productions that would be presented at the Opera House in the coming months. The planned attractions featured a number of well-known performers, including Roland Reed in *Peck's Bad Boy*, James O'Neill in *The Count of Monte Cristo*, and Annie Pixley in *Zara*. At the conclusion of this bit of promotion, the house orchestra struck up a tune, which I recognized as the chorus from *Das Build der Rose*. Finally, the melody trailed off; and the curtain parted slowly to reveal the opening scene of the play. Although the theme of the drama was rather prosaic, the actors made the most of their material and gave entertaining performances. Lizzie Mae Ulmer was especially engaging in the role of the daughter, and I could see why Mrs. Hutchins admired her. For an hour and a half, our attention was firmly held by the artful portrayals. Then, all too soon, we found ourselves applauding vigorously as the cast members emerged from the wings for their final bows.

In order to avoid the commotion of the departing crowd, Mrs. Hutchins and I remained seated until the aisles were fairly clear. While we waited, I asked if she would like to have lunch at the Bluebonnet Cafe.

"Why don't you let me prepare something at home?" she responded in her characteristic fashion.

"There is no sense in your slaving over a hot stove on such a fine day," I retorted. "After all, Amy is out with George, so you would just be cooking for the two of us. It will be much more convenient to stop at the Bluebonnet. Afterward, we can take a drive across the river and view the wildflowers on the far side."

"Very well. I can see that it's pointless to argue with you. Anyway, it *is* a nice day for a ride in the country."

We lingered until the theater was almost empty before getting up and walking to the lobby, where I asked an usher to have one of the hostlers retrieve the buggy. Shortly, we were rolling along Jackson Street toward Ervay. As we approached Browder Street, the array of carriages ahead indicated that the Bluebonnet

Cafe was doing a decent amount of business for a Sunday afternoon. Stopping a few doors away from the restaurant, we maneuvered along the walkway to the entrance, dodging a number of customers who were leaving. Fortunately, we were greeted by a waitress whom I knew from my frequent visits to the establishment. A fetching girl named Colette, who was always very solicitous of me, she wasted no time in clearing a table for us. There wasn't any need for me to look at a menu, since I knew the selections by heart; but I let Mrs. Hutchins take her time in surveying the list of entrees and accompaniments. She ended up ordering bisque soup and chicken salad, while I chose the veal loaf with shredded potatoes and stewed tomatoes. Due to the thriving trade, the food was slow in coming. That gave us an opportunity to chat about the play and the upcoming presentations at the Opera House. Once our meals were finally served, we both made rather quick work of them. In my case, at least, the haste was occasioned by the amount of time which had elapsed since breakfast. When we had cleaned our plates, Colette asked if we would care for dessert, recommending the cottage pudding with hard sauce. Mrs. Hutchins declined, however, saying that she planned to bake some apple tarts later and adding that she expected me for supper. After I had put down a generous tip and paid the bill, we walked back to the buggy and set off toward Main Street.

Some ten minutes later, we were clattering across the iron bridge over the Trinity River. On the far side, the road veered southwest through the hilly terrain that Tennyson and I had explored on foot. The wildflowers were beginning to fade a bit, but still provided a colorful contrast with the surrounding fields. Continuing for what I judged to be about two miles, we came to another road that appeared to run almost due south. Turning down it, we soon encountered a densely wooded area that extended for perhaps half a mile. The shade provided by the tall trees was welcome, and the resident mockingbirds treated us to a fine repertoire of songs.

Emerging into the sunlight again, we were confronted with a very different kind of landscape. Fields of prairie grass extended as far as the eye could see, interrupted only by an occasional small mound. This wide-open vista was punctuated by a moving column of smoke that obviously marked the passage of a train up ahead. I realized that we must be approaching the line of the Central Texas & Gulf, which meant that some of the property in view probably belonged to them. For a moment, I considered trying to follow the tracks southward, but concluded that I had better wait for another occasion to satisfy my curiosity. It was growing a bit warm, and I didn't want the drive to become tiresome for Mrs. Hutchins. Consequently, when we reached the railroad crossing, I turned the buggy around and headed back toward the city.

Not quite an hour later, I pulled to a stop next to the front steps of the Hutchins residence. Once we had climbed down, Mrs. Hutchins said, "Thank you so much for a delightful afternoon, Dr. Weston. I don't know when I've enjoyed myself as much."

"It was a pleasure," I returned. "You saved me from having to see the play alone, and I'm grateful that you agreed to accompany me on the drive."

"Don't forget about supper," she added. "We'll probably eat around seven, and I wouldn't be surprised if Amy asks George to join us."

"I can't wait to taste one of those apple tarts," I commented as Mrs. Hutchins went inside.

Driving around to the back of the house, I stowed the buggy and took care of the horse. Then I went upstairs to my bedroom and changed clothes. Although I would just as soon have forgotten about Jay Golden and his schemes, the papers in the dining room beckoned to me. It wasn't in my nature to leave a task unfinished; so, with a certain reluctance, I resumed the effort which I had begun that morning, looking for stockholders with addresses in Philadelphia or New York City. To save time and narrow the search, I decided to list only the individuals and companies that had purchased at least 500 shares of stock during the period covered by the records. It took about an hour and a half to finish transcribing the information. The final tally for Philadelphia was twenty-four individuals and three companies, while the count for New York City was twenty-seven individuals and five companies.

Reviewing the results of my labors, I observed that Golden's name didn't appear in the tabulation. This wasn't really surprising, since the man had a reputation for distancing himself from activities that might attract the attention of the authorities. However, there *was* an entry on the list that suggested a degree of carelessness among the conspirators: Martin Donlevy of Philadelphia, owner of 5170 shares of stock. Surely, there had to be a connection between this man and the Donlevy Company, I thought. If so, it strongly suggested that Tennyson had been right in his speculation about Golden using the land grants of the Central Texas & Gulf to reward his associates. My initial excitement over this find was quickly tempered, however, by the realization that the information would be of little use unless the gold were recovered soon.

As I sat in a momentary reverie of melancholy, a knock sounded at the front door. Answering it, I found Amy standing on the porch. The sight of her smiling face immediately chased away my feeling of dejection.

"Supper is served, Dr. Weston," she announced cheerfully.

"Thank you, Amy," I replied. "Did you enjoy your picnic?"

"Very much. We went to a beautiful spot on the lower part of Turtle Creek. It was quite peaceful and reminded me somehow of a scene from *Through the Looking Glass*."

"That sounds like a nice place to relax."

"I'd be glad to take you there sometime, as long as you agree not to disclose the location. Mother seems to have had a good time today as well. She went on at some length about the play. I hope you found it enjoyable as well."

"The production was nicely done, although I must confess to deriving as much pleasure from the drive that your mother and I took through the countryside. There is something about being out in the open that I find invigorating, especially when I am in the society of such a delightful companion."

"Mother is right about you having a way with words, Dr. Weston," Amy commented with a laugh. "If we don't hurry, though, there may not be anything left to eat. George has a pretty healthy appetite, you know."

Following her down the stairs and into the house, I saw George carrying a covered platter to the sideboard in the dining room while Mrs. Hutchins finished filling the glasses on the table. The plates had already been served with slices of baked ham accompanied by macaroni casserole and lima beans. In a lighthearted vein, I said, "Perhaps we should count those tarts if George has been left alone with them."

"Oh, I wouldn't be too concerned," Amy responded, with a wink at her mother. "There wasn't time for him to down more than one or two."

"I'll have you know that they haven't been touched," George retorted, trying to look indignant, but betraying himself with a slight grin.

Once we were all seated, Mrs. Hutchins asked me to say the blessing; but I deferred to George, who extemporized a prayer that was both sincere and reverent. When he had finished, I took a bite of the ham, which proved to be moist and tender, with a marvelous flavor. The macaroni casserole was also delicious, having a somewhat elastic texture and an unusual combination of ingredients. For the next twenty minutes or so, I savored each bite as the four of us conversed about a variety of inconsequential topics. Finally, it was time for dessert. Offering to do the honors, I retrieved the platter from the sideboard and placed it in the center of the table. Mrs. Hutchins then removed the cloth that covered it, revealing a mound of golden-brown pastries. I waited for the others to help themselves before selecting a particularly plump tart, which I consumed very slowly. It unquestionably tasted better than anything that we might have ordered at the Bluebonnet Cafe, and I complimented Mrs. Hutchins on her extraordinary skill in the kitchen. In return, she urged me to have another tart; but for the sake of my waistline, I declined. Despite the protests of the ladies, George and I insisted on helping to clear the table and wash the dishes. Afterward, we all adjourned to the parlor, where we played a game of whist.

Around a quarter past eight, we concluded the final hand of cards; and I rose to take my leave. "This has been a most congenial evening," I remarked, "but I had better be going. I want to thank all of you for your company and you especially, Mrs. Hutchins for another delectable meal. It was very considerate of you to include me."

"Oh, nonsense, Dr. Weston," Mrs. Hutchins replied. "You are always welcome to eat with us." Moving toward the dining room, she added, "Now don't rush off before I give you a couple of tarts to take along."

While we waited for her to return, George said, "I'll try to spend some time tomorrow looking for the information that you wanted at the County Courthouse."

"I'd greatly appreciate that if it isn't too much trouble, George," I responded. "Perhaps you could send word to my office if anything worthwhile results from your search."

"All right, I certainly will."

A moment later, I departed carrying a small basket laden with two tarts. Back upstairs, I left my treats on the table in the alcove and settled down in the library to think. A good deal of information had come to light since Tennyson left for Marshall, and I wanted to be certain that I could relate my discoveries to him in a coherent manner. To begin with, there were the property tax records showing that the Donlevy Company and Molloy & Wilber had acquired substantial acreage from the land grants of the Central Texas & Gulf Railroad. Then I had learned from Mr. Dillon that Molloy & Wilber was a building supply firm located in Waco and that it had been sold last year to a syndicate from Philadelphia. Next, the dossier which had been sent by Archer Pierce revealed that significant amounts of stock in the Texas & Louisiana Railway had been purchased by the Easton & Monroe Logging Company and by a man named Ralph Lawson from Waco. It seemed likely that this was the same Lawson who had visited Mr. Dillon in December of 1884 on behalf of the Belleville

Ironworks. Furthermore, the list of stockholders also included a Martin Donlevy of Philadelphia, who was very probably connected with the Donlevy Company. Another major shareholder was an Armand La Fourche, who resided near Houston. This was suggestive because a cotton cartel from that area had just leased a large amount of land in southern Dallas County, possibly from the holdings of Molloy & Wilber. Lastly, I had remembered hearing the name La Fourche mentioned by someone at the Whistle Stop Canteen in a context that now seemed decidedly suspicious. Admittedly, all of this evidence was circumstantial. Nevertheless, I was convinced that the identified men and businesses were participants in Golden's conspiracy.

For another ten or fifteen minutes, I sat in deep concentration, trying to think of any weaknesses in my reasoning that might be seized upon by Tennyson. Admittedly, several steps were missing from my chain of inferences; and the underlying assumptions remained to be proven. Even so, the conclusions were definitely plausible and consistent with the evidence. The question was whether these tentative deductions would stand up to my friend's critical scrutiny. After wrestling with this issue for a bit, I decided to avoid it by simply presenting the findings without commenting on them. To that end, I withdrew a sheet of paper from the center drawer of the desk and began writing down the sequence of facts in straightforward terms.

When I had finished, I folded the sheet in half and placed it back in the drawer for safekeeping. Then I opened the portfolio of property tax records in order to review the descriptions of the plats owned by Molloy & Wilber. I wanted to see if I could determine the location of their holdings in relation to the railroad crossing that Mrs. Hutchins and I had come upon that afternoon. It took a while to find a listing which was suitable for use as a reference, but I finally figured out that the northern boundary of their property was probably about four miles south of where I had turned the buggy around. If there were some way of verifying that this area corresponded to the lease mentioned in the article about the cotton cartel, it would certainly bolster the premises of my argument. My best hope for learning what I wanted to know was obviously Jack Lorentz, in view of his access to sources of obscure information. Remembering that I had other questions for him as well, I resolved to see if he would have lunch with me on the following day.

That seemed an appropriate point on which to end my deliberations, so I decided to retrieve one of my tarts and spend the remainder of the evening in light reading. As I scanned the shelves of the library for something suitable, Amy's comment concerning *Through the Looking Glass* came back to me. A bit of searching turned up an 1872 edition of this delightful volume, and I was soon engrossed in the enchanting world conjured by the good Reverend Dodgson. Shortly before ten, with my eyelids growing heavy, I laid the book aside and made ready for bed. In only a few minutes, I was fast asleep, my dreams filled with remarkable visions of Alice and her unusual companions.

CHAPTER 17

Supporting Evidence

On Monday morning, I woke up somewhat later than usual, owing to a heavy cloud cover that masked the appearance of dawn. Hurriedly dressing and gobbling my breakfast of scrambled eggs with bacon and biscuits, I set off for the central business area at a brisk cadence. Despite the threatening skies, I reached my destination of the Quincy Hotel without encountering any rainfall. Stepping up to the front desk, I quickly wrote a note inviting Jack Lorentz to meet me there at noon for lunch. After paying one of the attendants to deliver the message to the Dallas News Building, I proceeded to my office, arriving just as a few sprinkles began to fall. There were no patients waiting this time, but it wasn't long before one arrived. He was followed by another some seven or eight minutes later, then by two more after a further brief interval. This proved indicative of the day's pace, which was moderately busy, but not frenzied by any means.

Just as I was about to leave for my luncheon appointment, a messenger came by with a telegram. It turned out to be from Tennyson, advising me that his train was due in at 11:50 a.m. on Tuesday, but saying that I needn't bother with meeting him. Thinking that this last comment might be merely a polite dissimulation, I decided that I would have his buggy waiting at the station when he arrived. After all, it would not be a great inconvenience for me, since I could take advantage of my usual mid-day recess. Besides, I was anxious to find out what he had discovered during his five days in East Texas.

The earlier sprinkles had developed into a steady shower by that time, so I fetched an umbrella from my consulting room before starting out for the Quincy Hotel. At least the rain was accompanied by a drop in temperature, which made the walk rather refreshing. As soon as I entered the hotel lobby, I saw Jack standing near the desk, talking to an older man who was unfamiliar to me. Approaching them, I nodded and waited for a break in their conversation.

"Mr. Taylor, this is Dr. Jarvis Weston, a local physician with an office in the Curtis Building," Jack interjected after a moment. "Jarvis, this is Mr. Emery Taylor, the chairman of the Houston Mercantile Association. He's in Dallas today for a meeting with Ambrose Dillon."

Following the customary exchange of pleasantries, I seized the opportunity to ask Mr. Taylor whether he knew Armand La Fourche.

A frown stole across his brow as he replied with

obvious distaste, "It's been my misfortune to encounter him on occasion. Is he a friend of yours?"

"No, I've never met the man," I hastened to assert. "His name arose in connection with a business matter that I was handling for a friend. Since my sources indicated that La Fourche resides near Houston, I thought perhaps he might be a member of your organization."

"Thankfully, such is not the case. Mr. La Fourche, or *Monsieur* La Fourche as he prefers to be called, is hardly the sort of person who would be invited to join the Mercantile Association."

"If it isn't being too presumptuous, may I ask why?"

"Apparently you are unfamiliar with his reputation. He controls widespread gambling interests in Louisiana and is suspected of being engaged in various illegal activities, including a smuggling ring that operates along the coast."

"I had no idea that the fellow was involved in such things. Please accept my thanks for putting me straight about him. Perhaps you would allow me to buy your lunch as a small measure of gratitude?"

"The offer is appreciated, but I have another commitment in a few minutes. It was a pleasure meeting you, Dr. Weston. If there is anything that the Association can do to assist with your business affairs, please feel free to contact us. The address is on my card."

When Mr. Taylor had departed, Jack and I made our way to the dining room, where we managed to find a table against the back wall. Once we were seated, Jack smiled wryly and said, "I guess you're going to make me sing for my supper."

"Well, there *are* a couple of things that I want to ask you about," I admitted.

"Such is the life of the newspaperman. Nobody ever invites us out just for the pleasure of our company."

"Being misused doesn't seem to have affected your demeanor."

"Tell me, was that remark about the business deal with Armand La Fourche on the level?"

"Not in the strictest sense of the words. However, there was a good reason for the slight misrepresentation. La Fourche's name appeared on a list of individuals who have recently purchased significant amounts of stock in the Texas & Louisiana Railway. When I heard that Mr. Taylor was from Houston, it occurred to me that he might be able to supply some information about the man's activities."

"You're getting to be quite the detective, aren't you? So what can a humble reporter contribute to this undertaking?"

"My first question concerns the item in yesterday's newspaper about the cotton cartel from Houston that has announced an expansion into the Dallas area. Are you familiar with the article?"

"Yeah, but I don't know any of the details. That was Wayne Allen's story. Why are you interested in the cotton business?"

"If the report was accurate, the members of the cartel have leased a large tract of land in southern

Dallas County. I'd like to find out the location of that property."

"Thinking of investing in some real estate?"

"Try to be serious for a moment, Jack. The answer could play an important part in unravelling Jay Golden's conspiracy."

"Now there's a subject worthy of my attention. Kindly explain yourself."

"Very well, as long as it's understood that this must remain between the two of us until Tennyson returns. Based on several pieces of evidence, I suspect that a connection exists between the cotton cartel and a company by the name of Molloy & Wilber. The story is a rather elaborate one, which starts with a visit that Ambrose Dillon received in December of 1884."

"I'm all ears."

At that point, the waiter appeared; and we paused to give him our orders. Not feeling particularly hungry, I selected a sandwich of roasted turkey. Jack evidently had a heartier appetite, however, and chose the luncheon special of broiled catfish with scalloped potatoes and string beans.

When we were alone again, I continued, "Based on what Mr. Dillon told me, there are indications that Jay Golden began laying plans for the takeover of the Texas & Louisiana Railway well over a year ago. It appears that he recruited a number of Texas businessmen to assist him and induced them to start purchasing stock in the railroad on his behalf. As you know, Golden recently gained control of the Central Texas & Gulf, which received substantial acreage in the form of land grants when it built northward through the state. Tennyson speculated that some of this property might have been conveyed to Golden's associates in exchange for their collaboration. Young George Riley undertook to search the property tax records at the County Courthouse for indications of such transactions. One of the firms that showed prominently in his results was Molloy & Wilber, which acquired almost 4000 acres in the southern part of the county."

"And you believe the cotton producers from Houston may have leased some of that land?"

"The possibility shouldn't be ignored, in view of the implications."

"What implications would those be?"

"I suppose you know that Molloy & Wilber is a large building supply outfit located in Waco."

"Yeah, I've seen their facility down there."

"Are you aware that the two founders sold out last year to a syndicate from Philadelphia?"

"That's news to me. So you think this syndicate is part of Golden's empire, which means he now controls Molloy & Wilber. How does the cotton cartel come into the picture, though?"

"Through Armand La Fourche, who probably also had something to do with the theft of the locomotive that disappeared from Blanco siding."

"Whoa! That's a pretty big leap, isn't it?"

"Not at all. You see, when I encountered La Fourche's name on the list of Texas & Louisiana stockholders, it struck me as vaguely familiar. I finally remembered having heard it mentioned at the Whistle Stop Canteen in Longview. Tennyson and I ate lunch there when we were touring the line west of the spot where the engine was taken. Someone sitting within earshot of our table murmured, 'Tell La Fourche that we need money for expenses.' The comment made little impression on me at the time, since it didn't seem relevant to the investigation. However, when the fact came to light that the man owns more than 3000 shares of stock in the Texas & Louisiana, those words assumed new significance. Now Mr. Allen's comments about him have provided further support for my suspicions."

"You may well have enough there to interest the authorities in La Fourche's activities around the time of the theft, but I still don't see what the cotton growers have to do with the whole thing."

"This is nothing more than a hunch at the moment, but it seems to fit the facts. To begin with, we know that Golden's aims include dominating the markets for a wide range of products. Why shouldn't cotton be included among them? Suppose that La Fourche belongs to the cotton cartel, perhaps even controls it. If he *is* a key participant in Golden's conspiracy and if the land leased by the cartel turns out to be part of the Molloy & Wilber holdings, the transaction could be a clever means of rewarding La Fourche while keeping his name out of the county records."

"That's quite a scenario, Jarvis. Have you found anything else to support these speculations?"

"Not yet. I was hoping to enlist your help in establishing the needed proof. Of course, the bullion robbery has added a new urgency to the situation."

Jack's face took on a peculiar expression at this last remark, and he gave the impression of struggling to formulate a response. After an interval that must have been a good ten seconds, he said, "I'll see what Wayne can tell me about the land that was leased, but you really ought to stop worrying over the gold. The Secret Service folks claim to have the matter well in hand and obviously don't want any help from outsiders."

"Yes, Sheriff Lassiter made it quite clear that the subject was off limits to me. However, I'm a little disappointed in you, Jack. Since when does a good newspaperman let a little obstacle like the Treasury Department stand in the way of a story?"

"Could we move on to your next question?"

"Actually, it also relates to the raid on the bullion train. I'd like to know why there wasn't any mention in yesterday's newspaper about the effort to track down the robbers. The coverage amounted to little more than a rewording of what was printed on Friday."

"All I can say is that there was nothing new to report."

"Come now, Jack. Even if the lawmen hadn't picked up the trail by Saturday evening, an article could have been written about the leads that were being pursued."

"The fact is that the officials in charge of the investigation haven't released any details about their progress yet. We can only publish what they give us."

Jack looked rather uneasy as he uttered these words, which came across very much like a rehearsed statement. Fortunately, the awkwardness of the moment was dispelled by the delivery of our food. For several minutes, we ate without speaking. Then Jack broke the silence by saying, "I almost forgot that I have some information for you. When we had supper at Rousseau's last Thursday, you asked about the Easton & Monroe Logging Company. Well, I did a little digging into their background and learned that the firm was started in early 1857 by a man named Gilbert Donlevy. It apparently grew at a pretty steady pace as settlers streamed into Texas from back East. Then, following the end of the War Between the States, the company was incorporated and resumed its expansion, eventually becoming one of the largest logging outfits in the Piney Woods. The name, incidentally, was taken from the two towns that were the original endpoints of the railroad which was built for hauling logs to the mills."

At the mention of the name Donlevy, I had stopped eating in mid-bite. This was such an unexpected development that it left me momentarily at a loss for words. Presently, I recovered myself sufficiently to ask, "Does this Gilbert Donlevy still control the company?"

"No. He retired about two years ago and turned the operation of the business over to his son. However, the younger Donlevy reportedly was talked into some ill-advised investments and got himself in deep financial trouble. He ended up selling his interest in Easton & Monroe to a cousin."

"Would this cousin's first name happen to be Martin by any chance?"

With a look of candid surprise, Jack replied, "As a matter of fact, it would. How did you know that?"

"A Martin Donlevy from Philadelphia has acquired a substantial amount of stock in the Texas & Louisiana Railway within the last year. In addition, an enterprise called the Donlevy Company is listed in the Dallas County property tax records as the owner of record for more than 6000 acres from the land grants of the Central Texas & Gulf Railroad. If Tennyson is right about the missing engine being hidden on the Easton & Monroe property, what you've just told me could constitute a key piece of our puzzle."

"This problem has more twists than a barbed-wire fence, doesn't it? Let me make sure I understand what you're driving at. One: Armand La Fourche has bought a sizable number of shares in the Texas & Louisiana, which means he could be in league with Jay Golden. Two: A remark which you overheard at a restaurant in Longview seems to implicate La Fourche in the theft of the locomotive from Blanco siding. Three: The announced lease of some land in Dallas County by a cotton cartel from Houston might be a clandestine way of rewarding La Fourche, using the firm of Molloy & Wilber as a vehicle. Four: The fact that Martin Donlevy now controls the Easton & Monroe Logging Company suggests he may have been involved in the plan to steal the Mogul as well. Five: Donlevy's stock purchases and land acquisitions could also tie him to Golden's conspiracy. Is that a fair summary of your argument?"

"I'd say so, although there are several other considerations involved. For example, since Molloy & Wilber sells building supplies, the firm might well have a business relationship with the Ferguson Mill, which is now owned by Easton & Monroe. Then the role of the Hanley Brothers Mill in the overall scheme still remains to be determined. Last but certainly not least, the part played by Ralph Lawson deserves close attention."

"The name doesn't ring a bell. Have you told me about him?"

"Come to think of it, I guess not. He's the fellow who tried to get Ambrose Dillon to throw over his existing suppliers of hardware items and sign an exclusive contract with the Belleville Ironworks out of Illinois."

"That doesn't sound like a criminal act. Why do you think he's mixed up in the conspiracy?"

"One of the methods which Golden has used in growing his empire is buying interests in various manufacturers and then charging excessive freight rates to their competitors in order to corner the markets for those products. I'm betting that he has a financial stake in the Belleville Ironworks and that Lawson is working for him."

"Another hunch? Even if you're right, this guy would have to be pretty low on the totem pole."

"I might agree, except for one thing. Over the last four months, Lawson has purchased more than 2000 shares of stock in the Texas & Louisiana."

"Okay, we'll add him to the list of suspects. However, he still doesn't come across as a key figure in Golden's operation."

"Did I mention that his meeting with Mr. Dillon took place in December of 1884? My notion is that Lawson was sent to Texas back then as a kind of advance man for Golden and was tasked with recruiting some of the other conspirators."

Following a lengthy pause, Jack said, "All right, let's suppose that all of your conjectures are correct. What do you intend to do about them? Gathering enough evidence to bring charges against those people would be an awfully big task."

"Our major concern should be thwarting Golden's attempt to take over the Texas & Louisiana. I can see only one way of accomplishing that end, as much as you may not care for the idea. The man who organized the theft of the bullion must be apprehended before he has an opportunity to convert the gold into currency. All indications point to La Fourche as the most likely candidate. When Tennyson returns tomorrow, I hope he will agree with me and take the appropriate action."

Uttering an audible sigh, Jack said, "That's undoubtedly the wisest course at this point. With his extensive contacts, Tennyson will know the best way to proceed. It isn't clear to me, though, why you're convinced that the bullion robbery is associated with the attempt to gain control of the railroad."

"The connection eluded me for a while, but I finally realized that there is an obvious answer. With the proceeds from the sale of the gold, a majority of the outstanding stock can be acquired before the Texas & Louisiana completes its merger with the Missouri & Southwestern."

"I see. Don't you suppose that Golden probably has the resources to buy the needed shares anyway? After all, he's one of the richest men in the country."

"Also one of the greediest. Maybe his capital is tied up in other endeavors. Whatever the case, the threat to the railroad must be viewed as imminent now."

"Could be, but I think you're skating on pretty thin ice there."

Catching the waiter's attention as he passed a few tables away, I called for the bill and quickly paid it. Jack thanked me for buying lunch, then added, "Eating with you is an experienced not to be missed, Jarvis. I'll ask Wayne Allen about the land leased by the cotton cartel and let you know what turns up. In the meantime, promise me that you won't take any action until you've spoken with Tennyson."

"Don't worry, Jack," I reassured him. "Thanks for listening to me."

We parted company in front of the hotel; and I walked briskly back to my office, thankful that the rain had stopped. As I approached the door of the Curtis Building, I saw a young woman waiting there, with a little boy peering out bashfully from behind her skirt. The child had been stung by a wasp and was apparently suffering an allergic reaction to the bite, judging by the swollen condition of his left leg. Leading the way to my consulting room, I distracted the youngster with a lollipop while applying an ointment to the affected area and checking for any signs of impaired breathing. In the course of instructing his mother on how to care for the injury, I learned that she lived in the Cumberland Hill area and had been directed to me by Mrs. Wright. It was gratifying to know that word of my practice was beginning to spread independently of Dr. Everett's referrals.

For the remainder of the afternoon, the pace was somewhat slower than it had been during the morning. There were still a few cases of influenza, but it was clear that the outbreak had nearly run its course. Otherwise, the patients' complaints ranged from chronic dyspepsia to a sprained ankle. All in all, the day was quite typical of what a general practitioner might reasonably expect. Two weeks earlier, I would have been perfectly satisfied spending my time like this. However, as worries about Jay Golden and his audacious schemes continued to plague me, I was obliged to concede that my association with Tennyson had awakened new interests. Having been exposed to the varied and intriguing world of criminal investigation, I found myself no longer content with simply dispensing medical care.

My contemplations of this admission were interrupted by the tinkling of the bell over the outer door. With a glance at the clock on the wall, which showed not quite ten minutes before five, I stepped into the waiting room. Rather than the expected last-minute patient, though, it was an eager-looking George Riley who greeted me.

"Hello, Dr. Weston," he said. "Do you have time to talk?"

"Definitely, George," I replied. "Come on into my consulting room."

When we were seated, he continued, "I just wanted to deliver the results from my research at the courthouse."

"Did you manage to get the addresses we discussed?"

"One of them anyway. The other takes a little explaining." Handing a folded sheet of paper to me, he added, "Take a look at this, and you'll see what I mean."

In his customary fashion, George had organized the items on the page into neat columns, under the headings of "Company Name," "Place of Business," and "Property Tax Address." For Molloy & Wilber, the entries in the last two columns were identical, a location on McGregor Road in McLennan County. This tallied with what I had been told by Ambrose Dillon. In contrast, the information for the Donlevy Company included an unexpected bonus. While their place of business was listed simply as "various," the address for the firm's property tax statement proved enlightening: R. P. Lawson, in care of a box number at the Waco Post Office.

George's voice roused me from the musings induced by this significant piece of news. "You're probably wondering about the 'various' notation for the Donlevy Company," he remarked. "That's a direct quotation from the listing, but a footnote indicated the firm is an out-of-state business. Since their tax statements are being sent to Waco, though, they might be operating in Texas under another name. If you'd like, I could try searching through the files on business charters for a possible cross-reference."

"What you've given me is fine for the time being, George. In fact, it's far more than I had expected. If you'll promise not to share the information with anyone, I'll explain why."

"My lips are sealed, Dr. Weston. Mr. Pierce stressed the need for discretion when he told me the reason for his interest in the land grants."

"I assumed as much. Well, the signs are mounting that he was correct in his conjecture. It happens that a man from Philadelphia named Martin Donlevy holds a controlling interest in the Easton & Monroe Logging Company and has also purchased a good deal of stock in the Texas & Louisiana Railway. Furthermore, I have reason to believe that Ralph Lawson of Waco has been acting on Jay Golden's behalf in Texas for quite a while now. Your discovery of a relationship between the Donlevy Company and Lawson could very well turn out to be a key piece of evidence in the case."

"I'm glad that my efforts were of some use. Is there anything else which you need looked up?"

"Not just now, thanks. However, Mr. Pierce and I may have occasion to call on your services again before this affair is finished."

As George rose to go, I extended a five-dollar bill to him and said, "Perhaps this will serve as a retainer."

"No payment is necessary, Dr. Weston," he returned. "Mr. Pierce has already given me a generous fee."

"Consider this as a bonus then," I insisted. "I'm sure Amy would enjoy being treated to supper or the theater."

Reluctantly taking the money, he smiled and said, "You're a very thoughtful man, Doctor."

When George had left, I sat for several minutes, mulling over the implications of his findings. The unearthing of a link between the Donlevy Company and Lawson was consistent with my theory that the latter was a coordinator for Golden's activities in Texas. If a relationship between Lawson and La Fourche could also be established, it would pretty well substantiate my provisional deductions about the conspiracy. There was an undeniable sense of satisfaction at having made some real progress during Tennyson's absence. I only hoped that my conclusions could be acted upon in time to prevent these men from accomplishing their objective.

After taking time to straighten up the consulting room, I headed for Stockton's Restaurant to enjoy a good steak. The continuing threat of rain had evidently kept many of the establishment's usual clientele away, for the dining room was sparsely occupied. With my choice of tables, I decided to sit beside a window in order to watch the continually changing patterns of the clouds that were being blown across the evening sky. While thus engaged a short time later, I noticed a familiar figure pass by outside. It was Clair Whitman, and he was accompanied by a smartly-dressed man who appeared to be in his late thirties. The two of them entered the restaurant and stood near the door for a moment, surveying the room. Somewhat to my surprise, they then began walking directly toward me. Standing up as they approached, I said, "Good evening, Mr. Whitman. It's nice to see you again."

"Good evening, Dr. Weston," Whitman answered. "What an unexpected pleasure! Allow me to introduce Mr. Meredith Andrews, who manages the loan department at my bank. Meredith, this is Dr. Jarvis Weston."

"I'm happy to meet you, sir," I declared, extending my hand.

"Likewise," Andrews responded rather stifflly, presenting a grasp that was firm but brief.

"Dr. Weston is originally from Kansas City," Whitman commented. "His parents are old friends of Ambrose Dillon."

"If it won't intrude on your plans, you are more than welcome to join me," I offered.

"We would be glad of your company," Whitman remarked, taking a seat opposite me and ushering Andrews into the chair next to him.

Presently, the waiter observed the additions at my table and stopped by to take their orders. Thankfully, he brought an additional basket of cornbread, ensuring that we had an adequate supply to satisfy our appetites until the meals were delivered. The three of us passed an agreeable interval nibbling on the tasty squares and conversing about the local community.

Once our plates had been served, I undertook to

steer the discussion toward financial matters. Pretending that I was looking for an investment opportunity, I asked Whitman if he was familiar with the Donlevy Company.

"Why, yes, I know a little something about the enterprise," he answered. "It's a land development corporation that owns property in several states. The principal in the firm happens to be the nephew of a man I've known for three decades. Gil Donlevy came to Texas about the same time I did, but he stopped short of Dallas and settled over near Marshall. While Ambrose Dillon and I were trying to make our fortunes here on the banks of the Trinity, Gil was building a logging empire in the Piney Woods. You may have heard of his outfit: Easton & Monroe. Unfortunately, they're now a major competitor of mine."

"Mr. Pierce has mentioned them to me," I equivocated. "Is Mr. Donlevy still active in their operations?"

"As a matter of fact, Gil decided to retire a couple of years ago. His nephew subsequently acquired a majority position in Easton & Monroe and now serves as its president. The word in the banking community is that he wants to consolidate the lumber business with his real-estate holdings."

"What do you think of the proposal?"

"I consider it to be ill-advised. Martin Donlevy has a reputation for engaging in unbridled speculation with regard to some of his land purchases. That could lead to substantial losses for the corporation if he has misjudged the market. For someone who wants to earn a decent return while preserving capital, there are a number of better investment choices. Why don't you stop by the bank sometime and let us point out a few of the opportunities that exist right here in the city?"

"All right, I'll plan on doing that. It was certainly my good fortune that you decided to dine here this evening."

The remainder of the meal was spent in talking about the early days of Dallas and the adventures that Whitman had experienced as he struggled to make a living in the frontier environment. We lingered for a few minutes after the plates were cleared away, then paid our bills and took leave of one another.

It had started raining again, but my umbrella served to keep me reasonably dry as I strolled toward Routh Street in no great hurry. During the course of the day, several important facts had come to light, leaving me with a feeling of restless impatience. As a result, I welcomed the chance to amble along, listening to the soothing sound of the steadily falling drops and enjoying the unusually cool temperature.

Upon arriving at Number 211, I took a seat in the library and set about updating the summary which I had prepared on the previous evening. The new information concerning Martin Donlevy's role in Easton & Monroe and Ralph Lawson's connection with the Donlevy Company provided some of the supporting evidence that I needed for my chain of inferences. Resisting the temptation to state the apparent consequences, however,

I merely added these latest items to the list, leaving Tennyson to make his own assessment of them.

After completing this task, I decided to write several letters. The first was a brief note of thanks to Dr. Everett, expressing appreciation for his help in developing my practice. This was followed by overdue updates to three former classmates from St. Louis University, relating my experiences as a medical practitioner in the 'wild west' and inquiring about their professional activities. Once the correspondence was out of the way, I picked up the copy of *Through the Looking Glass* from the table and moved over to the padded leather chair. Before long, I was absorbed again in the curious world which had sprung so improbably from the mind of a shy Oxford mathematician. By the time I finished the chapter on Alice's encounter with the prideful Humpty Dumpty, I was ready to retire for the night.

CHAPTER 18

An Astonishing Admission

The following morning, I was awakened by a noisy group of sparrows who had chosen my window sill for a conference. Peering out, I observed that a few clouds were still visible to the south. However, a bright glow along the eastern horizon indicated that the sun would soon make an appearance. With a feeling of keen anticipation for what the day would bring, I quickly washed, shaved, and dressed, then waited anxiously for the clatter of the dumbwaiter. There was something appealing about the now-you-see-it, now-you-don't nature of this device; and I took an unreasonable pleasure in sliding open the door to discover the delights within. On this occasion, the bounty consisted of two poached eggs, a slice of ham, and a dish of stewed peaches, accompanied by the usual pot of tea. When I had consumed this tasty fare, I donned a pair of leggings and a light topcoat as protection against the muddy conditions of the streets. With these safeguards in place, I ventured into the backyard and hitched up Tennyson's buggy.

Driving slowly in order to minimize the splattering, it took about fifteen minutes to reach Hofstetter's Livery. After handing the rig over to the attendant there and telling him that I would return for it at approximately half-past eleven, I proceeded on foot to my office. For the first time since Dr. Everett had started referring patients to me, the day began with an empty waiting room. In fact, over the next couple of hours, the arrivals were few and far between. I assumed that people might be postponing their visits until the mud had dried a bit more, but felt disappointed nonetheless. This was a morning when I would very definitely have preferred staying busy, as a way of warding off my nervousness over Tennyson's return. To help pass the time, I double-checked the inventory of my medical supplies and set about generating a master index for the contents of my filing cabinets.

Around a quarter of eleven, I received a brief respite from the tedium. It was heralded by a prolonged jangling of the bell over the outer door, followed by a plaintive voice inquiring, "Is there a doctor in the house?" With a mixture of concern and annoyance, I stepped out of the consulting room to determine the cause of this disturbance. A hunched-over figure suddenly spun around, and I found myself looking into the grinning face of Jack Lorentz.

"I figured that would get your attention," he chuckled.

"Your behavior is appalling," I responded in an

affected tone of severity. "Suppose I had been with a patient?"

"I peeked in and made sure you were alone before raising that ruckus. Where is everybody today? Did we have a sudden outbreak of good health?"

"Either that, or they're waiting for the streets to dry out. But I'm sure you didn't stop by just to check on my caseload. What's on your mind?"

"I was passing this way and thought I'd let you know what Wayne Allen said about the land mentioned in that article on the cotton cartel. According to his informant, the lease covers about 2400 acres somewhere south of Five Mile Creek. Wayne is trying to find out if the boundaries can be pinned down any more precisely. I'll let you know when he gets back to me."

"Thanks, Jack. I appreciate your help. By the way, as long as we're on the subject of the investigation, something came up last night which provides further support for my contentions."

"You're determined to play detective, aren't you? Well, let's hear all about this latest clue."

"I was dining at Stockton's when Clair Whitman came in with another man who works at his bank. They joined me, and we had a nice conversation. At one point, I managed to insert a question about the Donlevy Company. Whitman informed me that it's a land development corporation controlled by none other than Martin Donlevy."

"Interesting, but hardly surprising. I guess there's some value in having the connection verified, though."

"Decidedly. It pretty well proves that Donlevy is involved with Golden and was given the property from the land grants in exchange for his services."

"Not necessarily. Those transactions could have been perfectly legitimate. I'm afraid you'll need a lot more than circumstantial evidence to convince a jury that Donlevy did anything illegal."

"All right, maybe I *am* extrapolating a bit. Still, all the indications point to the man having an important role in Golden's conspiracy."

"Could be, but a good reporter always makes sure of his facts. I'm not ready to pass judgment, at least until I've heard what Tennyson found out in East Texas."

"Well, we should both learn that soon enough, provided he's in a talkative mood. His train is scheduled to arrive less than an hour from now, and I plan to meet him at the station. You're welcome to come along."

"I wouldn't mind, but there are a couple of items at the office that require my attention first. Are you walking or riding?"

"Riding. Tennyson's buggy is at Hofstetter's Livery."

"What time should I be there?"

"Let's say half-past eleven. I want to make sure of reaching the depot with at least five minutes to spare."

"Okay. See you then."

Returning to my desk, I resumed the task of preparing a comprehensive index of my records. A short while later, I heard someone enter the waiting room and call out, "Dr. Weston!" This time, the visitor turned out to be an employee of Dillon Mercantile who had suffered a nasty cut on his left arm while loading a scythe into a customer's wagon. I cleaned the wound with carbolic acid, then applied eucaine to deaden the area and closed the gash with ten stitches. The clock on the wall showed almost twenty-five past eleven when I finished taping the bandages. With some final instructions to the patient on the care of his injury, I escorted him to the door, locked the office, and set out for the livery stable at a spirited pace.

True to his word, Jack was waiting for me when I arrived at Hofstetter's. As soon as the attendant brought the buggy out to the street, we were on our way to the depot. Although the mud had dried considerably by then, our progress down Jackson Street was still impeded by the remaining ruts. Fortunately, part of our route was paved with bois d'arc blocks, which allowed us to pick up the pace. As a result, it required only eight or nine minutes for us to reach our destination. Pulling up next to the boarding platform, I stopped in a spot where Tennyson would be able to see us when he stepped off the train.

It wasn't long before a column of smoke could be seen in the eastern sky, heralding the approach of the *Pecos Limited*. Soon we heard the mournful wailing of the whistle as the engineer signalled repeatedly for grade crossings. Finally, the locomotive appeared around the curve to the northeast and chuffed past us. As it braked to a stop, I looked at the station clock, which indicated 11:48. In less than a minute, passengers began streaming out of the cars, aided by a cadre of porters. For awhile,

I was concerned that Tennyson might not have been aboard, but he finally emerged from the second coach. While I waved to attract his attention, Jack jumped down and moved to intercept him. Presently, the two of them appeared through the crowd and climbed aboard. When they were seated, Tennyson said, "It was good of you to meet the train, Jarvis, but quite unnecessary. Was my telegram unclear?"

"Not at all," I replied. "However, I thought that you might have need of your buggy. Besides, driving down here really wasn't any trouble. May I inquire whether your trip produced the expected results?"

"Let's just say that several facts emerged during my absence which should be of material assistance in solving the puzzle of the missing locomotive. Evidently you've managed to make some progress as well."

"Why, yes I have. Did Jack tell you that?"

"No. Our friend here isn't one to violate a confidence. My surmise was based solely on observing your facial expression and overall demeanor. I'm afraid you wouldn't make a very good poker player, Jarvis."

"There's no need to rub it in. The inability to hide my reactions has played me false on more than one occasion. In any case, several items of possible interest did turn up while you were away. Rather than subjecting you to a lengthy verbal recounting of these discoveries, however, I have summarized them on two sheets of paper which may be found in the center drawer of your desk."

"Splendid! Such initiative is highly commendable."

Glancing over his shoulder, Tennyson added, "I take it that you are already privy to these facts, Jack."

"Yea, verily. For some reason, the good doctor decided to favor me with an account of both his findings and his theories about them."

"Then perhaps the three of us should review the information this evening in the privacy of Number 211. I'll ask Mrs. Hutchins to prepare something for supper. Shall we say half-past six?"

"You know my policy," Jack responded. "I never pass up a free meal."

"That will be fine with me," I concurred while heading the buggy out onto Houston Street.

Once we had turned up Commerce toward the Dallas News Building, I undertook to direct the conversation toward the subject which still preyed upon my mind. Affecting a casual air, I remarked, "The loss of the bullion was extremely unfortunate. Mr. Ward must be rather upset about it."

A slight twinkling was evident in Tennyson's eyes as he replied, "One would think as much. However, it shouldn't be too much longer before we receive some good news on that front."

"This fellow is as stubborn as they come," Jack interjected. "I've told him several times to stop fretting over the gold shipment, but he won't listen."

"Nor could he be expected to," Tennyson said. "Jarvis's perseverance is one of the traits that makes him a valuable colleague. However, if he can be patient for a few hours more, some of his concerns may be resolved."

"I sincerely hope so," I rejoined, ignoring the compliment. "The newspaper accounts of the robbery left a good many questions unanswered."

"Indeed they did. But tell me about the material which Archer sent. Have you had an opportunity to look through it?"

"As a matter of fact, I decided to open the package last Saturday evening and discovered that it contained around thirty pages of names. Since a list of that length was a bit cumbersome for ready use, I first extracted the entries for the individuals and companies with addresses in Texas, then added those from New York City and Philadelphia. My compilations are on the table in the dining room, along with the box containing the full roster."

"You *have* been industrious!"

"Two or three of the stockholders may deserve rather close attention," I commented quite matter-of-factly, hoping for some reaction from Tennyson. Instead, he forestalled further discussion of the topic by suggesting that we stop for a quick lunch at the Bluebonnet Cafe.

Hearing no objection from Jack, I proceeded to the intersection with Browder, turned right, and drew up just short of Jackson Street. Leaving the buggy at the curb, we walked around the corner to the restaurant and found seats at a table against the northeast wall. Momentarily, Colette spotted me and came over to take our orders. While we waited for our sandwiches and root beers, I asked Tennyson if Colin Drake had been able to supply any useful information concerning the Hanley Brothers Mill.

"My interview with him was most instructive," he answered. "It turns out that Drake has been acquainted for some time with Tom Buckley, the foreman at the Hanley Brothers. I learned that Buckley is a fearless gambler who has both won and lost considerable sums of money at the gaming tables in Caddo Parish, Louisiana. Over the past few months, he has had an extended run of bad luck and has been hard-pressed to pay his debts. Naturally, that would make him vulnerable to a compelling offer from the man behind the theft of Engine Number 35."

Although I had intended to let Tennyson peruse the written summary of my discoveries before discussing them with him, I couldn't contain myself when Buckley's gambling addiction was disclosed. In a voice which betrayed my excitement, I blurted out, "He must have been recruited by La Fourche!"

Tennyson arched his eyebrows somewhat as he commented, "You surprise me, Jarvis. How does a respectable medical practitioner come to be familiar with the nature of Armand La Fourche's business?"

"I encountered his name when going through the list of Texas & Louisiana stockholders and recalled having heard it somewhere. The circumstances finally came back to me. When we ate lunch at the Whistle Stop Canteen in Longview with Ted Wilson, someone sitting near us said 'Tell La Fourche that we need money for expenses.' Then yesterday, Jack introduced me to

Emery Taylor of the Houston Mercantile Association, who informed me that La Fourche controls a large number of gambling interests in Louisiana."

"I am impressed, dear fellow. It appears that you have a decided talent for investigative work, after all. Don't you agree, Jack?"

"Well, he has a decided imagination anyway."

"The comment at the restaurant in Longview certainly wasn't imagined. Together with this new information about Buckley, it establishes a strong case that La Fourche played a key role in the plan to steal the locomotive."

"Not a *strong* case, perhaps, but definitely a plausible one," Tennyson said. "At least I can assure Jack that the statement which you reported hearing was quite real, for it reached my ears as well. In fact, I probably took greater notice of the utterance than you did at the time, having encountered the exploits of Monsieur La Fourche on several previous occasions."

"Then you must be aware of the suspicions about his involvement in various illegal activities."

"Very much so. The fact is that I was instrumental in bringing several of his associates to trial. Unfortunately, La Fourche managed to avoid prosecution in each instance."

"What better reason to suspect him of being a key participant in Golden's conspiracy? He would obviously have access to the sort of men needed to carry out the theft at Blanco siding. Moreover, the scoundrel surely can't have had any legitimate purpose for buying a large amount of stock in the Texas & Louisiana Railway."

"La Fourche doesn't strike me as the sort of individual that Jay Golden would be likely to entrust with an important undertaking, though," Jack interposed. "His reputation is a little too tarnished for the Wall Street folks, even the dishonest ones. They're usually pretty concerned with maintaining a pose of respectability."

"Your point is a cogent one, Jack," Tennyson responded, as Colette appeared with our food. "However, I suggest that we postpone further discussion of it until this evening and concentrate instead on enjoying our meal."

Taking this advice, the three of us tucked into our sandwiches and made fairly quick work of them. When we had finished eating, Tennyson insisted on paying the bill. With a word of thanks, I took my leave and set out on foot toward Akard. As I covered the several blocks to the Curtis Building, I felt heartened by the news concerning Tom Buckley. It supplied another link in my chain of inferences and made me hopeful that the conspirators might be prevented from achieving their aim after all.

Although the afternoon patronage at my office proved to be fairly steady, time still passed far too slowly, much like waiting for the boiling of water in a teakettle. I was anxious to hear Tennyson's assessment of my discoveries, as well as to find out what else he had learned during his time in East Texas. In addition, I still intended to question him closely about the events associated with the bullion robbery. My eagerness over the evening's revelations made me wish that the hands of the clock on the wall would move more rapidly. Finally, around a quarter past five, I finished with my last patient of the day. After devoting a few minutes to my habit of straightening up the consulting room, I locked the office and headed for Routh Street. Despite my eagerness to confront Tennyson, I proceeded along Ross Avenue at an unhurried pace, taking the opportunity to organize my thoughts while walking.

Nearing the front steps of Number 211, I couldn't help smiling just a little in expectation of seeing Tennyson's surprise at my progress. If he agreed with my evaluation of the facts, all that remained to complete our investigation was to prove a connection between Lawson and La Fourche. That would surely give the authorities enough evidence to arrest Golden's confederates and foil the remainder of their plan. In this confident frame of mind, I climbed the staircase to the second story, rapped lightly on the door, and entered to find Tennyson sitting at the dining-room table. He was studying two sheets of paper, looking alternately at one and then the other while running his index fingers over the successive entries. The concentration which he brought to this task was so complete that a full half-minute must have passed before my presence was acknowledged.

Without looking up, he muttered a faint greeting, then paused and added, "Sincere compliments on a job well-done, Jarvis. It obviously took a good deal of effort to prepare these summaries from the records which my brother sent. The background information obtained from Ambrose Dillon and Clair Whitman also shows an admirable attention to detail."

"Thank you for saying so," I replied, "but the credit must be shared with George Riley. He took the trouble of organizing his notes from the property tax files in a way that made it easy to identify the owners of multiple parcels. Otherwise, I might not have noticed that Molloy & Wilber and the Donlevy Company had aggregated such large holdings."

"George *does* display a gratifying inclination to order and method in his endeavors. I definitely have high hopes for that young man. Your own contributions shouldn't be discounted, however. Some first-rate detective work was necessary to ferret out the underlying connections listed here. Are you prepared to share the remainder of your findings with me?"

"Frankly, I'm somewhat reluctant to discuss them just yet. Although my deductions seem perfectly plausible to me, Jack disagrees. I would prefer to hear what you learned in East Texas before taking the risk of sounding foolish."

"Please don't be concerned on that score, Jarvis. Your thoughts on the case are always of interest to me, and I am quite sure that they are consistent with the facts as you know them."

"Unfortunately, though, there are still a good many things about the situation that I *don't* know. However, I will hazard to tell you this much. The evidence suggests not only that Armand La Fourche organized the theft of the locomotive, but also that Martin Donlevy probably cooperated with him in the plan. If so, it's likely that the two of them were also involved in the gold robbery. What I can't understand is how they managed to succeed with all of the precautions that were arranged with Colonel Yarbrough. Can you explain how the raiders were able to get past the troopers who were stationed along the tracks?"

"Kindly take a chair, Jarvis. I have an announcement to make which may be somewhat distressing."

Sitting down opposite Tennyson, I said, "No one can foresee every possible contingency. You may have been wrong in thinking that the men who stole the engine were after something other than the bullion, but what happened certainly wasn't your fault. The responsibility for safeguarding the shipment unquestionably lay with the Treasury Department."

"That last statement is true enough," he remarked. "Nevertheless, if the alternative were available to me, I would gladly answer for the loss rather than having to perform this present duty."

"Your meaning eludes me. Why are you being so oblique?"

"One naturally tries to delay a disagreeable duty. Mine is admitting that I have perpetrated an inconsiderate deception."

"What sort of deception?"

"The truth is that the gold shipment was safely delivered to the state treasury on Saturday afternoon."

"Then it was recovered after all! Why in the world

wasn't there any mention of the fact in the newspaper stories?"

"I'm afraid you misunderstand me. Only a handful of people are aware that the bullion isn't missing. You see, there wasn't actually any robbery. The entire incident was staged, and the final act of the drama has yet to be played out."

Some Explanations at Last

Tennyson's announcement left me momentarily speechless. Even though I had entertained vague suspicions concerning the published accounts of the robbery, it had never entered my mind that the incident might have been a hoax. As the implications of this news began to sink in, the thought struck me that my assumption about the use of the gold had been completely erroneous. Feeling both discouraged and resentful, I finally brought myself to ask, "Why did you find it necessary to exclude me from your charade?"

"Please believe that the decision wasn't mine," Tennyson apologized. "When I suggested the ploy to Archer, he imposed a strict requirement for secrecy. Only those who had direct roles in the affair were permitted to know the details. While it hardly excuses my treatment of you, the telegram which I dispatched last Thursday *did* include a hint."

"Your message was a little too obscure for a simple doctor and only served to perplex me, especially in view of the curious omissions in the newspaper accounts. I suppose that Jack was a party to your plan?"

"Unfortunately, we were compelled to include him. Through an indiscretion on the part of Sheriff Lassiter, Jack began to ask some perceptive questions. In order to avoid the risk of having our goal compromised, Archer agreed to let him in on the ruse."

"That explains why he attempted to change the subject every time I asked something about the news coverage of the robbery. The sheriff was equally evasive when I questioned him on Sunday morning, but was considerably more effective in masking his reactions. So, what *was* the purpose of this elaborate pretense? Or do you still regard me as untrustworthy of being told the secret?"

"Not at all, dear fellow, although your sentiment is perfectly understandable. There is no denying that my actions constituted an abuse of our friendship, despite the obligation which governed them. I only hope that you will find the charity to pardon me once all of the circumstances have been related."

"It will take a great deal more than this to affect our friendship, but I would very much like to hear the circumstances."

"Before the evening is over, you shall. However, I'd like to reserve some of the points until Jack has arrived, so that the three of us can consider them together. For the moment, let me say that there were two basic reasons for undertaking such an audacious act of subterfuge. The first was to ensure the safety of the gold by making any would-be robbers believe that the shipment had been stolen before being handed off to the Central Texas & Gulf. It was this aspect of the plan which both my brother and Colonel Yarbrough found appealing."

"And the second reason?"

"I wanted to draw out the man behind the theft of the locomotive by giving the impression that his hirelings had gone into business for themselves. If he became concerned that his primary objective was in jeopardy due to the use of the stolen engine to make off with the bullion, he might well feel the need to visit the Piney Woods and take a personal hand in the matter."

"You certainly went to extreme lengths for a goal which is hardly assured of accomplishment. Besides, since Engine Number 35 was employed in your grand production, it has obviously been restored to the railroad. Isn't that sufficient to circumvent whatever intention this fellow may have had?"

"By no means. For one thing, the elusive Mogul is still at large somewhere south of Henderson, according to the last report sent by Choctaw Jones. Moreover, even if it *had* been recovered, the fact could scarcely be expected to deter our culprit from his purpose."

"But what about the published report that the missing engine was used in the attack on the bullion train? Was the story merely a fabrication?"

"Not a fabrication precisely, but a demonstration that things aren't always what they appear. Do you recall the telegram which I received from Mr. Ward last Tuesday?"

"Why, yes, as a matter of fact. You indicated that it contained a confirmation of some preparations for your trip to Marshall."

"Well, those preparations included having a sister engine painted to serve as a stand-in for Number 35."

"Apparently no detail was omitted in laying the groundwork for your drama. I am more than a little surprised, though, that Mr. Ward and the authorities would go along with such an unorthodox proposition. How did you persuade them to do so?"

"It wasn't as difficult as one might suppose. Bear in mind that the principal concern of those individuals was protecting the gold shipment. Once I raised the possibility that the missing engine might pose a threat in that regard, they were quite receptive to my plan. Incidentally, only Archer knew of the ulterior motive for the exercise."

"Wasn't Mr. Ward worried about the adverse affect which the published accounts of the robbery might have on the railroad's proposed merger?"

"The risk was considered slight, since the terms of that transaction are quite attractive for the underwriter. However, to remove the responsibility for the decision from Mr. Ward, my brother briefed the line's president on the strategem and obtained his concurrence."

"Apparently you had been thinking about this plan for some time. Sharing the basic intention with me surely couldn't have hurt. Instead, I was led to waste a considerable amount of time trying to deduce conclusions from a false premise. Furthermore, I am now left with no idea whatsoever of the real motive for stealing the locomotive."

"Please accept my assurance that your labors were not in vain, Jarvis. The information which you assembled is definitely worthwhile, and some of the resulting inferences are not far from the mark. As for the intended use of Engine Number 35, I have formed a satisfactory hypothesis concerning that and will share it with you over supper. While we await our friend from the fourth estate, though, I would like to hear more about your visit with Sheriff Lassiter."

"There isn't much to tell. I went to see him in order to find out what progress had been made in the search for the train robbers, as well as to discover how much he might know about your theories concerning Golden's conspiracy. The man played his part well, however; and I departed none the wiser for my trouble. As an example, the mention of the Easton & Monroe Logging Company failed to produce anything more than a passing comment."

"If he seemed uninformed on that subject, it's because I haven't seen fit to share my suspicions with him. When you have come to know the sheriff a little better, you may understand why."

"Is there some reason for doubting his integrity?"

"None whatsoever. Lassiter is a conscientious lawman and is quite effective when dealing with the commonplace sorts of crimes. However, his reasoning abilities are somewhat limited. He wouldn't be comfortable dealing with the intricate deliberations which we have had to consider in the pursuit of our investigation."

Ignoring this offhanded attempt at appeasement, I sought to redirect the conversation by inserting a question: "Before we get too far off the subject, would you mind explaining how the forwarding of the gold to Austin was managed?"

"Gladly," Tennyson answered. "When the train from St. Louis stopped in Marshall during the early hours of Friday morning to take on a fresh locomotive, the boxcar containing the bullion was clandestinely shunted onto a yard track and placed among several similar-looking pieces of rolling stock. Then on Saturday morning, that entire string of cars was added to the through-freight headed for Dallas, where an interchange with the Central Texas & Gulf took place in the normal fashion. The onboard crews members had no knowledge of the valuable cargo in their consist."

"I assume your brother's office was charged with guarding the bullion on behalf of the Treasury Department. Did he travel along with the shipment?"

"No. Archer remained in St. Louis for reasons which will become clear later. However, six of his men accompanied the train on its journey to Marshall; and two from that contingent rode in the boxcar for the final leg of the trip."

"Being cooped up like that all the way to Austin must have been decidedly unpleasant, especially if the doors were kept closed. Of course, Secret Service agents are probably accustomed to such hardships. In any event, it's disappointing that I won't have the pleasure of meeting your brother."

"The opportunity may yet arise before this matter is concluded."

Turning his head to look out one of the front windows, Tennyson added, "Here comes our city's number one reporter now. Let's clear these papers away and go see what delightful victuals Mrs. Hutchins has prepared for our supper."

Together, we gathered up the materials that rested on the table and carried them into the library. Presently, the familiar clattering noise in the alcove signaled the arrival of the dumbwaiter. While I moved to retrieve its contents, my friend proceeded to the front door in anticipation of Jack's knock.

In another couple of minutes, the three of us were seated in the dining room, facing plates laden with fried chicken, mashed potatoes, and green peas. After we had bowed our heads and silently given thanks for the sustenance, Jack was the first to speak. With a darting glance in my direction, he fixed his gaze on Tennyson and asked, "Have you told him yet?"

"Yes, and he took the news as well as might be expected."

"That's a relief," Jack continued. "Trying to fend off his questions about the robbery was starting to take a toll on my nerves. If you're planning any more shenanigans like this, do me a favor and find another accomplice. Writing two trumped-up stories in one week is more than I can handle."

"At least you knew the truth, Jack," I remarked. "Speaking of the newspaper articles, though, there's something which bothers me, Tennyson. It was my understanding that the improvised report concerning the negotiations over the freight rates was intended to serve as bait for the participants in Golden's conspiracy. Why was a second ruse necessary?"

"Your question goes to the very core of this rather convoluted affair, Jarvis," Tennyson replied. "The rudimentary answer is that the feigned robbery was directed at a different target than the story about my representation of the shippers. When the time comes to address the motive for stealing the locomotive, the distinction should become clear. First, however, I would very much like to hear what conclusions you have derived from your own inquiries."

"Get ready to be entertained with some uncommonly creative allegations," Jack interjected.

"A little creativity can be a useful adjunct to the strict application of logic," Tennyson commented. "We might benefit from imitating Jarvis's approach on occasion."

"Certainly not in the present instance," I responded. "My deductions were predicated on the conviction that Golden's associates had stolen the bullion in order to fund the takeover of the Texas & Louisiana Railway. Obviously, imagination got the better of me there. Since the basic premise has proven to be false, it's pointless to review the remainder of the argument."

"The notes which you left for me suggest otherwise," Tennyson observed. "In fact, I submit that your reaction to the supposed robbery actually played only a small part in the overall course of reasoning implied by the summary in question. Take this fellow Lawson, for example. It's apparent that you consider him as a pivotal figure in the case. Tell us why."

"The evidence against him is purely circumstantial, and I have undoubtedly made too much of some unsubstantiated points."

"You mustn't lose confidence in your instincts because of one small setback. There are times when following a hunch can pay worthwhile dividends."

"Well, it's true that I suspect Lawson of playing a major role in the scheme to establish a rail monopoly in Texas. My belief is based on three pieces of information which strike me as unlikely to be coincidental. First, as you already know, back in December of 1884, he tried to persuade Ambrose Dillon to sign an exclusive contract with a company in Illinois. Secondly, he owns a considerable amount of stock in the Texas & Louisiana. Lastly, he receives the tax statements for some 6000 acres of land that the Donlevy Company acquired from the Central Texas & Gulf."

"Those are suggestive points, to be sure," Tennyson acknowledged. "The last one concerning a connection with the Donlevy Company is of particular interest. Can you elaborate on the subject?"

"I came across several references to that name when looking through the notes which George Riley had assembled from the property tax records at the County Courthouse. It's one of two businesses listed as currently owning large tracts from the land grants originally awarded to the railroad. Trying to identify the owners of both operations led me to consult Ambrose Dillon."

"And was Mr. Dillon able to help you?"

"Only partially. He wasn't familiar with the Donlevy Company but gave me some very interesting news about the other firm, Molloy & Wilber."

"We'll return to them in a moment. Evidently you subsequently uncovered a noteworthy link between the Donlevy Company and the Easton & Monroe Logging Company. Tell us how that came about."

"When I compiled the summary of Texas & Louisiana stockholders with addresses in Philadelphia, Martin Donlevy's name caught my attention. It was natural to wonder if he might be associated with the Donlevy Company. This prospect grew more compelling when Jack told me the results of his research into the history of Easton & Monroe. Learning that Donlevy now holds the controlling interest in that enterprise obviously warranted finding out more about the man's activities. As luck would have it, an opportunity to do so arose yesterday evening. I was dining alone at Stockton's Restaurant when Clair Whitman came in with an employee from his bank. They joined me for supper, and we conversed on a variety of topics. Using the pretext of looking for an investment opportunity, I managed to introduce a question about the Donlevy Company. Mr. Whitman informed me that it's a land development corporation run by this same Martin

Donlevy, who apparently is regarded with a certain degree of disfavor in the financial community."

"Excellent, Jarvis! You've done a fine job pursuing the available leads and bringing out some important points. Now let's get back to Molloy & Wilber, which is supposedly a respectable purveyor of building materials. What part does it play in your construction of the case?"

"I'm not completely sure yet, but there are several indications that the current owners could be connected with Golden's scheme. For one thing, the business holds title to nearly 4000 acres of land previously owned by the Central Texas & Gulf in southern Dallas County. Then Mr. Dillon told me that the two founders, Arnold Molloy and Hiram Wilber, sold out last year to a syndicate from Philadelphia. It's also interesting to note that the operation is located in the same city where Ralph Lawson resides. Finally, although this may be reaching a bit, as an outlet for lumber products, the possibility of a tie-in with the Ferguson Mill shouldn't be ignored."

"You've raised some intriguing prospects. We shall have to see if anything comes of them. However, there is one final name on your list which deserves a few minutes of our attention: the infamous Armand La Fourche. Apart from the comments at lunch, what else should we know about him?"

"Here is where the theory becomes really fanciful," Jack threw in with an exaggerated grimace.

"All right, Jack," I retorted. "Your views on the subject have been made quite clear. Nevertheless, the evidence is convincing that La Fourche played a major part in the theft of the locomotive. His purpose is admittedly beyond me now, but I'm willing to bet a week's worth of lunches that it's connected somehow with Golden's conspiracy."

"Why do you think so?" Tennyson inquired in a supportive tone.

"I will readily concede that my reasoning is highly conjectural, but please bear with me. Last Sunday, an article was published in the *Dallas News* about a cotton cartel from Houston that has leased a large tract of land in southern Dallas County. The thought crossed my mind that the property in question might be part of the Molloy & Wilber holdings. If this is the case, it could indicate that the members of the syndicate are associated with Golden, probably through Lawson. To test the notion, I decided to review the list of Texas & Louisiana stockholders one more time, looking for addresses in or near Houston. That's when I found La Fourche's name, which prompted my recollection of the comment about him at the Whistle Stop Canteen. As I deliberated over the possibility of his involvement in this affair, a rather extraordinary idea came to me. Suppose that La Fourche controls the cotton cartel and that the announced lease is, in fact, a clever way of rewarding him for his role in stealing the engine. There may not be any firm evidence to support this contention yet, but it explains a lot and shouldn't be summarily dismissed without an objective evaluation."

"Your argument *does* embody a healthy dose of

ingenuity," Tennyson remarked. "Whether intentionally or not, you have employed an ancient and effective form of problem solving which the Greeks referred to as *heuristic*. One of the nine principal techniques utilized in this method is the introduction of auxiliary propositions as a means of stimulating the mind. The speculations concerning the cotton cartel are a prime example of this approach."

"Then you don't share Jack's opinion that my concept is ridiculous?"

"Certainly not, although I *do* regard it as somewhat tenuous. However, an auxiliary hypothesis need not be true in order to prove useful. The important consideration is whether it leads to a valid result. Since your interest in the cotton cartel indirectly caused you to consider La Fourche as a suspect in the theft of the locomotive, the technique clearly was helpful in this instance."

"Does that mean you agree with me about his involvement?"

"Concerning the removal of Engine Number 35 from Blanco siding, yes. As a matter of fact, my own efforts have turned up several facts which support such a contention."

"How very interesting," I said, casting a meaningful glance at Jack. "Will you share them with us?"

"Yes, but I must ask for your solemn promises that what is said this evening will not go beyond these walls. Much is still at stake in this affair, and we must be extremely careful to avoid scaring off our quarries."

"You certainly have *my* word," I replied.

"Mine, too," Jack added. "Just remember that you owe me an exclusive on the story when the time comes to go public with it."

"Very well. I've already told you about Tom Buckley's gambling losses at the casinos in western Louisiana. Since the majority of those establishments are controlled by Armand La Fourche, it was a reasonable surmise that he probably induced Buckley's cooperation in the plan to steal the locomotive. This presumption was strengthened by the results of an interview with Dennis King last Friday. As you may recall, he's the clerk who reportedly copied the telegraphed instructions directing the movement of the freight cars which derailed. By promising the youth immunity from prosecution for his part in the theft, I managed to extract a full confession. He admitted that the message was contrived and identified Buckley as the one who paid him to deliver it."

"Why was King willing to take such a risk?" I asked.

"As with Buckley, his addiction to games of chance had placed him in a vulnerable position. During a recent game of poker, which was undoubtedly rigged, the young man had rashly given a large IOU in the belief that he held a winning hand. When another player took the pot, Buckley offered King a way out of his dilemma. However, I'm satisfied that he was an unwitting accomplice and knew nothing about the planned derailment. Unfortunately, the same cannot be said of Buckley, who appears to have been an active, if not willing, participant in the carefully orchestrated events which took place at the Hanley Brothers Mill and the Marshall yard."

"So Buckley really *was* hired by La Fourche, just as I said."

"It certainly looks that way, particularly when two further pieces of evidence are taken into account. The more convincing resulted from Sheriff Peterson's interrogation of Abe McClure's hired hands. If you remember, McClure owns the farm which borders the woods directly north of Blanco siding. On the Saturday evening in question, a fellow named Dan Jacobs was repairing fence rails along the property's southwestern boundary. A little before seven o'clock, he saw three men on horseback enter the woods. They were too far away for him to discern their features, but one of the animals was quite recognizable. The mount was a pinto with distinctive markings, known to be ridden by the notorious outlaw Will Reed, who is the leader of a rowdy gang thought to have a hideout in the Indian Territory. La Fourche is a long-time associate of Reed's and is believed to have planned some of his escapades, including a train robbery near Denison."

"Now we're getting somewhere!" Jack exclaimed.

"You mentioned two pieces of evidence," I inserted. "What is the other?"

"It stems from one of those unconventional areas of knowledge which has been instrumental on several occasions in helping me link a suspect to a crime," Tennyson answered. "While tramping up and down the right-of-way along Blanco siding, I collected a number of discarded cigarettes and cigars. When these were subjected to the chemical tests that are described in my treatise on the subject, most of them were found to contain the common White Burley variety of tobacco. One of the cigars, however, exhibited a significantly higher percentage of oxidized matter than the others. This characteristic is unique to a type of tobacco called Perique, which is grown in only one place in the world: at Grand Points, Louisiana."

"Let me guess," Jack chimed in. "Armand La Fourche just happens to keep a stock of cigars made from this Perique tobacco."

"He does indeed. Besides smoking the cheroots himself, he occasionally hands them out to favored customers and associates. Of course, there is no way of proving that the remnant which I tested came from his supply. Even so, the result provides yet another reason for looking into the scoundrel's activities over the past few weeks."

"What about Lawson?" I inquired. "Do you think he could have planned the theft and engaged La Fourche to carry it out?"

"There's one major objection to that notion, provided Lawson actually *does* serve as Golden's primary representative in Texas. Jack touched upon the issue at lunch. Do you recall his remarks?"

"I remember him saying something to the effect that La Fourche didn't seem like the type of individual normally employed by Golden. Is that what you mean?"

"Yes. Perhaps Jack wouldn't mind expanding on the theme."

"Sure. Everything that I've read about Jay Golden portrays him as a very cautious individual who selects his cronies from the ranks of outwardly respectable businessmen. Those folks are probably extremely ruthless, and I don't doubt that they would swindle their own grandmothers to make a buck. So far, though, it doesn't look like any of them have gone in for the coarser sorts of crimes. La Fourche is a different breed altogether, with a reputation as someone who isn't beyond using violence to achieve his ends."

"Well-put. Your observations not only agree with the published accounts of Golden's business activities, but are borne out as well by what I have learned about him from my brother. It was this very aspect of the man's character which caused me to seek an alternative explanation for our problem."

"I don't understand," I confessed. "Are you implying that La Fourche was acting on behalf of someone other than Golden when he arranged to have the locomotive stolen?"

"The assertion shouldn't come as any real surprise, Jarvis. After all, you have already identified the individual in question and seemed quite certain of his implication in the affair."

"Are you referring to Martin Donlevy?"

"The same. Is there a more logical candidate for the role?"

"Frankly, I had regarded him as only a secondary

figure in the theft, due to the fact that he resides in Philadelphia. In any event, your challenge to my conjecture about Lawson applies equally to Donlevy, doesn't it? Whoever engaged La Fourche must have done so as part of Golden's plan."

"The information we've been reviewing this evening may seem to suggest as much. However, there is a little something about Martin Donlevy that you apparently don't know. It concerns the method by which he acquired control of the Easton & Monroe Logging Company."

"According to Jack, Donlevy bought a majority interest in the business from his cousin, who found himself in need of money. Isn't that right?"

"Yes, but it's the details of the transaction which have a bearing on the case. Through an inquiry which Archer was good enough to undertake for me, I learned that the purchase was financed by the investment banking firm of Woodward & Roche, with Donlevy's land holdings posted as collateral. An interesting provision of the note stipulates that it becomes immediately due and payable in full if the capital reserves of Easton & Monroe fall below a certain level. Moreover, Efram Woodward plans to call upon the firm and examine its accounts when he passes through Longview this week during his end-to-end inspection trip over the rails of the Texas & Louisiana. Does the imminent visit suggest anything to you?"

Before it dawned on me what Tennyson was implying, Jack chuckled and said, "I'll bet that someone is afraid of being caught with his hand in the till."

"Quite probably. Unless I am much mistaken, Donlevy has been draining the coffers of Easton & Monroe to fund his land acquisitions. Finding himself unable to replace the appropriated money before Woodward's visit, he has been placed in a position requiring desperate measures."

With our plates well-cleaned by that time, we decided to move into the parlor, where the accommodations were a bit more comfortable. Tennyson insisted on my sitting in the overstuffed chair, perhaps as a token reparation for his shabby treatment of me, while he and Jack took seats on the sofa. Once we were all settled, I resumed the discussion by posing a question: "What prompted your interest in Martin Donlevy?"

"There I must confess to having taken a shot in the dark. While seeking a plausible motive for the theft of Engine Number 35, I asked Archer to find out whether Woodward & Roche had ever dealt with any firms in the vicinity of the Piney Woods, aside from the Texas & Louisiana Railway. A telegram containing the answer was delivered to me at the Marshall Inn last Thursday. Up until that point, Donlevy hadn't entered into my thinking. However, I quickly learned a fair amount about his background from Colin Drake."

"Why did you decide to inquire about the dealings of Woodward & Roche, though? The relevance isn't obvious by any means."

"When Henry Ward told us of Mr. Woodward's upcoming trip to inspect the railroad's property and operations, I immediately focused on its possible link with our mystery. My initial hypothesis was that the individual who wanted the locomotive was bent on delaying the merger. However, as I learned more about Golden's previous tactics in such situations, it became necessary to abandon that idea and look for some other significant objective."

"You've lost me once more, I'm afraid. Apart from the embarassing publicity about the incident, I don't see how the stolen engine could pose any threat to the timely completion of the merger."

"Nevertheless, the risk still exists, although as an unfortunate consequence rather than a specific aim. Due to a quirk of fate, if Donlevy were to succeed in achieving his own goal, it would coincidentally serve Golden's purpose at the same time."

"For heaven's sake, stop beating around the bush, Tennyson. Please tell us what it is that you think Donlevy plans on doing."

"I'm reasonably certain he intends to employ the missing Mogul as a means of kidnapping Efram Woodward."

CHAPTER 20

A Bold Strategy

After a short silence, Jack snickered and said, "You two make quite a pair. This is almost as good as Jarvis's notion about La Fourche and the cotton cartel. I can understand Donlevy wanting to keep Woodward from getting a look at the Easton & Monroe ledgers, but there must be easier ways of doing that. Why use a locomotive to abduct him?"

"The answer should be obvious, Jack," Tennyson rejoined. "Think about the advantages of the iron horse over its four-legged counterpart."

"It can haul much heavier loads," I offered.

"True enough, but hardly pertinent. Come now, gentlemen. What has been the greatest contribution of steam power to the transportation of both goods and people?"

"Speed!" I exclaimed. "With a powerful engine like Number 35, Woodward could be spirited away very quickly."

"Precisely, Jarvis. A few miles south of Rusk, there is a little-used spur of the Beaumont & Carthage Railroad that crosses the Texas & Louisiana tracks at grade. This line runs to San Augustine and the wooded areas of Sabine County, where a secluded cabin would make an excellent hiding place. Choctaw Jones discovered a supply of rails and ties stashed under some brush near the junction. I believe that Donlevy proposes to intercept Woodward's business car on the Texas & Louisiana mainline, take it down the Crockett Branch, and divert it onto the Beaumont & Carthage by means of a shoo-fly track."

"That sounds pretty unlikely," Jack commented. "A lot of people would have to be involved."

"So they would. If I'm right about Donlevy, however, he faces ruin unless the Easton & Monroe treasury can be replenished before the accounts are audited. Removing Woodward to a distant location would afford the best chance of keeping him out of circulation long enough for some of the Donlevy Company's land holdings to be sold. Furthermore, the idea of employing a locomotive in the kidnapping may have been sparked by a demonstration which was recently conducted in New Jersey."

"What kind of a demonstration?" I asked.

"To promote its products, the Brooks Locomotive Works organized a special run between Philadelphia and Jersey City, a distance of about ninety miles. An engine similar to the Class D-3 Moguls built for the Texas & Louisiana, but with somewhat larger driving wheels, pulled an eight-car passenger train over that route in a mere seventy-six minutes. The performance was widely publicized in the Eastern newspapers."

"I can see where such an impressive exhibition might well have attracted Donlevy's attention. Even so, he presumably has access to the resources of the logging railroad operated by Easton & Monroe. Wouldn't it have been far simpler to draw from the available motive power on their roster?"

"Those are small-drivered beasts of burden which were designed for lugging heavy loads at slow speeds. Consequently, they are quite unsuited to the task in question. Moreover, Donlevy is presumably smart enough to avoid any action which might associate the kidnapping with him or his companies."

"Of course, I should have realized as much. All in all, it appears that your suspicions about the man are credible but lacking in substantiation. How do you propose to set about proving these allegations?"

"By catching his accomplices in the act."

"What! Surely you don't mean to put Mr. Woodward at risk?"

"Even I am not that imprudent, Jarvis. No, one further bit of deception will hopefully aid in trapping our culprits. When Mr. Woodward's business car arrives in St. Louis tomorrow afternoon, his place aboard it will be assumed by my brother, adorned in a suitable disguise."

"Isn't that taking an awful chance? Suppose the substitution is discovered."

"The men working for La Fourche aren't likely

to know their victim, except by description. In any case, Archer is well-accustomed to handling himself in dangerous situations."

"So where do you think the attempt to pounce on the inspection train will be made?" Jack inquired.

"The most likely place is on the curve just east of the spur into the Ferguson Mill. In fact, the raid may well be similar in execution to the staged attack on the bullion shipment."

"Speaking of that subject," I interjected, "you stated earlier that your two ruses were directed at separate targets. Apparently the feigned robbery was aimed at luring Donlevy to East Texas. However, under the circumstances as they now stand, the first ploy doesn't seem to have served any purpose. Am I missing something?"

"Perhaps it will help to consider the related events in sequence. The starting point may be taken as my meeting with Colonel Yarbrough at Fort Worth on the Saturday before last. He expressed concern about being able to provide adequate protection for the gold over the entire course of its route between Marshall and Austin, feeling that there had been an inordinate amount of publicity concerning the movement. I suggested that it might be wise to divert the car containing the bullion to another train, and the colonel liked the idea. As we discussed the details, the thought occurred to me that something might be gained by expanding the plan to include a mock holdup. However, I kept the notion to myself until all of the potential benefits and liabilities could be carefully evaluated. After an exchange of telegrams with Archer, the decision to proceed was made on the following Monday morning; and the necessary preparations were set in motion.

"Chance then intervened when you met Clyde Starrett and brought him back to the house. At that point in the investigation, my deliberations were still centered on Jay Golden's plot to establish a rail monopoly in Texas. Starrett's mission for the Panhandle Cattlemen's Association afforded a serendipitous opportunity to cause a little agitation among Golden's business associates, in the hope of exposing their identities. That goal is still an important one, incidentally, since the threat to the Texas & Louisiana remains.

"Keep in mind that I had no idea of Martin Donlevy's involvement in our problem before last Thursday. My 'grand production,' as you described it earlier, was simply intended to make the individual who instigated the theft of Engine Number 35 think that his objective had been jeopardized by the use of the locomotive in committing a conspicuous crime. There is something which smacks of fate in the way that Donlevy was provoked to his actions by the timing for Efram Woodward's trip."

"Enough about past history," Jack interposed. "What I'd like to know is how you plan on nabbing these folks in the act of making off with your brother."

"On Friday morning, the six Secret Service agents who accompanied the gold shipment to Marshall are going to be waiting in the woods about a half-mile east of the point where the Beaumont & Carthage Railroad crosses the Crockett Branch. Just around the following bend, the track will be blocked with logs. Hopefully, the element of surprise will allow the kidnappers to be captured without an exchange of gunfire when the engine is forced to stop."

"Wouldn't it be easier to apprehend them when they intercept the train near the Ferguson Mill?" I queried.

"Not really, in view of the potential for escape afforded by the terrain there. Besides, I want to make certain that the participants can be charged with kidnapping, not merely *attempted* kidnapping."

"Your trap may succeed in catching the hirelings," Jack observed, "but what are you going to do about La Fourche and Donlevy?"

"There's a pretty good chance that Reed and his men can be persuaded to incriminate La Fourche in exchange for a promise of more lenient sentences than they would otherwise face. The tradeoff is a sensible one, and Judge Fletcher of the U.S. District Court has already pledged his cooperation. Obtaining evidence against Donlevy won't be as easy, however. It's not inconceivable that La Fourche might choose to implicate him; but without corroboration, such testimony wouldn't carry much weight in court. Direct proof of Donlevy's involvement is needed, and I'm relying on Choctaw Jones to secure it."

"How do you expect him to do that?" I asked.

"Through careful surveillance. Donlevy appears to have taken the bait. I received word last night that he left

Philadelphia yesterday on the noon train to St. Louis. If his ultimate destination is Texas, as I expect, he should arrive in Longview tomorrow afternoon. Choctaw will be watching the station and will trail him as long as necessary. Sooner or later, Donlevy will probably visit the spot where the locomotive is hidden. An eyewitness account of his presence there should suffice to prove that he had a role in the kidnapping."

"So the entire matter could be resolved by Friday evening. Do you plan to be on hand for the unfolding of the anticipated events in East Texas?"

"By all means. Sheriff Peterson must be brought up to date, and there are several other details that require my attention. I'll be taking the early train to Marshall on Thursday morning and will probably return on Saturday. If you can manage to get away, I would be glad of your company, Jarvis. Yours, too, Jack. With a little persuasion, Donlevy might consent to an interview when he is brought in."

"An opportunity like that is too good to pass up," Jack responded.

"What about it, Jarvis? Can you get Dr. Everett to look after your patients for a couple of days?"

"I'll ask him at the first opportunity. Considering the aggravation this affair has caused me, I wouldn't like to miss its conclusion."

"Splendid! We'll make it a threesome, then; and you should both find the trip worthwhile. The final act of our drama promises to be an exciting one."

"Is it truly the final act, though? Arresting La

Fourche and Donlevy won't remove the threat to the Texas & Louisiana."

"No, but preventing the kidnapping of Mr. Woodward will help ensure that the merger with the Missouri & Southwestern can be completed on schedule, which should at least delay Golden's attempted takeover of the railroad. Of course, it's still important to expose the participants in his conspiracy and eventually bring them up on charges. The best chance for accomplishing that appears to rest on the transactions concerning the land grants. We will definitely have to pursue those clues more thoroughly once Donlevy's plan has been foiled. With the urgency removed from the situation, however, there should be adequate time to accumulate evidence against Golden and his collaborators before they can achieve their goal."

"I certainly hope you're right. It would provide some degree of consolation to have my suspicions about Lawson confirmed."

"He will definitely come in for an appreciable share of attention before our quest is concluded."

"Let's dispose of the present concerns before worrying about the future," Jack declared. "Is there anything which ought to be done in preparation for our journey?"

"Nothing other than packing your bags and getting adequate sleep. I'd like both of you to be well-rested in case a need arises for your services."

"Then I'm going to be on my way. This has been quite an evening, and a good newsman always outlines a story while the facts are fresh in his mind. That's doubly important with this muddle. Please tell Mrs. Hutchins that I enjoyed the meal."

"I'll walk part of the way with you, Jack," I offered. "A stroll in the night air may help dispel the unsettling effects of our friend's disclosures."

Leaving Tennyson to resume his perusal of the papers in the library, Jack and I set off toward the central business area, exchanging only a few words as we ambled along Ross Avenue. At the intersection with Pearl, I parted company with him and veered northwest toward Thomas Street. Within another few blocks, the effects of the day's tensions started to drain away. By the time my wanderings took me back to Number 211, the moderate exercise had largely served its purpose. Although the hour was still a bit early, I decided to turn in, after pausing to bid Tennyson a good night. Unfortunately, some little time elapsed before I finally nodded off. Worse yet, slumber came in only brief fragments, interrupted by what seemed like protracted periods of lying awake. Despite repeated efforts to concentrate on pleasant scenes, concerns about the latest developments in the investigation kept forcing themselves into my thoughts.

On Wednesday morning, I got up shortly before dawn and was surprised to find that Tennyson had already left. A note beside the washstand indicated that he would be at the Western Union office for the next several hours. Appended was an invitation to have supper with him at the Quincy Hotel around six that evening. With mild curiosity about what further news the day would bring, I drowsily went through the motions of washing and shaving, then dressed and took a seat in the library until the dumbwaiter arrived. In only a few minutes, a tray appeared, bearing another of Mrs. Hutchins's hearty breakfasts. As usual, this proved to be just the remedy needed for my sluggishness. Once fortified with the filling meal, I locked the front door and headed for Akard Street at a moderate pace.

Upon reaching the Curtis Building, it was a relief to see that two patients were already waiting at my door. Thankfully, the remainder of the morning was reasonably busy as well, which was certainly a welcome change from the previous day. About ten minutes before noon, an opportunity arose for a lunch break. After a hasty sandwich at the Bluebonnet Cafe, I proceeded to Harwood Street and stopped in for a brief chat with Dr. Everett. He readily consented to handle my caseload over the following three days, clearing the way for the proposed trip with Tennyson. Unburdened of this detail, I returned to my office in fairly good spirits, hopeful that the afternoon would pass as quickly as the morning had. Fortune failed me, however; and only six people sought medical attention during the balance of the day. Every so often, I found myself staring at the clock on the wall and pondering the fact that time always seems to behave in a manner contrary to one's desires. When the hands indicated at long last that 5:00 p.m. had arrived, I hung the "Closed" sign in the front window and deliberately tarried over the chore of putting the consulting room in order. This still left nearly fifty minutes until my supper appointment with Tennyson, so I decided to call on Jack and ask him a few questions.

The familiar attendant was on duty in the lobby of the Dallas News Building that evening and voiced a friendly greeting as I entered. Walking past him to the corridor where the reporters' offices were located, it was apparent from a distance that Jack's door was closed. However, a peek through the frosted glass pane revealed a vague image of his profile. Satisfied that no one else was present, I knocked twice before sticking my head in and asking if he could spare a few minutes.

"Sure, come on in and have a seat," he replied, moving a pile of papers from the chair beside his desk. "I wasn't expecting to see you until supper, but the timing of your visit is actually pretty good. There's something that I want to get off my chest. You've got every right to be sore about the stories on the bullion robbery, and I'd like to apologize for my part in the deception. Tennyson and Archer put me in a difficult position by imposing a pledge of secrecy. On a couple of occasions, I came awfully close to letting you in on the trick because your questions were making me feel foolish. In the final analysis, though, I couldn't bring myself to violate their trust."

"No apology is necessary, Jack. You clearly were honor-bound to comply with Tennyson's instructions. It's just disappointing that he didn't have enough faith in my discretion to share his intentions."

"In all fairness, it wasn't Tennyson's idea to keep

you in the dark. Archer is pretty slow to trust people, which has to be expected in his line of work."

"Speaking of Archer, what are your thoughts about this plan to have him impersonate Mr. Woodward?"

"I sure wouldn't want to be in his boots if the Reed gang is involved in the kidnapping attempt. They have the reputation of being a very tough bunch of hombres."

"It seems to me that letting them carry off the business car is taking an unnecessary chance with Archer's safety. I may be a rank amateur at this sort of thing, but Tennyson's strategies sometimes strike me as a bit reckless."

"A better word might be 'daring.' Take it from me that he always weighs the risks carefully before deciding on a course of action. I've never seen him do anything rash."

"There's always a first time. I'd feel a lot better about the situation if his plan were altered to have the outlaws arrested as soon as they stop the train."

"That would probably be my inclination, too; but Tennyson obviously has what he considers valid reasons to take a different approach."

"Maybe so. I just hope there aren't any unpleasant surprises."

"Well, keep in mind that Archer has a good deal of experience with matters like this. Besides, six of his agents will be on hand to see that everything turns out all right."

"A lot could happen between the Ferguson Mill and Rusk, though. Of course, it's not really my business. I should probably confine myself to medical subjects and leave the task of catching criminals to those trained for the work. Unfortunately, the investigation has become downright addictive."

"You're not alone in experiencing that problem. Tennyson's cases frequently encompass challenging puzzles which make them hard to ignore. Luckily for me, they usually provide appealing material for front-page articles; and the present affair should yield a sensational one."

"It definitely has enough points of interest, anyway. Have you worked out a suitable way to present the details?"

"Not entirely. The stumbling block is writing the story without mentioning Golden's conspiracy. I promised Tennyson to keep it quiet until he's ready to identify the participants."

Withdrawing his pocket watch and looking at the dial for a moment, Jack stood up and said, "We'd better be going. It's almost time for our supper engagement."

"I gather that Tennyson summoned you to dine at the Quincy as well," I observed, slowly getting to my feet. "He left a note for me this morning, but didn't give any indication of his purpose. Do you happen to know what's in store for us?"

"My guess is that this is just a last-minute briefing for tomorrow's trip. Then again, maybe he has some fresh reports from his sources in the field. There's only one way to find out."

"You have a knack for getting right to the heart of

things, Jack," I responded with a smile as we headed toward the front of the building.

Once outside, we made quick work of the six blocks to the Quincy Hotel, arriving for our appointment with several minutes to spare. Seeing no sign of Tennyson in the lobby and anxious to avoid a group of cigar-smoking patrons, I suggested that we wait on the sidewalk. A couple of people who knew Jack stopped to chat as we stood near the entrance. Finally, the lanky form of our friend appeared around the corner from the direction of Akard Street. As he came nearer, I noticed an unmistakable gleam in his eyes, although his overall demeanor seemed decidedly purposeful.

"Good evening, gentlemen," he greeted us. "Today has brought encouraging news. Our quarries have broken cover, and the hunt is afield."

"Then your assumption about Donlevy's destination has been confirmed?" I inquired.

"For all intents and purposes," Tennyson replied. "Let's get something to eat, and you shall hear the particulars."

Proceeding into the dining room, we managed to obtain a table at the far end of the south wall, which allowed us to talk in reasonable privacy. Even so, I kept my voice low while urging Tennyson to expand on his remarks.

Speaking in scarcely more than a whisper, he said, "I received word from one of Archer's agents that Martin Donlevy left St. Louis last night on the Missouri & Southwestern's Ozark Special, which provides express service to Little Rock. From there, he can continue to Shreveport on the Ouachita and then catch the Pecos Limited to Longview. It looks very much like he is headed for the Easton & Monroe property."

"You said *quarries*, plural," Jack noted. "What else has happened?"

"Choctaw Jones sent a coded message via the Texas & Louisiana telegraph operator at Henderson, indicating that Will Reed and four other men were spotted riding toward the location where the missing locomotive is hidden."

"Your plan appears to be coming together," I commented.

"More so than I had anticipated."

"In what way?"

"The possibility now looms that Choctaw may be able to sight Donlevy in the company of Reed, as well as observing him with the stolen engine. A jury should find such evidence extremely convincing."

"Do you think La Fourche might also show up while Donlevy is there?"

"Probably not. It's far more likely that those two intend to meet elsewhere, perhaps at one of La Fourche's gaming establishments, once Donlevy has satisfied himself that the preparations for the kidnapping are in readiness. If they do, Choctaw will be nearby to keep an eye on them."

At that moment, the waiter appeared to take our orders. With more interest in the ongoing discussion than in the menu selections, all three of us settled for the daily special, which consisted of baked ham with sweet potatoes and okra. When the server had departed toward the kitchen, Jack was the first to speak.

"So what can Jarvis and I do to make ourselves useful while we're in East Texas?" he asked.

"There *are* a couple of assignments that remain to be filled if you feel disposed to undertake them," Tennyson answered. "Someone must be stationed along the Crockett Branch near Gallatin on Friday to alert Archer's men when the kidnappers pass on their way south. This duty will require transmitting a simple code from a lineside telegraph key. Although no real danger is involved, the waiting might prove tiresome. On the other hand, the second commission could entail some degree of risk; so I will certainly understand if neither of you wishes to volunteer for it. A reliable observer is needed to take up a position in the woods a short distance east of the Ferguson Mill, where he can provide an independent eyewitness account of the events which take place when the train is stopped."

"No reporter worth his salt would pass up a chance like that," Jack said. "You know, I still have my old Colt Peacemaker; and I'm not a bad shot if the need arises. Just tell me where to hide."

"Your help would certainly be welcome, Jack; but you must promise not to take any undue chances for the sake of a story. No matter what happens at trackside, the person who takes on this task must avoid being seen by Reed and his men."

"I can manage that. Anyway, who else could you get to sit in the bushes all morning?"

Feeling slightly miffed over Jack's appropriation of the more exciting job, I declared an equal willingness to assume the responsibility, adding that my Smith & Wesson Schofield had served me well in several sharpshooting contests.

"It's reassuring to learn that both of you are capable marksmen," Tennyson rejoined. "However, all things considered, your services would be of greater value at the spot near Gallatin, Jarvis. Having a doctor on hand there may be a wise precaution in the event someone is injured when the kidnappers are confronted by Archer's men."

"Naturally, I'll do whatever you think best; but my knowledge of Morse code is rather limited."

"That won't be a hindrance. You'll be supplied with the required sequence of dots and dashes, and an experienced telegrapher will demonstrate how to operate the key when we visit the railroad's Division Office tomorrow."

"All right. One question remains: How am I supposed to locate the remote sending station in an area which is totally unfamiliar to me?"

"Arrangements have been made for an 'extra' to set out from the Marshall yard at 6:00 a.m. on Friday, officially bound for a quarry near Laneville. A long spur to the site diverges from the Crockett Branch about twenty-five miles north of Rusk. The train will deliver you to the outskirts of Gallatin before backtracking to its destination and tying up there until late afternoon.

If all goes according to plan, your return passage will be aboard Woodward's business car with my brother and his men after the kidnappers have been captured. In a similar fashion, Jack will be transported to the vicinity of the Ferguson Mill aboard the regular morning through-freight for Dallas, with a scheduled departure time of 6:37 a.m.

"This exercise seems to have been organized quite thoroughly. Can you tell us how long we may have to remain at our posts?"

"The inspection train will leave the Marshall depot at 7:20 a.m. and proceed at a restricted speed consistent with its supposed objective. As a result, it should reach the expected site of the attack right around eight o'clock. Allowing time for the necessary shunting activities there and assuming that the kidnappers will run down the Crockett Branch pretty rapidly, I would expect the missing Mogul and its newly acquired consist to pass through Gallatin shortly after nine. Another half an hour should see the outlaws in custody."

"And where are you going to be while Jarvis and I enjoy the delights of the countryside?" Jack queried.

Tennyson's response came as a considerable surprise: "Aboard the last coach on the inspection train, handling the conductor's functions."

"It hadn't occurred to me that Archer won't be the only one who is risking his neck," I admitted. "Do the other members of the crew know about the danger facing them?"

"Of course. In view of Reed's reputation, I wasn't

about to put the railroad's operating employees in jeopardy. The positions of engineer and fireman will be handled by two volunteers from Colonel Yarbrough's command who have railroading backgrounds, a Sergeant Brubaker and a Corporal Nelson. They arrived in Marshall yesterday to begin learning the timetable and rulebook in preparation for Friday's run."

"Will there be anyone else on board?"

"No. The three of us will be enough to handle the train. Additional personnel would only get in the way."

"Your plan seems to be well thought-out," I remarked, "but allowing Reed and his men to carry your brother away still strikes me as an unnecessary risk. I can't help thinking that it would be preferable to confront the outlaws when they stop the train, even if one or two of them might escape."

"Such a course could very easily provoke a shootout, Jarvis. My approach is intended to avoid a potentially violent encounter while ensuring that we obtain sufficient evidence to put Armand La Fourche behind bars for a good long time."

"No one can take issue with the objective, but the method of achieving it must be viewed as extraordinary. In any case, I'll defer to your judgment and

provide whatever assistance is needed."

"Splendid! The ability to rely on staunch friends is an invaluable asset, and it's certainly fitting that you and Jack should both play important parts in the final act of this drama. Aside from earning my gratitude, contributing to the conviction of La Fourche can be counted as a public service."

Presently, the waiter returned carrying three plates heaped with food; and conversation was suspended while we gave our full attention to consuming the generous portions. When the last morsels were gone, Tennyson called for the bill and suggested that we adjourn for the evening.

After leaving the hotel, the three of us sauntered down Akard together until we came to the intersection with Patterson Street, where Jack needed to turn off toward his boarding house. As parting words were exchanged, I asked if he would like a ride to the Houston Street depot the next morning.

"You bet," Jack said. "Lugging my valise all that way on foot isn't a very inviting prospect. What time shall I expect my carriage?"

"The first eastbound train is scheduled to depart at 7:04 a.m.," Tennyson answered. "We ought to be at the station about ten or fifteen minutes ahead of time, which means calling for you not much later than half-past six."

"I'll be waiting with bells on. Thanks for another instructive evening."

Once Jack had departed, Tennyson and I proceeded to Routh Street via our customary route. Upon arrival at Number 211, we went straight to our respective bedrooms and began preparing for the journey to East Texas. Withdrawing a locked container from the bottom drawer of the dresser, I took out my seldom-used Schofield .45 and a box of ammunition. Following a careful inspection of the pistol, I placed these items in the bottom of my valise. Then I added some clothing suitable for the occasion, along with the usual toiletries. With my packing completed, I repaired to the library, where I was soon joined by Tennyson.

For the better part of an hour, we discussed the steps required to complete the unmasking of Golden's confederates. Relieved that my efforts hadn't been entirely in vain after all, I began to feel a renewed sense of enthusiasm for the investigation. As speculations concerning the relationship between Ralph Lawson and the firm of Molloy & Wilber began to consume my attention, Tennyson brought me back to the more pressing business which lay ahead. His face was a study in determination as he reviewed the plans to capture the kidnappers and secure the desired testimony against La Fourche. Finally, about half-past nine, we retired in order to get a good night's rest before embarking on the implementation of his bold stategy.

CHAPTER 21

Return to the Piney Woods

On Thursday morning, something woke me abruptly from a brief period of sound sleep while the room was still cloaked in darkness. Opening the door, a faint glow from across the hall revealed that Tennyson was already dressed and sitting in the library, with head bowed and fingers tented. He appeared completely lost in thought, so I went about my preparations at the washstand and then donned a comfortable traveling suit before joining him. For several minutes, I sat there without speaking, to avoid interrupting his concentration. Finally, he looked up and said, "Please excuse my distraction, Jarvis. Are you ready for our little adventure?"

"Ready, but still a bit worried," I replied. "Would it be an imposition to ask what was occupying your attention so thoroughly a moment ago?"

"Not at all. I was simply reexamining the various contingencies which might arise tomorrow, trying to make certain that nothing has been overlooked. The major challenge will be maintaining close coordination among all those participating in the exercise."

"If there's anything you need my help with, please don't hesitate to say so."

"Volunteering to serve as the lookout near Gallatin is assistance enough. The task may seem a simple one, but it could well be instrumental in enabling the capture of the kidnappers without gunplay. Having a reliable and resourceful individual at the post is a considerable relief."

"Hopefully, your confidence will prove justified. Jack's role concerns me, though. With his apparent zeal for reporting the news, I'm afraid he might be disposed to take some unwise risks when the inspection train is stopped by the outlaws."

"Despite an occasional tendency to put on a show of bravado, Jack is usually very careful. Whenever any real danger is involved, his good sense generally prevails over his exuberance. As an added precaution, however, I intend to have him accompanied tomorrow by one of Sheriff Peterson's deputies."

"That makes me feel better about the situation," I conceded as a rattling sound from across the hall heralded the arrival of the dumbwaiter.

Fetching the welcome tray of food, I immediately carried it into the dining room, with Tennyson trailing behind me. Once the plates, mugs, and utensils were arranged on the table, we said grace and began devouring the delicious selections provided by Mrs. Hutchins. As soon as both of us had finished eating, I started clearing things away while Tennyson went down to hitch up the buggy. Then I quickly collected our bags, locked the front door, and descended the stairway just as the horse's head appeared from behind the house. In another moment, we were on our way toward Jack's quarters at a good clip.

It was still rather dark, but the eastern sky was beginning to turn a deep azure as sunrise rapidly approached. By the time we turned onto Patterson Street, a band of golden light spreading above the horizon announced the imminent start of the day. Jack was waiting in front of his rooming house and greeted us with a hearty "Morning, gents" as the buggy rolled to a stop. After tossing his valise aboard and climbing into the rear seat beside it, he shouted "Tallyho," which provoked a surprisingly sharp crack of the reins.

A drive of about twelve minutes put us at the Houston Street depot, where a hostler promptly took charge of the buggy. Walking up to the ticket window, Tennyson purchased three first-class seats to Marshall on the *Fleur de Lis*, then excused himself and went inside to send several telegrams. With a good quarter of an hour remaining before our scheduled departure, I left Jack sitting on a bench and wandered down the platform to watch a switch engine at work. This activity engaged my attention until another locomotive chuffed into view from the south, pulling a string of five passenger cars. As a single long note sounded from its whistle, I observed with more than casual interest that the motive power for our journey to East Texas was a Class D-3 Mogul. Walking back to the station, I found Jack slouched with his eyes closed. Momentarily, Tennyson returned from the telegraph office and suggested that it might be wise to board before a line formed. Proceeding to the last coach, we settled into accommodations near the aft door. I chose the side overlooking the adjacent tracks in order to continue my scrutiny of the shunting movements, which were quite fascinating in their complexity. Far sooner than I expected, two long blasts from the whistle signaled the release of the brakes; and the train started moving. My face remained glued to the window as we threaded our way through the central business district and on into the outlying residential areas. It wasn't until the open country east of the city came into view that I turned to look across the aisle.

Tennyson had already adopted the trance-like pose which signified a long period of intense deliberation, while Jack appeared to be dozing again. Since there was clearly no prospect for holding a conversation with either one, I withdrew the journal from my bag and occupied myself in making notes about the passing sights. After some little time, the conductor came through the car punching tickets, awakening Jack from his nap. Once roused, he took out a pack of cards and challenged me to a game of penny-ante poker. We continued playing until the train paused for its station stop in Grand Saline. Feeling a need to stretch my legs at that point, I stepped out onto the rear platform and rode there for the next half an hour or so, enjoying the fresh air. On the way back to my seat, I noticed a new face among the passengers at the forward end of our car. He was an older man, well-dressed, but with the leathery complexion of someone who has been exposed to the elements for a good many years. Even from a distance, the grim set of his jaw could be seen, leading me to conclude that he was on a determined mission of some sort. Little did I know then that his objective was bound up with our own.

Jack was busy editing some pages of typescript, and Tennyson was peering intently out of the window; so I returned to jotting down comments on the trackside views. It seemed only a short time before I heard the conductor announce that we were approaching Longview. Reaching over and tapping Jack on the shoulder, I mentioned that he might want to start getting the lay of the land, since we were nearing the area of interest for our undertaking. As the train rolled to a stop at the station, the man with the weather-worn features rose and moved to the exit. After watching him get off and stride directly to a waiting buggy, I crossed the aisle and took up a position where key features could be pointed out as they came into sight. Once we were underway again, it was only a few minutes before we reached the first of these, the wye leading to the Crockett Branch. This didn't seem to interest Jack very much, but he took more notice a short while later when I drew his attention to the site of the Ferguson Mill. Presently, as the train slowed perceptibly for a curve, Tennyson murmured, "That's the most likely place," gesturing toward a small clearing adjacent to the right-of-way. It was a location well-suited for a holdup, thanks to the topography and the cover afforded by the surrounding woods. Glancing behind me, I also noted that there appeared to be several places on the opposite side of the track which could be used for surveillance. Shortly, the scene passed out of view as we rounded the bend and hurried on toward Marshall. Despite having to brake again a few miles later for the restricted speed within the city limits, the engineer brought us into the station slightly ahead of schedule.

Gathering up our belongings, my companions and I disembarked through the forward door and proceeded into the station. Several people were milling around near the train board, evidently checking the schedule for connections. As one rather stout gentleman moved out of the way, the familiar form of Ted Wilson emerged from behind him. Spotting us, he maneuvered his way to where we were standing and said, "It's good to see you again, Mr. Pierce. You, too, Dr. Weston. I hope everything was satisfactory on your journey from Dallas."

"The Texas & Louisiana provided its usual fine service," Tennyson replied. "Allow me to introduce my friend Jack Lorentz, who is a journalist with the *Dallas News*. Jack, this is Ted Wilson, the stationmaster here at Marshall."

When the two had shaken hands, Wilson continued, "There's a buggy out front for your use. Mr. Ward would like to see all of us in his office at three o'clock this afternoon, provided that's not inconvenient. In the meantime, if you need anything else, just let me know."

"Thank you. The buggy should suffice for the present; and unless there are some unexpected developments during the next few hours, I see no difficulty in meeting at the suggested time."

Without further discussion, Wilson accompanied us to the carriage, which Tennyson drove the short distance down the street to the Marshall Inn. After registering and depositing our luggage in the rooms, we headed directly for the sheriff's office. While Tennyson and Sheriff Peterson were closeted in private discussion, Jack and I wandered around the perimeter of the town square. Then I led the way to the Harrison County Land Office and pointed out that this was where the name of the Easton & Monroe Logging Company had first entered the investigation.

Ever the working reporter, Jack insisted on going in and seeing the records for himself. Without any hesitation, he opened the door, marched up to the counter, and presented his calling card. As Howard Newton greeted him and offered to be of assistance, I stepped forward and said, "Please excuse this intrusion, Mr. Newton. You may recall that I was here not long ago with Ted Wilson on some business for the Texas & Louisiana. Dr. Jarvis Weston."

"Sure, I remember your visit, Dr. Weston. Not many people are interested in the routes of the logging railroads in the county."

"Would it be too much trouble for Mr. Lorentz here to have a look at the survey covering the property immediately southwest of the Ferguson Mill? I believe it was in binder number 137."

"No trouble at all. I'll get it for you."

In just a moment, Newton returned from the records room with a folder, which he laid on the counter in front of us. Opening it and turning over a few pages, he pointed at an area and said, "This ought to be what you want."

I bent closer and saw that he was indicating the northeast sector of the plat, where the customary representation for a rail line appeared. "Yes, that's the one, all right," I responded. "You have a good memory."

"Well, an unusual request like yours naturally had a tendency to stick in a person's mind. Then, too, Ted Wilson told me the interest in my records was connected with the search for the missing locomotive; and it ended up being used in the gold robbery. Is that why you're back in Marshall?"

"No, Mr. Lorentz and I have some other business here today," I prevaricated while running my index finger over the name at the bottom of the page. Nodding in recognition, Jack took out a sheet of paper, made a quick sketch, and wrote several lines. After he had finished, I leafed over to the survey covering the site of the Ferguson Mill and mentioned that the location was interesting in relation to the logging railroad. Feigning an air of disinterest, Jack scribbled another note and replaced the paper in his pocket. Both of us then thanked Howard Newton for his assistance and took our leave.

When we arrived back at the sheriff's office, Tennyson was waiting outside, impatient to get underway. He related that Sheriff Peterson had pledged his full cooperation with the plan for trapping the kidnappers, particularly since it would afford the opportunity of arresting Will Reed. Climbing aboard our transportation once more, we returned to Grand Street and followed it all the way past the western boundary of the city before veering southeast on a narrow road which was nearly overgrown with weeds. Continuing along this path for what I judged was about four miles, we came upon a secluded cabin that stood among a sizable cluster of live-oak trees. As Tennyson drew to a stop near it, a very large man clad in buckskin appeared from the far side, carrying a rifle and squinting in our direction. Suddenly, he broke into a smile and hollered, "Is that Mr. Pierce over there?"

"Hello, Kiowa," Tennyson shouted in reply. "How are you getting along?"

Approaching the buggy, this rough-looking character said, "Cain't complain overly much, 'cept that the town's gittin' too close fer a loner like me."

"I'm afraid there's no stopping progress these days. Let me introduce you to my friends, Dr. Jarvis Weston and Jack Lorentz. Gentlemen, this is Kiowa Jones, Choctaw's brother."

Following an exchange of greetings, Tennyson continued, "I need to get in touch with Choctaw before the end of the day. Can you carry a message to him for me? He should be down near Henderson, somewhere in the vicinity of the logging railroad."

"Yep. He passed through here 'round noon yesterd'y,

expectin' to be headin' that way later. It won't be no problem findin' the ol' coot."

Tennyson then handed over an envelope along with some currency, adding that the dispatch was fairly urgent. In response, Jones promptly set about saddling a good-sized roan horse. Once he had mounted it and ridden off in a southerly direction at a gallop, we started back to town.

By the time that the central business area was in view again, it was nearly one o'clock. Feeling the need for some nourishment, I suggested finding a place to dine. Tennyson agreed and stopped in front of the Delmont House, where he and I had enjoyed a filling supper with Mr. Ward during our earlier visit to Marshall. Choosing a table beside a window, all three of us ordered roast beef sandwiches with potato salad and sarsaparilla. While waiting for the delivery of our food, Jack asked what remained on the day's schedule.

"First, I need to go by the telegraph office," Tennyson answered. "A report should have arrived this morning from Roy Sullivan, who is directing the contingent of Secret Service agents near Rusk. After that, we'll return to the hotel for an appointment with Colin Drake at two o'clock. He's bringing me some information concerning sales of lumber products from the Ferguson Mill to Molloy & Wilber. If time permits, our final stop before the meeting with Mr. Ward will be the crew shanty in the railroad yard to see Sergeant Brubaker and Corporal Nelson for a few minutes."

It was gratifying to hear the unexpected revelation

that my suspicions about Molloy & Wilber had been taken seriously, and I was naturally anxious to find out what Colin Drake could tell us. The prospect of obtaining some corroborating facts from him caused me to momentarily focus once more on speculations about Golden's conspiracy, but such thoughts were cut short by the appearance of the waiter with our meals. Concern over the time led us to eat quickly and without much conversation. As soon as Tennyson had paid the bill, we set out for the Western Union office, which was located just a few blocks away, near the courthouse.

The anticipated telegram from Agent Sullivan was waiting, but it took a little while for Tennyson to decode the contents. Nodding in apparent satisfaction at the resulting message, he wrote out an encrypted response and handed it to the operator for immediate transmission. We then returned to the buggy and hurried off toward the Marshall Inn. Along the way there, I inquired whether the news from Rusk had been encouraging.

"Very much so," Tennyson answered. "Sullivan reported that construction on the shoo-fly track was started early this morning, pretty well confirming my conjecture about the kidnappers' plans. In addition, he had received word from Choctaw Jones saying Martin Donlevy arrived yesterday afternoon at the Easton & Monroe maintenance facility south of Henderson. It appears the stage is well and truly set for the final act of our drama."

"Thank goodness," I commented, feeling a decided

sense of relief that my friend's deductions had been borne out. "Let's hope the denouement doesn't deviate from the script."

"It won't, as long as all of us concentrate on our duties and stay alert. The odds favor a successful outcome, provided Reed and his men can be taken by surprise. Your role is particularly important in that respect, Jarvis."

"I'll certainly give my best effort, but there isn't much time left to rehearse for the role."

"Don't worry. Immediately following our meeting with Mr. Ward, Brian Simpson will be on hand to explain the use of the lineside telegraph key and assist you in practicing at one of the desks in the dispatching center."

Another minute or two found us at the hotel. Leaving the buggy in the alley on the west side of the building, we proceeded into the lobby and took chairs which afforded a view of the entrance. It wasn't long before our visitor came through the door and quickly surveyed the surroundings. He was a rather good-looking man of medium height and build, with sandy-colored hair and a closely-cropped beard. This last feature made it difficult to judge his age, but I guessed him to be in his late thirties or early forties. Tennyson rose and went forward to greet him, while Jack and I hovered a discreet distance behind. When the introductions had been made, the four of us adjourned to my room at the far end of the second floor, in order to have some privacy for our discussion.

"Well, Colin, were you able to learn anything of interest?" Tennyson asked as I closed the door.

"Some would probably think so," Drake responded, a mild brogue betraying his Irish ancestry.

"Please continue, then," Tennyson urged. "My friends can be trusted to treat your disclosures as confidential. In fact, it was Dr. Weston's researches that led me to make the inquiry."

Looking at Jack with an air of skepticism, Drake said, "I guess there's really no reason to keep this a secret, although it took a bit of cajolery to extract the information from my sources. As you know, Arnold Molloy and Hiram Wilber sold their business last year to an outfit from Philadelphia. Within two months of the sale, there was a sharp upturn in the amount of finished lumber that the company was receiving from the Ferguson Mill. At the present time, better than forty percent of the mill's output is going to Molloy & Wilber."

"Just the proof that we needed!" I exclaimed imprudently, excited to hear this verification that a connection existed between the two firms.

"At least it adds to the plausibility of your hypothesis," Tennyson remarked. "Do you happen to know, Colin, whether Ferguson's overall production has increased as a result of these shipments?"

"Apparently not. The word from buyers is that their total output has been pretty flat for quite some time."

"A significant point perhaps. You've been extremely helpful, and I sincerely appreciate your cooperation in coming here. The reported dealings may not be secret, but they could prove compromising to those involved. As a result, no one else must know we're looking into the situation."

"That goes without saying, Mr. Pierce. If there's anything else you'd like to find out about the timber operations in East Texas, just ask."

"Thank you for the offer."

After a brief exchange of pleasantries, we escorted Drake down to the lobby, said our goodbyes, and set out for the railroad yard. The crew shanty was located a short distance from the tower, and reaching it required crossing several tracks. This could be hazardous because of the frequent switching moves, so I kept a sharp lookout as Tennyson threaded the buggy along the network of gravel roads. Presently, we drew up by a small cream-colored building where several men wearing striped overalls were sitting on benches. Stopping next to them, Tennyson asked whether Jeb Brubaker was around.

"Yeah, Brubaker and Nelson are both inside catchin' a little shut-eye," one of the men answered.

Tennyson thanked him, set the brake, and stepped to the ground, telling us that he would only be a moment. A good five or six minutes later, he came out of the shanty and said, "Those two seem to be thoroughly versed in their duties for tomorrow. If the remainder of the preparations have gone as well, the plan should come off without a hitch."

CHAPTER 22

Final Instructions

Continuing along the gravel road for another hundred yards or so, we traversed the switching leads again and came to a stop beside the Division Office. Jack and I followed Tennyson through the double door and up the stairway to the second floor, where the daunting Mrs. Freeman was on duty at her post. Regarding us with an air which suggested that we weren't on the list of approved visitors, she maintained a determined silence until Tennyson spoke.

"Good afternoon, madam," he intoned with exaggerated politeness. "Would you be good enough to inform Superintendent Ward that Mr. Pierce and his associates have arrived?"

"Very well," the secretary responded in a condescending voice before slowly getting up and turning around. Tapping lightly on the door behind her, she opened it part way and murmured something. Almost immediately, Henry Ward scurried into the alcove and voiced a hearty greeting.

"Come in, gentlemen!" he boomed, ushering us into

his office. "The others should be along shortly. Would any of you care for some liquid refreshment? Whisky or brandy perhaps?"

Tennyson and I declined; but after being introduced, Jack accepted a shot of Kentucky sipping whisky. Once we were all settled in our chairs, Mr. Ward said, "The inspection train passed through Hope, Arkansas not quite twenty minutes ago, which should put it into Marshall right around 8:00 p.m. I'll be on hand for the arrival and will escort our substitute Mr. Woodward to the hotel. Tomorrow morning, he'll be picked up by Ted Wilson and taken back to his business car in time for a departure at 7:20 a.m. Brian Simpson has been assigned as the dispatcher, with instructions to maintain a safe window of open track around the train at all points west of here."

"I assume that the provisions are also in place for the 'extra' to Laneville," Tennyson remarked.

"Yes, and it will be the only movement authorized over the Crockett Branch tomorrow. Steve Ellis, Will Gossett, and Frank Springer have been called for the crew; but they don't know yet about carrying a passenger to Gallatin. Have you decided who's going?"

"Dr. Weston has graciously volunteered for the duty."

"It will mean a pretty early day, Doctor. The train is slated to leave from Track 2 in the yard at 6:00 a.m. sharp, which calls for being on board at least ten minutes before that. I'll have Frank Springer wait at the entrance of this building to walk over with you. When we've finished our discussions this afternoon, stop by Brian Simpson's desk for a short indoctrination on the art of using a telegraph key."

"All right," I acknowledged as a tap sounded at the door. It was followed by the appearance of Mrs. Freeman, who wearily proclaimed the arrival of Ted Wilson and Sheriff Peterson.

"Please show them in," Ward instructed.

When the two men had taken seats, Tennyson commented that Jack and one of the sheriff's deputies would be riding the first westbound freight of the next day to a location near the Ferguson Mill.

"I've asked Rick Minton to accompany your friend," Peterson noted. "He's very familiar with that area and can recommend a good spot for observing the happenings without being seen."

Although his face betrayed undeniable surprise at this announcement, Jack refrained from commenting, but simply requested further instructions.

"Train 81 is scheduled to depart at 6:37 a.m. from Track 4," Ward stated. "Since it's a regularly scheduled run, the conductor will be busy checking waybills; but I'll have someone else waiting to show you and Deputy Minton where to go. Please make sure that you're here no later than 6:15, since the caboose is liable to be a good distance east of the yard lead."

"Maybe I should just plan on coming down with Jarvis, then," Jack said. "In fact, it might be a good idea if Minton met us at the hotel around half-past five and we all rode together. With a little inducement, Tennyson might even be persuaded to drive us."

"By all means," Tennyson replied. "However, let's move on to the remainder of the preparations for tomorrow's events. How much has Captain Stevens been told, Mr. Ward?"

"As usual when a dignitary is expected, instructions were issued for Stevens and his men to carry out a special check of the property, which was started yesterday," Ward answered. "The usual procedure in such cases will be observed, with two guards posted to keep watch over the inspection train while it's parked in the yard overnight. Otherwise, nothing has been said to him concerning the suspected kidnapping attempt."

"Good. The precaution may prove to be well-advised. What about *your* tasks in coordinating the run, Mr. Wilson? Are you satisfied that the train can be handled acceptably by its novice crew?"

"I'm fairly comfortable there, Mr. Pierce. Brubaker and Nelson both have a respectable amount of railroading experience, and they've certainly learned the rulebook well enough to make a short trip over the line west of here on their own. There are still one or two things that I need to tell you about the conductor's job, though."

"Once we're finished here, I'll be at your disposal for whatever tutoring is required. Were you able to find a uniform for me?"

"As a matter of fact, Sam Duggan had a spare which ought to fit reasonably well. He's about your height but just a little heavier. It'll be waiting at the depot in the morning, along with one of my caps."

"Excellent. The arrangements for our undertaking are progressing nicely. Is there anything you'd like to add, Sheriff Peterson?"

"This is your show, Mr. Pierce; but I'd sure feel better having a couple of my men on the train."

"The offer is appreciated. However, the risk is too great that a deputy might be recognized by one of the outlaws, which could lead to gunplay. It will be safer for those on board without any lawmen around."

"You may have a point there. At least let me put a couple of sharpshooters over near the Ferguson Mill in case things don't go according to plan. Ben Gibson and Clay Holden can ride over tonight and pick out a suitable spot for ambushing the kidnappers if the situation starts looking bad."

"Are these two men capable of exercising good judgment?"

"I'd trust them with my life."

"They'll have to understand that any interference must be avoided unless the circumstances leave no alternative."

"Don't worry, Mr. Pierce. Ben and Clay have been around long enough to know what's required when baiting a trap."

"Go ahead, then. A little added insurance won't do any harm, although the resources might be better used elsewhere. How do matters stand regarding the measures which we discussed this morning?"

"I telegraphed the U. S. Marshal in Shreveport, like you asked. He agreed to have La Fourche watched and will move in for the arrest him as soon as we give the word."

"Did you learn La Fourche's current whereabouts?"

"According to the last message from Marshal Jennings, he's at his casino in Greenwood, which is just across the state line, about twenty-five miles from here."

"That's probably where Donlevy intends to meet him. It would definitely strengthen our evidence and be a fitting way of concluding this exercise if the two of them could be apprehended together. I'd dearly like to be on hand for such an event and would welcome your company, Sheriff. Perhaps the railroad can be prevailed upon to provide an engine and caboose for a run to Greenwood around half-past nine in the morning."

"Gladly," Ward responded. "Please attend to it, Wilson."

"Yes, sir. Tom Burleson should be available for the hogger's seat, and I can handle the fireman's duties myself. If it's all right with Mr. Pierce, we'll be waiting on the siding behind the depot."

"That will be fine, thank you. I believe the stage is set then, gentlemen. Do you have anything further to say, Mr. Ward?"

"Only that the Texas & Louisiana is pleased to cooperate in the capture of these scoundrels, and our full resources are at your disposal."

"The railroad's support has been more than generous. Now, Jarvis and I had better get on with our lessons. Why don't you tag along with Mr. Wilson and me, Jack."

Following some brief parting words, we withdrew from Ward's office and filed past Mrs. Freeman, who stared at us in her deprecating manner. Once clear of the alcove, Tennyson took me aside and pressed a calling card into my hand, murmuring that the required code was written on the reverse side. With a quick glance at the succession of dots and dashes, I proceeded to the adjacent dispatching center, while the others headed for the stairway. As promised, Brian Simpson was waiting to provide a lesson in the rudiments of railroad telegraphy. He handed me a carefully-drawn map showing the sending station near Gallatin, as well as a key to the lock on its enclosure, then demonstrated the timing and rhythm required in transmitting a message. For the better part of an hour, I sat at a desk beside him, making repeated attempts to imitate his fluid cadence. Despite a rather ungainly technique, my results were finally pronounced as "adequate." After thanking Simpson for his time and patience, I went downstairs.

The sound of Jack's voice, which carried rather well, led me to a room off the main hallway. There I discovered him holding forth on the problems facing President Cleveland's administration while Tennyson and Ted Wilson listened with apparent indifference. My interruption of this discourse was obviously welcomed by the captive audience; and Tennyson immediately seized the opportunity to change the subject, asking how the practice had gone.

"Well enough for the intended purpose," I answered, "although no one is apt to offer me any plaudits for speed or finesse. What about your session? Did Mr. Wilson succeed in teaching you the responsibilities of a conductor?"

"He made a determined effort within the time available and managed to get across the basic aspects of the job."

Tennyson then closed the door and continued, "Before we leave, it would be advisable to spend a few minutes going through a step-by-step review of what can be expected tomorrow. Timing will play an important part in the achievement of our objectives, and all of you should understand how your responsibilities fit into the overall events."

Moving to the blackboard at the far end of the room, he drew several diagrams representing track arrangements and used these to illustrate the various train movements that would probably take place as the kidnapping unfolded. His detailed explanation of the actions involved in this sequence consumed a good half an hour. When it was completed, Jack helped erase all traces of the artwork; and the four of us departed the building together.

Wilson had come down from the depot via handcar and planned on getting back the same way, so we parted company with him and drove straight to the Marshall Inn. Pausing near the front desk, Tennyson suggested taking a brief respite before supper to rinse off the dust and relax a bit. The idea was a welcome one; and after agreeing on a rendezvous at six o'clock, we all went up to our rooms. In my case, most of the interlude was consumed in writing notes concerning the day's activities.

With five or six minutes remaining till the hour, I felt the need for a little exercise and headed downstairs. Stepping into the lobby, my attention was caught by two men in the far corner who were standing very close together and conversing in subdued voices. As the nearer one shifted position slightly, a familiar face came into view: Captain Stevens. A closer look at his confidant revealed the weathered features of the older gentleman who had boarded our coach at Grand Saline that morning.

Finding these two together seemed cause for suspicion, and I decided it best to retreat before Stevens saw me. Hurriedly retracing my steps to the upper landing, I went directly to the second room and knocked somewhat too insistently. In a moment, Tennyson opened the door and said, "Calm down, Jarvis. Whatever is the matter?"

"Please excuse my excitement," I apologized, "but something has occurred which may be important. During the meeting in Mr. Ward's office, you made a remark which seemed to indicate a certain distrust of Captain Stevens. Well, I just observed him in the lobby having a very private chat with the leathery-faced man who was on the train with us between Grand Saline and Longview."

Tennyson displayed only the slightest surprise at

this news, commenting that it provided support for one of his ideas, but offering no particulars. By the time we roused Jack from his nap and started off to supper, Stevens and his acquaintance had disappeared.

The evening was quite pleasant, and I enjoyed the four-block walk to Mrs. Barton's Restaurant. This establishment turned out to be a homey place offering friendly service and a decent variety of plainly-cooked food. My choice was the meatloaf with brown rice and asparagus, while Tennyson and Jack both ordered sirloin steaks with baked potatoes and English peas. All of us gladly accepted the waitress's suggestion to try the specialty of the house, a frothy beverage called Sophie's Syllabub.

Despite intense curiosity over the idea which Tennyson had mentioned in his room, I refrained from pressing the issue, assuming that he would disclose the details when the time was right. Before long, Jack began to monopolize the conversation with tales about some of the colorful individuals whose dreams and daring had laid the groundwork for the logging industry in the Piney Woods. While listening to the anecdotes, it dawned on me that Gilbert Donlevy was prominent among those pioneers and that the company which he had built might now be lost through his nephew's recklessness.

At the conclusion of the meal, Tennyson indicated the need for a few words with Sheriff Peterson. Having nothing better to occupy our time, Jack and I tagged along. Upon reaching the town square, we spotted the sheriff entering his office and followed him inside. Manning the desk was a rugged-looking deputy who introduced himself as Rick Minton. While he and Jack began talking about their mutual assignment of the next day, Peterson ushered Tennyson into the back room and closed the door. It was a good while before they returned and stated that matters were progressing satisfactorily. After some further discussion concerning coordination with the lawmen in Louisiana, we left and started toward the hotel, taking a roundabout route which enabled seeing a little more of the town.

My pocket watch showed not quite ten minutes until eight o'clock when our trek brought us back to the front steps of the Marshall Inn. Since Mr. Ward and Archer were expected shortly, we decided to wait outside for them and took seats on the wooden benches near the entrance. Jack wasted little time in resuming his stories concerning the area's early settlers, quickly garnering a wider audience as several passersby stopped to listen and add comments. A moderate breeze blowing from the east provided a soothing environment and made me start feeling drowsy. This congenial interval was finally interrupted by an approaching buggy. As it drew up a few yards away, I received my first glimpse of Tennyson's impressive brother.

Archer's true appearance may have been masked by his disguise, but hardly anything about him suggested a kinship with Tennyson. A broad forehead dominated a squarish face adorned with muttonchops; and he was not only a good deal heavier than my friend, but larger-boned as well. In fact, the only indication of a possible family relationship between the two came from a slight similarity in the shapes of their noses.

Mr. Ward played the solicitous host, helping the visiting dignitary to the sidewalk and introducing him as "the distinguished Mr. Efram Woodward from Philadelphia."

"I am very pleased to meet you, sir," Tennyson extemporized. "These are my colleagues, Dr. Jarvis Weston and Mr. Jack Lorentz. May we extend an invitation for a spot of brandy with us once you've settled in? Just come by Number 22 at your convenience."

"That's a most hospitable offer," came the well-acted response. "It's been a long day, and a restorative would be welcome."

Going along with the charade, Jack and I retrieved two sizable traveling bags from the buggy and carried them into the hotel. When Archer had signed the register and received his key, Ward bid us good night and left. We then escorted the ersatz Mr. Woodward to quarters at the rear of the first floor and convened in Tennyson's room.

The next fifteen or twenty minutes were spent in running over our duties of the following day one more time, with particular emphasis on Jack's role in documenting the events at trackside during the kidnapping. Tennyson had just finished warning again about the need for maintaining cover no matter what occurred when a loud rap on the door announced his brother's arrival. As soon as Archer was admitted, he began asking questions regarding the latest reports from Agent Sullivan and Choctaw Jones. The answers led to a further review of the preparations for capturing the outlaws and arresting the men who hired them. A little before 9:00 p.m., the discussions concluded; and we disbanded for the evening.

Back in my room, I laid out a pair of denim trousers and a broadcloth shirt, set the Seth Thomas alarm for five o'clock, and made ready for bed. It was a good long time before sleep came, however; and I would get little rest that night due to the natural anxiety brought on by our impending adventure.

CHAPTER 23

A Diminished Success

Mr. Ward's counsel about an "early morning" struck home when the insistent ringing of a clamorous bell awakened me from a light slumber. Sitting up, I groped in the darkness for the clock and eventually succeeded in making the noise stop. After lighting the oil lamp on the nightstand, I struggled across to the washbowl and immersed my face for a moment, then quickly shaved and dressed. An unfamiliar accessory completed the day's attire: a cavalryman's holster that had been a gift from a relative. With the Schofield .45 carefully secured in this, I headed downstairs, ready for whatever lay ahead.

Tennyson was standing near a window on the far side of the lobby, his face a study in calm determination. Noticing my approach, he uttered a perfunctory greeting and remarked that the buggy had already been brought around. Shortly, Jack showed up, wearing a beige Stetson that had seen better days and toting his Peacemaker in a low-slung rig decorated with a small silver medallion. I couldn't resist ribbing him about looking like a dangerous gunslinger, but elicited nothing more than a halfhearted retort. Before long, we sighted Deputy Minton walking toward the hotel and went outside to meet him. In short order, the four of us were rolling down Grand Street at a fairly good rate, bound for the railroad yard.

Some ten minutes later, Tennyson pulled up beside the Texas & Louisiana Division Office. As Minton, Jack, and I climbed down, Frank Springer stepped forward and said, "Good morning, gentlemen. If you'll come with me, Dr. Weston, our train isn't too far away. Rick, Bill Collins should be along directly. He'll take you and this other fellow over to Track 4."

Uttering some final words of caution, Tennyson turned the buggy around and started back for the depot, where he still needed to change into his conductor's uniform before boarding the inspection train. Springer promptly led the way across the yard throat and along a gravel path to the caboose that would serve as my transportation. On the way, I noted that our locomotive was a small Ten-Wheeler and that the remainder of the "extra" consisted of two boxcars and three gondolas. Hoping for a chance to ride in the cupola, I asked if it would be all right and was delighted at the consenting nod. While Springer set about inspecting the running gear and couplers, I clambered up to the elevated perch. In due course, the conductor returned, signaled the engineer with a lantern, and climbed onto the rear platform. Momentarily, two long blasts sounded from the whistle; and the train started moving.

Our progress was unhurried until we reached the marker denoting the city limit, where Steve Ellis evidently opened the throttle a substantial amount, judging from the pronounced acceleration. With the increase in speed, the caboose started rocking from side to side, forcing the use of the handholds. Although the motion was amplified by my position atop the car, I enjoyed watching the surroundings from this unusual vantage point. A brief respite from the lurching was afforded when Ellis slowed for the speed restriction at Blanco siding. Once clear of the west turnout there, however, the running pace quickened noticeably; and bracing myself became more difficult.

For the next quarter of an hour or so, we practically raced toward Longview, braking only at the curve where Tennyson expected the kidnappers to strike. I kept a sharp lookout as the Ferguson Mill neared, but the site passed by too quickly for any conclusive observations about suspicious activities there. The remaining six or seven miles until the junction with the Crockett Branch were reeled off in about as many minutes. Then a sharp deceleration brought us to a halt with the engine standing just east of the wye.

Someone, presumably Will Gossett, climbed down from the left-hand side of the cab and walked forward to line up the turnout for the diverging route. Presently, the fireman swung aboard the locomotive once more; and the train inched ahead until the caboose had crossed the frog. At that point, Springer ran back and realigned the switch. After completing this chore, he gave the signal to proceed and rejoined me inside the caboose.

Soon we were highballing south through unfamiliar country. Tall evergreens began crowding the right of way, their lower branches occasionally brushing against the cupola's windows. By and by, a long lake emerged into view on our left, providing a welcome change in the scenery. This rare discontinuity in the sylvan landscape made me start thinking about the difficulties which must have confronted the men who undertook to construct a railroad through such terrain. The accomplishment of their vision had clearly required both fortitude and hard work. Moreover, the result would bolster local commerce for many generations. I couldn't help reflecting on the marked contrast with the underhanded tactics employed by opportunists like Jay Golden in acquiring the products of others' labors. These musings must have absorbed my attention for some time before the sound of Springer's voice intruded.

"Dr. Weston! The Hanley Brothers Mill is coming up on the right, in case you're interested," he informed me.

Thanking him for the advisory, I focused on watching the indicated side of the track. Presently, a broad clearing appeared, occupied by three good-sized buildings and a long loading dock. The overall layout was similar to that at the Ferguson Mill, with a spur running into the largest structure. Several wagons were in evidence, and quite a few workers could be seen bustling about the grounds. As the successful-looking enterprise passed from sight, I glanced at my pocket watch and noted that we had been underway for approximately fifty-five minutes.

"How much farther is it to Gallatin?" I called down to Springer.

"Roughly forty miles," he replied. "If Steve keeps running at this rate, we should be there by a quarter of eight."

"Where does the line for Laneville cut off?"

"About twenty-three miles ahead. Backtracking to it after dropping you off will take a good half an hour, since our speed is restricted when reversing."

Remembering Tennyson's comment that he expected the inspection train to reach Gallatin around nine, I ran through some quick mental calculations and concluded that we were cutting the timing pretty close. If my figuring was correct, there would be a margin of no more than twenty minutes for the "extra" to clear the line before the kidnappers came through with Archer. That certainly didn't leave much latitude on our part for unexpected delays.

Over the following ten or twelve miles, there was little to see but a dense expanse of timber. Then I spotted the signpost for Henderson and realized that we must be approaching the vicinity where Choctaw Jones had been keeping watch. Apparently the Easton & Monroe property was well off to the west, however, since nothing at hand indicated the presence of a logging railroad nearby. Our speed slackened briefly as the train passed a short siding which served a general store and a cotton oil dealer, but Ellis quickly made up the time.

The remainder of the trip offered no change in the rather monotonous vista, apart from crossing a short trestle that spanned a shallow creek. Not long afterward, the track curved fairly sharply to the left; and Springer hollered, "Your stop's coming up, Dr. Weston."

A few minutes later, we jerked to a standstill in what looked like a very remote spot. Glancing around before descending from the cupola, I noticed a small tan enclosure mounted against a telegraph pole on the left-hand side of the track. "That must be the sending station," I observed while collecting my medical bag. "Where is the town ?"

With a confirming nod, Springer answered, "It's about a mile further on. There isn't a whole lot to the place; but if you get hungry, the Lumberman's Saloon serves pretty fair ham and eggs all day."

"Good. Please thank the head-end crew for an interesting ride."

When I had stepped off the rear platform and moved aside, Springer leaned out and swung his lantern in a circle. Ellis responded with three short toots of the whistle, and the train started moving backward. Once the locomotive disappeared around the bend, I walked over to the trackside box and tried the key which Brian Simpson had provided. The padlock was rusted from exposure to the elements, necessitating a certain amount of fiddling before it finally opened. My efforts were rewarded with access to an apparatus not much different from those installed at the dispatching center. Satisfied that all was ready for the task ahead, I closed the door of the housing, but left the lock undone. Then I walked a short distance into the woods and found a suitable place to wait for the missing Mogul's appearance.

Sitting in the shade and enjoying the tranquil sounds of the forest, it would have been easy to doze off. As a preventive measure, I began reviewing the evidence concerning Jay Golden's conspiracy. The information supplied by Colin Drake on the previous day had unquestionably been a significant step forward, providing reliable support for one of my tentative conclusions. However, there remained a pressing need to identify the principals in the syndicate that had purchased Molloy & Wilber. Ralph Lawson still struck me as the best prospect for linking that firm with Golden, and I pondered how more could be learned about his activities. For some reason, a comment made by George Riley suddenly came to mind. While discussing out-of-state corporations operating in Texas, he had mentioned a file containing business charters at the Dallas County Courthouse. The notion dawned on me that McLennan County probably maintained similar records. An excursion to Waco might yield some useful results; and if the trip were made on a Saturday, perhaps George could come with me. Feeling rather pleased with myself for having formulated a plan, I decided to do some exploring.

The surrounding wilderness featured several different types of pine trees, as well as a good many flowers and shrubs. Dogwood, wild onion, and winecup plants were well-represented, along with some unfamiliar bushes that bore clusters of reddish-purple berries. Under other circumstances, I could have been quite contented to spend the entire morning cataloguing the assorted botanical attractions. As it was, conscious that Archer's men were depending on me, I roamed through the thick growth for about forty minutes before returning to my chosen lookout post.

While continuing the vigil for the kidnappers, I occupied myself in watching the clouds overhead, which were being swept into ever-changing patterns by the winds aloft. Eventually, a new sight appeared in the sky to the northeast: black smoke. At first, the plume was barely visible above the treetops; but its discernible extent expanded noticeably as the source advanced toward me. Shortly, the telltale chuffing sound of a locomotive could be heard faintly echoing through the woodland. Stretching out flat on the ground to avoid being detected, I felt my muscles involuntarily tighten in anticipation. The noise grew increasingly louder until the onrushing train charged by, barely six yards away from where I was watching. Although the business car passed too quickly for the faces of those aboard to be seen clearly, the numeral "35" was plainly evident on the tender.

When a safe interval had elapsed, I got up and walked over to the telegraph sending station. Extracting Tennyson's calling card from my shirt pocket, I studied the code for a moment and carefully tapped out the message. As a precaution, I also waited approximately ten seconds and then repeated the transmission before locking the door of the housing. With my assignment completed, there seemed no particular reason to remain there; and having a belated breakfast in Gallatin struck me as a good idea.

The Lumberman's Saloon wasn't difficult to find, standing with just a few other buildings on a dirt street about twenty yards west of the track. A gaze through the opening above the double doors revealed only one patron, a scruffy-looking individual who was sitting at a table near the back of the room, taking swigs from a whisky bottle. This character may have been perfectly harmless, but having a pistol at my side felt reassuring under the circumstances. Pushing through the entrance, I walked up to the counter and asked for a plate of ham and eggs. The barkeeper responded by shouting the order through an aperture behind him and filling a mug with strong-smelling coffee, which evidently was served as standard fare whether wanted or not.

"Can't recall seeing your face around these parts before," the man declared, eyeing my medical bag with obvious curiosity.

"Just passing through," I returned in a nonchalant tone. "A friend who works for the railroad recommended this place to me."

"Whereabouts are you headed?"

"I have some business down near Rusk. How far from here is that?"

"Ten or eleven miles by road, a little less if you follow the T&L rails."

Surprised to discover the distance wasn't any greater, I staved off further conversation by reluctantly sipping the pungent coffee, at the same time carrying out some hurried arithmetic in my head. Considering the amount of time it had taken for me to walk into town, Archer's men might have already intercepted the kidnappers. If so, they could be returning through Gallatin aboard Woodward's business car within another fifteen or twenty minutes, assuming that nothing untoward had occurred. This raised the possibility of missing my ride back to Marshall unless I ate rather quickly.

Fortunately, very little time elapsed before the still-sizzling food was placed in front of me. As soon as the grease stopped splattering, I dug in, gobbling the meal much more rapidly than recommended for proper digestion. When nothing but gristle remained on the plate, I deposited thirty-five cents on the counter, thanked the barkeeper, and strode out the door.

Heading straight toward the Texas & Louisiana track, I briefly considered walking south to meet the returning train somewhere between Rusk and Gallatin. However, the deeply rooted habit of obeying instructions overcame that impulse and pointed my steps in the opposite direction. After trodding along the rock-strewn ground beside the ballast for six or seven minutes, I detected a muted sound which could only have been the Mogul's whistle. Looking behind me, a column of grayish smoke was visible in the distance. This telltale sign provided the first positive indication that the confrontation with the kidnappers had been successful. Continuing along the right-of-way at a reduced pace, I kept glancing over my shoulder, watching for the engine's approach. When it had closed to within a few hundred yards, I stopped, turned around, and waved both hands in the air.

Thankfully, the locomotive began slowing and finally stopped with the business car about ten feet ahead of me. Archer promptly emerged onto the rear platform and shouted, "Good morning, Dr. Weston. Hop aboard."

Hurrying forward, I climbed the steps to join him and said, "You're certainly a welcome sight, Mr. Pierce! Did the capture go smoothly?"

"Thanks to your telegraph message, Sullivan and the others executed the plan quite satisfactorily. There *was* a little unpleasantness, however. In fact, we have some slight need for your medical services. One of the outlaws suffered a minor wound when he foolishly brandished a pistol at me."

Leading the way inside, Archer pointed out the injured man, who had a bandana wrapped around his left arm just above the elbow. He was sitting at the forward end of the car in company with the other gang members, all secured to their chairs by handcuffs. Four Secret Service agents were seated across the aisle from them, cradling rifles.

"Where are the rest of your men?" I inquired a little

anxiously, remembering that six were supposed to have participated in the ambush.

"Bridger and McCullough are up in the cab, riding herd on the engineer and the fireman. Incidentally, the two crewmen don't act like habitual criminals. My guess is that they were recruited from the Easton & Monroe logging railroad for this escapade."

"That would make sense in view of Donlevy's involvement. In any case, I'd better see about the fellow who was shot."

Moving on down the car, I knelt and examined the wound, which turned out to be relatively benign. Even so, it needed a good cleansing with carbolic acid as a safeguard against infection. After applying a proper bandage and receiving a grunted word of thanks, I rejoined Archer in the lounge area.

Our journey back along the Crockett Branch was somewhat tedious, the only conversation being occasional brief exchanges on various casual topics. We also seemed to be traveling relatively slowly; and, in fact, about an hour and a quarter elapsed before the wye near Longview came into sight. As one of Archer's men went out to throw the switch, I warily asked whether clearance had been obtained for running over the mainline.

"Yes, it has," Archer replied, looking at his pocket watch. "The dispatcher was contacted from Rusk and gave us a one-hour window for an eastward movement, beginning at 10:50. We're within that now and shouldn't have any trouble reaching Marshall before the authorization expires."

Presently, two prolonged notes issued from the whistle; and our movement resumed. Within a mile, the telegraph poles were flitting past at a rate which seemed noticeably brisker than the previous one. I focused my attention on the south side of our route, hoping to see some evidence remaining from the holdup and subsequent events. However, the only detectable sign was a cinder pile between the rails leading into the Ferguson Mill. Recalling the newspaper story about the supposed bullion robbery, I concluded that these remnants probably marked the spot where Brubaker and Nelson had been forced to dump the contents of their firebox. This made me wonder how the disabled engine could have been removed and what had taken place since then. Several possibilities occurred to me and occupied my thoughts until we slowed for the speed restriction at the Marshall outskirts.

Upon entering the central section of the city, our train was shunted onto a secondary track that ran behind the depot, coming to a jolting halt there around a quarter till noon. While Sullivan and the other agents looked after the prisoners, Archer and I exited through the rear door and started walking across to the station. We were met halfway by a greeting party consisting of Ted Wilson, Jack Lorentz, and Deputy Minton. Although I was relieved at finding that Jack had survived his assignment unscathed, my first comment was addressed to Wilson: "I thought you'd be in Greenwood by now."

"Been and returned," he replied. "As a matter of fact, we got in about twenty minutes ago. Mr. Pierce and

Sheriff Peterson are down at the courthouse questioning the three men they brought back. An old army scout named Choctaw Jones is with them, too."

"*Three* men did you say?" I queried in surprise.

"That's right. One of them was that casino owner, Armand La Fourche. His picture has been in the Shreveport newspaper a time or two. The others were strangers to me."

"La Fourche was expected, along with Martin Donlevy, but nobody else. Do you have any information concerning another accomplice, Mr. Pierce?"

"No, I don't. However, my brother often springs surprises of this sort."

"What about it, Jack? Did Tennyson confide in you?"

"Afraid not. Our friend was decidedly tight-lipped when he returned from his foray, and the sheriff hustled their prisoners away so quickly that I didn't get a good look at them. Don't worry, though. More than likely, we'll be given the whole story over lunch."

"You're probably right, but there's an idea which I'd like to confirm before then. If Mr. Pierce has no objection, why don't we start on down toward the courthouse?"

"By all means," Archer responded. "I wouldn't mind seeing these fellows myself and also need a word with Tennyson before he questions Reed."

Taking his cue, Minton went over to confer with Sullivan. Presently, the entourage of outlaws and Secret Service agents marched off behind the deputy in the direction of the sheriff's office. Archer, Jack, and I followed at a discreet distance, separating from the others as they passed the courthouse. Approaching the building's main entrance, Archer said, "You'd better wait outside until I see how matters stand with the interrogations."

Nearly half an hour must have elapsed before he reappeared and invited us to accompany him. Our destination was a room on the second floor, bearing a sign labeled "Authorized Personnel Only." As we walked toward it along the deserted corridor, Tennyson stepped out, took me aside, and murmured, "No more than a quick peek, Jarvis. The individual of interest is on the far right."

Placing a hand on my back, he guided me forward and opened the door just a crack. As I carefully peered through the aperture in the indicated direction, my hunch was confirmed by the sight of the gray-haired gentleman who had boarded the *Fleur de Lis* in Grand Saline on Thursday. For a brief moment, I stared at the weathered countenance, then drew back. When we had removed ourselves a safe distance, Tennyson asked quietly, "Was that the man you observed having a conversation with Captain Stevens yesterday evening?"

"The very same," I answered. "Who is he?"

"All in good time, Jarvis. I must get over to the jail now for what could be a pivotal discussion with Will Reed. Meet me at the Delmont House around half-past one, and your curiosity shall be satisfied."

"Very well, if the delay is truly necessary. Remaining in suspense seems my customary plight lately."

"When can I see Donlevy?" Jack interjected before Tennyson could escape.

"Be patient. The chances are good that you'll have a first-hand account from him before the day ends. It may even include some unexpected admissions."

With this provocative remark, Tennyson turned and moved rapidly toward the stairway while the rest of us trailed behind. At the landing on the first floor, Archer paused and said, "Trying to match my brother's pace is a lost cause when he's in a hurry. I could stand a little fortification just now. Is there a respectable saloon nearby?"

"Haggerty's comes well-recommended, and it's only about three blocks from here," Jack offered.

"Splendid! Will you gentlemen join me in a small libation?"

Jack promptly accepted the invitation, so I consented as well, rather than appear impolite. Several minutes later found us sitting at a four-place table in an establishment which was apparently a popular gathering place for local businessmen. My companions both ordered bourbon whisky, while I chose a glass of port. As we sipped our drinks, Archer commented that the case had taken a rather distressing turn.

"Do the circumstances involve the third suspect?" I ventured.

"Regrettably so. One can't help feeling a certain

ambivalence when required to arrest such a respected member of the community."

"That remark suggests you know the man's identity."

"I learned it from Tennyson at the courthouse, but must let him disclose the name. He wants to confer with Judge Fletcher first. In any event, the full particulars will come out soon enough."

"Well perhaps in the meantime, Jack might be persuaded to summarize his observations of what took place this morning out near the Ferguson Mill."

"Sure, on the condition that you don't spill the beans before the story is published. My vigil in the brambles should have *some* reward."

Archer and I both assured Jack that his confidence would be respected, and he launched into an entertaining description of the circumstances which had attended the abduction. The preliminary events weren't much different from those reported in the *Dallas News* coverage about the feigned gold robbery. One noteworthy point, however, was that the inspection train's locomotive and combine returned to the scene of the holdup only a short time after the outlaws' departure. Apparently, Corporal Nelson had somehow succeeded in keeping the boiler's fire lit despite the contrary indication on the spur at the Ferguson Mill. As a result, Jack and Deputy Minton were picked up a good deal sooner than anticipated and accompanied Tennyson back to Marshall. When they reached the depot around ten minutes past nine, Sheriff Peterson was there with a fresh report concerning Martin Donlevy's whereabouts.

Following a brief discussion in private, Tennyson and the sheriff boarded the waiting caboose provided by Ted Wilson and left for Greenwood.

"And that's the unmitigated truth from an eyewitness," Jack pronounced at the conclusion of his narrative. "Now, turnabout is fair play, Mr. Pierce. Let's have the victim's perspective on the kidnapping."

"The experience held no real surprises," Archer responded. "Reed and two other men kept a close watch over me the whole time; but they didn't tie my hands, which turned out to be a mistake. Our run down the Crockett Branch went off without incident, although the speed felt pretty fast and made the ride less than comfortable. Dr. Weston must have selected a good hiding place, because I didn't see a soul at trackside around Gallatin. Going through Rusk, though, the train attracted a few stares. Then we braked hard and crawled across the shoo-fly construction onto the Beaumont & Carthage line. A short distance past the junction, just beyond a fairly sharp bend, the rails were blocked by some sizable logs, forcing an abrupt stop. Sullivan and the others were aboard in an instant, and Reed wisely surrendered. However, Buck Cravens grabbed me and stuck a pistol against my head. Using a maneuver from the Oriental discipline of jujitsu, I managed to escape his grasp and disarm him. During the scuffle, the weapon discharged, wounding Cravens in the left arm. Thankfully, that was the only casualty incurred."

"It's a wonder you weren't shot yourself," I commented.

"Perhaps, but such hazards are all in a day's work for me," Archer returned. "Besides, the results were well worth the slight risk incurred. Consider the benefits: We have captured an outlaw who is wanted in several states and secured the evidence needed to finally put Armand La Fourche behind bars."

"Testimony from a prominent citizen would probably go a long way toward ensuring a conviction," Jack suggested. "Do you think that old fellow will cooperate?"

"Quite possibly, depending on how much discretion Judge Fletcher shows. Tennyson may have the answer when he joins us at the Delmont House. Let's wander on over there and stake out a suitable table."

Archer and Jack polished off their drinks with gusto, while I took one more sip from mine. Then the three of us exited the saloon and started ambling toward the restaurant. Once there, we asked to be seated in an area which afforded some privacy; and a cooperative waiter obliged. Before too long, Tennyson walked through the door, looking a bit melancholy. When I held up a hand to attract his attention, he came across the room and took the chair opposite me.

"Were you able to see the judge?" Archer inquired straightaway.

"Yes, I spent about fifteen minutes with him, explaining the situation and proposing compromises. His reaction was generally sympathetic, although the serious nature of the offense doesn't permit much leeway in assessing a penalty. Even so, he promised due consideration in exchange for a signed statement detailing La Fourche's connection with the kidnapping plan."

"That sounds like a fair deal," Jack interjected, "but you still owe us a name. Hasn't the time come to identify this mysterious third culprit?"

"All right, as much as the obligation pains me. Occasionally, an honest man becomes caught up in an illegal activity through someone else's weakness. Such a predicament occurred today, diminishing an otherwise successful result. The gentleman who has provoked your curiosity is Gil Donlevy, the founder of the Easton & Monroe Logging Company and an individual held in high regard throughout East Texas."

CHAPTER 24

Epilogue

After an extended pause during which no one said anything, I asked, "How did he get drawn into his nephew's scheme?"

"Why don't we go ahead and order?" Tennyson proposed, motioning to the waiter. "While the food is being prepared, I'll answer your question and relate a decent man's undoing at the hands of a scoundrel."

A quick glance at the menu decided me on the baked trout with new potatoes and black-eyed peas, complemented by ice-cold lemonade. When the others had made their selections and we were free from potential eavesdropping, Tennyson embarked on a chronicle that paralleled a Greek tragedy in some ways.

"This twisted affair was triggered by Martin Donlevy's unbridled ambition," he began. "As you know, the younger Donlevy made enough money through land speculation to purchase his cousin's controlling interest in the Easton & Monroe firm, albeit with a large note outstanding. The daring tactics he employed also caught the attention of several Philadelphia businessmen who were affiliated with Jay Golden, and they recruited him for the plot to take over the Texas & Louisiana Railway.

"Perhaps influenced by these high-living manipulators, Donlevy became bolder in his investments and began using funds from the Easton & Monroe coffers to acquire additional acreage, including large tracts situated on the border between Iowa and Nebraska. Then the unprecedented flooding along the Missouri River two months ago rendered those holdings unsaleable for a good long time.

"Even such a serious setback might eventually have been overcome, but fate intervened a second time. A letter arrived announcing that Efram Woodward would be coming through Texas in the near future and planned on stopping off at the Easton & Monroe offices to review the accounting records. This placed Donlevy in a very precarious position. He tried borrowing money against his remaining assets, but was evidently considered a poor risk by the banking community because of the situation concerning the floods. The only recourse left was requesting a loan from Uncle Gilbert, despite the fact that doing so might expose the underlying embezzlement.

"As luck would have it, the elder Donlevy wasn't in a position to provide the needed amount anyway, having recently invested a substantial sum in a new Colorado mining venture. However, he naturally wondered what misfortune lay behind his nephew's untimely request. Some discreet inquiries, initiated with the help of a trusted former employee, ultimately uncovered the truth about the Easton & Monroe reserves.

"Determined to prevent the company he had founded from falling into the hands of outsiders and to avoid a scandal involving the family name, Gil Donlevy reluctantly approached Armand La Fourche for financial assistance. The two had known each other for many years, having met at the casinos in Caddo Parish. It was La Fourche who initially suggested the kidnapping as a solution to Martin's dilemma and then convinced the Donlevys that they had no other choice. His real objective was ingratiating himself with Jay Golden by thwarting the completion of the merger between the Texas & Louisiana and the Missouri & Southwestern. However, Martin Donlevy embraced the notion with little hesitation and subsequently devised the plan for employing a locomotive to carry Woodward away. Of course, the scheme's execution was left in La Fourche's hands."

"I'm still a bit unclear on the role played by Donlevy's uncle," I observed. "Did he really go along with the proposal?"

"Not willingly, Jarvis. Apart from obtaining the inspection train's schedule from Captain Stevens, his participation was minimal. Nevertheless, he had full knowledge of the undertaking and took no steps to prevent it. In the eyes of the law, that constitutes collaboration as an accessory before the fact; and the indiscretion will cost him dearly, even if Judge Fletcher hands down a lenient sentence. Therein lies my one regret over today's outcome: Seeing a good man ruined is a high price to pay for putting La Fourche in prison."

Additional discussion on this sobering topic was forestalled by the waiter's return with our plates, and conversation was sporadic while we ate. At the conclusion of the meal, Tennyson turned to Jack and said, "By the way, arrangements have been made on your behalf for a private interview with Gil Donlevy at the courthouse. He'll be waiting in that same room on the second floor about twenty minutes from now. While you're busy extracting his candid story, Jarvis and I will stop by Mr. Ward's office and conclude our business with the railroad. Barring any unforeseen developments, we might then try catching the afternoon train back to Dallas."

"That suits me," Jack replied with a smile, as Archer requested the bill. When the tab had been paid, we all rose and walked outside together. Jack immediately started toward the courthouse, while the rest of us headed west along Grand Street. Upon reaching the Marshall Inn, Tennyson and I parted company with his brother and set out for the Texas & Louisiana Division Office in the buggy provided by Ted Wilson. Despite having to endure the withering gaze of Mrs. Freeman again, the visit was highly satisfactory. It concluded with Mr. Ward expressing heartfelt gratitude for our assistance and Tennyson pocketing a generous check for his services.

By a quarter past three, he and I were sitting in the hotel lobby with our valises packed for the journey home. In another ten minutes, just after Archer had joined us minus his disguise, Jack walked through the entrance looking like the cat that ate the canary. He quickly gathered his belongings; and we all drove to the depot, where the Western Express arrived from Shreveport at 3:47. Following a short wait, during which the two brothers conferred privately, Tennyson led the way to our seats at the rear of the last coach. As the train left the station, he leaned across the aisle and said, "Well, Jarvis, your initial experience in the field of criminal investigation has certainly been a trying one. If you still have a taste for the work, however, an even greater challenge lies ahead. Unmasking the remaining participants in Jay Golden's conspiracy is apt to require our combined energies for a good long while."

So it turned out when all was said and done, but the telling of that tale must be left for another time.

– Jarvis B. Weston, M.D.
August, 1892

Appendix of Historical Notes

(Numbers in brackets refer to the
entries in the List of References.)

Chapter 1

a) William Brown Miller (1807 to 1899) came to Dallas in 1846, after spending his early years in Alabama and Tennessee. He purchased some acreage on the southeast side of the Trinity River and succeeded in establishing a prosperous farming enterprise there. In addition, he operated a ferry which provided the sole means of crossing the river until a wooden toll bridge was built at the west end of Main Street in 1855. That same year, in order to ensure a proper education for his five daughters, Miller brought a teacher from Kentucky and then invited other families of the county to send their children to classes at his home. The resulting school operated for four years. In 1870, Miller served as president of the fifth State Fair. [1], [2], [5]

b) Dallas had its origins in a settlement at the three forks of the Trinity River, where John Neely Brian opened a trading post in the fall of 1841. As people looking for new opportunities flocked to the area, the fledgling township expanded first to the northeast, then almost due north toward the present route of Oak Lawn Avenue. By the late 1880's, the population had grown to some 30,000 (the official census figure for 1890 was 38,097); and the signs of "suburban sprawl" were already in evidence. A map from that period shows a street layout for the central portion of the city which differs only slightly from today's (with rail lines where the freeways now run). [1], [4]

c) Routh Street was named by John M. Howell for his father-in-law, Jacob Routh, who came to North Texas from Tennessee in 1851 and settled along Spring Creek in Collin County. In the early 1870's, after marrying Routh's daughter, Howell purchased some suburban acreage extending from Turtle Creek to McKinney Road (later McKinney Avenue), platted it for streets, and began selling lots. [3], [4]

Chapter 2

a) The Houston & Texas Central Railroad reached Dallas in 1872 on a north-south alignment; and a year later, the Texas & Pacific came through on its route to El Paso. By 1886, the city could boast six rail lines, each with its own depot. It wasn't until 1916 that the railroads (whose number had grown to eight by then) joined together to build Union Station as a common terminal for passenger trains. [3]

b) Locomotives of the Ten-Wheeler type, which are designated as 4-6-0's under the Whyte classification system, were first produced in the late 1840's. By the 1870's, this configuration had become the preferred power for passenger service, especially in hilly terrain. [7]

c) c) In 1871, the Texas & Pacific Railroad was granted a special charter by the United States Congress for a line between Marshall, Texas and San Diego, California. It never reached the western terminus, but Marshall became a major center of operations for the carrier, which built a large maintenance complex there. The route traveled by Pierce and Weston in the story can be retraced today aboard Amtrak's Texas Eagle. [9]

Chapter 3

a) By the mid-1860's, increasing freight tonnage on America's railroads called for new motive power with greater tractive effort. Locomotive builders responded with the Mogul configuration, which was referred to as the 2-6-0 in the parlance of the Whyte system. This type was particularly favored by the Missouri, Kansas & Texas Railway, which owned 74 of them by 1886. The number on their roster eventually grew to a total of 357, with some of these reliable "hogs" continuing in service through the early 1950's. [10]

b) The first telegraph line in the United States was placed into service on May 24, 1844, linking Washington and Baltimore. This rapid means of communication soon became the preferred method for dispatching trains, and the expansion of the telegraph network generally paralleled the routes of the railroads. [3]

Chapter 4

a) After the infamous "Black Friday" of September 24, 1869, which was triggered by the efforts of Daniel Drew and his cronies in the "Erie Ring" to corner the gold market, considerably more attention was paid to the outflow of bullion from the federal treasury. [8]

b) Following the completion of the nation's first transcontinental railroad in 1869, the rail network west of the Mississippi River grew by leaps and bounds. As it did so, the "robber barons" who controlled most of the lines in the northeastern states sought to add the new companies to their portfolios. Perhaps the most notorious of these early "corporate raiders" was Jay Gould, who is reported to have bragged that he didn't build railroads, he bought them. After bankrupting the Erie in 1872, he exploited the coffers of the Union Pacific, then went on to acquire more than 8000 miles of lines in the Southwest. [8]

Chapter 5

a) The rolling stock of railroads in the late nineteenth century rode on trucks with iron or steel axles whose ends were supported in iron journal boxes. It was common practice to lubricate the moving parts with sperm oil or castor oil which was wicked up from a reservoir by packing material made of cotton waste. Due to the constant vibrations experienced by a car moving over jointed rails, the packing often settled away from its intended position. When this occurred, the result was a "hot box," which could lead to a derailment if the affected axle seized. [11]

b) In engineering terms, railroad track constitutes a beam on an elastic foundation (the soil over which it is laid). Changes in temperature and humidity cause the metal rails, the ties, and the roadbed to move, with effects ranging from mild waviness to severe misalignments. For this reason, track maintenance has always played an important role in the efforts to achieve reliable railroad operations. By the latter part of the nineteenth century, it was recognized that materials containing loams or clays shouldn't be used for ballast, while white oak, chestnut, and Southern yellow pine had become the preferred woods for ties.[11]

c) The Texas & Pacific Railroad came through Longview in 1873 on its way west, but local cotton farmers wanted a more direct way of shipping their crops to Houston. The first attempt to achieve this had been the chartering of the International Railroad in 1871, which was intended to provide a connection with the Houston & Texas Central at Hearne (about 20 miles northwest of Bryan). When this effort fell short of its goal, the Longview and Sabine Valley

Railway took up the challenge of reaching the Gulf. However, its backers also ran out of money, as did those of several successor companies. More than thirty years would pass before the original goal was realized. Today, the rails of the Union Pacific connect Longview with Hearne enroute to Austin, while a separate line diverges for Houston at Palestine. [9]

d) A number of logging railroads were built in the Piney Woods during the late nineteenth century, and we are fortunate that one of them has survived to the present day. This wonderful relic from a bygone era is the Moscow, Camden & San Augustine Railway, which celebrated its centennial in 1998. Although dieselized in 1964, at that date there were still ten steam engines on the property. Two of them, which just happen to be Moguls, still operate today, pulling tourist trains on the Eureka Springs & North Arkansas Railway in Eureka Springs, Arkansas. [12]

Chapter 8

a) As late as 1911, medical practitioners believed that influenza was caused by a "vapor" which emanated from the ground in the aftermath of prolonged rainy spells.

Despite that curious notion, the symptoms were treated much as they are today, with bedrest, plenty of fluids, chest salves, and inhalants to open the breathing passages. [6]

b) In early 1874, six nuns from the Ursuline convent in Galveston came to Dallas at the request of Father Joseph Martiniere, the pastor of Sacred Heart Church. On February 2 of that year, they began teaching classes in a four-room house which stood on the site later occupied by the Federal Building. Less than two years later, increasing enrollment in their school forced the construction of a much larger two-story facility. An official charter for the Ursuline Academy of Dallas was granted by the Texas legislature in 1878. [1], [3]

c) The *Dallas Herald* (not to be confused with the later *Dallas Times Herald*) was the city's first newspaper. It was founded by James Wellington Latimer in 1849 as a weekly publication, graduating to the status of a daily in 1874. On October 1, 1885, the first issue of a fresh rival appeared on Dallas streets. This was the *Dallas Morning News*, an offshoot of the *Galveston News* under the direction of Colonel Alfred H. Belo. Less than two months later, after more than 36 years of service to the community, the *Dallas Herald* was acquired by the newcomer. [1], [2]

Chapter 9

a) The Secret Service is the oldest non-military law enforcement agency of the federal government. It was established in 1865 as a bureau of the Treasury Department charged with investigating incidents of counterfeiting, forgery, and other irregularities relating to interstate commerce. [6]

b) Father Sebastion Augugneur from Nacogdoches celebrated the first Mass in Dallas at the home of Maxime Guillot in 1859. For the next thirteen years, circuit-riding priests dispatched from the diocese of Galveston attended to the spiritual needs of the city's Catholics. By 1872, however, it was clear that a permanent parish was warranted; and Father M. Perrier was tasked with organizing one. Services were initially held in the Odd Fellows Hall; but in 1873, Sacred Heart Church was built on the northeast corner of Bryan and Ervay Streets. The following year, Father Joseph Martiniere was designated as the initial pastor of the new parish. [1], [3]

c) In 1882, a group of twenty-two citizens joined together to form the Dallas Opera House Association and succeeded in having a theater erected on the southeast corner of Commerce and Austin Streets. The building, which was three stories high with a seating capacity of 1200, featured a parterre and two galleries. *Fortune's Fool*, a melodrama written by Will C. Marion, who also played the leading role, was staged there in the fall of 1885 by the well-known Rial Biggers troupe. [2]

d) The first bridge across the Trinity River in the Dallas area was a privately-owned wooden span built in 1855 at the west end of Main Street (about where the Commerce Street viaduct stands today). In 1872, its place was taken by an iron toll bridge, erected by the Dallas Bridge Company at a reported cost of $65,000. The components for this structure were fabricated in St. Louis and shipped via barge to Houston, then loaded onto cars of the Houston & Texas Central Railroad for transport to Corsicana. Ox-drawn wagons were used for the final leg of the journey. Responding to the complaints of residents who objected to the fees charge by the bridge's owners, the County of Dallas purchased the span in 1882. [1], [3]

e) Sometime between 1865 and 1868, the first privately-owned financial institution in Dallas was organized by T. C. Jordan and E. G. Mays with a capitalization of

$20,000. By 1873, several competitors had appeared on the scene; and the stage was set for a seemingly unending series of mergers which have continued unabated to the present day. Banking deposits increased markedly during the decade of the 1870's, thanks to the growth in commerce spurred by the coming of the railroads. In 1885, there were six banks in the city: Adams & Leonard, the American National Bank, the City National Bank, the Dallas National Bank, the Exchange Bank, and Oliver & Griggs. [1]

Chapter 10

a) The cattle industry in Texas expanded to the plains of the Panhandle around 1876; and over the following decade, approximately 400,000 beeves per year left West Texas for northern markets. Initially, these herds were driven along the route of the Chisolm Trail or the Dodge City Trail, with the principal destinations being the Union Stockyard in Chicago and the Armour Packing House in Kansas City. During the administration of Governor John Ireland (1883 - 1887), a law was enacted by the state legislature forbidding the cutting of barbed-wire fences. This was a major factor in bringing the era of the long trail drive to an end. [6]

b) The first attempt at countering the excesses of the "robber barons" was the rather weak Interstate Commerce Act of 1887. This legislation required the railroads to publish their freight rates, but merely stipulated that the charges should be "reasonable and just." [8]

Chapter 11

a) Although Dallas had emerged from its humble beginnings to become the state's largest city by the late 1880's, it retained something of a wild and wooly reputation, due in part to the many gambling halls and saloons which lined the north side of Main Street for several blocks. The city's proximity to the Indian Territory, where many desperadoes of the day took refuge from the law, didn't help matters either. For a time, the notorious Belle Starr took up residence at the Planter's Hotel. She shocked some of the citizenry by periodically donning an outfit of fringed buckskin and riding her horse at full speed through the central business district. [2]

b) The Le Grand Hotel, owned by Tom Smith and designed by the noted architect James E.

Flanders, was completed in the fall of 1875 on the southwest corner of Commerce and Austin Streets. It was advertised as "the most elegant hotel in the South" and included features such as a chandelier more than nine feet in diameter, a fountain adorned by a bronze figure of Neptune, and a parlor with a grand piano. Four years later, the rival Windsor Hotel opened on the northeast corner of Main and Austin Streets. In 1882, Colonel William E. Hughes purchased the two properties and joined them with a second-story bridge across Austin Street, creating the Grand Windsor. A four-story addition, also designed by Flanders, was added in 1885. The combined hotel was particularly noted for its elaborate menus, which included all of the selections ordered by Pierce and Weston in the story. [1], [4]

Chapter 12

a) Dallas officially became the seat for the county of the same name in 1850, and a log cabin measuring 16 by 32 feet was built to serve as the courthouse. By 1857, a need for more space prompted the erection of a red brick building on the same site. However, rapid deterioration required its replacement in 1871. The new structure, which was made of gray stone and capped with an elegant bell tower, survived only nine years before burning to the ground. Its place was taken in 1881 by a supposedly fireproof edifice designed in the Second Empire style, which also succumbed to a blaze after another nine years. [4]

b) In 1865, the Texas legislature enacted a law stipulating that any railroad building through the state was to receive sixteen sections of land (10,240 acres) for each mile of track completed. This was a form of inducement commonly used by both the states and the federal government at that time to fund rail construction, since land was abundantly available, while capital was in short supply. The Houston & Texas Central ultimately received over four million acres, and the proceeds from selling this property enabled finishing the line to Dallas. [1]

c) The Commonwealth Commercial College was founded in January of 1874 by Professor E. B. Lawrence as a business school offering both day and evening classes. It was housed in a two-story building situated at 317 Main Street. In addition to his academic credentials, Professor Lawrence was an accomplished musician. He organized one of the city's first bands, which often played at dances held in the main hall on the college's second floor. [1], [3]

d) The name "Oak Lawn" was adopted in 1874 for a suburb which came to be bounded by Turtle Creek, Lemmon Avenue, Maple Avenue, and Oak Lawn Avenue. This land had originally been homesteaded by Obadiah Knight during the days before Texas became a state. It was his eldest son, Epps Knight, who began selling the acreage to settlers wanting to escape the growing congestion within the central part of the city. Four men from Tennessee (John Dickason, Henry Sale, George Mellersh, and the Reverend Marcus Cullum) and one from Central Texas (John Andrews) moved their families to the area in the early 1870's and became instrumental in its further development. [2]

Chapter 14

a) The University of Texas was established at Austin in 1881, but the affiliated medical school at Galveston didn't open until ten years later. A bit of literary license has been used to advance that date for the purposes of the story. During the latter part of the nineteenth century, it was possible to embark on the study of medicine with no more background than a high-school education or its equivalent. [6]

b) The nation's first ice-making plant was set up at New Orleans in 1868. That same year, the railroads introduced refrigerator cars, making it possible to transport fresh meats, fruits, and vegetables over long distances without risk of spoilage. In 1878, H. A. Fleuss invented a vacuum-based machine for domestic use which, with about three minutes of pumping, could produce enough ice to fill a carafe. As a result of these developments, iced tea had become a popular beverage with Texans by the 1880's (as had iced beer). [6]

c) The character of Dallas has always been associated more closely with commerce than with art. Nevertheless, talented artists have been a part of the community since at least the 1870's. One of the early notables was Frank Reaugh, who moved to the city in 1876 at the age of fifteen and began making sketches of farm scenes. He later studied at the Julien School in Paris and became intrigued with the work of the Dutch painter Anton Mauve. Upon returning home, he brought the Impressionist technique to the depiction of various Texas subjects, especially the great herds of longhorn cattle. The unique motifs of the state also served to attract visits by artists from other regions. In May of 1884, for example, Professor L. R. Bromley's "The Siege of the Alamo" was exhibited by the Star Art Gallery. [1], [2]

Chapter 16

a) The jail which is mentioned in the story was constructed in 1879 on the southwest corner of Houston and Jackson Streets. It was an impressive three-story structure with a central tower. [4]

b) In the fall of 1885, the Greenwall brothers of New Orleans assumed control of the Dallas Opera House and installed George W. Anzy as manager. Under his direction, a number of well-known theater troupes were engaged to put on shows such as *Dad's Girl, Sis! Sis! Sis!, The Professor, Il Trovatore, The Black Crook, The Mikado, Richelieu, Peck's Bad Boy,* and *The Count of Monte Cristo.* [1]

c) *Through the Looking Glass,* the wonderfully imaginative allegorical tale written by Charles Lutwidge Dodgson under the pseudonym of Lewis Carroll, was first published in 1871. A sequel to the very well-received *Alice's Adventures in Wonderland,* which had appeared in 1865, it proved even more popular than its predecessor. [6]

Chapter 18

a) From the earliest days of Dallas, bois d'arc trees abounded in the area. They were well-adapted to the "black gumbo" of the North Texas prairie and grew rapidly. In the late 1870's, City Engineer William M. Johnson developed a method of cutting and treating the wood from these trees for use as paving blocks. The first chance to demonstrate the benefits of his development came in 1881 when Tom L. Marsalis, then a wholesale grocer, agreed to pay for installing the blocks in front of his store on Elm Street. The result was so well-received that the process was extended to portions of Main, Akard, Jefferson, Lamar, Murphy, and Poydras Streets. [1], [3]

b) The site of the fictional Houston Street depot is that of the present Union Station, which Amtrak's Texas Eagle still approaches from the east along the route followed by the Pecos Limited in the story. This line runs roughly parallel to Military Parkway and Haskell Avenue on its way to the downtown area.

Chapter 19

a) From the 1850's onward, cotton was an

important crop in the Dallas area. With the coming of the railroads in the early 1870's, cotton brokers were attracted to the city in large numbers; and a sizable trade in the commodity soon developed. In 1884, the Gaston Building was constructed at the corner of Commerce and Lamar Streets to house the growing community of "spot" traders, futures speculators, exporting firms, and representative of compresses. [1]

b) Until the opening of the Indian Territory for homesteading on April 22, 1889, this sparsely populated area served as a refuge for numerous outlaws who preyed on banks and railroads in the northern part of Texas and the southern part of Kansas. These hallmarks of the "Wild West" included Sam Bass, Belle Starr, and the Dalton gang. [1], [13]

c) The high content of oxidized matter found in Perique tobacco derives from the practice of pressing the leaves daily and then allowing them to absorb their expressed juices. [6]

Chapter 20

a) The Brooks Locomotive Works of Dunkirk, New York manufactured steam engines from 1869 until 1901, when it was merged into the American Locomotive Company together with eight other builders. The firm's products included a handsome Mogul featuring 55-inch drivers, cylinders measuring 19 by 24 inches, and a total weight of 118,000 pounds. [7]

b) The Colt Peacemaker was introduced in 1873 and quickly became the preferred weapon of Western gunfighters due to its balance and durability. It was a good-looking gun, particularly in the long-barreled version; and purchasers often ordered options such as handles made from ivory or mother-of-pearl, as well as ornate scrollwork on the body. In 1875, competitor Smith & Wesson countered with the rather ungraceful-appearing Schofield .45, which gained a measure of fame as the gun used by Jesse James. [14]

Chapter 22

a) Prior to the adoption of Centralized Traffic Control, which was first introduced on forty miles of the New York Central in 1927, railroads were dispatched using timetables and train orders. Any movement not listed in a timetable was designated as an "extra," and the locomotives of such trains were typically required to carry a pair of white flags indicating their status. [15]

b) During the late nineteenth century, it wasn't unusual for individuals of means to own private railroad cars, either for business purposes or for travel with their families. The majority of these were built to order by the Pullman Company, an enterprise founded by George M. Pullman in 1867 that became the dominant supplier of passenger cars through the early years of the twentieth century. Such conveyances were generally outfitted with oil lamps, hot-water heating systems, overstuffed chairs and settees, marble basins, gold fixtures, and sidewalls of carved walnut. [16]

List of References

[1]   Maxine Holmes and Gerald D. Saxon, editors, *The WPA Dallas Guide and History* (Dallas: Dallas Public Library and University of North Texas Press, 1992).

[2]   John William Rogers, *The Lusty Texans of Dallas* (New York: E.P. Dutton and Company, 1951).

[3]   Sam Acheson, *Dallas Yesterday* (Dallas: S. M. U. Press, 1977).

[4]   William L. McDonald, *Dallas Rediscovered: A Photographic Chronicle of Urban Expansion 1870 - 1925* (Dallas: The Dallas Historical Society, 1978).

[5]   Evelyn Miller Crowell, *Texas Childhood* (Dallas: The Kaleidograph Press, 1941).

[6]   Encyclopaedia Britannica, Inc., Eleventh Edition (New York: 1911). [This version was employed because of the proximity of its publication date to the time period of the story.]

[7]   Edwin P. Alexander, *Iron Horses* (New York: Bonanza Books, 1941).

[8] Oliver Jensen, *American Heritage History of Railroads in America* (New York: American Heritage Wings Books, 1975).

[9] Richard K. Troxell, *Texas Trains* (Plano, Texas: Republic of Texas Press, 2002).

[10] Joe G. Collias and Raymond B. George, Jr., *Katy Power* (Crestwood, Missouri: MM Books, 1986).

[11] Charles Paine, *The Art of Railroading* (Chevy Chase, Maryland: Claycomb Press, Inc., 1987). [Reprinted from *The Railroad Gazette* of 1884.]

[12] Glen Brewer, "Ghosts in the Piney Woods," *Classic Trains* Magazine, Vol. 3, No.1 (Spring, 2002).

[13] The Missouri-Kansas-Texas Railroad Company, *The Opening of the Great Southwest* (Dallas: 1970). [The Missouri, Kansas & Texas Railway was reorganized into the Missouri-Kansas-Texas Railroad on July 6, 1922.]

[14] Paul Trachtman and the Editors of Time-Life Books, *The Gunfighters* (New York: Time-Life Books, 1974).

[15] John H. Armstrong, "All About Signals," *Trains* Magazine (June and July, 1957).

[16] J. B. Hollingsworth and P. B. Whitehouse, *American Railroads* (London: Bison Books Limited, 1977).